TOP NOTCH TALES

TOP NOTCH TALES

A Selection of the World's Greatest Short Stories

Edited by Jonathan Macpherson

TOP NOTCH BOOKS

Edited and published by Top Notch Books
Perth, Western Australia
www.jonathanmacpherson.com

First Edition

CONTENTS

PREFACE

Ever since I read Ambrose Bierce's *An Occurrence at Owl Creek Bridge* in high school, I've been hooked on short stories, reading thousands across every genre and era. This collection brings together eighteen stories that I consider to be among the very best.

These timeless gems have left their mark on modern bestsellers, Oscar-winning films, and acclaimed television, from Hollywood's golden age to today's streaming hits.

For your convenience, the stories are grouped into four parts: Adventure, Mystery & Suspense; Comedy, Mischief & Wit; Horror & the Supernatural; Romance & Redemption. Read straight through, or open to whichever mood strikes you.

For me, every story here is riveting, entertaining, and unforgettable. These are tales I return to every so often, many years after first enjoying them. I hope they offer the same experience to you and you agree they are truly top-notch.

Jonathan Macpherson

PART I
Adventure, Mystery & Suspense

RICHARD CONNELL

Richard Connell (1893–1949) was an American journalist, screenwriter and author whose pulse-pounding tales gripped the pulp era. A Harvard graduate and World War I veteran, he produced novels, screenplays, and hundreds of short stories for magazines like *The Saturday Evening Post* and *Collier's*. His masterpiece, "*The Most Dangerous Game*," is a high-stakes thriller of survival and cunning that redefined adventure fiction. The story's gripping premise sparked the 1932 film adaptation, episodes of *The Twilight Zone* and *Alfred Hitchcock Presents*, and endless echoes in modern thrillers. He later thrived in Hollywood, but this primal classic cemented his legacy as a master of high-concept suspense. Connell is said to have dashed off *The Most Dangerous Game* in one feverish sitting after returning from a hunting trip.

The Most Dangerous Game

Richard Connell

First published in *Collier's*, 1924.

Off there to the right—somewhere—is a large island," said Whitney. "It's rather a mystery—"

"What island is it?" Rainsford asked.

"The old charts call it 'Ship-Trap Island,'" Whitney replied. "A suggestive name, isn't it? Sailors have a curious dread of the place. I don't know why. Some superstition—"

"Can't see it," remarked Rainsford, trying to peer through the dank tropical night that was palpable as it pressed its thick warm blackness in upon the yacht.

"You've good eyes," said Whitney, with a laugh, "and I've seen you pick off a moose moving in the brown fall bush at four hundred yards, but even you can't see four miles or so through a moonless Caribbean night."

"Nor four yards," admitted Rainsford. "Ugh! It's like moist black velvet."

"It will be light enough in Rio," promised Whitney. "We should make it in a few days. I hope the jaguar guns have come from Purdey's. We should have some good hunting up the Amazon. Great sport, hunting."

"The best sport in the world," agreed Rainsford.

"For the hunter," amended Whitney. "Not for the jaguar."

"Don't talk rot, Whitney," said Rainsford. "You're a big-game hunter, not a philosopher. Who cares how a jaguar feels?"

"Perhaps the jaguar does," observed Whitney.

"Bah! They've no understanding."

"Even so, I rather think they understand one thing—fear. The fear of pain and the fear of death."

"Nonsense," laughed Rainsford. "This hot weather is making you soft, Whitney. Be a realist. The world is made up of two classes—the hunters and the huntees. Luckily, you and I are hunters. Do you think we've passed that island yet?"

"I can't tell in the dark. I hope so."

"Why?" asked Rainsford.

"The place has a reputation—a bad one."

"Cannibals?" suggested Rainsford.

"Hardly. Even cannibals wouldn't live in such a God-forsaken place. But it's gotten into sailor lore, somehow. Didn't you notice that the crew's nerves seemed a bit jumpy to-day?"

"They were a bit strange, now you mention it. Even Captain Nielsen—"

"Yes, even that tough-minded old Swede, who'd go up to the devil himself and ask him for a light. Those fishy blue eyes held a look I never saw there before. All I could get out of him was: 'This place has an evil name among sea-faring men, sir.' Then he said to me, very gravely: 'Don't you feel anything?'—as if the air about us was actually poisonous. Now, you mustn't laugh when I tell you this—I did feel something like a sudden chill.

"There was no breeze. The sea was as flat as a plate-glass window. We were drawing near the island then. What I felt was a—a mental chill; a sort of sudden dread."

"Pure imagination," said Rainsford. "One superstitious sailor can taint the whole ship's company with his fear."

"Maybe. But sometimes I think sailors have an extra sense that tells them when they are in danger. Sometimes I think evil is a tangible thing—with wave lengths, just as sound and light have. An evil place can, so to speak, broadcast vibrations of evil. Anyhow, I'm glad we're getting out of this zone. Well, I think I'll turn in now, Rainsford."

"I'm not sleepy," said Rainsford. "I'm going to smoke another pipe up on the after deck."

"Good-night, then, Rainsford. See you at breakfast."

"Right. Good-night, Whitney."

There was no sound in the night as Rainsford sat there but the muffled throb of the engine that drove the yacht swiftly through the darkness, and the swish and ripple of the wash of the propeller.

Rainsford, reclining in a steamer chair, indolently puffed on his favourite brier. The sensuous drowsiness of the night was on him. "It's so dark," he thought, "that I could sleep without closing my eyes; the night would be my eyelids—"

An abrupt sound startled him. Off to the right he heard it, and his ears, expert in such matters, could not be mistaken. Again he heard the sound, and again. Somewhere, off in the blackness, someone had fired a gun three times.

Rainsford sprang up and moved quickly to the rail, mystified. He strained his eyes in the direction from which the reports had come, but it was like trying to see through a blanket. He leaped upon the rail and balanced himself there, to get greater elevation; his pipe, striking a rope, was knocked from his mouth. He lunged for it; a short, hoarse cry came from his lips as he realized he had reached too far and had lost his balance. The cry was pinched off short as the blood-warm waters of the Caribbean Sea closed over his head.

He struggled up to the surface and tried to cry out, but the wash from the speeding yacht slapped him in the face and the salt water in his open mouth made him gag and strangle. Desperately he struck out with strong strokes after the receding lights of the yacht, but he stopped before he had swum fifty feet. A certain cool-headedness had come to him; it was not the first time he had been in a tight place. There was a chance that his cries could be heard by someone aboard the yacht, but that chance was slender, and grew more slender as the yacht raced on. He wrestled himself out of his clothes, and shouted with all his power. The lights of the yacht became faint and ever-vanishing fireflies; then they were blotted out entirely by the night.

Rainsford remembered the shots. They had come from the right, and doggedly he swam in that direction, swimming with slow, deliberate strokes, conserving his strength. For a seemingly endless time he fought the sea. He began to count his strokes; he could do possibly a hundred more and then—

Rainsford heard a sound. It came out of the darkness, a high, screaming sound, the sound of an animal in an extremity of anguish and terror.

He did not recognize the animal that made the sound; he did not try to; with fresh vitality he swam toward the sound. He heard it again; then it was cut short by another noise, crisp, staccato.

"Pistol shot," muttered Rainsford, swimming on.

Ten minutes of determined effort brought another sound to his ears—the most welcome he had ever heard—the muttering and growling of the sea breaking on a rocky shore. He was almost on the rocks before he saw them: on a night less calm he would have been shattered against them. With his remaining strength he dragged himself from the swirling waters. Jagged crags appeared to jut up into the opaqueness; he forced himself upward, hand over hand. Gasping, his hands raw, he reached a flat place at the top. Dense jungle came down to the very edge of the cliffs. What perils that tangle of trees and underbrush might hold for him did not concern Rainsford just then. All he knew was that he was safe from his enemy, the sea, and that utter weariness was on him. He flung himself down at the jungle edge and tumbled headlong into the deepest sleep of his life.

When he opened his eyes he knew from the position of the sun that it was late in the afternoon. Sleep had given him new vigour; a sharp hunger was picking at him. He looked about him, almost cheerfully.

"Where there are pistol shots, there are men. Where there are men, there is food," he thought. But what kind of men, he wondered, in so forbidding a place? An unbroken front of snarled and ragged jungle fringed the shore.

He saw no sign of a trail through the closely knit web of weeds and trees; it was easier to go along the shore, and Rainsford floundered along by the water. Not far from where he had landed, he stopped.

Some wounded thing, by the evidence a large animal, had thrashed about in the underbrush; the jungle weeds were crushed down and the moss was lacerated; one patch of weeds was stained crimson. A small, glittering object not far away caught Rainsford's eye and he picked it up. It was an empty cartridge.

"A twenty-two," he remarked. "That's odd. It must have been a fairly large animal, too. The hunter had his nerve with him to tackle it with a light gun. It's clear that the brute put up a fight. I suppose the first three shots I heard was when the hunter flushed his quarry and wounded it. The last shot was when he trailed it here and finished it."

He examined the ground closely and found what he had hoped to find—the print of hunting boots. They pointed along the cliff in the direction he had been going. Eagerly he hurried along, now slipping on a rotten log or a loose stone, but making headway; night was beginning to settle down on the island.

Bleak darkness was blacking out the sea and jungle when Rainsford sighted the lights. He came upon them as he turned a crook in the coast line, and his first thought was that he had come upon a village, for there were many lights. But as he forged along he saw to his great astonishment that all the lights were in one enormous building—a lofty structure with pointed towers plunging upward into the gloom. His eyes made out the shadowy outlines of a palatial château; it was set on a high bluff, and on three sides of it cliffs dived down to where the sea licked greedy lips in the shadows.

"Mirage," thought Rainsford. But it was no mirage, he found, when he opened the tall spiked iron gate. The stone steps were real enough; the massive door with a leering gargoyle for a knocker was real enough; yet about it all hung an air of unreality.

He lifted the knocker, and it creaked up stiffly as if it had never before been used. He let it fall, and it startled him with its booming loudness. He thought he heard steps within; the door remained closed. Again Rainsford lifted the heavy knocker, and let it fall. The door opened then, opened as suddenly as if it were on a spring, and Rainsford stood blinking in the river of glaring gold light that poured out. The first thing Rainsford's eyes discerned was the largest man Rainsford had ever seen—a gigantic creature, solidly made and black-bearded to the waist. In his hand the man held a long-barrelled revolver, and he was pointing it straight at Rainsford's heart.

Out of the snarl of beard two small eyes regarded Rainsford.

"Don't be alarmed," said Rainsford, with a smile which he hoped was disarming. "I'm no robber. I fell off a yacht. My name is Sanger Rainsford of New York City."

The menacing look in the eyes did not change. The revolver pointed as rigidly as if the giant were a statue. He gave no sign that he understood Rainsford's words, or that he had even heard them. He was dressed in uniform, a black uniform trimmed with gray astrakhan.

"I'm Sanger Rainsford of New York," Rainsford began again. "I fell off a yacht. I am hungry."

The man's only answer was to raise with his thumb the hammer of his revolver. Then Rainsford saw the man's free hand go to his forehead in a military salute, and he saw him click his heels together and stand at attention. Another man was coming down the broad marble steps, an erect, slender man in evening clothes. He advanced to Rainsford and held out his hand.

In a cultivated voice marked by a slight accent that gave it added precision and deliberateness, he said: "It is a very great pleasure and honour to welcome Mr. Sanger Rainsford, the celebrated hunter, to my home."

Automatically Rainsford shook the man's hand.

"I've read your book about hunting snow leopards in Tibet, you see," explained the man. "I am General Zaroff."

Rainsford's first impression was that the man was singularly handsome; his second was that there was an original, almost bizarre quality about the general's face. He was a tall man past middle age, for his hair was a vivid white; but his thick eyebrows and pointed military moustache were as black as the night from which Rainsford had come. His eyes, too, were black and very bright. He had high cheek bones, a sharp-cut nose, a spare, dark face, the face of a man used to giving orders, the face of an aristocrat. Turning to the giant in uniform, the general made a sign. The giant put away his pistol, saluted, withdrew.

"Ivan is an incredibly strong fellow," remarked the general, "but he has the misfortune to be deaf and dumb. A simple fellow, but, I'm afraid, like all his race, a bit of a savage."

"Is he Russian?"

"He is a Cossack," said the general, and his smile showed red lips and pointed teeth. "So am I.

"Come," he said, "we shouldn't be chatting here. We can talk later. Now you want clothes, food, rest. You shall have them. This is a most restful spot."

Ivan had reappeared, and the general spoke to him with lips that moved but gave forth no sound.

"Follow Ivan, if you please, Mr. Rainsford," said the general. "I was about to have my dinner when you came. I'll wait for you. You'll find that my clothes will fit you, I think."

It was to a huge, beam-ceilinged bedroom with a canopied bed big enough for six men that Rainsford followed the silent giant. Ivan laid out an evening suit, and Rainsford, as he put it on, noticed that it came from a London tailor who ordinarily cut and sewed for none below the rank of duke.

The dining room to which Ivan conducted him was in many ways remarkable. There was a medieval magnificence about it; it suggested a baronial hall of feudal times with its oaken panels, its high ceiling, its vast refectory table where two score men could sit down to eat. About the hall were the mounted heads of many animals—lions, tigers, elephants, moose, bears; larger or more perfect specimens Rainsford had never seen. At the great table the general was sitting, alone.

"You'll have a cocktail, Mr. Rainsford," he suggested. The cocktail was surpassingly good, and, Rainsford noted, the table appointments were of the finest—the linen, the crystal, the silver, the china.

They were eating *borsch*, the rich red soup with whipped cream so dear to Russian palates. Half apologetically General Zaroff said: "We do our best to preserve the amenities of civilization here. Please forgive any lapses. We are well off the beaten track, you know. Do you think the champagne has suffered from its long ocean trip?"

"Not in the least," declared Rainsford. He was finding the general a most thoughtful and affable host, a true cosmopolite. But there was one small trait of the general's that made Rainsford uncomfortable. Whenever he looked up from his plate he found the general studying him, appraising him narrowly.

"Perhaps," said General Zaroff, "you were surprised that I recognized your name. You see, I read all books on hunting published in English, French, and Russian. I have but one passion in my life, Mr. Rainsford, and it is the hunt."

"You have some wonderful heads here," said Rainsford as he ate a particularly well-cooked filet mignon. "That Cape buffalo is the largest I ever saw."

"Oh, that fellow. Yes, he was a monster."

"Did he charge you?"

"Hurled me against a tree," said the general. "Fractured my skull. But I got the brute."

"I've always thought," said Rainsford, "that the Cape buffalo is the most dangerous of all big game."

For a moment the general did not reply; he was smiling his curious red-lipped smile. Then he said slowly: "No. You are wrong, sir. The Cape buffalo is not the most dangerous big game." He sipped his wine. "Here in my preserve on this island," he said, in the same slow tone, "I hunt more dangerous game."

Rainsford expressed his surprise. "Is there big game on this island?"

The general nodded. "The biggest."

"Really?"

"Oh, it isn't here naturally, of course. I have to stock the island."

"What have you imported, General?" Rainsford asked. "Tigers?"

The general smiled. "No," he said. "Hunting tigers ceased to interest me some years ago. I exhausted their possibilities, you see. No thrill left in tigers, no real danger. I live for danger, Mr. Rainsford."

The general took from his pocket a gold cigarette case and offered his guest a long black cigarette with a silver tip; it was perfumed and gave off a smell like incense.

"We will have some capital hunting, you and I," said the general. "I shall be most glad to have your society."

"But what game—" began Rainsford.

"I'll tell you," said the general. "You will be amused, I know. I think I may say, in all modesty, that I have done a rare thing. I have invented a new sensation. May I pour you another glass of port, Mr. Rainsford?"

"Thank you, General."

The general filled both glasses, and said: "God makes some men poets. Some He makes kings, some beggars. Me He made a hunter. My hand was made for the trigger, my father said. He was a very rich man with a quarter of a million acres in the Crimea, and he was an ardent sportsman. When I was only five years old he gave me a little gun, specially made in Moscow for me, to shoot sparrows with. When I shot some of his prize turkeys with it, he did not punish me; he complimented me on my marksmanship. I killed my first bear in the Caucasus when I was ten. My whole life has been one prolonged hunt. I went into the army—it was expected of noblemen's sons—and for a time commanded a division of Cossack cavalry, but my real interest was always the hunt. I have hunted every kind of game in every land. It would be impossible for me to tell you how many animals I have killed."

The general puffed at his cigarette.

"After the debacle in Russia I left the country, for it was imprudent for an officer of the Tsar to stay there. Many noble

Russians lost everything. I, luckily, had invested heavily in American securities, so I shall never have to open a tea room in Monte Carlo or drive a taxi in Paris. Naturally, I continued to hunt—grizzlies in your Rockies, crocodiles in the Ganges, rhinoceroses in East Africa. It was in Africa that the Cape buffalo hit me and laid me up for six months. As soon as I recovered I started for the Amazon to hunt jaguars, for I had heard they were unusually cunning. They weren't." The Cossack sighed. "They were no match at all for a hunter with his wits about him, and a high-powered rifle. I was bitterly disappointed. I was lying in my tent with a splitting headache one night when a terrible thought pushed its way into my mind. Hunting was beginning to bore me! And hunting, remember, had been my life. I have heard that in America business men often go to pieces when they give up the business that has been their life."

"Yes, that's so," said Rainsford.

The general smiled. "I had no wish to go to pieces," he said. "I must do something. Now, mine is an analytical mind, Mr. Rainsford. Doubtless that is why I enjoy the problems of the chase."

"No doubt, General Zaroff."

"So," continued the general, "I asked myself why the hunt no longer fascinated me. You are much younger than I am, Mr. Rainsford, and have not hunted as much, but you perhaps can guess the answer."

"What was it?"

"Simply this: hunting had ceased to be what you call 'a sporting proposition.' It had become too easy. I always got my quarry. Always. There is no greater bore than perfection."

The general lit a fresh cigarette.

"No animal had a chance with me any more. That is no boast; it is a mathematical certainty. The animal had nothing but his legs and his instinct. Instinct is no match for reason. When I thought of this it was a tragic moment for me, I can tell you."

Rainsford leaned across the table, absorbed in what his host was saying.

"It came to me as an inspiration what I must do," the general went on.

"And that was?"

The general smiled the quiet smile of one who has faced an obstacle and surmounted it with success. "I had to invent a new animal to hunt," he said.

"A new animal? You're joking."

"Not at all," said the general. "I never joke about hunting. I needed a new animal. I found one. So I bought this island, built this house, and here I do my hunting. The island is perfect for my purposes—there are jungles with a maze of trails in them, hills, swamps—"

"But the animal, General Zaroff?"

"Oh," said the general, "it supplies me with the most exciting hunting in the world. No other hunting compares with it for an instant. Every day I hunt, and I never grow bored now, for I have a quarry with which I can match my wits."

Rainsford's bewilderment showed in his face.

"I wanted the ideal animal to hunt," explained the general. "So I said: 'What are the attributes of an ideal quarry?' And the answer was, of course: 'It must have courage, cunning, and, above all, it must be able to reason.'"

"But no animal can reason," objected Rainsford.

"My dear fellow," said the general, "there is one that can."

"But you can't mean—" gasped Rainsford.

"And why not?"

"I can't believe you are serious, General Zaroff. This is a grisly joke."

"Why should I not be serious? I am speaking of hunting."

"Hunting? Good God, General Zaroff, what you speak of is murder."

The general laughed with entire good nature. He regarded Rainsford quizzically. "I refuse to believe that so modern and civilized a young man as you seem to be harbours romantic ideas about the value of human life. Surely your experiences in the war—"

"Did not make me condone cold-blooded murder," finished Rainsford, stiffly.

Laughter shook the general. "How extraordinarily droll you are!" he said. "One does not expect nowadays to find a young man of the educated class, even in America, with such a naïve, and, if I may say so, mid-Victorian point of view. It's like finding a snuffbox in a limousine. Ah, well, doubtless you had Puritan ancestors. So many Americans appear to have had. I'll wager you'll forget your notions when you go hunting with me. You've a genuine new thrill in store for you, Mr. Rainsford."

"Thank you, I'm a hunter, not a murderer."

"Dear me," said the general, quite unruffled, "again that unpleasant word. But I think I can show you that your scruples are quite ill founded."

"Yes?"

"Life is for the strong, to be lived by the strong, and, if needs be, taken by the strong. The weak of the world were put here to give the strong pleasure. I am strong. Why should I not use my gift? If I wish to hunt, why should I not? I hunt the scum of the earth—sailors from tramp ships—lascars, blacks, Chinese, whites, mongrels—a thoroughbred horse or hound is worth more than a score of them."

"But they are men," said Rainsford, hotly.

"Precisely," said the general. "That is why I use them. It gives me pleasure. They can reason, after a fashion. So they are dangerous."

"But where do you get them?"

The general's left eyelid fluttered down in a wink. "This island is called Ship Trap," he answered. "Sometimes an angry god of the high seas sends them to me. Sometimes, when Providence is not so kind, I help Providence a bit. Come to the window with me."

Rainsford went to the window and looked out toward the sea.

"Watch! Out there!" exclaimed the general, pointing into the night. Rainsford's eyes saw only blackness, and then, as the general pressed a button, far out to sea Rainsford saw the flash of lights.

The general chuckled. "They indicate a channel," he said, "where there's none: giant rocks with razor edges crouch like a sea monster with wide-open jaws. They can crush a ship as easily as I crush this nut." He dropped a walnut on the hardwood floor and brought his heel grinding down on it. "Oh, yes," he said, casually, as if in answer to a question. "I have electricity. We try to be civilized here."

"Civilized? And you shoot down men?"

A trace of anger was in the general's black eyes, but it was there for but a second, and he said, in his most pleasant manner: "Dear me, what a righteous young man you are! I assure you I do not do the thing you suggest. That would be barbarous. I treat these visitors with every consideration. They get plenty of good food and exercise. They get into splendid physical condition. You shall see for yourself tomorrow."

"What do you mean?"

"We'll visit my training school," smiled the general. "It's in the cellar. I have about a dozen pupils down there now. They're from the Spanish bark *Sanlúcar* that had the bad luck to go on the rocks cut there. A very inferior lot, I regret to say. Poor specimens and more accustomed to the deck than to the jungle."

He raised his hand, and Ivan, who served as waiter, brought thick Turkish coffee. Rainsford, with an effort, held his tongue in check.

"It's a game, you see," pursued the general, blandly. "I suggest to one of them that we go hunting. I give him a supply of food and an excellent hunting knife. I give him three hours' start. I am to follow, armed only with a pistol of the smallest calibre and range. If my quarry eludes me for three whole days, he wins the game. If I find him"—the general smiled—"he loses."

"Suppose he refuses to be hunted?"

"Oh," said the general, "I give him his option, of course. He need not play that game if he doesn't wish to. If he does not wish to hunt, I turn him over to Ivan. Ivan once had the honour of serving as official knouter to the Great White Tsar, and he has his own ideas of sport. Invariably, Mr. Rainsford, invariably they choose the hunt."

"And if they win?"

The smile on the general's face widened. "To date I have not lost," he said.

Then he added, hastily: "I don't wish you to think me a braggart, Mr. Rainsford. Many of them afford only the most elementary sort of problem. Occasionally I strike a tartar. One almost did win. I eventually had to use the dogs."

"The dogs?"

"This way, please. I'll show you."

The general steered Rainsford to a window. The lights from the windows sent a flickering illumination that made grotesque patterns on the courtyard below, and Rainsford could see moving about there a dozen or so huge black shapes; as they turned toward him, their eyes glittered greenly.

"A rather good lot, I think," observed the general. "They are let out at seven every night. If any one should try to get into my house—or out of it—something extremely regrettable would occur to him." He hummed a snatch of song from the Folies Bergère.

"And now," said the general, "I want to show you my new collection of heads. Will you come with me to the library?"

"I hope," said Rainsford, "that you will excuse me tonight, General Zaroff. I'm really not feeling at all well."

"Ah, indeed?" the general inquired, solicitously. "Well, I suppose that's only natural, after your long swim. You need a good, restful night's sleep. To-morrow you'll feel like a new man, I'll wager. Then we'll hunt, eh? I've one rather promising prospect—"

Rainsford was hurrying from the room.

"Sorry you can't go with me to-night," called the general. "I expect rather fair sport—a big, strong black. He looks resourceful— Well, good-night, Mr. Rainsford; I hope you have a good night's rest."

The bed was good, and the pajamas of the softest silk, and he was tired in every fibre of his being, but nevertheless Rainsford could not quiet his brain with the opiate of sleep. He lay, eyes wide open. Once he thought he heard stealthy steps in the corridor outside his room. He sought to throw open the door; it would not open. He went to the window and looked out. His room was high up in one of the towers. The lights of the château were out now, and it was dark and silent, but there was a fragment of sallow moon, and by its wan light he could see, dimly, the courtyard; there, weaving in and out in the pattern of shadow, were black, noiseless forms; the hounds heard him at the window and looked up, expectantly, with their green eyes. Rainsford went back to the bed and lay down. By many methods he tried to put himself to sleep. He had achieved a doze when, just as morning began to come, he heard, far off in the jungle, the faint report of a pistol.

General Zaroff did not appear until luncheon. He was dressed faultlessly in the tweeds of a country squire. He was solicitous about the state of Rainsford's health.

"As for me," sighed the general, "I do not feel so well. I am worried, Mr. Rainsford. Last night I detected traces of my old complaint."

To Rainsford's questioning glance the general said: "Ennui. Boredom."

Then, taking a second helping of Crêpes Suzette, the general explained: "The hunting was not good last night. The fellow lost his head. He made a straight trail that offered no problems at all. That's the trouble with these sailors; they have dull brains to begin with, and they do not know how to get about in the woods. They do excessively stupid and obvious things. It's most annoying. Will you have another glass of Chablis, Mr. Rainsford?"

"General," said Rainsford, firmly, "I wish to leave this island at once."

The general raised his thickets of eyebrows; he seemed hurt. "But, my dear fellow," the general protested, "you've only just come. You've had no hunting—"

"I wish to go to-day," said Rainsford. He saw the dead black eyes of the general on him, studying him. General Zaroff's face suddenly brightened.

He filled Rainsford's glass with venerable Chablis from a dusty bottle.

"To-night," said the general, "we will hunt—you and I."

Rainsford shook his head. "No, General," he said. "I will not hunt."

The general shrugged his shoulders and delicately ate a hothouse grape. "As you wish, my friend," he said. "The choice rests entirely with you. But may I not venture to suggest that you will find my idea of sport more diverting than Ivan's?"

He nodded toward the corner to where the giant stood, scowling, his thick arms crossed on his hogshead of chest.

"You don't mean—" cried Rainsford.

"My dear fellow," said the general, "have I not told you I always mean what I say about hunting? This is really an inspiration. I drink to a foeman worthy of my steel—at last."

The general raised his glass, but Rainsford sat staring at him.

"You'll find this game worth playing," the general said, enthusiastically. "Your brain against mine. Your woodcraft against mine. Your strength and stamina against mine. Out-door chess! And the stake is not without value, eh?"

"And if I win—" began Rainsford, huskily.

"I'll cheerfully acknowledge myself defeated if I do not find you by midnight of the third day," said General Zaroff. "My sloop will place you on the mainland near a town."

The general read what Rainsford was thinking.

"Oh, you can trust me," said the Cossack. "I will give you my word as a gentleman and a sportsman. Of course, you, in turn, must agree to say nothing of your visit here."

"I'll agree to nothing of the kind," said Rainsford.

"Oh," said the general, "in that case— But why discuss that now? Three days hence we can discuss it over a bottle of Veuve Cliquot, unless—"

The general sipped his wine.

Then a businesslike air animated him. "Ivan," he said to Rainsford, "will supply you with hunting clothes, food, a knife. I suggest you wear moccasins; they leave a poorer trail. I suggest, too, that you avoid the big swamp in the south-east corner of the island. We call it Death Swamp. There's quicksand there. One foolish fellow tried it. The deplorable part of it was that Lazarus followed him. You can imagine my feelings, Mr. Rainsford. I loved Lazarus; he was the finest hound in my pack. Well, I must beg you to excuse me now. I always take a siesta after lunch. You'll hardly have time for a nap, I fear. You'll want to start, no doubt. I shall not follow till dusk. Hunting at night is so much more exciting than by day, don't you think? Au revoir, Mr. Rainsford, au revoir."

General Zaroff, with a deep, courtly bow, strolled from the room.

From another door came Ivan. Under one arm he carried khaki hunting clothes, a haversack of food, a leather sheath containing a long-bladed hunting knife; his right hand rested on a cocked revolver thrust in the crimson sash about his waist.

Rainsford had fought his way through the bush for two hours. "I must keep my nerve. I must keep my nerve," he said, through tight teeth.

He had not been entirely clear-headed when the château gates snapped shut behind him. His whole idea at first was to put distance between himself and General Zaroff, and, to this end, he had plunged along, spurred on by the sharp rowels of something very like panic. Now he had got a grip on himself, had stopped, and was taking stock of himself and the situation.

He saw that straight flight was futile; inevitably it would bring him face to face with the sea. He was in a picture with a frame of water, and his operations, clearly, must take place within that frame.

"I'll give him a trail to follow," muttered Rainsford, and he struck off from the rude path he had been following into the trackless wilderness. He executed a series of intricate loops; he doubled on his tail again and again, recalling all the lore of the fox hunt, and all the dodges of the fox. Night found him leg-weary, with hands and face lashed by the branches, on a thickly wooded ridge. He knew it would be insane to blunder on through the dark, even if he had the strength. His need for rest was imperative and he thought: "I have played the fox, now I must play the cat of the fable." A big tree with a thick trunk and outspread branches was near by, and, taking care to leave not the slightest mark, he climbed up into the crotch, and stretching out on one of the broad limbs, after a fashion, rested. Rest brought him new confidence and almost a feeling of security. Even so zealous a hunter as General Zaroff could not trace him there, he told himself; only the devil himself could follow that complicated trail through the jungle after dark. But perhaps the general was a devil—

An apprehensive night crawled slowly by like a wounded snake, and sleep did not visit Rainsford, although the silence of a dead world was on the jungle. Toward morning, when a dingy gray was varnishing the sky, the cry of some startled bird focussed Rainsford's attention in that direction. Something was coming through the bush, coming slowly, carefully, coming by the same winding way Rainsford had come. He flattened himself down on the limb, and through a screen of leaves almost as thick as tapestry, he watched. The thing that was approaching was a man.

It was General Zaroff. He made his way along with his eyes fixed in utmost concentration on the ground before him. He paused, almost beneath the tree, dropped to his knees, and studied the ground. Rainsford's impulse was to hurl himself down like a panther, but he saw that the general's right hand held something metallic—a small automatic pistol.

The hunter shook his head several times, as if he were puzzled. Then he straightened up and took from his case one of his black cigarettes; its pungent incense-like smoke floated up to Rainsford's nostrils.

Rainsford held his breath. The general's eyes had left the ground and were travelling inch by inch up the tree. Rainsford froze there, every muscle tensed for a spring. But the sharp eyes of the hunter stopped before they reached the limb where Rainsford lay; a smile spread over his brown face.

Very deliberately he blew a smoke ring into the air; then he turned his back on the tree and walked carelessly away, back along the trail he had come. The swish of the underbrush against his hunting boots grew fainter and fainter.

The pent-up air burst hotly from Rainsford's lungs. His first thought made him feel sick and numb. The general could follow a trail through the woods at night; he could follow an extremely difficult trail; he must have uncanny powers; only by the merest chance had the Cossack failed to see his quarry.

Rainsford's second thought was even more terrible. It sent a shudder of cold horror through his whole being. Why had the general smiled? Why had he turned back?

Rainsford did not want to believe what his reason told him was true, but the truth was as evident as the sun that had by now pushed through the morning mists. The general was playing with him! The general was saving him for another day's sport! The Cossack was the cat; he was the mouse. Then it was that Rainsford knew the full meaning of terror.

"I will not lose my nerve. I will not."

He slid down from the tree, and struck off again into the woods. His face was set and he forced the machinery of his mind to function. Three hundred yards from his hiding place he stopped where a huge dead tree leaned precariously on a smaller, living one. Throwing off his sack of food, Rainsford took his knife from its sheath and began to work with all his energy.

The job was finished at last, and he threw himself down behind a fallen log a hundred feet away. He did not have to wait long. The cat was coming again to play with the mouse.

Following the trail with the sureness of a bloodhound came General Zaroff. Nothing escaped those searching black eyes, no crushed blade of grass, no bent twig, no mark, no matter how faint, in the moss. So intent was the Cossack on his stalking that he was upon the thing Rainsford had made before he saw it. His foot touched the protruding bough that was the trigger. Even as he touched it, the general sensed his danger and leaped back with the agility of an ape. But he was not quite quick enough; the dead tree, delicately adjusted to rest on the cut living one, crashed down and struck the general a glancing blow on the shoulder as it fell; but for his alertness, he must have been smashed beneath it. He staggered, but he did not fall; nor did he drop his revolver. He stood there, rubbing his injured shoulder, and Rainsford, with fear again gripping his heart, heard the general's mocking laugh ring through the jungle.

"Rainsford," called the general, "if you are within sound of my voice, as I suppose you are, let me congratulate you. Not many men know how to make a Malay man-catcher. Luckily for me I, too, have hunted in Malacca. You are proving interesting, Mr. Rainsford. I am going now to have my wound dressed; it's only a slight one. But I shall be back. I shall be back."

When the general, nursing his bruised shoulder, had gone, Rainsford took up his flight again. It was flight now, a desperate, hopeless flight, that carried him on for some hours. Dusk came, then darkness, and still he pressed on. The ground grew softer under his moccasins; the vegetation grew ranker, denser; insects bit him savagely. Then, as he stepped forward, his foot sank into the ooze. He tried to wrench it back, but the muck sucked viciously at his foot as if it were a giant leech. With a violent effort he tore his foot loose. He knew where he was now. Death Swamp and its quicksand.

His hands were tight closed as if his nerve were something tangible that someone in the darkness was trying to tear from his grip. The softness of the earth had given him an idea. He stepped back from the quicksand a dozen feet or so and, like some huge prehistoric beaver, he began to dig.

Rainsford had dug himself in in France when a second's delay meant death. That had been a placid pastime compared to his digging now. The pit grew deeper; when it was above his shoulders, he climbed out and from some hard saplings cut stakes and sharpened them to a fine point. These stakes he planted in the bottom of the pit with the points sticking up. With flying fingers he wove a rough carpet of weeds and branches and with it he covered the mouth of the pit. Then, wet with sweat and aching with tiredness, he crouched behind the stump of a lightning-charred tree.

He knew his pursuer was coming; he heard the padding sound of feet on the soft earth, and the night breeze brought him the perfume of the general's cigarette. It seemed to Rainsford that the general was coming with unusual swiftness; he was not feeling his way along, foot by foot. Rainsford, crouching there, could not see the general, nor could he see the pit. He lived a year in a minute. Then he felt an impulse to cry aloud with joy, for he heard the sharp crackle of the breaking branches as the cover of the pit gave way; he heard the sharp scream of pain as the pointed stakes found their mark. He leaped up from his place of concealment. Then he cowered back. Three feet from the pit a man was standing, with an electric torch in his hand.

"You've done well, Rainsford," the voice of the general called. "Your Burmese tiger pit has claimed one of my best dogs. Again you score. I think, Mr. Rainsford, I'll see what you can do against my whole pack. I'm going home for a rest now. Thank you for a most amusing evening."

At daybreak Rainsford, lying near the swamp, was awakened by a sound that made him know that he had new things to learn about fear. It was a distant sound, faint and wavering, but he knew it. It was the baying of a pack of hounds.

Rainsford knew he could do one of two things. He could stay where he was and wait. That was suicide. He could flee. That was postponing the inevitable. For a moment he stood there, thinking. An idea that held a wild chance came to him, and, tightening his belt, he headed away from the swamp.

The baying of the hounds drew nearer, then still nearer, nearer, ever nearer. On a ridge Rainsford climbed a tree. Down a watercourse, not a quarter of a mile away, he could see the bush moving. Straining his eyes, he saw the lean figure of General Zaroff; just ahead of him, Rainsford made out another figure whose wide shoulders surged through the tall jungle weeds; it was the giant Ivan, and he seemed pulled forward by some unseen force; Rainsford knew that Ivan must be holding the pack in leash.

They would be on him any minute now. His mind worked frantically. He thought of a native trick he had learned in Uganda. He slid down the tree. He caught hold of a springy young sapling and to it he fastened his hunting knife, with the blade pointing down the trail; with a bit of wild grapevine he tied back the sapling. Then he ran for his life. The hounds raised their voices as they hit the fresh scent. Rainsford knew now how an animal at bay feels.

He had to stop to get his breath. The baying of the hounds stopped abruptly, and Rainsford's heart stopped, too. They must have reached the knife.

He shinned excitedly up a tree and looked back. His pursuers had stopped. But the hope that was in Rainsford's brain when he climbed died, for he saw in the shallow valley that General Zaroff was still on his feet. But Ivan was not. The knife, driven by the recoil of the springing tree, had not wholly failed.

Rainsford had hardly tumbled to the ground when the pack took up the cry again.

"Nerve, nerve, nerve!" he panted, as he dashed along. A blue gap showed between the trees dead ahead. Ever nearer drew the hounds. Rainsford forced himself on toward that gap. He reached it. It was the shore of the sea. Across a cove he could see the gloomy gray stone of the château. Twenty feet below him the sea rumbled and hissed. Rainsford hesitated. He heard the hounds. Then he leaped far out into the sea.

When the general and his pack reached the place by the sea, the Cossack stopped. For some minutes he stood regarding the blue-green expanse of water. He shrugged his shoulders. Then he sat down, took a drink of brandy from a silver flask, lit a perfumed cigarette, and hummed a bit from "Madama Butterfly."

General Zaroff had an exceedingly good dinner in his great panelled dining hall that evening. With it he had a bottle of Pol Roger and half a bottle of Chambertin. Two slight annoyances kept him from perfect enjoyment. One was the thought that it would be difficult to replace Ivan; the other was that his quarry had escaped him; of course the American hadn't played the game—so thought the general as he tasted his after-dinner liqueur. In his library he read, to soothe himself, from the works of Marcus Aurelius. At ten he went up to his bedroom. He was deliciously tired, he said to himself, as he locked himself in. There was a little moonlight, so before turning on his light he went to the window and looked down at the courtyard. He could see the great hounds, and he called: "Better luck another time," to them. Then he switched on the light.

A man, who had been hiding in the curtains of the bed, was standing there.

"Rainsford!" screamed the general. "How in God's name did you get here?"

"Swam," said Rainsford. "I found it quicker than walking through the jungle."

The general sucked in his breath and smiled. "I congratulate you," he said. "You have won the game."

Rainsford did not smile. "I am still a beast at bay," he said, in a low, hoarse voice. "Get ready, General Zaroff."

The general made one of his deepest bows. "I see," he said. "Splendid! One of us is to furnish a repast for the hounds. The other will sleep in this very excellent bed. On guard, Rainsford."

He had never slept in a better bed, Rainsford decided.

SAKI (H.H. MUNRO)

H. H. Munro (1870–1916), better known by his pen name Saki, was a master of irony, wit, and the darker undercurrents of Edwardian society. Born in Burma, he was raised by strict aunts in rural England. He worked as a foreign correspondent before turning to fiction, often lampooning characters much like his aunts and avenging his childhood with merciless satire. His compact stories fuse sly humour, biting irony, and abrupt reversals that leave a sardonic sting. At forty-four, Munro enlisted in World War I, refused a commission, and fought as a private. A sniper killed him in the trenches near Beaumont-Hamel; his reputed last words were a curt "Put that bloody cigarette out."

THE INTERLOPERS

SAKI

First published in *The Bystander*, 1912.

In a forest of mixed growth somewhere on the eastern spurs of the Carpathians, a man stood one winter night watching and listening, as though he waited for some beast of the woods to come within the range of his vision, and later, of his rifle. But the game for whose presence he kept so keen an outlook was none that figured in the sportsman's calendar as lawful and proper for the chase; Ulrich von Gradwitz patrolled the dark forest in quest of a human enemy.

The forest lands of Gradwitz were of wide extent and well stocked with game; the narrow strip of precipitous woodland that lay on its outskirt was not remarkable for the game it harboured or the shooting it afforded, but it was the most jealously guarded of all its owner's territorial possessions. A famous lawsuit, in the days of his grandfather, had wrested it from the illegal possession of a neighbouring family of petty landowners; the dispossessed party had never acquiesced in the judgment of the courts, and a long series of poaching affrays and similar scandals had embittered the relationships between the families for three generations.

The neighbour feud had grown into a personal one since Ulrich had come to be head of his family; if there was a man in the world whom he detested and wished ill to, it was Georg Znaeym, the inheritor of the quarrel and the tireless game-snatcher and raider of the disputed border-forest. The feud might, perhaps, have died down or been compromised if the personal ill-will of the two men had not stood in the way; as boys they had thirsted for one another's blood, as men each prayed that misfortune might fall on the other, and this wind-scourged winter night Ulrich had banded together his foresters to watch the dark forest—not in quest of four-footed quarry, but to keep a lookout for the prowling thieves whom he suspected of being afoot from across the land boundary.

The roebuck, which usually kept in the sheltered hollows during a storm-wind, were running like driven things to-night, and there was movement and unrest among the creatures that were wont to sleep through the dark hours. Assuredly there was a disturbing element in the forest, and Ulrich could guess the quarter from whence it came.

He strayed away by himself from the watchers whom he had placed in ambush on the crest of the hill, and wandered far down the steep slopes amid the wild tangle of undergrowth, peering through the tree trunks and listening through the whistling and skirling of the wind and the restless beating of the branches for sight and sound of the marauders. If only on this wild night, in this dark, lone spot, he might come across Georg Znaeym, man to man, with none to witness—that was the wish that was uppermost in his thoughts. And as he stepped round the trunk of a huge beech he came face to face with the man he sought.

The two enemies stood glaring at one another for a long, silent moment. Each had a rifle in his hand, each had hate in his heart and murder uppermost in his mind. The chance had come to give full play to the passions of a lifetime. But a man who has been brought up under the code of a restraining civilisation cannot easily nerve himself to shoot down his neighbour in cold blood and without word spoken, except for an offence against his hearth and honour. And before the moment of hesitation had given way to action, a deed of Nature's own violence overwhelmed them both.

A fierce shriek of the storm had been answered by a splitting crash over their heads, and ere they could leap aside a mass of falling beech tree had thundered down on them. Ulrich von Gradwitz found himself stretched on the ground, one arm numb beneath him and the other held almost as helplessly in a tight tangle of forked branches, while both legs were pinned beneath the fallen mass. His heavy shooting-boots had saved his feet from being crushed to pieces, but if his fractures were not as serious as they might have been, at least it was evident that he could not move from his present position till someone came to release him.

The descending twig had slashed the skin of his face, and he had to wink away some drops of blood from his eyelashes before he could take in a general view of the disaster. At his side, so near that under ordinary circumstances he could almost have touched him, lay Georg Znaeym, alive and struggling, but obviously as helplessly pinioned down as himself. All round them lay a thick-strewn wreckage of splintered branches and broken twigs.

Relief at being alive and exasperation at his captive plight brought a strange medley of pious thank-offerings and sharp curses to Ulrich's lips. Georg, who was early blinded with the blood which trickled across his eyes, stopped his struggling for a moment to listen, and then gave a short, snarling laugh.

"So you're not killed, as you ought to be, but you're caught, anyway," he cried. "Caught fast. Ho, what a jest—Ulrich von Gradwitz snared in his stolen forest. There's real justice for you!"

And he laughed again, mockingly and savagely.

"I'm caught in my own forest-land," retorted Ulrich. "When my men come to release us you will wish, perhaps, that you were in a better plight than caught poaching on a neighbour's land—shame on you."

Georg was silent for a moment; then he answered quietly:

"Are you sure that your men will find much to release? I have men, too, in the forest to-night, close behind me, and they will be here first and do the releasing. When they drag me out from under these damned branches it won't need much clumsiness on their part to roll this mass of trunk right over on the top of you. Your men will find you dead under a fallen beech tree. For form's sake I shall send my condolences to your family."

"It is a useful hint," said Ulrich fiercely. "My men had orders to follow in ten minutes' time—seven of which must have gone by already—and when they get me out, I will remember the hint. Only, as you will have met your death poaching on my lands, I don't think I can decently send any message of condolence to your family."

"Good," snarled Georg, "good. We fight this quarrel out to the death, you and I and our foresters, with no cursed interlopers to come between us. Death and damnation to you, Ulrich von Gradwitz."

"The same to you, Georg Znaeym—forest-thief, game-snatcher."

Both men spoke with the bitterness of possible defeat before them, for each knew that it might be long before his men would seek him out or find him; it was a bare matter of chance which party would arrive first on the scene.

Both had now given up the useless struggle to free themselves from the mass of wood that held them down; Ulrich limited his endeavours to an effort to bring his one partially free arm near enough to his outer coat pocket to draw out his wine-flask. Even when he had accomplished that operation it was long before he could manage the unscrewing of the stopper or get any of the liquid down his throat. But what a heaven-sent draught it seemed!

It was an open winter, and little snow had fallen as yet; hence the captives suffered less from the cold than might have been the case at that season of the year. Nevertheless, the wine was warming and reviving to the wounded man, and he looked across with something like a throb of pity to where his enemy lay, just keeping the groans of pain and weariness from crossing his lips.

"Could you reach this flask if I threw it over to you?" asked Ulrich suddenly. "There is good wine in it, and one may as well be as comfortable as one can. Let us drink, even if to-night one of us dies."

"No, I can scarcely see anything; there is so much blood caked round my eyes," said Georg, "and in any case I don't drink wine with an enemy."

Ulrich was silent for a few minutes and lay listening to the weary screeching of the wind. An idea was slowly forming and growing in his brain, an idea that gained strength every time that he looked across at the man who was fighting so grimly against pain and exhaustion. In the pain and languor that Ulrich himself was feeling, the old fierce hatred seemed to be dying down.

"Neighbour," he said presently, "do as you please if your men come first. It was a fair compact. But as for me, I've changed my mind. If my men are the first to come, you shall be the first to be helped, as though you were my guest. We have quarrelled like devils all our lives over this stupid strip of forest, where the trees can't even stand upright in a breath of wind. Lying here to-night thinking, I've come to think we've been rather fools; there are better things in life than getting the better of a boundary dispute. Neighbour, if you will help me to bury the old quarrel, I—I will ask you to be my friend."

Georg Znaeym was silent for so long that Ulrich thought, perhaps, he had fainted with the pain of his injuries. Then he spoke slowly and in jerks.

"How the whole region would stare and gabble if we rode into the market-square together. No one living can remember seeing a Znaeym and a von Gradwitz talking to one another in friendship. And what peace there would be among the forester folk if we ended our feud to-night! And if we choose to make peace among our people there is none other to interfere, no interlopers from outside.

"You would come and keep the Sylvester night beneath my roof, and I would come and feast on some high day at your castle. I would never fire a shot on your land, save when you invited me as a guest; and you should come and shoot with me down in the marshes where the wild-fowl are. In all the countryside there are none that could hinder if we willed to make peace. I never thought to have wanted to do other than hate you all my life, but I think I have changed my mind about things too, this last half-hour. And you offered me your wine-flask... Ulrich von Gradwitz, I will be your friend."

For a space both men were silent, turning over in their minds the wonderful changes that this dramatic reconciliation would bring about. In the cold, gloomy forest, with the wind tearing in fitful gusts through the naked branches and whistling round the tree-trunks, they lay and waited for the help that would now bring release and succour to both parties. And each prayed a private prayer that his men might be the first to arrive, so that he might be the first to show honourable attention to the enemy that had become a friend.

Presently, as the wind dropped for a moment, Ulrich broke silence.

"Let's shout for help," he said. "In this lull our voices may carry a little way."

"They won't carry far through the trees and undergrowth," said Georg, "but we can try. Together, then."

The two raised their voices in a prolonged hunting call.

"Together again," said Ulrich a few minutes later, after listening in vain for an answering halloo.

"I heard nothing but the pestilential wind," said Georg hoarsely.

There was silence again for some minutes, and then Ulrich gave a joyful cry.

"I can see figures coming through the wood. They are following in the way I came down the hillside."

Both men raised their voices in as loud a shout as they could muster.

"They hear us! They've stopped. Now they see us. They're running down the hill towards us," cried Ulrich.

"How many of them are there?" asked Georg.

"I can't see distinctly," said Ulrich. "Nine or ten."

"Then they are yours," said Georg. "I had only seven out with me."

"They are making all the speed they can—brave lads," said Ulrich gladly.

"Are they your men?" asked Georg. "Are they your men?" he repeated impatiently as Ulrich did not answer.

"No," said Ulrich with a laugh—the idiotic, chattering laugh of a man unstrung with hideous fear.

"Who are they?" asked Georg quickly, straining his eyes to see what the other would gladly not have seen.

"Wolves."

Ambrose Bierce

Ambrose Bierce (1842–circa 1914) was an American soldier, journalist, and satirist whose sharp wit earned him the nickname "Bitter Bierce." A Union veteran of the Civil War, he brought first-hand knowledge of battlefield horrors to his fiction, writing with precision, irony, and dark insight. *An Occurrence at Owl Creek Bridge* stands as his masterpiece. Kurt Vonnegut described it as the "greatest American short story," and "a flawless example of American genius." Adapted into a 1962 Oscar-winning short film, it was featured on *The Twilight Zone*. In 1913, at seventy-one, Bierce crossed into Mexico during the revolution and was never seen again. His last known letter ended, "As to me, I leave here tomorrow for an unknown destination."

An Occurrence at Owl Creek Bridge

Ambrose Bierce

First published in *The San Francisco Examiner*, 1890.

I

A man stood upon a railroad bridge in northern Alabama, looking down into the swift water twenty feet below. The man's hands were behind his back, the wrists bound with a cord. A rope closely encircled his neck. It was attached to a stout cross-timber above his head and the slack fell to the level of his knees. Some loose boards laid upon the sleepers supporting the metals of the railway supplied a footing for him and his executioners--two private soldiers of the Federal army, directed by a sergeant who in civil life may have been a deputy sheriff. At a short remove upon the same temporary platform was an officer in the uniform of his rank, armed. He was a captain. A sentinel at each end of the bridge stood with his rifle in the position known as "support," that is to say, vertical in front of the left shoulder, the hammer resting on the forearm thrown straight across the chest--a formal and unnatural position, enforcing an erect carriage of the body. It did not appear to be the duty of these two men to know what was occurring at the center of the bridge; they merely blockaded the two ends of the foot planking that traversed it.

Beyond one of the sentinels nobody was in sight; the railroad ran straight away into a forest for a hundred yards, then, curving, was lost to view. Doubtless there was an outpost farther along. The other bank of the stream was open ground--a gentle acclivity topped with a stockade of vertical tree trunks, loopholed for rifles, with a single embrasure through which protruded the muzzle of a brass cannon commanding the bridge. Midway of the slope between the bridge and fort were the spectators--a single company of infantry in line, at "parade rest," the butts of the rifles on the ground, the barrels inclining slightly backward against the right shoulder, the hands crossed upon the stock. A lieutenant stood at the right of the line, the point of his sword upon the ground, his left hand resting upon his right. Excepting the group of four at the center of the bridge, not a man moved. The company faced the bridge, staring stonily, motionless. The sentinels, facing the banks of the stream, might have been statues to adorn the bridge. The captain stood with folded arms, silent, observing the work of his subordinates, but making no sign. Death is a dignitary who when he comes announced is to be received with formal manifestations of respect, even by those most familiar with him. In the code of military etiquette silence and fixity are forms of deference.

The man who was engaged in being hanged was apparently about thirty-five years of age. He was a civilian, if one might judge from his habit, which was that of a planter. His features were good--a straight nose, firm mouth, broad forehead, from which his long, dark hair was combed straight back, falling behind his ears to the collar of his well-fitting frock coat. He wore a mustache and pointed beard, but no whiskers; his eyes were large and dark gray, and had a kindly expression which one would hardly have expected in one whose neck was in the hemp. Evidently this was no vulgar assassin. The liberal military code makes provision for hanging many kinds of persons, and gentlemen are not excluded.

The preparations being complete, the two private soldiers stepped aside and each drew away the plank upon which he had been standing. The sergeant turned to the captain, saluted and placed himself immediately behind that officer, who in turn moved apart one pace. These movements left the condemned man and the sergeant standing on the two ends of the same plank, which spanned three of the cross-ties of the bridge. The end upon which the civilian stood almost, but not quite, reached a fourth. This plank had been held in place by the weight of the captain; it was now held by that of the sergeant. At a signal from the former the latter would step aside, the plank would tilt and the condemned man go down between two ties. The arrangement commended itself to his judgment as simple and effective. His face had not been covered nor his eyes bandaged. He looked a moment at his "unsteadfast footing," then let his gaze wander to the swirling water of the stream racing madly beneath his feet. A piece of dancing driftwood caught his attention and his eyes followed it down the current. How slowly it appeared to move! What a sluggish stream!

He closed his eyes in order to fix his last thoughts upon his wife and children. The water, touched to gold by the early sun, the brooding mists under the banks at some distance down the stream, the fort, the soldiers, the piece of drift--all had distracted him. And now he became conscious of a new disturbance. Striking through the thought of his dear ones was a sound which he could neither ignore nor understand, a sharp, distinct, metallic percussion like the stroke of a blacksmith's hammer upon the anvil; it had the same ringing quality. He wondered what it was, and whether immeasurably distant or near by--it seemed both. Its recurrence was regular, but as slow as the tolling of a death knell. He awaited each stroke with impatience and--he knew not why--apprehension. The intervals of silence grew progressively longer, the delays became maddening. With their greater infrequency the sounds increased in strength and sharpness. They hurt his ear like the thrust of a knife; he feared he would shriek. What he heard was the ticking of his watch.

He unclosed his eyes and saw again the water below him. "If I could free my hands," he thought, "I might throw off the noose and spring into the stream. By diving I could evade the bullets and, swimming vigorously, reach the bank, take to the woods and get away home. My home, thank God, is as yet outside their lines; my wife and little ones are still beyond the invader's farthest advance."

As these thoughts, which have here to be set down in words, were flashed into the doomed man's brain rather than evolved from it the captain nodded to the sergeant. The sergeant stepped aside.

II

Peyton Farquhar was a well-to-do planter, of an old and highly respected Alabama family. Being a slave owner and like other slave owners a politician he was naturally an original secessionist and ardently devoted to the Southern cause. Circumstances of an imperious nature, which it is unnecessary to relate here, had prevented him from taking service with the gallant army that had fought the disastrous campaigns ending with the fall of Corinth, and he chafed under the inglorious restraint, longing for the release of his energies, the larger life of the soldier, the opportunity for distinction. That opportunity, he felt, would come, as it comes to all in war time. Meanwhile he did what he could. No service was too humble for him to perform in aid of the South, no adventure too perilous for him to undertake if consistent with the character of a civilian who was at heart a soldier, and who in good faith and without too much qualification assented to at least a part of the frankly villainous dictum that all is fair in love and war.

One evening while Farquhar and his wife were sitting on a rustic bench near the entrance to his grounds, a gray-clad soldier rode up to the gate and asked for a drink of water. Mrs. Farquhar was only too happy to serve him with her own white hands. While she was fetching the water her husband approached the dusty horseman and inquired eagerly for news from the front.

"The Yanks are repairing the railroads," said the man, "and are getting ready for another advance. They have reached the Owl Creek bridge, put it in order and built a stockade on the north bank. The commandant has issued an order, which is posted everywhere, declaring that any civilian caught interfering with the railroad, its bridges, tunnels or trains will be summarily hanged. I saw the order."

"How far is it to the Owl Creek bridge?" Farquhar asked.

"About thirty miles."

"Is there no force on this side the creek?"

"Only a picket post half a mile out, on the railroad, and a single sentinel at this end of the bridge."

"Suppose a man--a civilian and student of hanging--should elude the picket post and perhaps get the better of the sentinel," said Farquhar, smiling, "what could he accomplish?"

The soldier reflected. "I was there a month ago," he replied. "I observed that the flood of last winter had lodged a great quantity of driftwood against the wooden pier at this end of the bridge. It is now dry and would burn like tow."

The lady had now brought the water, which the soldier drank. He thanked her ceremoniously, bowed to her husband and rode away. An hour later, after nightfall, he repassed the plantation, going northward in the direction from which he had come. He was a Federal scout.

III

As Peyton Farquhar fell straight downward through the bridge he lost consciousness and was as one already dead. From this state he was awakened--ages later, it seemed to him--by the pain of a sharp pressure upon his throat, followed by a sense of suffocation. Keen, poignant agonies seemed to shoot from his neck downward through every fiber of his body and limbs. These pains appeared to flash along well-defined lines of ramification and to beat with an inconceivably rapid periodicity. They seemed like streams of pulsating fire heating him to an intolerable temperature. As to his head, he was conscious of nothing but a feeling of fulness--of congestion. These sensations were unaccompanied by thought. The intellectual part of his nature was already effaced; he had power only to feel, and feeling was torment. He was conscious of motion. Encompassed in a luminous cloud, of which he was now merely the fiery heart, without material substance, he swung through unthinkable arcs of oscillation, like a vast pendulum. Then all at once, with terrible suddenness, the light about him shot upward with the noise of a loud splash; a frightful roaring was in his ears, and all was cold and dark. The power of thought was restored; he knew that the rope had broken and he had fallen into the stream. There was no additional strangulation; the noose about his neck was already suffocating him and kept the water from his lungs. To die of hanging at the bottom of a river!--the idea seemed to him ludicrous. He opened his eyes in the darkness and saw above him a gleam of light, but how distant, how inaccessible! He was still sinking, for the light became fainter and fainter until it was a mere glimmer. Then it began to grow and brighten, and he knew that he was rising toward the surface--knew it with reluctance, for he was now very comfortable. "To be hanged and drowned," he thought, "that is not so bad; but I do not wish to be shot. No; I will not be shot; that is not fair."

He was not conscious of an effort, but a sharp pain in his wrist apprised him that he was trying to free his hands.

He gave the struggle his attention, as an idler might observe the feat of a juggler, without interest in the outcome. What splendid effort!--what magnificent, what superhuman strength! Ah, that was a fine endeavor! Bravo! The cord fell away; his arms parted and floated upward, the hands dimly seen on each side in the growing light. He watched them with a new interest as first one and then the other pounced upon the noose at his neck. They tore it away and thrust it fiercely aside, its undulations resembling those of a water snake. "Put it back, put it back!" He thought he shouted these words to his hands, for the undoing of the noose had been succeeded by the direst pang that he had yet experienced. His neck ached horribly; his brain was on fire; his heart, which had been fluttering faintly, gave a great leap, trying to force itself out at his mouth. His whole body was racked and wrenched with an insupportable anguish! But his disobedient hands gave no heed to the command. They beat the water vigorously with quick, downward strokes, forcing him to the surface. He felt his head emerge; his eyes were blinded by the sunlight; his chest expanded convulsively, and with a supreme and crowning agony his lungs engulfed a great draught of air, which instantly he expelled in a shriek!

He was now in full possession of his physical senses. They were, indeed, preternaturally keen and alert. Something in the awful disturbance of his organic system had so exalted and refined them that they made record of things never before perceived. He felt the ripples upon his face and heard their separate sounds as they struck. He looked at the forest on the bank of the stream, saw the individual trees, the leaves and the veining of each leaf--saw the very insects upon them: the locusts, the brilliant-bodied flies, the grey spiders stretching their webs from twig to twig. He noted the prismatic colors in all the dewdrops upon a million blades of grass. The humming of the gnats that danced above the eddies of the stream, the beating of the dragon flies' wings, the strokes of the water-spiders' legs, like oars which had lifted their boat--all these made audible music. A fish slid along beneath his eyes and he heard the rush of its body parting the water.

He had come to the surface facing down the stream; in a moment the visible world seemed to wheel slowly round, himself the pivotal point, and he saw the bridge, the fort, the soldiers upon the bridge, the captain, the sergeant, the two privates, his executioners. They were in silhouette against the blue sky. They shouted and gesticulated, pointing at him. The captain had drawn his pistol, but did not fire; the others were unarmed. Their movements were grotesque and horrible, their forms gigantic.

Suddenly he heard a sharp report and something struck the water smartly within a few inches of his head, spattering his face with spray. He heard a second report, and saw one of the sentinels with his rifle at his shoulder, a light cloud of blue smoke rising from the muzzle. The man in the water saw the eye of the man on the bridge gazing into his own through the sights of the rifle. He observed that it was a grey eye and remembered having read that grey eyes were keenest, and that all famous marksmen had them. Nevertheless, this one had missed.

A counter-swirl had caught Farquhar and turned him half round; he was again looking into the forest on the bank opposite the fort. The sound of a clear, high voice in a monot-onous singsong now rang out behind him and came across the water with a distinctness that pierced and subdued all other sounds, even the beating of the ripples in his ears. Although no soldier, he had frequented camps enough to know the dread significance of that deliberate, drawling, aspirated chant; the lieutenant on shore was taking a part in the morning's work. How coldly and pitilessly--with what an even, calm intonation, presaging, and enforcing tranquillity in the men--with what accurately measured intervals fell those cruel words:

"Attention, company! . . . Shoulder arms! . . . Ready! . . . Aim! . . . Fire!"

Farquhar dived--dived as deeply as he could. The water roared in his ears like the voice of Niagara, yet he heard the dulled thunder of the volley and, rising again toward the surface, met shining bits of metal, singularly flattened, oscillating slowly downward. Some of them touched him on the face and hands, then fell away, continuing their descent. One lodged between his collar and neck; it was uncomfortably warm and he snatched it out.

As he rose to the surface, gasping for breath, he saw that he had been a long time under water; he was perceptibly farther down stream nearer to safety. The soldiers had almost finished reloading; the metal ramrods flashed all at once in the sunshine as they were drawn from the barrels, turned in the air, and thrust into their sockets. The two sentinels fired again, independently and ineffectually.

The hunted man saw all this over his shoulder; he was now swimming vigorously with the current. His brain was as energetic as his arms and legs; he thought with the rapidity of lightning.

"The officer," he reasoned, "will not make that martinet's error a second time. It is as easy to dodge a volley as a single shot. He has probably already given the command to fire at will. God help me, I cannot dodge them all!"

An appalling splash within two yards of him was followed by a loud, rushing sound, diminuendo, which seemed to travel back through the air to the fort and died in an explosion which stirred the very river to its deeps!

A rising sheet of water curved over him, fell down upon him, blinded him, strangled him! The cannon had taken a hand in the game. As he shook his head free from the commotion of the smitten water he heard the deflected shot humming through the air ahead, and in an instant it was cracking and smashing the branches in the forest beyond.

"They will not do that again," he thought; "the next time they will use a charge of grape. I must keep my eye upon the gun; the smoke will apprise me--the report arrives too late; it lags behind the missile. That is a good gun."

Suddenly he felt himself whirled round and round--spinning like a top. The water, the banks, the forests, the now distant bridge, fort and men--all were commingled and blurred. Objects were represented by their colors only; circular horizontal streaks of color--that was all he saw. He had been caught in a vortex and was being whirled on with a velocity of advance and gyration that made him giddy and sick. In a few moments he was flung upon the gravel at the foot of the left bank of the stream--the southern bank--and behind a projecting point which concealed him from his enemies. The sudden arrest of his motion, the abrasion of one of his hands on the gravel, restored him, and he wept with delight. He dug his fingers into the sand, threw it over himself in handfuls and audibly blessed it. It looked like diamonds, rubies, emeralds; he could think of nothing beautiful which it did not resemble. The trees upon the bank were giant garden plants; he noted a definite order in their arrangement, inhaled the fragrance of their blooms. A strange, roseate light shone through the spaces among their trunks and the wind made in their branches the music of aeolian harps. He had no wish to perfect his escape--was content to remain in that enchanting spot until retaken.

A whiz and rattle of grapeshot among the branches high above his head roused him from his dream. The baffled cannoneer had fired him a random farewell. He sprang to his feet, rushed up the sloping bank, and plunged into the forest.

All that day he traveled, laying his course by the rounding sun. The forest seemed interminable; nowhere did he discover a break in it, not even a woodman's road. He had not known that he lived in so wild a region. There was something uncanny in the revelation.

By nightfall he was fatigued, footsore, famishing. The thought of his wife and children urged him on. At last he found a road which led him in what he knew to be the right direction. It was as wide and straight as a city street, yet it seemed untraveled. No fields bordered it, no dwelling anywhere. Not so much as the barking of a dog suggested human habitation. The black bodies of the trees formed a straight wall on both sides, terminating on the horizon in a point, like a diagram in a lesson in perspective. Overhead, as he looked up through this rift in the wood, shone great garden stars looking unfamiliar and grouped in strange constellations. He was sure they were arranged in some order which had a secret and malign significance. The wood on either side was full of singular noises, among which--once, twice, and again--he distinctly heard whispers in an unknown tongue.

His neck was in pain and lifting his hand to it found it horribly swollen. He knew that it had a circle of black where the rope had bruised it. His eyes felt congested; he could no longer close them. His tongue was swollen with thirst; he relieved its fever by thrusting it forward from between his teeth into the cold air. How softly the turf had carpeted the untraveled avenue--he could no longer feel the roadway beneath his feet!

Doubtless, despite his suffering, he had fallen asleep while walking, for now he sees another scene--perhaps he has merely recovered from a delirium. He stands at the gate of his own home. All is as he left it, and all bright and beautiful in the morning sunshine. He must have traveled the entire night. As he pushes open the gate and passes up the wide white walk, he sees a flutter of female garments; his wife, looking fresh and cool and sweet, steps down from the veranda to meet him. At the bottom of the steps she stands waiting, with a smile of ineffable joy, an attitude of matchless grace and dignity. Ah, how beautiful she is! He springs forward with extended arms. As he is about to clasp her he feels a stunning blow upon the back of the neck; a blinding white light blazes all about him with a sound like the shock of a cannon--then all is darkness and silence!

Peyton Farquhar was dead; his body, with a broken neck, swung gently from side to side beneath the timbers of the Owl Creek bridge.

JACK LONDON

Jack London (1876–1916) was an American adventurer, journalist, and novelist whose life was as raw and relentless as his fiction. A sailor, gold prospector, and war correspondent, he mined his own hardscrabble exploits from the Klondike to the South Seas for tales of survival, primal instinct, and unyielding will. When his early pieces were steadily rejected, he began pinning each slip to the wall at Heinold's First and Last Chance Saloon in Oakland. He nailed up six hundred before his story *To the Man on Trail* sold to *The Overland Monthly* in 1898. The slips still hang there today. *Lost Face* captures London at his visceral peak.

LOST FACE

JACK LONDON

First published in *Lost Face* (Macmillan), 1910.

It was the end. Subienkow had travelled a long trail of bitterness and horror, homing like a dove for the capitals of
Europe, and here, farther away than ever, in Russian America,
the trail ceased. He sat in the snow, arms tied behind him,
waiting the torture. He stared curiously before him at a huge
Cossack, prone in the snow, moaning in his pain. The men
had finished handling the giant and turned him over to the
women. That they exceeded the fiendishness of the men, the
man's cries attested.

Subienkow looked on, and shuddered. He was not afraid
to die. He had carried his life too long in his hands, on
that weary trail from Warsaw to Nulato, to shudder at mere
dying. But he objected to the torture. It offended his soul.
And this offence, in turn, was not due to the mere pain he
must endure, but to the sorry spectacle the pain would make
of him. He knew that he would pray, and beg, and entreat,
even as Big Ivan and the others that had gone before. This
would not be nice. To pass out bravely and cleanly, with
a smile and a jest—ah! that would have been the way. But

to lose control, to have his soul upset by the pangs of the flesh, to screech and gibber like an ape, to become the veriest beast—ah, that was what was so terrible.

There had been no chance to escape. From the beginning, when he dreamed the fiery dream of Poland's independence, he had become a puppet in the hands of Fate. From the beginning, at Warsaw, at St. Petersburg, in the Siberian mines, in Kamtchatka, on the crazy boats of the fur-thieves, Fate had been driving him to this end. Without doubt, in the foundations of the world was graved this end for him—for him, who was so fine and sensitive, whose nerves scarcely sheltered under his skin, who was a dreamer, and a poet, and an artist. Before he was dreamed of, it had been determined that the quivering bundle of sensitiveness that constituted him should be doomed to live in raw and howling savagery, and to die in this far land of night, in this dark place beyond the last boundaries of the world.

He sighed. So that thing before him was Big Ivan—Big Ivan the giant, the man without nerves, the man of iron, the Cossack turned freebooter of the seas, who was as phlegmatic as an ox, with a nervous system so low that what was pain to ordinary men was scarcely a tickle to him. Well, well, trust these Nulato Indians to find Big Ivan's nerves and trace them to the roots of his quivering soul. They were certainly doing it. It was inconceivable that a man could suffer so much and yet live. Big Ivan was paying for his low order of nerves. Already he had lasted twice as long as any of the others.

Subienkow felt that he could not stand the Cossack's sufferings much longer. Why didn't Ivan die? He would go mad if that screaming did not cease. But when it did cease, his turn would come. And there was Yakaga awaiting him, too, grinning at him even now in anticipation—Yakaga, whom only last week he had kicked out of the fort, and upon whose face he had laid the lash of his dog-whip. Yakaga would attend to him. Doubtlessly Yakaga was saving for him more refined tortures, more exquisite nerve-racking. Ah! that must have been a good one, from the way Ivan screamed. The squaws bending over him stepped back with laughter and clapping of hands. Subienkow saw the monstrous thing that had been perpetrated, and began to laugh hysterically. The Indians looked at him in wonderment that he should laugh. But Subienkow could not stop.

This would never do. He controlled himself, the spasmodic twitchings slowly dying away. He strove to think of other things, and began reading back in his own life. He remembered his mother and his father, and the little spotted pony, and the French tutor who had taught him dancing and sneaked him an old worn copy of Voltaire. Once more he saw Paris, and dreary London, and gay Vienna, and Rome. And once more he saw that wild group of youths who had dreamed, even as he, the dream of an independent Poland with a king of Poland on the throne at Warsaw. Ah, there it was that the long trail began. Well, he had lasted longest. One by one, beginning with the two executed at St. Petersburg, he took up the count of the passing of those brave spirits. Here one had been beaten to death by a jailer, and there, on that bloodstained highway of the exiles, where they had marched for endless months, beaten and maltreated by their Cossack guards, another had dropped by the way. Always it had been savagery—brutal, bestial savagery. They had died—of fever, in the mines, under the knout. The last two had died after the escape, in the battle with the Cossacks, and he alone had won to Kamtchatka with the stolen papers and the money of a traveller he had left lying in the snow.

It had been nothing but savagery. All the years, with his heart in studios, and theatres, and courts, he had been hemmed in by savagery. He had purchased his life with blood. Everybody had killed. He had killed that traveller for his passports. He had proved that he was a man of parts by duelling with two Russian officers on a single day. He had had to prove himself in order to win to a place among the fur-thieves. He had had to win to that place. Behind him lay the thousand-years-long road across all Siberia and Russia. He could not escape that way. The only way was ahead, across the dark and icy sea of Bering to Alaska. The way had led from savagery to deeper savagery. On the scurvy-rotten ships of the fur-thieves, out of food and out of water, buffeted by the interminable storms of that stormy sea, men had become animals. Thrice he had sailed east from Kamtchatka. And thrice, after all manner of hardship and suffering, the survivors had come back to Kamtchatka. There had been no outlet for escape, and he could not go back the way he had come, for the mines and the knout awaited him.

Again, the fourth and last time, he had sailed east. He had been with those who first found the fabled Seal Islands; but he had not returned with them to share the wealth of furs in the mad orgies of Kamtchatka. He had sworn never to go back. He knew that to win to those dear capitals of Europe he must go on. So he had changed ships and remained in the dark new land. His comrades were Slavonian hunters and Russian adventurers, Mongols and Tartars and Siberian aborigines; and through the savages of the new world they had cut a path of blood. They had massacred whole villages that refused to furnish the fur-tribute; and they, in turn, had been massacred by ships' companies. He, with one Finn, had been the sole survivor of such a company. They had spent a winter of solitude and starvation on a lonely Aleutian isle, and their rescue in the spring by another fur-ship had been one chance in a thousand.

But always the terrible savagery had hemmed him in. Passing from ship to ship, and ever refusing to return, he had come to the ship that explored south. All down the Alaska coast they had encountered nothing but hosts of savages. Every anchorage among the beetling islands or under the frowning cliffs of the mainland had meant a battle or a storm. Either the gales blew, threatening destruction, or the war canoes came off, manned by howling natives with the war-paint on their faces, who came to learn the bloody virtues of the sea-rovers' gunpowder. South, south they had coasted, clear to the myth-land of California. Here, it was said, were Spanish adventurers who had fought their way up from Mexico. He had had hopes of those Spanish adventurers. Escaping to them, the rest would have been easy—a year or two, what did it matter more or less—and he would win to Mexico, then a ship, and Europe would be his. But they had met no Spaniards. Only had they encountered the same impregnable wall of savagery. The denizens of the confines of the world, painted for war, had driven them back from the shores. At last, when one boat was cut off and every man killed, the commander had abandoned the quest and sailed back to the north.

The years had passed. He had served under Tebenkoff when Michaelovski Redoubt was built. He had spent two years in the Kuskokwim country. Two summers, in the month of June, he had managed to be at the head of Kotzebue Sound. Here, at this time, the tribes assembled for barter; here were to be found spotted deerskins from Siberia, ivory from the Diomedes, walrus skins from the shores of the Arctic, strange stone lamps, passing in trade from tribe to tribe, no one knew whence, and, once, a hunting-knife of English make; and here, Subienkow knew, was the school in which to learn geography. For he met Eskimos from Norton Sound, from King Island and St. Lawrence Island, from Cape Prince of Wales, and Point Barrow. Such places had other names, and their distances were measured in days.

It was a vast region these trading savages came from, and a vaster region from which, by repeated trade, their stone lamps and that steel knife had come. Subienkow bullied, and cajoled, and bribed. Every far-journeyer or strange tribesman was brought before him. Perils unaccountable and unthinkable were mentioned, as well as wild beasts, hostile tribes, impenetrable forests, and mighty mountain ranges; but always from beyond came the rumour and the tale of white-skinned men, blue of eye and fair of hair, who fought like devils and who sought always for furs. They were to the east—far, far to the east. No one had seen them. It was the word that had been passed along.

It was a hard school. One could not learn geography very well through the medium of strange dialects, from dark minds that mingled fact and fable and that measured distances by "sleeps" that varied according to the difficulty of the going. But at last came the whisper that gave Subienkow courage. In the east lay a great river where were these blue-eyed men. The river was called the Yukon. South of Michaelovski Redoubt emptied another great river which the Russians knew as the Kwikpak. These two rivers were one, ran the whisper.

Subienkow returned to Michaelovski. For a year he urged an expedition up the Kwikpak. Then arose Malakoff, the Russian half-breed, to lead the wildest and most ferocious of the hell's broth of mongrel adventurers who had crossed from Kamtchatka. Subienkow was his lieutenant. They threaded the mazes of the great delta of the Kwikpak, picked up the first low hills on the northern bank, and for half a thousand miles, in skin canoes loaded to the gunwales with trade-goods and ammunition, fought their way against the five-knot current of a river that ran from two to ten miles wide in a channel many fathoms deep. Malakoff decided to build the fort at Nulato. Subienkow urged to go farther. But he quickly reconciled himself to Nulato. The long winter was coming on. It would be better to wait. Early the following summer, when the ice was gone, he would disappear up the Kwikpak and work his way to the Hudson Bay Company's posts. Malakoff had never heard the whisper that the Kwikpak was the Yukon, and Subienkow did not tell him.

Came the building of the fort. It was enforced labour. The tiered walls of logs arose to the sighs and groans of the Nulato Indians. The lash was laid upon their backs, and it was the iron hand of the freebooters of the sea that laid on the lash. There were Indians that ran away, and when they were caught they were brought back and spread-eagled before the fort, where they and their tribe learned the efficacy of the knout. Two died under it; others were injured for life; and the rest took the lesson to heart and ran away no more. The snow was flying ere the fort was finished, and then it was the time for furs. A heavy tribute was laid upon the tribe. Blows and lashings continued, and that the tribute should be paid, the women and children were held as hostages and treated with the barbarity that only the fur-thieves knew.

Well, it had been a sowing of blood, and now was come the harvest. The fort was gone. In the light of its burning, half the fur-thieves had been cut down. The other half had passed under the torture. Only Subienkow remained, or Subienkow and Big Ivan, if that whimpering, moaning thing in the snow could be called Big Ivan. Subienkow caught Yakaga grinning at him. There was no gainsaying Yakaga. The mark of the lash was still on his face. After all, Subienkow could not blame him, but he disliked the thought of what Yakaga would do to him. He thought of appealing to Makamuk, the head-chief; but his judgment told him that such appeal was useless. Then, too, he thought of bursting his bonds and dying fighting. Such an end would be quick. But he could not break his bonds. Caribou thongs were stronger than he. Still devising, another thought came to him. He signed for Makamuk, and that an interpreter who knew the coast dialect should be brought.

"Oh, Makamuk," he said, "I am not minded to die. I am a great man, and it were foolishness for me to die. In truth, I shall not die. I am not like these other carrion."

He looked at the moaning thing that had once been Big Ivan, and stirred it contemptuously with his toe.

"I am too wise to die. Behold, I have a great medicine. I alone know this medicine. Since I am not going to die, I shall exchange this medicine with you."

"What is this medicine?" Makamuk demanded.

"It is a strange medicine."

Subienkow debated with himself for a moment, as if loth to part with the secret.

"I will tell you. A little bit of this medicine rubbed on the skin makes the skin hard like a rock, hard like iron, so that no cutting weapon can cut it. The strongest blow of a cutting weapon is a vain thing against it. A bone knife becomes like a piece of mud; and it will turn the edge of the iron knives we have brought among you. What will you give me for the secret of the medicine?"

"I will give you your life," Makamuk made answer through the interpreter.

Subienkow laughed scornfully.

"And you shall be a slave in my house until you die."

The Pole laughed more scornfully.

"Untie my hands and feet and let us talk," he said.

The chief made the sign; and when he was loosed Subienkow rolled a cigarette and lighted it.

"This is foolish talk," said Makamuk. "There is no such medicine. It cannot be. A cutting edge is stronger than any medicine."

The chief was incredulous, and yet he wavered. He had seen too many deviltries of fur-thieves that worked. He could not wholly doubt.

"I will give you your life; but you shall not be a slave," he announced.

"More than that."

Subienkow played his game as coolly as if he were bartering for a foxskin.

"It is a very great medicine. It has saved my life many times. I want a sled and dogs, and six of your hunters to travel with me down the river and give me safety to one day's sleep from Michaelovski Redoubt."

"You must live here, and teach us all of your deviltries," was the reply.

Subienkow shrugged his shoulders and remained silent. He blew cigarette smoke out on the icy air, and curiously regarded what remained of the big Cossack.

"That scar!" Makamuk said suddenly, pointing to the Pole's neck, where a livid mark advertised the slash of a knife in a Kamtchatkan brawl. "The medicine is not good. The cutting edge was stronger than the medicine."

"It was a strong man that drove the stroke." (Subienkow considered.) "Stronger than you, stronger than your strongest hunter, stronger than he."

Again, with the toe of his moccasin, he touched the Cossack—a grisly spectacle, no longer conscious—yet in whose dismembered body the pain-racked life clung and was loth to go.

"Also, the medicine was weak. For at that place there were no berries of a certain kind, of which I see you have plenty in this country. The medicine here will be strong."

"I will let you go down river," said Makamuk; "and the sled and the dogs and the six hunters to give you safety shall be yours."

"You are slow," was the cool rejoinder. "You have committed an offence against my medicine in that you did not at once accept my terms. Behold, I now demand more. I want one hundred beaver skins." (Makamuk sneered.)

"I want one hundred pounds of dried fish." (Makamuk nodded, for fish were plentiful and cheap.) "I want two sleds—one for me and one for my furs and fish. And my rifle must be returned to me. If you do not like the price, in a little while the price will grow."

Yakaga whispered to the chief.

"But how can I know your medicine is true medicine?" Makamuk asked.

"It is very easy. First, I shall go into the woods—"

Again Yakaga whispered to Makamuk, who made a suspicious dissent.

"You can send twenty hunters with me," Subienkow went on. "You see, I must get the berries and the roots with which to make the medicine. Then, when you have brought the two sleds and loaded on them the fish and the beaver skins and the rifle, and when you have told off the six hunters who will go with me—then, when all is ready, I will rub the medicine on my neck, so, and lay my neck there on that log. Then can your strongest hunter take the axe and strike three times on my neck. You yourself can strike the three times."

Makamuk stood with gaping mouth, drinking in this latest and most wonderful magic of the fur-thieves.

"But first," the Pole added hastily, "between each blow I must put on fresh medicine. The axe is heavy and sharp, and I want no mistakes."

"All that you have asked shall be yours," Makamuk cried in a rush of acceptance. "Proceed to make your medicine."

Subienkow concealed his elation. He was playing a desperate game, and there must be no slips. He spoke arrogantly.

"You have been slow. My medicine is offended. To make the offence clean you must give me your daughter."

He pointed to the girl, an unwholesome creature, with a cast in one eye and a bristling wolf-tooth. Makamuk was angry, but the Pole remained imperturbable, rolling and lighting another cigarette.

"Make haste," he threatened. "If you are not quick, I shall demand yet more."

In the silence that followed, the dreary northland scene faded before him, and he saw once more his native land, and France, and, once, as he glanced at the wolf-toothed girl, he remembered another girl, a singer and a dancer, whom he had known when first as a youth he came to Paris.

"What do you want with the girl?" Makamuk asked.

"To go down the river with me." Subienkow glanced over her critically. "She will make a good wife, and it is an honour worthy of my medicine to be married to your blood."

Again he remembered the singer and dancer and hummed aloud a song she had taught him. He lived the old life over, but in a detached, impersonal sort of way, looking at the memory-pictures of his own life as if they were pictures in a book of anybody's life. The chief's voice, abruptly breaking the silence, startled him

"It shall be done," said Makamuk. "The girl shall go down the river with you. But be it understood that I myself strike the three blows with the axe on your neck."

"But each time I shall put on the medicine," Subienkow answered, with a show of ill-concealed anxiety.

"You shall put the medicine on between each blow. Here are the hunters who shall see you do not escape. Go into the forest and gather your medicine."

Makamuk had been convinced of the worth of the medicine by the Pole's rapacity. Surely nothing less than the greatest of medicines could enable a man in the shadow of death to stand up and drive an old-woman's bargain.

"Besides," whispered Yakaga, when the Pole, with his guard, had disappeared among the spruce trees, "when you have learned the medicine you can easily destroy him."

"But how can I destroy him?" Makamuk argued. "His medicine will not let me destroy him."

"There will be some part where he has not rubbed the medicine," was Yakaga's reply. "We will destroy him through that part. It may be his ears. Very well; we will thrust a spear in one ear and out the other. Or it may be his eyes. Surely the medicine will be much too strong to rub on his eyes."

The chief nodded. "You are wise, Yakaga. If he possesses no other devil-things, we will then destroy him."

Subienkow did not waste time in gathering the ingredients for his medicine, he selected whatsoever came to hand such as spruce needles, the inner bark of the willow, a strip of birch bark, and a quantity of moss-berries, which he made the hunters dig up for him from beneath the snow. A few frozen roots completed his supply, and he led the way back to camp.

Makamuk and Yakaga crouched beside him, noting the quantities and kinds of the ingredients he dropped into the pot of boiling water.

"You must be careful that the moss-berries go in first," he explained.

"And—oh, yes, one other thing—the finger of a man. Here, Yakaga, let me cut off your finger."

But Yakaga put his hands behind him and scowled.

"Just a small finger," Subienkow pleaded.

"Yakaga, give him your finger," Makamuk commanded.

"There be plenty of fingers lying around," Yakaga grunted, indicating the human wreckage in the snow of the score of persons who had been tortured to death.

"It must be the finger of a live man," the Pole objected.

"Then shall you have the finger of a live man." Yakaga strode over to the Cossack and sliced off a finger.

"He is not yet dead," he announced, flinging the bloody trophy in the snow at the Pole's feet. "Also, it is a good finger, because it is large."

Subienkow dropped it into the fire under the pot and began to sing. It was a French love-song that with great solemnity he sang into the brew.

"Without these words I utter into it, the medicine is worthless," he explained. "The words are the chiefest strength of it. Behold, it is ready."

"Name the words slowly, that I may know them," Makamuk commanded.

"Not until after the test. When the axe flies back three times from my neck, then will I give you the secret of the words."

"But if the medicine is not good medicine?" Makamuk queried anxiously.

Subienkow turned upon him wrathfully.

"My medicine is always good. However, if it is not good, then do by me as you have done to the others. Cut me up a bit at a time, even as you have cut him up." He pointed to the Cossack. "The medicine is now cool. Thus, I rub it on my neck, saying this further medicine."

With great gravity he slowly intoned a line of the "Marseillaise," at the same time rubbing the villainous brew thoroughly into his neck.

An outcry interrupted his play-acting. The giant Cossack, with a last resurgence of his tremendous vitality, had arisen to his knees. Laughter and cries of surprise and applause arose from the Nulatos, as Big Ivan began flinging himself about in the snow with mighty spasms.

Subienkow was made sick by the sight, but he mastered his qualms and made believe to be angry.

"This will not do," he said. "Finish him, and then we will make the test. Here, you, Yakaga, see that his noise ceases."

While this was being done, Subienkow turned to Makamuk.

"And remember, you are to strike hard. This is not baby-work. Here, take the axe and strike the log, so that I can see you strike like a man."

Makamuk obeyed, striking twice, precisely and with vigour, cutting out a large chip.

"It is well." Subienkow looked about him at the circle of savage faces that somehow seemed to symbolize the wall of savagery that had hemmed him about ever since the Czar's police had first arrested him in Warsaw. "Take your axe, Makamuk, and stand so. I shall lie down. When I raise my hand, strike, and strike with all your might. And be careful that no one stands behind you. The medicine is good, and the axe may bounce from off my neck and right out of your hands."

He looked at the two sleds, with the dogs in harness, loaded with furs and fish. His rifle lay on top of the beaver skins. The six hunters who were to act as his guard stood by the sleds.

"Where is the girl?" the Pole demanded. "Bring her up to the sleds before the test goes on."

When this had been carried out, Subienkow lay down in the snow, resting his head on the log like a tired child about to sleep. He had lived so many dreary years that he was indeed tired.

"I laugh at you and your strength, O Makamuk," he said. "Strike, and strike hard."

He lifted his hand. Makamuk swung the axe, a broadaxe for the squaring of logs. The bright steel flashed through the frosty air, poised for a perceptible instant above Makamuk's head, then descended upon Subienkow's bare neck. Clear through flesh and bone it cut its way, biting deeply into the log beneath. The amazed savages saw the head bounce a yard away from the blood-spouting trunk.

There was a great bewilderment and silence, while slowly it began to dawn in their minds that there had been no medicine. The fur-thief had outwitted them. Alone, of all their prisoners, he had escaped the torture. That had been the stake for which he played. A great roar of laughter went up. Makamuk bowed his head in shame. The fur-thief had fooled him. He had lost face before all his people. Still they continued to roar out their laughter. Makamuk turned, and with bowed head stalked away. He knew that thenceforth he would be no longer known as Makamuk. He would be Lost Face; the record of his shame would be with him until he died; and whenever the tribes gathered in the spring for the salmon, or in the summer for the trading, the story would pass back and forth across the camp-fires of how the fur-thief died peaceably, at a single stroke, by the hand of Lost Face.

"Who was Lost Face?" he could hear, in anticipation, some insolent young buck demand, "Oh, Lost Face," would be the answer, "he who once was Makamuk in the days before he cut off the fur-thief's head."

Sir Arthur Conan Doyle

Sir Arthur Conan Doyle (1859–1930) was a Scottish physician turned writer who revolutionised detective fiction. After serving as a ship's surgeon on an Arctic whaler, he published his first Sherlock Holmes tale, *A Study in Scarlet*, in *Beeton's Christmas Annual* (1887) at age twenty-eight. The story introduced the razor-sharp consulting detective and his loyal chronicler, Dr. Watson. Doyle produced fifty-six short stories and four novels in the canon, fusing forensic logic with irresistible narrative drive. He famously tried to kill off Holmes in 1893 but revived him a decade later under public pressure. Sherlock Holmes remains the gold standard for detectives worldwide, inspiring countless adaptations and a devoted global following. Later in life, Doyle became a passionate spiritualist, engaging Houdini in spirited debates on the existence of the supernatural.

SHERLOCK HOLMES: THE ADVENTURE OF THE DYING DETECTIVE

ARTHUR CONAN DOYLE

First published in *Beeton's Christmas Annual*, 1887.

Mrs. Hudson, the landlady of Sherlock Holmes, was a long-suffering woman. Not only was her first-floor flat invaded at all hours by throngs of singular and often undesirable characters but her remarkable lodger showed an eccentricity and irregularity in his life which must have sorely tried her patience. His incredible untidiness, his addiction to music at strange hours, his occasional revolver practice within doors, his weird and often malodorous scientific experiments, and the atmosphere of violence and danger which hung around him made him the very worst tenant in London. On the other hand, his payments were princely. I have no doubt that the house might have been purchased at the price which Holmes paid for his rooms during the years that I was with him.

The landlady stood in the deepest awe of him and never dared to interfere with him, however outrageous his proceedings might seem. She was fond of him, too, for he had a remarkable gentleness and courtesy in his dealings with women. He disliked and distrusted the sex, but he was always a chivalrous opponent. Knowing how genuine was her regard for him, I listened earnestly to her story when she came to my rooms in the second year of my married life and told me of the sad condition to which my poor friend was reduced.

"He's dying, Dr. Watson," said she. "For three days he has been sinking, and I doubt if he will last the day. He would not let me get a doctor. This morning when I saw his bones sticking out of his face and his great bright eyes looking at me I could stand no more of it. 'With your leave or without it, Mr. Holmes, I am going for a doctor this very hour,' said I. 'Let it be Watson, then,' said he. I wouldn't waste an hour in coming to him, sir, or you may not see him alive."

I was horrified for I had heard nothing of his illness. I need not say that I rushed for my coat and my hat. As we drove back I asked for the details.

"There is little I can tell you, sir. He has been working at a case down at Rotherhithe, in an alley near the river, and he has brought this illness back with him. He took to his bed on Wednesday afternoon and has never moved since. For these three days neither food nor drink has passed his lips."

"Good God! Why did you not call in a doctor?"

"He wouldn't have it, sir. You know how masterful he is. I didn't dare to disobey him. But he's not long for this world, as you'll see for yourself the moment that you set eyes on him."

He was indeed a deplorable spectacle. In the dim light of a foggy November day the sick room was a gloomy spot, but it was that gaunt, wasted face staring at me from the bed which sent a chill to my heart. His eyes had the brightness of fever, there was a hectic flush upon either cheek, and dark crusts clung to his lips; the thin hands upon the coverlet twitched incessantly, his voice was croaking and spasmodic. He lay listlessly as I entered the room, but the sight of me brought a gleam of recognition to his eyes.

"Well, Watson, we seem to have fallen upon evil days," said he in a feeble voice, but with something of his old carelessness of manner.

"My dear fellow!" I cried, approaching him.

"Stand back! Stand right back!" said he with the sharp imperiousness which I had associated only with moments of crisis. "If you approach me, Watson, I shall order you out of the house."

"But why?"

"Because it is my desire. Is that not enough?"

Yes, Mrs. Hudson was right. He was more masterful than ever. It was pitiful, however, to see his exhaustion.

"I only wished to help," I explained.

"Exactly! You will help best by doing what you are told."

"Certainly, Holmes."

He relaxed the austerity of his manner.

"You are not angry?" he asked, gasping for breath.

Poor devil, how could I be angry when I saw him lying in such a plight before me?

"It's for your own sake, Watson," he croaked.

"For my sake?"

"I know what is the matter with me. It is a coolie disease from Sumatra—a thing that the Dutch know more about than we, though they have made little of it up to date. One thing only is certain. It is infallibly deadly, and it is horribly contagious."

He spoke now with a feverish energy, the long hands twitching and jerking as he motioned me away.

"Contagious by touch, Watson—that's it, by touch. Keep your distance and all is well."

"Good heavens, Holmes! Do you suppose that such a consideration weighs with me of an instant? It would not affect me in the case of a stranger. Do you imagine it would prevent me from doing my duty to so old a friend?"

Again I advanced, but he repulsed me with a look of furious anger.

"If you will stand there I will talk. If you do not you must leave the room."

I have so deep a respect for the extraordinary qualities of Holmes that I have always deferred to his wishes, even when I least understood them. But now all my professional instincts were aroused. Let him be my master elsewhere, I at least was his in a sick room.

"Holmes," said I, "you are not yourself. A sick man is but a child, and so I will treat you. Whether you like it or not, I will examine your symptoms and treat you for them."

He looked at me with venomous eyes.

"If I am to have a doctor whether I will or not, let me at least have someone in whom I have confidence," said he.

"Then you have none in me?"

"In your friendship, certainly. But facts are facts, Watson, and, after all, you are only a general practitioner with very limited experience and mediocre qualifications. It is painful to have to say these things, but you leave me no choice."

I was bitterly hurt.

"Such a remark is unworthy of you, Holmes. It shows me very clearly the state of your own nerves. But if you have no confidence in me I would not intrude my services. Let me bring Sir Jasper Meek or Penrose Fisher, or any of the best men in London. But someone you must have, and that is final. If you think that I am going to stand here and see you die without either helping you myself or bringing anyone else to help you, then you have mistaken your man."

"You mean well, Watson," said the sick man with something between a sob and a groan. "Shall I demonstrate your own ignorance? What do you know, pray, of Tapanuli fever? What do you know of the black Formosa corruption?"

"I have never heard of either."

"There are many problems of disease, many strange pathological possibilities, in the East, Watson." He paused after each sentence to collect his failing strength. "I have learned so much during some recent researches which have a medico-criminal aspect. It was in the course of them that I contracted this complaint. You can do nothing."

"Possibly not. But I happen to know that Dr. Ainstree, the greatest living authority upon tropical disease, is now in London. All remonstrance is useless, Holmes, I am going this instant to fetch him." I turned resolutely to the door.

Never have I had such a shock! In an instant, with a tiger-spring, the dying man had intercepted me. I heard the sharp snap of a twisted key. The next moment he had staggered back to his bed, exhausted and panting after his one tremendous outflame of energy.

"You won't take the key from be by force, Watson, I've got you, my friend. Here you are, and here you will stay until I will otherwise. But I'll humour you." (All this in little gasps, with terrible struggles for breath between.) "You've only my own good at heart. Of course I know that very well. You shall have your way, but give me time to get my strength. Not now, Watson, not now. It's four o'clock. At six you can go."

"This is insanity, Holmes."

"Only two hours, Watson. I promise you will go at six. Are you content to wait?"

"I seem to have no choice."

"None in the world, Watson. Thank you, I need no help in arranging the clothes. You will please keep your distance. Now, Watson, there is one other condition that I would make. You will seek help, not from the man you mention, but from the one that I choose."

"By all means."

"The first three sensible words that you have uttered since you entered this room, Watson. You will find some books over there. I am somewhat exhausted; I wonder how a battery feels when it pours electricity into a non-conductor? At six, Watson, we resume our conversation."

But it was destined to be resumed long before that hour, and in circumstances which gave me a shock hardly second to that caused by his spring to the door. I had stood for some minutes looking at the silent figure in the bed. His face was almost covered by the clothes and he appeared to be asleep. Then, unable to settle down to reading, I walked slowly round the room, examining the pictures of celebrated criminals with which every wall was adorned. Finally, in my aimless perambulation, I came to the mantelpiece. A litter of pipes, tobacco-pouches, syringes, penknives, revolver-cartridges, and other debris was scattered over it. In the midst of these was a small black and white ivory box with a sliding lid. It was a neat little thing, and I had stretched out my hand to examine it more closely when—

It was a dreadful cry that he gave—a yell which might have been heard down the street. My skin went cold and my hair bristled at that horrible scream. As I turned I caught a glimpse of a convulsed face and frantic eyes. I stood paralyzed, with the little box in my hand.

"Put it down! Down, this instant, Watson—this instant, I say!" His head sank back upon the pillow and he gave a deep sigh of relief as I replaced the box upon the mantelpiece. "I hate to have my things touched, Watson. You know that I hate it. You fidget me beyond endurance. You, a doctor—you are enough to drive a patient into an asylum. Sit down, man, and let me have my rest!"

The incident left a most unpleasant impression upon my mind. The violent and causeless excitement, followed by this brutality of speech, so far removed from his usual suavity, showed me how deep was the disorganization of his mind. Of all ruins, that of a noble mind is the most deplorable. I sat in silent dejection until the stipulated time had passed. He seemed to have been watching the clock as well as I, for it was hardly six before he began to talk with the same feverish animation as before.

"Now, Watson," said he. "Have you any change in your pocket?"

"Yes."

"Any silver?"

"A good deal."

"How many half-crowns?"

"I have five."

"Ah, too few! Too few! How very unfortunate, Watson! However, such as they are you can put them in your watch-pocket. And all the rest of your money in your left trouser pocket. Thank you. It will balance you so much better like that."

This was raving insanity. He shuddered, and again made a sound between a cough and a sob.

"You will now light the gas, Watson, but you will be very careful that not for one instant shall it be more than half on. I implore you to be careful, Watson. Thank you, that is excellent. No, you need not draw the blind. Now you will have the kindness to place some letters and papers upon this table within my reach. Thank you. Now some of that litter from the mantelpiece. Excellent, Watson! There is a sugar-tongs there. Kindly raise that small ivory box with its assistance. Place it here among the papers. Good! You can now go and fetch Mr. Culverton Smith, of 13 Lower Burke Street."

To tell the truth, my desire to fetch a doctor had somewhat weakened, for poor Holmes was so obviously delirious that it seemed dangerous to leave him. However, he was as eager now to consult the person named as he had been obstinate in refusing.

"I never heard the name," said I.

"Possibly not, my good Watson. It may surprise you to know that the man upon earth who is best versed in this disease is not a medical man, but a planter. Mr. Culverton Smith is a well-known resident of Sumatra, now visiting London. An outbreak of the disease upon his plantation, which was distant from medical aid, caused him to study it himself, with some rather far-reaching consequences. He is a very methodical person, and I did not desire you to start before six, because I was well aware that you would not find him in his study. If you could persuade him to come here and give us the benefit of his unique experience of this disease, the investigation of which has been his dearest hobby, I cannot doubt that he could help me."

I gave Holmes's remarks as a consecutive whole and will not attempt to indicate how they were interrupted by gaspings for breath and those clutchings of his hands which indicated the pain from which he was suffering. His appearance had changed for the worse during the few hours that I had been with him. Those hectic spots were more pronounced, the eyes shone more brightly out of darker hollows, and a cold sweat glimmered upon his brow. He still retained, however, the jaunty gallantry of his speech. To the last gasp he would always be the master.

"You will tell him exactly how you have left me," said he. "You will convey the very impression which is in your own mind—a dying man—a dying and delirious man. Indeed, I cannot think why the whole bed of the ocean is not one solid mass of oysters, so prolific the creatures seem. Ah, I am wondering! Strange how the brain controls the brain! What was I saying, Watson?"

"My directions for Mr. Culverton Smith."

"Ah, yes, I remember. My life depends upon it. Plead with him, Watson. There is no good feeling between us. His nephew, Watson—I had suspicions of foul play and I allowed him to see it. The boy died horribly. He has a grudge against me. You will soften him, Watson. Beg him, pray him, get him here by any means. He can save me—only he!"

"I will bring him in a cab, if I have to carry him down to it."

"You will do nothing of the sort. You will persuade him to come. And then you will return in front of him. Make any excuse so as not to come with him. Don't forget, Watson. You won't fail me. You never did fail me. No doubt there are natural enemies which limit the increase of the creatures. You and I, Watson, we have done our part. Shall the world, then, be overrun by oysters? No, no; horrible! You'll convey all that is in your mind."

I left him full of the image of this magnificent intellect babbling like a foolish child. He had handed me the key, and with a happy thought I took it with me lest he should lock himself in. Mrs. Hudson was waiting, trembling and weeping, in the passage. Behind me as I passed from the flat I heard Holmes's high, thin voice in some delirious chant. Below, as I stood whistling for a cab, a man came on me through the fog.

"How is Mr. Holmes, sir?" he asked.

It was an old acquaintance, Inspector Morton, of Scotland Yard, dressed in unofficial tweeds.

"He is very ill," I answered.

He looked at me in a most singular fashion. Had it not been too fiendish, I could have imagined that the gleam of the fanlight showed exultation in his face.

"I heard some rumour of it," said he.

The cab had driven up, and I left him.

Lower Burke Street proved to be a line of fine houses lying in the vague borderland between Notting Hill and Kensington. The particular one at which my cabman pulled up had an air of smug and demure respectability in its old-fashioned iron railings, its massive folding-door, and its shining brasswork. All was in keeping with a solemn butler who appeared framed in the pink radiance of a tinted electrical light behind him.

"Yes, Mr. Culverton Smith is in. Dr. Watson! Very good, sir, I will take up your card."

My humble name and title did not appear to impress Mr. Culverton Smith. Through the half-open door I heard a high, petulant, penetrating voice.

"Who is this person? What does he want? Dear me, Staples, how often have I said that I am not to be disturbed in my hours of study?"

There came a gentle flow of soothing explanation from the butler.

"Well, I won't see him, Staples. I can't have my work interrupted like this. I am not at home. Say so. Tell him to come in the morning if he really must see me."

Again the gentle murmur.

"Well, well, give him that message. He can come in the morning, or he can stay away. My work must not be hindered."

I thought of Holmes tossing upon his bed of sickness and counting the minutes, perhaps, until I could bring help to him. It was not a time to stand upon ceremony. His life depended upon my promptness. Before the apologetic butler had delivered his message I had pushed past him and was in the room.

With a shrill cry of anger a man rose from a reclining chair beside the fire. I saw a great yellow face, coarse-grained and greasy, with heavy, double-chin, and two sullen, menacing gray eyes which glared at me from under tufted and sandy brows. A high bald head had a small velvet smoking-cap poised coquettishly upon one side of its pink curve. The skull was of enormous capacity, and yet as I looked down I saw to my amazement that the figure of the man was small and frail, twisted in the shoulders and back like one who has suffered from rickets in his childhood.

"What's this?" he cried in a high, screaming voice. "What is the meaning of this intrusion? Didn't I send you word that I would see you to-morrow morning?"

"I am sorry," said I, "but the matter cannot be delayed. Mr. Sherlock Holmes—"

The mention of my friend's name had an extraordinary effect upon the little man. The look of anger passed in an instant from his face. His features became tense and alert.

"Have you come from Holmes?" he asked.

"I have just left him."

"What about Holmes? How is he?"

"He is desperately ill. That is why I have come."

The man motioned me to a chair, and turned to resume his own. As he did so I caught a glimpse of his face in the mirror over the mantelpiece. I could have sworn that it was set in a malicious and abominable smile. Yet I persuaded myself that it must have been some nervous contraction which I had surprised, for he turned to me an instant later with genuine concern upon his features.

"I am sorry to hear this," said he. "I only know Mr. Holmes through some business dealings which we have had, but I have every respect for his talents and his character. He is an amateur of crime, as I am of disease. For him the villain, for me the microbe. There are my prisons," he continued, pointing to a row of bottles and jars which stood upon a side table. "Among those gelatine cultivations some of the very worst offenders in the world are now doing time."

"It was on account of your special knowledge that Mr. Holmes desired to see you. He has a high opinion of you and thought that you were the one man in London who could help him."

The little man started, and the jaunty smoking-cap slid to the floor.

"Why?" he asked. "Why should Mr. Homes think that I could help him in his trouble?"

"Because of your knowledge of Eastern diseases."

"But why should he think that this disease which he has contracted is Eastern?"

"Because, in some professional inquiry, he has been working among Chinese sailors down in the docks."

Mr. Culverton Smith smiled pleasantly and picked up his smoking-cap.

"Oh, that's it—is it?" said he. "I trust the matter is not so grave as you suppose. How long has he been ill?"

"About three days."

"Is he delirious?"

"Occasionally."

"Tut, tut! This sounds serious. It would be inhuman not to answer his call. I very much resent any interruption to my work, Dr. Watson, but this case is certainly exceptional. I will come with you at once."

I remembered Holmes's injunction.

"I have another appointment," said I.

"Very good. I will go alone. I have a note of Mr. Holmes's address. You can rely upon my being there within half an hour at most."

It was with a sinking heart that I reentered Holmes's bedroom. For all that I knew the worst might have happened in my absence. To my enormous relief, he had improved greatly in the interval. His appearance was as ghastly as ever, but all trace of delirium had left him and he spoke in a feeble voice, it is true, but with even more than his usual crispness and lucidity.

"Well, did you see him, Watson?"

"Yes; he is coming."

"Admirable, Watson! Admirable! You are the best of messengers."

"He wished to return with me."

"That would never do, Watson. That would be obviously impossible. Did he ask what ailed me?"

"I told him about the Chinese in the East End."

"Exactly! Well, Watson, you have done all that a good friend could. You can now disappear from the scene."

"I must wait and hear his opinion, Holmes."

"Of course you must. But I have reasons to suppose that this opinion would be very much more frank and valuable if he imagines that we are alone. There is just room behind the head of my bed, Watson."

"My dear Holmes!"

"I fear there is no alternative, Watson. The room does not lend itself to concealment, which is as well, as it is the less likely to arouse suspicion. But just there, Watson, I fancy that it could be done." Suddenly he sat up with a rigid intentness upon his haggard face. "There are the wheels, Watson. Quick, man, if you love me! And don't budge, whatever happens—whatever happens, do you hear? Don't speak! Don't move! Just listen with all your ears." Then in an instant his sudden access of strength departed, and his masterful, purposeful talk droned away into the low, vague murmurings of a semi-delirious man.

From the hiding-place into which I had been so swiftly hustled I heard the footfalls upon the stair, with the opening and the closing of the bedroom door. Then, to my surprise, there came a long silence, broken only by the heavy breathings and gaspings of the sick man. I could imagine that our visitor was standing by the bedside and looking down at the sufferer. At last that strange hush was broken.

"Holmes!" he cried. "Holmes!" in the insistent tone of one who awakens a sleeper. "Can't you hear me, Holmes?" There was a rustling, as if he had shaken the sick man roughly by the shoulder.

"Is that you, Mr. Smith?" Holmes whispered. "I hardly dared hope that you would come."

The other laughed.

"I should imagine not," he said. "And yet, you see, I am here. Coals of fire, Holmes—coals of fire!"

"It is very good of you—very noble of you. I appreciate your special knowledge."

Our visitor sniggered.

"You do. You are, fortunately, the only man in London who does. Do you know what is the matter with you?"

"The same," said Holmes.

"Ah! You recognize the symptoms?"

"Only too well."

"Well, I shouldn't be surprised, Holmes. I shouldn't be surprised if it were the same. A bad lookout for you if it is. Poor Victor was a dead man on the fourth day—a strong, hearty young fellow. It was certainly, as you said, very surprising that he should have contracted and out-of-the-way Asiatic disease in the heart of London—a disease, too, of which I had made such a very special study. Singular coincidence, Holmes. Very smart of you to notice it, but rather uncharitable to suggest that it was cause and effect."

"I knew that you did it."

"Oh, you did, did you? Well, you couldn't prove it, anyhow. But what do you think of yourself spreading reports about me like that, and then crawling to me for help the moment you are in trouble? What sort of a game is that—eh?"

I heard the rasping, laboured breathing of the sick man. "Give me the water!" he gasped.

"You're precious near your end, my friend, but I don't want you to go till I have had a word with you. That's why I give you water. There, don't slop it about! That's right. Can you understand what I say?"

Holmes groaned.

"Do what you can for me. Let bygones be bygones," he whispered. "I'll put the words out of my head—I swear I will. Only cure me, and I'll forget it."

"Forget what?"

"Well, about Victor Savage's death. You as good as admitted just now that you had done it. I'll forget it."

"You can forget it or remember it, just as you like. I don't see you in the witnessbox. Quite another shaped box, my good Holmes, I assure you. It matters nothing to me that you should know how my nephew died. It's not him we are talking about. It's you."

"Yes, yes."

"The fellow who came for me—I've forgotten his name—said that you contracted it down in the East End among the sailors."

"I could only account for it so."

"You are proud of your brains, Holmes, are you not? Think yourself smart, don't you? You came across someone who was smarter this time. Now cast your mind back, Holmes. Can you think of no other way you could have got this thing?"

"I can't think. My mind is gone. For heaven's sake help me!"

"Yes, I will help you. I'll help you to understand just where you are and how you got there. I'd like you to know before you die."

"Give me something to ease my pain."

"Painful, is it? Yes, the coolies used to do some squealing towards the end. Takes you as cramp, I fancy."

"Yes, yes; it is cramp."

"Well, you can hear what I say, anyhow. Listen now! Can you remember any unusual incident in your life just about the time your symptoms began?"

"No, no; nothing."

"Think again."

"I'm too ill to think."

"Well, then, I'll help you. Did anything come by post?"

"By post?"

"A box by chance?"

"I'm fainting—I'm gone!"

"Listen, Holmes!" There was a sound as if he was shaking the dying man, and it was all that I could do to hold myself quiet in my hiding-place. "You must hear me. You shall hear me. Do you remember a box—an ivory box? It came on Wednesday. You opened it—do you remember?"

"Yes, yes, I opened it. There was a sharp spring inside it. Some joke—"

"It was no joke, as you will find to your cost. You fool, you would have it and you have got it. Who asked you to cross my path? If you had left me alone I would not have hurt you."

"I remember," Holmes gasped. "The spring! It drew blood. This box—this on the table."

"The very one, by George! And it may as well leave the room in my pocket. There goes your last shred of evidence. But you have the truth now, Holmes, and you can die with the knowledge that I killed you. You knew too much of the fate of Victor Savage, so I have sent you to share it. You are very near your end, Holmes. I will sit here and I will watch you die."

Holmes's voice had sunk to an almost inaudible whisper.

"What is that?" said Smith. "Turn up the gas? Ah, the shadows begin to fall, do they? Yes, I will turn it up, that I may see you the better." He crossed the room and the light suddenly brightened. "Is there any other little service that I can do you, my friend?"

"A match and a cigarette."

I nearly called out in my joy and my amazement. He was speaking in his natural voice—a little weak, perhaps, but the very voice I knew. There was a long pause, and I felt that Culverton Smith was standing in silent amazement looking down at his companion.

"What's the meaning of this?" I heard him say at last in a dry, rasping tone.

"The best way of successfully acting a part is to be it," said Holmes. "I give you my word that for three days I have tasted neither food nor drink until you were good enough to pour me out that glass of water. But it is the tobacco which I find most irksome. Ah, here are some cigarettes." I heard the striking of a match. "That is very much better. Halloa! halloa! Do I hear the step of a friend?"

There were footfalls outside, the door opened, and Inspector Morton appeared.

"All is in order and this is your man," said Holmes.

The officer gave the usual cautions.

"I arrest you on the charge of the murder of one Victor Savage," he concluded.

"And you might add of the attempted murder of one Sherlock Holmes," remarked my friend with a chuckle. "To save an invalid trouble, Inspector, Mr. Culverton Smith was good enough to give our signal by turning up the gas. By the way, the prisoner has a small box in the right-hand pocket of his coat which it would be as well to remove. Thank you. I would handle it gingerly if I were you. Put it down here. It may play its part in the trial."

There was a sudden rush and a scuffle, followed by the clash of iron and a cry of pain.

"You'll only get yourself hurt," said the inspector. "Stand still, will you?" There was the click of the closing handcuffs.

"A nice trap!" cried the high, snarling voice. "It will bring you into the dock, Holmes, not me. He asked me to come here to cure him. I was sorry for him and I came. Now he will pretend, no doubt, that I have said anything which he may invent which will corroborate his insane suspicions. You can lie as you like, Holmes. My word is always as good as yours."

"Good heavens!" cried Holmes. "I had totally forgotten him. My dear Watson, I owe you a thousand apologies. To think that I should have overlooked you! I need not introduce you to Mr. Culverton Smith, since I understand that you met somewhat earlier in the evening. Have you the cab below?

I will follow you when I am dressed, for I may be of some use at the station.

"I never needed it more," said Holmes as he refreshed himself with a glass of claret and some biscuits in the intervals of his toilet. "However, as you know, my habits are irregular, and such a feat means less to me than to most men. It was very essential that I should impress Mrs. Hudson with the reality of my condition, since she was to convey it to you, and you in turn to him. You won't be offended, Watson? You will realize that among your many talents dissimulation finds no place, and that if you had shared my secret you would never have been able to impress Smith with the urgent necessity of his presence, which was the vital point of the whole scheme. Knowing his vindictive nature, I was perfectly certain that he would come to look upon his handiwork."

"But your appearance, Holmes—your ghastly face?"

"Three days of absolute fast does not improve one's beauty, Watson. For the rest, there is nothing which a sponge may not cure. With vaseline upon one's forehead, belladonna in one's eyes, rouge over the cheek-bones, and crusts of beeswax round one's lips, a very satisfying effect can be produced. Malingering is a subject upon which I have sometimes thought of writing a monograph. A little occasional talk about half-crowns, oysters, or any other extraneous subject produces a pleasing effect of delirium."

"But why would you not let me near you, since there was in truth no infection?"

"Can you ask, my dear Watson? Do you imagine that I have no respect for your medical talents? Could I fancy that your astute judgment would pass a dying man who, however weak, had no rise of pulse or temperature? At four yards,

I could deceive you. If I failed to do so, who would bring my Smith within my grasp? No, Watson, I would not touch that box. You can just see if you look at it sideways where the sharp spring like a viper's tooth emerges as you open it. I dare say it was by some such device that poor Savage, who stood between this monster and a reversion, was done to death. My correspondence, however, is, as you know, a varied one, and I am somewhat upon my guard against any packages which reach me. It was clear to me, however, that by pretending that he had really succeeded in his design I might surprise a confession. That pretence I have carried out with the thoroughness of the true artist. Thank you, Watson, you must help me on with my coat. When we have finished at the police-station I think that something nutritious at Simpson's would not be out of place."

PART II

Comedy, Mischief & Wit

O. Henry (William Sydney Porter)

O. Henry (1862–1910) was the pen name of William Sydney Porter, an American short-story master whose own life twisted like his plots. A pharmacist, draftsman, and bank clerk by turns, he faced embezzlement charges in 1898 and served three years in an Ohio federal prison. There, confined yet inspired, he penned his first tales under the borrowed name of a guard, "O. Henry." Freed in 1901, he settled in New York and churned out over three hundred stories famed for witty irony, warm humanity, and his signature twist endings. He published prolifically in magazines, earning just pennies per word yet leaving an indelible mark on the form. The annual O. Henry Award, launched in his honour in 1918, continues to recognise outstanding short stories, keeping his legacy alive in American letters.

The Ransom of Red Chief

O. Henry

First published in *The Saturday Evening Post*, 1907.

It looked like a good thing—but wait till I tell you. We were down South, in Alabama—Bill Driscoll and myself—when this kidnapping idea struck us. It was, as Bill afterward expressed it, "during a moment of temporary mental apparition"; but we didn't find that out till later.

There was a town down there, as flat as a flannel-cake, and called Summit, of course. It contained inhabitadassantnts of as undeleterious and self-satisfied a class of peasantry as ever clustered around a Maypole.

Bill and me had a joint capital of about six hundred dollars, and we needed just two thousand dollars more to pull off a fraudulent town-lot scheme in Western Illinois with. We talked it over on the front steps of the hotel. Philoprogenitiveness, says we, is strong in semi-rural communities; therefore and for other reasons, a kidnapping project ought to do better there than in the radius of newspapers that send reporters out in plain clothes to stir up talk about such things. We knew that Summit couldn't get after us with anything stronger than constables and maybe some lackadaisical bloodhounds and a diatribe or two in the Weekly Farmers' Budget. So, it looked good.

We selected for our victim the only child of a prominent citizen named Ebenezer Dorset. The father was respectable and tight, a mortgage fancier and a stern, upright collection-plate passer and forecloser. The kid was a boy of ten, with bas-relief freckles and hair the colour of the cover of the magazine you buy at the news-stand when you want to catch a train. Bill and me figured that Ebenezer would melt down for a ransom of two thousand dollars to a cent. But wait till I tell you.

About two miles from Summit was a little mountain, covered with a dense cedar brake. On the rear elevation of this mountain was a cave. There we stored provisions. One evening after sundown, we drove in a buggy past old Dorset's house. The kid was in the street, throwing rocks at a kitten on the opposite fence.

"Hey, little boy!" says Bill, "would you like to have a bag of candy and a nice ride?"

The boy catches Bill neatly in the eye with a piece of brick.

"That will cost the old man an extra five hundred dollars," says Bill, climbing over the wheel.

That boy put up a fight like a welter-weight cinnamon bear; but at last we got him down in the bottom of the buggy and drove away. We took him up to the cave and I hitched the horse in the cedar brake. After dark I drove the buggy to the little village, three miles away, where we had hired it, and walked back to the mountain.

Bill was pasting court-plaster over the scratches and bruises on his features. There was a fire burning behind the big rock at the entrance of the cave, and the boy was watching a pot of boiling coffee, with two buzzard tail-feathers stuck in his red hair. He points a stick at me when I come up, and says:

"Ha! Cursed paleface, do you dare to enter the camp of Red Chief, the terror of the plains?"

"He's all right now," says Bill, rolling up his trousers and examining some bruises on his shins. "We're playing Indian. We're making Buffalo Bill's show look like magic-lantern views of Palestine in the town hall. I'm Old Hank, the Trapper, Red Chief's captive, and I'm to be scalped at daybreak. By Geronimo! that kid can kick hard."

Yes, sir, that boy seemed to be having the time of his life. The fun of camping out in a cave had made him forget that he was a captive himself. He immediately christened me Snake-eye, the Spy, and announced that when his braves returned from the warpath, I was to be broiled at the stake at the rising of the sun.

Then we had supper; and he filled his mouth full of bacon and bread and gravy, and began to talk. He made a during-dinner speech something like this:

"I like this fine. I never camped out before; but I had a pet 'possum once, and I was nine last birthday. I hate to go to school. Rats ate up sixteen of Jimmy Talbot's aunt's speckled hen's eggs. Are there any real Indians in these woods? I want some more gravy. Does the trees moving make the wind blow? We had five puppies. What makes your nose so red, Hank? My father has lots of money. Are the stars hot? I whipped Ed Walker twice Saturday. I don't like girls. You dassent catch toads unless with a string. Do oxen make any noise? Why are oranges round? Have you got beds to sleep on in this cave? Amos Murray has got six toes. A parrot can talk, but a monkey or a fish can't. How many does it take to make twelve?"

Every few minutes he would remember that he was a pesky redskin, and pick up his stick rifle and tiptoe to the mouth of the cave to rubber for the scouts of the hated paleface. Now and then he would let out a war-whoop that made Old Hank the Trapper shiver. That boy had Bill terrorized from the start.

"Red Chief," says I to the kid, "would you like to go home?"

"Aw, what for?" says he. "I don't have any fun at home. I hate to go to school. I like to camp out. You won't take me back home again, Snake-eye, will you?"

"Not right away," says I. "We'll stay here in the cave a while."

"All right!" says he. "That'll be fine. I never had such fun in all my life."

We went to bed about eleven o'clock. We spread down some wide blankets and quilts and put Red Chief between us. We weren't afraid he'd run away. He kept us awake for three hours, jumping up and reaching for his rifle and screeching, "Hist! Pard," in mine and Bill's ears, as the fancied crackle of a twig or the rustle of a leaf revealed to his young imagination the stealthy approach of the outlaw band. At last, I fell into a troubled sleep, and dreamed that I had been kidnapped and chained to a tree by a ferocious pirate with red hair.

Just at daybreak, I was awakened by a series of awful screams from Bill. They weren't yells, or howls, or shouts, or whoops, or yawps, such as you'd expect from a manly set of vocal organs—they were simply indecent, terrifying, humiliating screams, such as women emit when they see ghosts or caterpillars. It's an awful thing to hear a strong, desperate, fat man scream incontinently in a cave at daybreak.

I jumped up to see what the matter was. Red Chief was sitting on Bill's chest, with one hand twined in Bill's hair. In the other he had the sharp case-knife we used for slicing bacon, and he was industriously and realistically trying to take Bill's scalp, according to the sentence that had been pronounced upon him the evening before.

I got the knife away from the kid and made him lie down again. But from that moment, Bill's spirit was broken. He laid down on his side of the bed, but he never closed an eye again in sleep as long as that boy was with us. I dozed off for a while, but along toward sun-up I remembered that Red Chief had said I was to be burned at the stake at the rising of the sun. I wasn't nervous or afraid; but I sat up and lit my pipe and leaned against a rock.

"What you getting up so soon for, Sam?" asked Bill.

"Me?" says I. "Oh, I got a kind of a pain in my shoulder. I thought sitting up would rest it."

"You're a liar!" says Bill. "You're afraid. You was to be burned at sunrise, and you was afraid he'd do it. And he would, too, if he could find a match. Ain't it awful, Sam? Do you think anybody will pay out money to get a little imp like that back home?"

"Sure," said I. "A rowdy kid like that is just the kind that parents dote on. Now, you and the Chief get up and cook breakfast, while I go up on the top of this mountain and reconnoitre."

I went up on the peak of the little mountain and ran my eye over the contiguous vicinity. Over toward Summit I expected to see the sturdy yeomanry of the village armed with scythes and pitchforks beating the countryside for the dastardly kidnappers. But what I saw was a peaceful landscape dotted with one man ploughing with a dun mule. Nobody was dragging the creek; no couriers dashed hither and yon bringing tidings of no news to the distracted parents. There was a sylvan attitude of somnolent sleepiness pervading that section of Alabama that lay exposed to my view.

"Perhaps," says I to myself, "it has not yet been discovered that the wolves have borne away the tender lambkin from the fold. Heaven help the wolves!" says I, and I went down the mountain to breakfast.

When I got to the cave I found Bill backed up against the side of it, breathing hard, and the boy threatening to smash him with a rock half as big as a cocoanut.

"He put a red-hot boiled potato down my back," explained Bill, "and then mashed it with his foot; and I boxed his ears. Have you got a gun about you, Sam?"

I took the rock away from the boy and kind of patched up the argument.

"I'll fix you," says the kid to Bill. "No man ever yet struck the Red Chief but what he got paid for it. You better beware!"

After breakfast the kid takes a piece of leather with strings wrapped around it out of his pocket and goes outside the cave unwinding it.

"What's he up to now?" says Bill, anxiously. "You don't think he'll run away, do you, Sam?"

"No fear of it," says I. "He don't seem to be much of a home body. But we've got to fix up some plan about the ransom. There don't seem to be much excitement around Summit on account of his disappearance; but maybe they haven't realized yet that he's gone. His folks may think he's spending the night with Aunt Jane or one of the neighbours. Anyhow, he'll be missed to-day. To-night we must get a message to his father demanding the two thousand dollars for his return."

Just then we heard a kind of war-whoop, such as David might have emitted when he knocked out the champion Goliath. It was a sling that Red Chief had pulled out of his pocket, and he was whirling it around his head.

I dodged, and heard a heavy thud and a kind of a sigh from Bill, like a horse gives out when you take his saddle off. A rock the size of an egg had caught Bill just behind his left ear. He loosened himself all over and fell in the fire across the frying-pan of hot water for washing the dishes. I dragged him out and poured cold water on his head for half an hour.

By and by, Bill sits up and feels behind his ear and says: "Sam, do you know who my favourite Biblical character is?"

"Take it easy," says I. "You'll come to your senses presently."

"King Herod," says he. "You won't go away and leave me here alone, will you, Sam?"

I went out and caught that boy and shook him until his freckles rattled.

"If you don't behave," says I, "I'll take you straight home. Now, are you going to be good, or not?"

"I was only funning," says he sullenly. "I didn't mean to hurt Old Hank. But what did he hit me for? I'll behave, Snake-eye, if you won't send me home, and if you'll let me play the Black Scout to-day."

"I don't know the game," says I. "That's for you and Mr. Bill to decide. He's your playmate for the day. I'm going away for a while, on business. Now, you come in and make friends with him and say you are sorry for hurting him, or home you go, at once."

I made him and Bill shake hands, and then I took Bill aside and told him I was going to Poplar Cove, a little village three miles from the cave, and find out what I could about how the kidnapping had been regarded in Summit. Also, I thought it best to send a peremptory letter to old man Dorset that day, demanding the ransom and dictating how it should be paid.

"You know, Sam," says Bill, "I've stood by you without batting an eye in earthquakes, fire and flood—in poker games, dynamite outrages, police raids, train robberies and cyclones. I never lost my nerve yet till we kidnapped that two-legged skyrocket of a kid. He's got me going. You won't leave me long with him, will you, Sam?"

"I'll be back some time this afternoon," says I. "You must keep the boy amused and quiet till I return. And now we'll write the letter to old Dorset."

Bill and I got paper and pencil and worked on the letter while Red Chief, with a blanket wrapped around him, strutted up and down, guarding the mouth of the cave. Bill begged me tearfully to make the ransom fifteen hundred dollars instead of two thousand. "I ain't attempting," says he, "to decry the celebrated moral aspect of parental affection, but we're dealing with humans, and it ain't human for anybody to give up two thousand dollars for that forty-pound chunk of freckled wildcat. I'm willing to take a chance at fifteen hundred dollars. You can charge the difference up to me."

So, to relieve Bill, I acceded, and we collaborated a letter that ran this way:

Ebenezer Dorset, Esq.:

We have your boy concealed in a place far from Summit. It is useless for you or the most skilful detectives to attempt to find him. Absolutely the only terms on which you can have him restored to you are these: We demand fifteen hundred dollars in large bills for his return; the money to be left at midnight to-night at the same spot and in the same box as your reply—as hereinafter described. If you agree to these terms, send your answer in writing by a solitary messenger to-night at half-past eight o'clock. After crossing Owl Creek, on the road to Poplar Cove, there are three large trees about a hundred yards apart, close to the fence of the wheat-field on the right-hand side. At the bottom of the fence-post, opposite the third tree, will be found a small pasteboard box.

The messenger will place the answer in this box and return immediately to Summit.

If you attempt any treachery or fail to comply with our demand as stated, you will never see your boy again.

If you pay the money as demanded, he will be returned to you safe and well within three hours. These terms are final, and if you do not accede to them no further communication will be attempted.

TWO DESPERATE MEN.

I addressed this letter to Dorset and put it in my pocket. As I was about to start, the kid comes up to me and says:

"Aw, Snake-eye, you said I could play the Black Scout while you was gone."

"Play it, of course," says I. "Mr. Bill will play with you. What kind of a game is it?"

"I'm the Black Scout," says Red Chief, "and I have to ride to the stockade to warn the settlers that the Indians are coming. I'm tired of playing Indian myself. I want to be the Black Scout."

"All right," says I. "It sounds harmless to me. I guess Mr. Bill will help you foil the pesky savages."

"What am I to do?" asks Bill, looking at the kid suspiciously.

"You are the hoss," says Black Scout. "Get down on your hands and knees. How can I ride to the stockade without a hoss?"

"You'd better keep him interested," said I, "till we get the scheme going. Loosen up."

Bill gets down on his all fours, and a look comes in his eye like a rabbit's when you catch it in a trap.

"How far is it to the stockade, kid?" he asks, in a husky manner of voice.

"Ninety miles," says the Black Scout. "And you have to hump yourself to get there on time. Whoa, now!"

The Black Scout jumps on Bill's back and digs his heels in his side.

"For Heaven's sake," says Bill, "hurry back, Sam, as soon as you can. I wish we hadn't made the ransom more than a thousand. Say, you quit kicking me or I'll get up and warm you good."

I walked over to Poplar Cove and sat around the post-office and store, talking with the chawbacons that came in to trade. One whiskerando says that he hears Summit is all upset on account of Elder Ebenezer Dorset's boy having been lost or stolen. That was all I wanted to know. I bought some smoking tobacco, referred casually to the price of black-eyed peas, posted my letter surreptitiously, and came away. The postmaster said the mail-carrier would come by in an hour to take the mail on to Summit.

When I got back to the cave Bill and the boy were not to be found. I explored the vicinity of the cave, and risked a yodel or two, but there was no response.

So I lighted my pipe and sat down on a mossy bank to await developments.

In about half an hour I heard the bushes rustle, and Bill wabbled out into the little glade in front of the cave. Behind him was the kid, stepping softly like a scout, with a broad grin on his face. Bill stopped, took off his hat and wiped his face with a red handkerchief. The kid stopped about eight feet behind him.

"Sam," says Bill, "I suppose you'll think I'm a renegade, but I couldn't help it. I'm a grown person with masculine proclivities and habits of self-defense, but there is a time when all systems of egotism and predominance fail. The boy is gone. I have sent him home. All is off."

"There were martyrs in old times," goes on Bill, "that suffered death rather than give up the particular graft they enjoyed. None of 'em ever was subjugated to such supernatural tortures as I have been. I tried to be faithful to our articles of depredation; but there came a limit."

"What's the trouble, Bill?" I asks him.

"I was rode," says Bill, "the ninety miles to the stockade, not barring an inch. Then, when the settlers was rescued, I was given oats. Sand ain't a palatable substitute. And then, for an hour, I had to try to explain to him why there was nothin' in holes, how a road can run both ways, and what makes the grass green. I tell you, Sam, a human can only stand so much. I takes him by the neck of his clothes and drags him down the mountain. On the way he kicks my legs black-and-blue from the knees down; and I've got to have two or three bites on my thumb and hand cauterized.

"But he's gone," continues Bill—"gone home. I showed him the road to Summit and kicked him about eight feet nearer there at one kick. I'm sorry we lose the ransom; but it was either that or Bill Driscoll to the madhouse."

Bill is puffing and blowing, but there is a look of ineffable peace and growing content on his rose-pink features.

"Bill," says I, "there isn't any heart disease in your family, is there?"

"No," says Bill, "nothing chronic except malaria and accidents. Why?"

"Then you might turn around," says I, "and have a look behind you."

Bill turns and sees the boy, and loses his complexion and sits down plump on the ground and begins to pluck aimlessly at grass and little sticks. For an hour I was afraid for his mind. And then I told him that my scheme was to put the whole job through immediately and that we would get the ransom and be off with it by midnight if old Dorset fell in with our proposition. So Bill braced up enough to give the kid a weak sort of a smile and a promise to play the Russian in a Japanese war with him as soon as he felt a little better.

I had a scheme for collecting that ransom without danger of being caught by counterplots that ought to commend itself to professional kidnappers. The tree under which the answer was to be left—and the money later on—was close to the road fence with big, bare fields on all sides. If a gang of constables should be watching for any one to come for the note they could see him a long way off crossing the fields or in the road. But no, sirree! At half-past eight I was up in that tree as well hidden as a tree toad, waiting for the messenger to arrive.

Exactly on time, a half-grown boy rides up the road on a bicycle, locates the pasteboard box at the foot of the fence-post, slips a folded piece of paper into it and pedals away again back toward Summit.

I waited an hour and then concluded the thing was square. I slid down the tree, got the note, slipped along the fence till I struck the woods, and was back at the cave in another half an hour. I opened the note, got near the lantern and read it to Bill. It was written with a pen in a crabbed hand, and the sum and substance of it was this:

Two Desperate Men:

Gentlemen: I received your letter to-day by post, in regard to the ransom you ask for the return of my son. I think you are a little high in your demands, and I hereby make you a counter-proposition, which I am inclined to believe you will accept. You bring Johnny home and pay me two hundred and fifty dollars in cash, and I agree to take him off your hands. You had better come at night, for the neighbours believe he is lost, and I couldn't be responsible for what they would do to anybody they saw bringing him back.

Very respectfully,
EBENEZER DORSET.

"Great pirates of Penzance!" says I; "of all the impudent—"

But I glanced at Bill, and hesitated. He had the most appealing look in his eyes I ever saw on the face of a dumb or a talking brute.

"Sam," says he, "what's two hundred and fifty dollars, after all? We've got the money. One more night of this kid will send me to a bed in Bedlam. Besides being a thorough gentleman,

I think Mr. Dorset is a spendthrift for making us such a liberal offer. You ain't going to let the chance go, are you?"

"Tell you the truth, Bill," says I, "this little he ewe lamb has somewhat got on my nerves too. We'll take him home, pay the ransom and make our get-away."

We took him home that night. We got him to go by telling him that his father had bought a silver-mounted rifle and a pair of moccasins for him, and we were going to hunt bears the next day.

It was just twelve o'clock when we knocked at Ebenezer's front door. Just at the moment when I should have been abstracting the fifteen hundred dollars from the box under the tree, according to the original proposition, Bill was counting out two hundred and fifty dollars into Dorset's hand.

When the kid found out we were going to leave him at home he started up a howl like a calliope and fastened himself as tight as a leech to Bill's leg. His father peeled him away gradually, like a porous plaster.

"How long can you hold him?" asks Bill.

"I'm not as strong as I used to be," says old Dorset, "but I think I can promise you ten minutes."

"Enough," says Bill. "In ten minutes I shall cross the Central, Southern and Middle Western States, and be legging it trippingly for the Canadian border."

And, as dark as it was, and as fat as Bill was, and as good a runner as I am, he was a good mile and a half out of Summit before I could catch up with him.

The Cop and the Anthem

O. Henry

First published in *The New York World*, 1904.

On his bench in Madison Square Soapy moved uneasily. When wild geese honk high of nights, and when women without sealskin coats grow kind to their husbands, and when Soapy moves uneasily on his bench in the park, you may know that winter is near at hand.

A dead leaf fell in Soapy's lap. That was Jack Frost's card. Jack is kind to the regular denizens of Madison Square, and gives fair warning of his annual call. At the corners of four streets he hands his pasteboard to the North Wind, footman of the mansion of All Outdoors, so that the inhabitants thereof may make ready.

Soapy's mind became cognizant of the fact that the time had come for him to resolve himself into a singular Committee of Ways and Means to provide against the coming rigour. And therefore he moved uneasily on his bench.

The hibernatorial ambitions of Soapy were not of the highest. In them were no considerations of Mediterranean cruises, of soporific southern skies, or drifting in the Vesuvian Bay. Three months on the Island was what his soul craved. Three months of assured board and bed and congenial company, safe from Boreas and bluecoats, seemed to Soapy the essence of things desirable.

For years the hospitable Blackwell's had been his winter quarters. Just as his more fortunate fellow New Yorkers had bought their tickets to Palm Beach and the Riviera each winter, so Soapy had made his humble arrangements for his annual hegira to the Island. And now the time was come. On the previous night three Sabbath newspapers, distributed beneath his coat, about his ankles, and over his lap, had failed to repulse the cold as he slept on his bench near the spurting fountain in the ancient square.

So the Island loomed large and timely in Soapy's mind. He scorned the provisions made in the name of charity for the city's dependents. In Soapy's opinion the Law was more benign than Philanthropy. There was an endless round of institutions, municipal and eleemosynary, on which he might set out and receive lodging and food accordant with the simple life. But to one of Soapy's proud spirit the gifts of charity are encumbered. If not in coin you must pay in humiliation of spirit for every benefit received at the hands of philanthropy.

As Cæsar had his Brutus, every bed of charity must have its toll of a bath; every loaf of bread its compensation of a private and personal inquisition. Wherefore it is better to be a guest of the Law, which, though conducted by rules, does not meddle unduly with a gentleman's private affairs.

Soapy, having decided to go to the Island, at once set about accomplishing his desire. There were many easy ways of doing this. The pleasantest was to dine luxuriously at some expensive restaurant, and then, after declaring insolvency, be handed over quietly and without uproar to a policeman. An accommodating magistrate would do the rest.

Soapy left his bench and strolled out of the square and across the level sea of asphalt, where Broadway and Fifth Avenue flow together. Up Broadway he turned, and halted at a glittering café, where were gathered together nightly the choicest products of the grape, the silkworm, and the protoplasm.

Soapy had confidence in himself from the lowest button of his vest upward. He was shaven, and his coat was decent, and his neat black, ready-tied four-in-hand had been presented to him by a lady missionary on Thanksgiving Day. If he could reach a table in the restaurant unsuspected, success would be his. The portion of him that would show above the table would raise no doubt in the waiter's mind.

A roasted mallard duck, thought Soapy, would be about the thing—with a bottle of Chablis, and then Camembert, a demi-tasse and a cigar. One dollar for the cigar would be enough. The total would not be so high as to call forth any supreme manifestation of revenge from the café management; and yet the meal would leave him filled and happy for the journey to his winter refuge.

But as Soapy set foot inside the restaurant door the head waiter's eye fell upon his frayed trousers and decadent shoes. Strong and ready hands turned him about and conveyed him in silence and haste to the sidewalk, and averted the ignoble fate of the menaced mallard.

Soapy turned off Broadway. It seemed that his route to the coveted Island was not to be an epicurean one. Some other way of entering limbo must be thought of.

At a corner of Sixth Avenue electric lights and cunningly displayed wares behind plate-glass made a shop window conspicuous. Soapy took a cobblestone and dashed it through the glass. People came running round the corner, a policeman in the lead. Soapy stood still, with his hands in his pockets, and smiled at the sight of brass buttons.

"Where's the man that done that?" inquired the officer excitedly.

"Don't you figure out that I might have had something to do with it?" said Soapy, not without sarcasm, but friendly, as one greets good fortune.

The policeman's mind refused to accept Soapy even as a clue. Men who smash windows do not remain to parley with the Law's minions—they take to their heels. The policeman saw a man halfway down the block running to catch a car. With drawn club he joined in the pursuit.

Soapy, with disgust in his heart, loafed along—twice unsuccessful.

On the opposite side of the street was a restaurant of no great pretensions. It catered to large appetites and modest purses. Its crockery and atmosphere were thick; its soup and napery thin. Into this place Soapy took his accusive shoes and tell-tale trousers without challenge.

At a table he sat and consumed beefsteak, flapjacks, doughnuts, and pie. And then to the waiter he betrayed the fact that the minutest coin and himself were strangers.

"Now, get busy and call a cop," said Soapy. "And don't keep a gentleman waiting."

"No cop for youse," said the waiter, with a voice like butter cakes and an eye like the cherry in a Manhattan cocktail. "Hey, Con!"

Neatly upon his left ear on the callous pavement two waiters pitched Soapy. He arose, joint by joint, as a carpenter's rule opens, and beat the dust from his clothes. Arrest seemed but a rosy dream. The Island seemed very far away. A policeman who stood before a drug store two doors away laughed and walked down the street.

Five blocks Soapy travelled before his courage permitted him to woo capture again. This time the opportunity presented what he fatuously termed to himself a "cinch." A young woman of a modest and pleasing guise was standing before a show window gazing with sprightly interest at its display of shaving mugs and inkstands, and two yards from the window a large policeman of severe demeanour leaned against a water-plug.

It was Soapy's design to assume the rôle of the despicable and execrated "masher." The refined and elegant appearance of his victim and the contiguity of the conscientious cop encouraged him to believe that he would soon feel the pleasant official clutch upon his arm that would ensure his winter quarters on the little, tight island.

Soapy straightened the lady missionary's ready-made tie, dragged his shrinking cuffs into the open, set his hat at a killing cant and sidled toward the young woman. He made eyes at her, was taken with sudden coughs and "hems," smiled, smirked, and went brazenly through the impudent and contemptible litany of the "masher."

With half an eye Soapy saw that the policeman was watching him fixedly. The young woman moved away a few steps, and again bestowed her absorbed attention upon the shaving mugs. Soapy followed, boldly stepping to her side, raised his hat and said:

"Ah there, Bedelia! Don't you want to come and play in my yard?"

The policeman was still looking. The persecuted young woman had but to beckon a finger and Soapy would be practically en route for his insular haven. Already he imagined he could feel the cosy warmth of the station-house.

The young woman faced him and, stretching out a hand, caught Soapy's coat sleeve.

"Sure, Mike," she said joyfully, "if you'll blow me to a pail of suds. I'd have spoke to you sooner, but the cop was watching."

With the young woman playing the clinging ivy to his oak, Soapy walked past the policeman overcome with gloom. He seemed doomed to liberty.

At the next corner he shook off his companion and ran. He halted in the district where by night are found the lightest streets, hearts, vows, and librettos. Women in furs and men in greatcoats moved gaily in the wintry air.

A sudden fear seized Soapy that some dreadful enchantment had rendered him immune to arrest. The thought brought a little of panic upon it, and when he came upon another policeman lounging grandly in front of a transplendent theatre he caught at the immediate straw of "disorderly conduct."

On the sidewalk Soapy began to yell drunken gibberish at the top of his harsh voice. He danced, howled, raved, and otherwise disturbed the welkin.

The policeman twirled his club, turned his back to Soapy and remarked to a citizen:

"'Tis one of them Yale lads celebratin' the goose egg they gave to Hartford College. Noisy, but no harm. We've instructions to lave them be."

Disconsolate, Soapy ceased his unavailing racket. Would never a policeman lay hands on him? In his fancy the Island seemed an unattainable Arcadia. He buttoned his thin coat against the chilling wind.

In a cigar store he saw a well-dressed man lighting a cigar at a swinging light. His silk umbrella he had set by the door on entering. Soapy stepped inside, secured the umbrella and sauntered off with it slowly. The man at the cigar light followed hastily.

"My umbrella," he said sternly.

"Oh, is it?" sneered Soapy, adding insult to petit larceny. "Well, why don't you call a policeman? I took it. Your umbrella! Why don't you call a cop? There stands one on the corner."

The umbrella owner slowed his steps. Soapy did likewise, with a presentiment that luck would run against him.

The policeman looked at the two curiously.

"Of course," said the umbrella man, "that is—well, you know how these mistakes occur—if it's your umbrella, I hope you'll excuse me—I picked it up this morning in a restaurant—if you recognize it as yours, why—I hope you'll—"

"Of course it's mine," said Soapy viciously.

The ex-umbrella man retreated. The policeman hurried to assist a tall blonde in an opera cloak across the street in front of a streetcar that was approaching two blocks away.

Soapy walked eastward through a street damaged by improvements. He hurled the umbrella wrathfully into an excavation. He muttered against the men who wear helmets and carry clubs. Because he wanted to fall into their clutches, they seemed to regard him as a king who could do no wrong.

At length Soapy reached one of the avenues to the east where the glitter and turmoil was but faint. He set his face down this toward Madison Square, for the homing instinct survives even when the home is a park bench.

But on an unusually quiet corner Soapy came to a standstill. Here was an old church, quaint and rambling and gabled. Through one violet-stained window a soft light glowed, where, no doubt, the organist loitered over the keys, making sure of his mastery of the coming Sabbath anthem.

For there drifted out to Soapy's ears sweet music that caught and held him transfixed against the convolutions of the iron fence. The moon was above, lustrous and serene; vehicles and pedestrians were few; sparrows twittered sleepily in the eaves—for a little while the scene might have been a country churchyard.

And the anthem that the organist played cemented Soapy to the iron fence, for he had known it well in the days when his life contained such things as mothers and roses and ambitions and friends and immaculate thoughts and collars.

The conjunction of Soapy's receptive state of mind and the influences about the old church wrought a sudden and wonderful change in his soul. He viewed with swift horror the pit into which he had tumbled—the degraded days, unworthy desires, dead hopes, wrecked faculties, and base motives that made up his existence.

And also in a moment his heart responded thrillingly to this novel mood. An instantaneous and strong impulse moved him to battle with his desperate fate. He would pull himself out of the mire; he would make a man of himself again; he would conquer the evil that had taken possession of him.

There was time; he was comparatively young yet; he would resurrect his old eager ambitions and pursue them without faltering. Those solemn but sweet organ notes had set up a revolution in him. To-morrow he would go into the roaring downtown district and find work.

A fur importer had once offered him a place as driver. He would find him to-morrow and ask for the position. He would be somebody in the world. He would—

Soapy felt a hand laid on his arm. He looked quickly round into the broad face of a policeman.

"What are you doin' here?" asked the officer.

"Nothin'," said Soapy.

"Then come along," said the policeman.

"Three months on the Island," said the Magistrate in the Police Court the next morning.

THE OPEN WINDOW

SAKI

First published in *The Westminster Gazette*, 1911.

"My aunt will be down presently, Mr. Nuttel," said a very self-possessed young lady of fifteen; "in the meantime you must try and put up with me."

Framton Nuttel endeavoured to say the correct something which should duly flatter the niece of the moment without unduly discounting the aunt that was to come. Privately he doubted more than ever whether these formal visits on a succession of total strangers would do much towards helping the nerve cure which he was supposed to be undergoing.

"I know how it will be," his sister had said when he was preparing to migrate to this rural retreat; "you will bury yourself down there and not speak to a living soul, and your nerves will be worse than ever from moping. I shall just give you letters of introduction to all the people I know there. Some of them, as far as I can remember, were quite nice."

Framton wondered whether Mrs. Sappleton, the lady to whom he was presenting one of the letters of introduction came into the nice division.

"Do you know many of the people round here?" asked the niece, when she judged that they had had sufficient silent communion.

"Hardly a soul," said Framton. "My sister was staying here, at the rectory, you know, some four years ago, and she gave me letters of introduction to some of the people here."

He made the last statement in a tone of distinct regret.

"Then you know practically nothing about my aunt?" pursued the self-possessed young lady.

"Only her name and address," admitted the caller. He was wondering whether Mrs. Sappleton was in the married or widowed state. An undefinable something about the room seemed to suggest masculine habitation.

"Her great tragedy happened just three years ago," said the child; "that would be since your sister's time."

"Her tragedy?" asked Framton; somehow in this restful country spot tragedies seemed out of place.

"You may wonder why we keep that window wide open on an October afternoon," said the niece, indicating a large French window that opened on to a lawn.

"It is quite warm for the time of the year," said Framton; "but has that window got anything to do with the tragedy?"

"Out through that window, three years ago to a day, her husband and her two young brothers went off for their day's shooting. They never came back. In crossing the moor to their favourite snipe-shooting ground they were all three engulfed in a treacherous piece of bog. It had been that dreadful wet summer, you know, and places that were safe in other years gave way suddenly without warning. Their bodies were never recovered. That was the dreadful part of it." Here the child's voice lost its self-possessed note and became falteringly human. "Poor aunt always thinks that they will come back someday, they and the little brown spaniel that was lost with them, and walk in at that window just as they used to do. That is why the window is kept open every evening till it is quite dusk. Poor dear aunt, she has often told me how they went out, her husband with his white waterproof coat over his arm, and Ronnie, her youngest brother, singing 'Bertie, why do you bound?' as he always did to tease her, because she said it got on her nerves. Do you know, sometimes on still, quiet evenings like this, I almost get a creepy feeling that they will all walk in through that window - "

She broke off with a little shudder. It was a relief to Framton when the aunt bustled into the room with a whirl of apologies for being late in making her appearance.

"I hope Vera has been amusing you?" she said.

"She has been very interesting," said Framton.

"I hope you don't mind the open window," said Mrs. Sappleton briskly; "my husband and brothers will be home directly from shooting, and they always come in this way. They've been out for snipe in the marshes today, so they'll make a fine mess over my poor carpets. So like you menfolk, isn't it?"

She rattled on cheerfully about the shooting and the scarcity of birds, and the prospects for duck in the winter. To Framton it was all purely horrible. He made a desperate but only partially successful effort to turn the talk on to a less ghastly topic, he was conscious that his hostess was giving him only a fragment of her attention, and her eyes were constantly straying past him to the open window and the lawn beyond. It was certainly an unfortunate coincidence that he should have paid his visit on this tragic anniversary.

"The doctors agree in ordering me complete rest, an absence of mental excitement, and avoidance of anything in the nature of violent physical exercise," announced Framton, who laboured under the tolerably widespread delusion that total strangers and chance acquaintances are hungry for the least detail of one's ailments and infirmities, their cause and cure. "On the matter of diet they are not so much in agreement," he continued.

"No?" said Mrs. Sappleton, in a voice which only replaced a yawn at the last moment. Then she suddenly brightened into alert attention - but not to what Framton was saying.

"Here they are at last!" she cried. "Just in time for tea, and don't they look as if they were muddy up to the eyes!"

Framton shivered slightly and turned towards the niece with a look intended to convey sympathetic comprehension. The child was staring out through the open window with a dazed horror in her eyes. In a chill shock of nameless fear Framton swung round in his seat and looked in the same direction.

In the deepening twilight three figures were walking across the lawn towards the window, they all carried guns under their arms, and one of them was additionally burdened with a white coat hung over his shoulders. A tired brown spaniel kept close at their heels. Noiselessly they neared the house, and then a hoarse young voice chanted out of the dusk: "I said, Bertie, why do you bound?"

Framton grabbed wildly at his stick and hat; the hall door, the gravel drive, and the front gate were dimly noted stages in his headlong retreat. A cyclist coming along the road had to run into the hedge to avoid imminent collision.

"Here we are, my dear," said the bearer of the white mackin-tosh, coming in through the window, "fairly muddy, but most of it's dry. Who was that who bolted out as we came up?"

"A most extraordinary man, a Mr. Nuttel," said Mrs. Sappleton; "could only talk about his illnesses, and dashed off without a word of goodby or apology when you arrived. One would think he had seen a ghost."

"I expect it was the spaniel," said the niece calmly; "he told me he had a horror of dogs. He was once hunted into a cemetery somewhere on the banks of the Ganges by a pack of pariah dogs, and had to spend the night in a newly dug grave with the creatures snarling and grinning and foaming just above him. Enough to make anyone lose their nerve."

Romance at short notice was her speciality.

THE LUMBER ROOM

SAKI

First published in *The Morning Post*, 1914.

The children were to be driven, as a special treat, to the sands at Jagborough. Nicholas was not to be of the party; he was in disgrace. Only that morning he had refused to eat his wholesome bread-and-milk on the seemingly frivolous ground that there was a frog in it.

Older and wiser and better people had told him that there could not possibly be a frog in his bread-and-milk and that he was not to talk nonsense; he continued, nevertheless, to talk what seemed the veriest nonsense, and described with much detail the coloration and markings of the alleged frog. The dramatic part of the incident was that there really was a frog in Nicholas's basin of bread-and-milk; he had put it there himself, so he felt entitled to know something about it.

The sin of taking a frog from the garden and putting it into a bowl of wholesome bread-and-milk was enlarged on at great length, but the fact that stood out clearest in the whole affair, as it presented itself to the mind of Nicholas, was that the older, wiser, and better people had been proved to be profoundly in error in matters about which they had expressed the utmost assurance.

"You said there couldn't possibly be a frog in my bread-and-milk; there was a frog in my bread-and-milk," he repeated, with the insistence of a skilled tactician who does not intend to shift from favourable ground.

So his boy-cousin and girl-cousin and his quite uninteresting younger brother were to be taken to Jagborough sands that afternoon and he was to stay at home. His cousins' aunt, who insisted, by an unwarranted stretch of imagination, in styling herself his aunt also, had hastily invented the Jagborough expedition in order to impress on Nicholas the delights that he had justly forfeited by his disgraceful conduct at the breakfast-table.

It was her habit, whenever one of the children fell from grace, to improvise something of a festival nature from which the offender would be rigorously debarred; if all the children sinned collectively they were suddenly informed of a circus in a neighbouring town, a circus of unrivalled merit and uncounted elephants, to which, but for their depravity, they would have been taken that very day.

A few decent tears were looked for on the part of Nicholas when the moment for the departure of the expedition arrived. As a matter of fact, however, all the crying was done by his girl-cousin, who scraped her knee rather painfully against the step of the carriage as she was scrambling in.

"How she did howl," said Nicholas cheerfully, as the party drove off without any of the elation of high spirits that should have characterized it.

"She'll soon get over that," said the soi-disant aunt; "it will be a glorious afternoon for racing about over those beautiful sands. How they will enjoy themselves!"

"Bobby won't enjoy himself much, and he won't race much either," said Nicholas with a grim chuckle; "his boots are hurting him. They're too tight."

"Why didn't he tell me they were hurting?" asked the aunt with some asperity.

"He told you twice, but you weren't listening. You often don't listen when we tell you important things."

"You are not to go into the gooseberry garden," said the aunt, changing the subject.

"Why not?" demanded Nicholas.

"Because you are in disgrace," said the aunt loftily.

Nicholas did not admit the flawlessness of the reasoning; he felt perfectly capable of being in disgrace and in a gooseberry garden at the same moment. His face took on an expression of considerable obstinacy.

It was clear to his aunt that he was determined to get into the gooseberry garden, "only," as she remarked to herself, "because I have told him he is not to."

Now the gooseberry garden had two doors by which it might be entered, and once a small person like Nicholas could slip in there he could effectually disappear from view amid the masking growth of artichokes, raspberry canes, and fruit bushes.

The aunt had many other things to do that afternoon, but she spent an hour or two in trivial gardening operations among flower-beds and shrubberies, whence she could watch the two doors that led to the forbidden paradise. She was a woman of few ideas, with immense powers of concentration.

Nicholas made one or two sorties into the front garden, wriggling his way with obvious stealth of purpose towards one or other of the doors, but never able for a moment to evade the aunt's watchful eye. As a matter of fact, he had no intention of trying to get into the gooseberry garden, but it was extremely convenient for him that his aunt should believe that he had; it was a belief that would keep her on self-imposed sentry-duty for the greater part of the afternoon.

Having thoroughly confirmed and fortified her suspicions, Nicholas slipped back into the house and rapidly put into execution a plan of action that had long germinated in his brain.

By standing on a chair in the library one could reach a shelf on which reposed a fat, important-looking key. The key was as important as it looked; it was the instrument which kept the mysteries of the lumber-room secure from unauthorized intrusion, which opened a way only for aunts and such-like privileged persons.

Nicholas had not had much experience of the art of fitting keys into keyholes and turning locks, but for some days past he had practised with the key of the schoolroom door; he did not believe in trusting too much to luck and accident.

The key turned stiffly in the lock, but it turned. The door opened, and Nicholas was in an unknown land, compared with which the gooseberry garden was a stale delight, a mere material pleasure.

Often and often Nicholas had pictured to himself what the lumber-room might be like, that region that was so carefully sealed from youthful eyes and concerning which no questions were ever answered. It came up to his expectations.

In the first place it was large and dimly lit, one high window opening onto the forbidden garden being its only source of illumination. In the second place it was a storehouse of unimagined treasures. The aunt-by-assertion was one of those people who think that things spoil by use and consign them to dust and damp by way of preserving them.

Such parts of the house as Nicholas knew best were rather bare and cheerless, but here there were wonderful things for the eye to feast on.

First and foremost there was a piece of framed tapestry that was evidently meant to be a fire-screen. To Nicholas it was a living, breathing story; he sat down on a roll of Indian hangings, glowing in wonderful colours beneath a layer of dust, and took in all the details of the tapestry picture.

A man, dressed in the hunting costume of some remote period, had just transfixed a stag with an arrow; it could not have been a difficult shot because the stag was only one or two paces away from him.

In the thickly growing vegetation that the picture suggested it would not have been difficult to creep up to a feeding stag, and the two spotted dogs that were springing forward to join in the chase had evidently been trained to keep to heel till the arrow was discharged.

That part of the picture was simple, if interesting, but did the huntsman see, what Nicholas saw, that four galloping wolves were coming in his direction through the wood? There might be more than four of them hidden behind the trees, and in any case would the man and his dogs be able to cope with the four wolves if they made an attack?

The man had only two arrows left in his quiver, and he might miss with one or both of them; all one knew about his skill in shooting was that he could hit a large stag at a ridiculously short range. Nicholas sat for many golden minutes revolving the possibilities of the scene; he was inclined to think that there were more than four wolves and that the man and his dogs were in a tight corner.

But there were other objects of delight and interest claiming his instant attention; there were quaint twisted candlesticks in the shape of snakes, and a teapot fashioned like a china duck, out of whose open beak the tea was supposed to come. How dull and shapeless the nursery teapot seemed in comparison!

And there was a carved sandalwood box packed tight with aromatic cotton-wool, and between the layers of cotton-wool were little brass figures—hump-necked bulls, and peacocks and goblins, delightful to see and to handle.

Less promising in appearance was a large square book with plain black covers; Nicholas peeped into it, and, behold, it was full of coloured pictures of birds. And such birds!

In the garden, and in the lanes when he went for a walk, Nicholas came across a few birds, of which the largest were an occasional magpie or wood-pigeon; here were herons and bustards, kites, toucans, tiger-bitterns, brush-turkeys, ibises, golden pheasants—a whole portrait gallery of undreamed-of creatures.

And as he was admiring the colouring of the mandarin duck and assigning a life-history to it, the voice of his aunt in shrill vociferation of his name came from the gooseberry garden without.

She had grown suspicious at his long disappearance, and had leapt to the conclusion that he had climbed over the wall behind the sheltering screen of the lilac bushes: she was now engaged in energetic and rather hopeless search for him among the artichokes and raspberry canes.

"Nicholas, Nicholas!" she screamed. "You are to come out of this at once. It's no use trying to hide there; I can see you all the time."

It was probably the first time for twenty years that any one had smiled in that lumber-room.

Presently the angry repetitions of Nicholas's name gave way to a shriek, and a cry for somebody to come quickly. Nicholas shut the book, restored it carefully to its place in a corner, and shook some dust from a neighbouring pile of newspapers over it. Then he crept from the room, locked the door, and replaced the key exactly where he had found it.

His aunt was still calling his name when he sauntered into the front garden.

"Who's calling?" he asked.

"Me," came the answer from the other side of the wall; "didn't you hear me? I've been looking for you in the gooseberry garden, and I've slipped into the rain-water tank. Luckily there's no water in it, but the sides are slippery and I can't get out. Fetch the little ladder from under the cherry-tree—"

"I was told I wasn't to go into the gooseberry garden," said Nicholas promptly.

"I told you not to, and now I tell you that you may," came the voice from the rain-water tank, rather impatiently.

"Your voice doesn't sound like aunt's," objected Nicholas; "you may be the Evil One tempting me to be disobedient.

Aunt often tells me that the Evil One tempts me and that I always yield. This time I'm not going to yield."

"Don't talk nonsense," said the prisoner in the tank; "go and fetch the ladder."

"Will there be strawberry jam for tea?" asked Nicholas innocently.

"Certainly there will be," said the aunt, privately resolving that Nicholas should have none of it.

"Now I know that you are the Evil One and not aunt," shouted Nicholas gleefully; "when we asked aunt for strawberry jam yesterday she said there wasn't any. I know there are four jars of it in the store cupboard, because I looked, and of course you know it's there, but she doesn't, because she said there wasn't any. Oh, Devil, you have sold yourself!"

There was an unusual sense of luxury in being able to talk to an aunt as though one was talking to the Evil One, but Nicholas knew, with childish discernment, that such luxuries were not to be over-indulged in.

He walked noisily away, and it was a kitchen-maid, in search of parsley, who eventually rescued the aunt from the rain-water tank.

Tea that evening was partaken of in a fearsome silence. The tide had been at its highest when the children had arrived at Jagborough Cove, so there had been no sands to play on—a circumstance that the aunt had overlooked in the haste of organizing her punitive expedition.

The tightness of Bobby's boots had had a disastrous effect on his temper the whole of the afternoon, and altogether the children could not have been said to have enjoyed themselves.

The aunt maintained the frozen muteness of one who has suffered undignified and unmerited detention in a rain-water tank for thirty-five minutes.

As for Nicholas, he, too, was silent, in the absorption of one who has much to think about; it was just possible, he considered, that the huntsman would escape with his hounds while the wolves feasted on the stricken stag.

SHERLOCK HOLMES: A SCANDAL IN BOHEMIA

ARTHUR CONAN DOYLE

First published in *The Strand Magazine*, 1891.

I

To Sherlock Holmes she is always *the woman*. I have seldom heard him mention her under any other name. In his eyes she eclipses and predominates the whole of her sex. It was not that he felt any emotion akin to love for Irene Adler. All emotions, and that one particularly, were abhorrent to his cold, precise but admirably balanced mind. He was, I take it, the most perfect reasoning and observing machine that the world has seen, but as a lover he would have placed himself in a false position. He never spoke of the softer passions, save with a gibe and a sneer. They were admirable things for the observer—excellent for drawing the veil from men's motives and actions. But for the trained reasoner to admit such intrusions into his own delicate and finely adjusted temperament was to introduce a distracting factor which might throw a doubt upon all his mental results. Grit in a sensitive instrument, or a crack in one of his own high-power lenses, would not be more disturbing than a strong emotion in a nature such as his. And yet there was but one woman to him, and that woman was the late Irene Adler, of dubious and questionable memory.

I had seen little of Holmes lately. My marriage had drifted us away from each other. My own complete happiness, and the home-centred interests which rise up around the man who first finds himself master of his own establishment, were sufficient to absorb all my attention, while Holmes, who loathed every form of society with his whole Bohemian soul, remained in our lodgings in Baker Street, buried among his old books, and alternating from week to week between cocaine and ambition, the drowsiness of the drug, and the fierce energy of his own keen nature. He was still, as ever, deeply attracted by the study of crime, and occupied his immense faculties and extraordinary powers of observation in following out those clues, and clearing up those mysteries which had been abandoned as hopeless by the official police. From time to time I heard some vague account of his doings: of his summons to Odessa in the case of the Trepoff murder, of his clearing up of the singular tragedy of the Atkinson brothers at Trincomalee, and finally of the mission which he had accomplished so delicately and successfully for the reigning family of Holland. Beyond these signs of his activity, however, which I merely shared with all the readers of the daily press, I knew little of my former friend and companion.

One night—it was on the twentieth of March, 1888—I was returning from a journey to a patient (for I had now returned to civil practice), when my way led me through Baker Street. As I passed the well-remembered door, which must always be associated in my mind with my wooing, and with the dark incidents of the *Study in Scarlet*, I was seized with a keen desire to see Holmes again, and to know how he was employing his extraordinary powers. His rooms were brilliantly lit, and, even as I looked up, I saw his tall, spare figure pass twice in a dark silhouette against the blind. He was pacing the room swiftly, eagerly, with his head sunk upon his chest and his hands clasped behind him. To me, who knew his every mood and habit, his attitude and manner told their own story. He was at work again. He had risen out of his drug-created dreams and was hot upon the scent of some new problem.

I rang the bell and was shown up to the chamber which had formerly been in part my own.

His manner was not effusive. It seldom was; but he was glad, I think, to see me. With hardly a word spoken, but with a kindly eye, he waved me to an arm-chair, threw across his case of cigars, and indicated a spirit case and a gasogene in the corner. Then he stood before the fire and looked me over in his singular introspective fashion.

"Wedlock suits you," he remarked. "I think, Watson, that you have put on seven and a half pounds since I saw you."

"Seven!" I answered.

"Indeed, I should have thought a little more. Just a trifle more, I fancy, Watson. And in practice again, I observe. You did not tell me that you intended to go into harness."

"Then, how do you know?"

"I see it, I deduce it. How do I know that you have been getting yourself very wet lately, and that you have a most clumsy and careless servant girl?"

"My dear Holmes," said I, "this is too much. You would certainly have been burned, had you lived a few centuries ago. It is true that I had a country walk on Thursday and came home in a dreadful mess, but as I have changed my clothes I can't imagine how you deduce it. As to Mary Jane, she is incorrigible, and my wife has given her notice, but there, again, I fail to see how you work it out."

He chuckled to himself and rubbed his long, nervous hands together.

"It is simplicity itself," said he; "my eyes tell me that on the inside of your left shoe, just where the firelight strikes it, the leather is scored by six almost parallel cuts. Obviously they have been caused by someone who has very carelessly scraped round the edges of the sole in order to remove crusted mud from it. Hence, you see, my double deduction that you had been out in vile weather, and that you had a particularly malignant boot-slitting specimen of the London slavey. As to your practice, if a gentleman walks into my rooms smelling of iodoform, with a black mark of nitrate of silver upon his right forefinger, and a bulge on the right side of his top-hat to show where he has secreted his stethoscope, I must be dull, indeed, if I do not pronounce him to be an active member of the medical profession."

I could not help laughing at the ease with which he explained his process of deduction.

"When I hear you give your reasons," I remarked, "the thing always appears to me to be so ridiculously simple that I could easily do it myself, though at each successive instance of your reasoning I am baffled until you explain your process. And yet I believe that my eyes are as good as yours."

"Quite so," he answered, lighting a cigarette, and throwing himself down into an arm-chair. "You see, but you do not observe. The distinction is clear. For example, you have frequently seen the steps which lead up from the hall to this room."

"Frequently."

"How often?"

"Well, some hundreds of times."

"Then how many are there?"

"How many? I don't know."

"Quite so! You have not observed. And yet you have seen. That is just my point. Now, I know that there are seventeen steps, because I have both seen and observed. By-the-way, since you are interested in these little problems, and since you are good enough to chronicle one or two of my trifling experiences, you may be interested in this." He threw over a sheet of thick, pink-tinted notepaper which had been lying open upon the table. "It came by the last post," said he. "Read it aloud."

The note was undated, and without either signature or address.

"There will call upon you to-night, at a quarter to eight o'clock," it said, "a gentleman who desires to consult you upon a matter of the very deepest moment. Your recent services to one of the royal houses of Europe have shown that you are one who may safely be trusted with matters which are of an importance which can hardly be exaggerated. This account of you we have from all quarters received. Be in your chamber then at that hour, and do not take it amiss if your visitor wear a mask."

"This is indeed a mystery," I remarked. "What do you imagine that it means?"

"I have no data yet. It is a capital mistake to theorise before one has data. Insensibly one begins to twist facts to suit theories, instead of theories to suit facts. But the note itself. What do you deduce from it?"

I carefully examined the writing, and the paper upon which it was written.

"The man who wrote it was presumably well-to-do," I remarked, endeavouring to imitate my companion's processes. "Such paper could not be bought under half a crown a packet. It is peculiarly strong and stiff."

"Peculiar—that is the very word," said Holmes. "It is not an English paper at all. Hold it up to the light."

I did so, and saw a large E with a small *g*, a P, and a large G with a small *t* woven into the texture of the paper.

"What do you make of that?" asked Holmes.

"The name of the maker, no doubt; or his monogram, rather."

"Not at all. The 'G' with the small 't' stands for *Gesellschaft*, which is the German for 'Company.' It is a customary contraction like our 'Co.' 'P,' of course, stands for *Papier*. Now for the 'Eg.' Let us glance at our Continental Gazetteer." He took down a heavy brown volume from his shelves. "Eglow, Eglonitz—here we are, Egria. It is in a German-speaking country—in Bohemia, not far from Carlsbad. 'Remarkable as being the scene of the death of Wallenstein, and for its numerous glass-factories and paper-mills.' Ha, ha, my boy, what do you make of that?" His eyes sparkled, and he sent up a great blue triumphant cloud from his cigarette.

"The paper was made in Bohemia," I said.

"Precisely. And the man who wrote the note is a German. Do you note the peculiar construction of the sentence—'This account of you we have from all quarters received'? A Frenchman or Russian could not have written that. It is the German who is so uncourteous to his verbs. It only remains, therefore, to discover what is wanted by this German who writes upon Bohemian paper and prefers wearing a mask to showing his face. And here he comes, if I am not mistaken, to resolve all our doubts."

As he spoke there was the sharp sound of horses' hoofs and grating wheels against the curb, followed by a pull at the bell. Holmes whistled.

"A pair, by the sound," said he. "Yes," he continued, glancing out of the window. "A nice little brougham and a pair of beauties. A hundred and fifty guineas apiece. There's money in this case, Watson, if there is nothing else."

"I think that I had better go, Holmes."

"Not a bit, Doctor. Stay where you are. I am lost without my Boswell. And this promises to be interesting. It would be a pity to miss it."

"But your client—"

"Never mind him. I may want your help, and so may he. Here he comes. Sit down in that arm-chair, Doctor, and give us your best attention."

A slow and heavy step, which had been heard upon the stairs and in the passage, paused immediately outside the door. Then there was a loud and authoritative tap.

"Come in!" said Holmes.

A man entered who could hardly have been less than six feet six inches in height, with the chest and limbs of a Hercules. His dress was rich with a richness which would, in

England, be looked upon as akin to bad taste. Heavy bands of astrakhan were slashed across the sleeves and fronts of his double-breasted coat, while the deep blue cloak which was thrown over his shoulders was lined with flame-coloured silk and secured at the neck with a brooch which consisted of a single flaming beryl. Boots which extended halfway up his calves, and which were trimmed at the tops with rich brown fur, completed the impression of barbaric opulence which was suggested by his whole appearance. He carried a broad-brimmed hat in his hand, while he wore across the upper part of his face, extending down past the cheekbones, a black vizard mask, which he had apparently adjusted that very moment, for his hand was still raised to it as he entered. From the lower part of the face he appeared to be a man of strong character, with a thick, hanging lip, and a long, straight chin suggestive of resolution pushed to the length of obstinacy.

"You had my note?" he asked with a deep, harsh voice and a strongly marked German accent. "I told you that I would call." He looked from one to the other of us, as if uncertain which to address.

"Pray take a seat," said Holmes. "This is my friend and colleague, Dr. Watson, who is occasionally good enough to help me in my cases. Whom have I the honour to address?"

"You may address me as the Count Von Kramm, a Bohemian nobleman. I understand that this gentleman, your friend, is a man of honour and discretion, whom I may trust with a matter of the most extreme importance. If not, I should much prefer to communicate with you alone."

I rose to go, but Holmes caught me by the wrist and pushed me back into my chair. "It is both, or none," said he. "You may say before this gentleman anything which you may say to me."

The Count shrugged his broad shoulders. "Then I must begin," said he, "by binding you both to absolute secrecy for two years; at the end of that time the matter will be of no importance. At present it is not too much to say that it is of such weight it may have an influence upon European history."

"I promise," said Holmes.

"And I."

"You will excuse this mask," continued our strange visitor. "The august person who employs me wishes his agent to be unknown to you, and I may confess at once that the title by which I have just called myself is not exactly my own."

"I was aware of it," said Holmes dryly.

"The circumstances are of great delicacy, and every precaution has to be taken to quench what might grow to be an immense scandal and seriously compromise one of the reigning families of Europe. To speak plainly, the matter implicates the great House of Ormstein, hereditary kings of Bohemia."

"I was also aware of that," murmured Holmes, settling himself down in his arm-chair and closing his eyes.

Our visitor glanced with some apparent surprise at the languid, lounging figure of the man who had been no doubt depicted to him as the most incisive reasoner and most energetic agent in Europe. Holmes slowly reopened his eyes and looked impatiently at his gigantic client.

"If your Majesty would condescend to state your case," he remarked, "I should be better able to advise you."

The man sprang from his chair and paced up and down the room in uncontrollable agitation. Then, with a gesture of desperation, he tore the mask from his face and hurled it upon the ground.

"You are right," he cried; "I am the King. Why should I attempt to conceal it?"

"Why, indeed?" murmured Holmes. "Your Majesty had not spoken before I was aware that I was addressing Wilhelm Gottsreich Sigismond von Ormstein, Grand Duke of Cassel-Felstein, and hereditary King of Bohemia."

"But you can understand," said our strange visitor, sitting down once more and passing his hand over his high white forehead, "you can understand that I am not accustomed to doing such business in my own person. Yet the matter was so delicate that I could not confide it to an agent without putting myself in his power. I have come incognito from Prague for the purpose of consulting you."

"Then, pray consult," said Holmes, shutting his eyes once more.

"The facts are briefly these: Some five years ago, during a lengthy visit to Warsaw, I made the acquaintance of the well-known adventuress, Irene Adler. The name is no doubt familiar to you."

"Kindly look her up in my index, Doctor," murmured Holmes without opening his eyes. For many years he had adopted a system of docketing all paragraphs concerning men and things, so that it was difficult to name a subject or a person on which he could not at once furnish information. In this case I found her biography sandwiched in between that of a Hebrew rabbi and that of a staff-commander who had written a monograph upon the deep-sea fishes.

"Let me see!" said Holmes. "Hum! Born in New Jersey in the year 1858. Contralto—hum! La Scala, hum! Prima donna Imperial Opera of Warsaw—yes! Retired from operatic stage—ha! Living in London—quite so! Your Majesty, as I understand, became entangled with this young person, wrote her some compromising letters, and is now desirous of getting those letters back."

"Precisely so. But how—"

"Was there a secret marriage?"

"None."

"No legal papers or certificates?"

"None."

"Then I fail to follow your Majesty. If this young person should produce her letters for blackmailing or other purposes, how is she to prove their authenticity?"

"There is the writing."

"Pooh, pooh! Forgery."

"My private note-paper."

"Stolen."

"My own seal."

"Imitated."

"My photograph."

"Bought."

"We were both in the photograph."

"Oh, dear! That is very bad! Your Majesty has indeed committed an indiscretion."

"I was mad—insane."

"You have compromised yourself seriously."

"I was only Crown Prince then. I was young. I am but thirty now."

"It must be recovered."

"We have tried and failed."

"Your Majesty must pay. It must be bought."

"She will not sell."

"Stolen, then."

"Five attempts have been made. Twice burglars in my pay ransacked her house. Once we diverted her luggage when she travelled. Twice she has been waylaid. There has been no result."

"No sign of it?"

"Absolutely none."

Holmes laughed. "It is quite a pretty little problem," said he.

"But a very serious one to me," returned the King reproach-fully.

"Very, indeed. And what does she propose to do with the photograph?"

"To ruin me."

"But how?"

"I am about to be married."

"So I have heard."

"To Clotilde Lothman von Saxe-Meningen, second daughter of the King of Scandinavia. You may know the strict principles of her family. She is herself the very soul of delicacy. A shadow of a doubt as to my conduct would bring the matter to an end."

"And Irene Adler?"

"Threatens to send them the photograph. And she will do it. I know that she will do it. You do not know her, but she has a soul of steel. She has the face of the most beautiful of women, and the mind of the most resolute of men. Rather than I should marry another woman, there are no lengths to which she would not go—none."

"You are sure that she has not sent it yet?"

"I am sure."

"And why?"

"Because she has said that she would send it on the day when the betrothal was publicly proclaimed. That will be next Monday."

"Oh, then we have three days yet," said Holmes with a yawn. "That is very fortunate, as I have one or two matters of importance to look into just at present. Your Majesty will, of course, stay in London for the present?"

"Certainly. You will find me at the Langham under the name of the Count Von Kramm."

"Then I shall drop you a line to let you know how we progress."

"Pray do so. I shall be all anxiety."

"Then, as to money?"

"You have *carte blanche*."

"Absolutely?"

"I tell you that I would give one of the provinces of my kingdom to have that photograph."

"And for present expenses?"

The King took a heavy chamois leather bag from under his cloak and laid it on the table.

"There are three hundred pounds in gold and seven hundred in notes," he said.

Holmes scribbled a receipt upon a sheet of his note-book and handed it to him.

"And Mademoiselle's address?" he asked.

"Is Briony Lodge, Serpentine Avenue, St. John's Wood."

Holmes took a note of it. "One other question," said he. "Was the photograph a cabinet?"

"It was."

"Then, good-bye, your Majesty, and I trust that we shall soon have some good news for you."

"And good-bye, Watson," he added, as the wheels of the royal brougham rolled down the street. "If you will be good enough to call to-morrow afternoon at three o'clock I should like to chat this little matter over with you."

II

At three o'clock precisely I was at Baker Street, but Holmes had not yet returned. The landlady informed me that he had left the house shortly after eight o'clock in the morning. I sat down beside the fire, however, with the intention of awaiting him, however long he might be. I was already deeply interested in his inquiry, for, though it was surrounded by none of the grim and strange features which were associated with the two crimes which I have already recorded, still, the nature of the case and the exalted station of his client gave it a character of its own. Indeed, apart from the nature of the investigation which my friend had on hand, there was something in his masterly grasp of a situation, and his keen, incisive reasoning, which made it a pleasure to me to study his system of work, and to follow the quick, subtle methods by which he disentangled the most inextricable mysteries. So accustomed was I to his invariable success that the very possibility of his failing had ceased to enter into my head.

It was close upon four before the door opened, and a drunken-looking groom, ill-kempt and side-whiskered, with an inflamed face and disreputable clothes, walked into the room. Accustomed as I was to my friend's amazing powers in the use of disguises, I had to look three times before I was certain that it was indeed he. With a nod he vanished into the bedroom, whence he emerged in five minutes tweed-suited and respectable, as of old. Putting his hands into his pockets, he stretched out his legs in front of the fire and laughed heartily for some minutes.

"Well, really!" he cried, and then he choked and laughed again until he was obliged to lie back, limp and helpless, in the chair.

"What is it?"

"It's quite too funny. I am sure you could never guess how I employed my morning, or what I ended by doing."

"I can't imagine. I suppose that you have been watching the habits, and perhaps the house, of Miss Irene Adler."

"Quite so; but the sequel was rather unusual. I will tell you, however. I left the house a little after eight o'clock this morning in the character of a groom out of work. There is a wonderful sympathy and freemasonry among horsey men. Be one of them, and you will know all that there is to know. I soon found Briony Lodge. It is a bijou villa, with a garden at the back, but built out in front right up to the road, two sto-ries. Chubb lock to the door. Large sitting-room on the right side, well furnished, with long windows almost to the floor, and those preposterous English window fasteners which a child could open. Behind there was nothing remarkable, save that the passage window could be reached from the top of the coach-house. I walked round it and examined it closely from every point of view, but without noting anything else of interest.

"I then lounged down the street and found, as I expected, that there was a mews in a lane which runs down by one wall of the garden. I lent the ostlers a hand in rubbing down their horses, and received in exchange twopence, a glass of half and half, two fills of shag tobacco, and as much information as I could desire about Miss Adler, to say nothing of half a dozen other people in the neighbourhood in whom I was not in the least interested, but whose biographies I was compelled to listen to."

"And what of Irene Adler?" I asked.

"Oh, she has turned all the men's heads down in that part. She is the daintiest thing under a bonnet on this planet. So say the Serpentine-mews, to a man. She lives quietly, sings at concerts, drives out at five every day, and returns at seven sharp for dinner. Seldom goes out at other times, except when she sings. Has only one male visitor, but a good deal of him. He is dark, handsome, and dashing, never calls less than once a day, and often twice. He is a Mr. Godfrey Norton, of the Inner Temple. See the advantages of a cabman as a confidant. They had driven him home a dozen times from Serpentine-mews, and knew all about him. When I had listened to all they had to tell, I began to walk up and down near Briony Lodge once more, and to think over my plan of campaign.

"This Godfrey Norton was evidently an important factor in the matter. He was a lawyer. That sounded ominous. What was the relation between them, and what the object of his repeated visits? Was she his client, his friend, or his mistress? If the former, she had probably transferred the photograph to his keeping. If the latter, it was less likely. On the issue of this question depended whether I should continue my work at Briony Lodge, or turn my attention to the gentle-man's chambers in the Temple. It was a delicate point, and it widened the field of my inquiry. I fear that I bore you with these details, but I have to let you see my little difficulties, if you are to understand the situation."

"I am following you closely," I answered.

"I was still balancing the matter in my mind when a hansom cab drove up to Briony Lodge, and a gentleman sprang out. He was a remarkably handsome man, dark, aquiline, and moustached—evidently the man of whom I had heard. He appeared to be in a great hurry, shouted to the cabman to wait, and brushed past the maid who opened the door with the air of a man who was thoroughly at home.

"He was in the house about half an hour, and I could catch glimpses of him in the windows of the sitting-room, pacing up and down, talking excitedly, and waving his arms. Of her I could see nothing. Presently he emerged, looking even more flurried than before. As he stepped up to the cab, he pulled a gold watch from his pocket and looked at it earnestly, 'Drive like the devil,' he shouted, 'first to Gross & Hankey's in Regent Street, and then to the Church of St. Monica in the Edgeware Road. Half a guinea if you do it in twenty minutes!'

"Away they went, and I was just wondering whether I should not do well to follow them when up the lane came a neat little landau, the coachman with his coat only half-buttoned, and his tie under his ear, while all the tags of his harness were sticking out of the buckles. It hadn't pulled up before she shot out of the hall door and into it. I only caught a glimpse of her at the moment, but she was a lovely woman, with a face that a man might die for.

"'The Church of St. Monica, John,' she cried, 'and half a sovereign if you reach it in twenty minutes.'"

"This was quite too good to lose, Watson. I was just balancing whether I should run for it, or whether I should perch behind her landau when a cab came through the street. The driver looked twice at such a shabby fare, but I jumped in before he could object. 'The Church of St. Monica,' said I, 'and half a sovereign if you reach it in twenty minutes.' It was twenty-five minutes to twelve, and of course it was clear enough what was in the wind.

"My cabby drove fast. I don't think I ever drove faster, but the others were there before us. The cab and the landau with their steaming horses were in front of the door when I arrived. I paid the man and hurried into the church. There was not a soul there save the two whom I had followed and a surpliced clergyman, who seemed to be expostulating with them. They were all three standing in a knot in front of the altar. I lounged up the side aisle like any other idler who has dropped into a church. Suddenly, to my surprise, the three at the altar faced round to me, and Godfrey Norton came running as hard as he could towards me.

"□'Thank God,' he cried. 'You'll do. Come! Come!'

"□'What then?' I asked.

"□'Come, man, come, only three minutes, or it won't be legal.'

"I was half-dragged up to the altar, and before I knew where I was I found myself mumbling responses which were whispered in my ear, and vouching for things of which I knew nothing, and generally assisting in the secure tying up of Irene Adler, spinster, to Godfrey Norton, bachelor. It was all done in an instant, and there was the gentleman thanking me on the one side and the lady on the other, while the clergyman beamed on me in front. It was the most preposterous position in which I ever found myself in my life, and it was the thought of it that started me laughing just now. It seems that there had been some informality about their license, that the clergyman absolutely refused to marry them without a witness of some sort, and that my lucky appearance saved the bridegroom from having to sally out into the streets in search of a best man. The bride gave me a sovereign, and I mean to wear it on my watch-chain in memory of the occasion."

"This is a very unexpected turn of affairs," said I; "and what then?"

"Well, I found my plans very seriously menaced. It looked as if the pair might take an immediate departure, and so necessitate very prompt and energetic measures on my part. At the church door, however, they separated, he driving back to the Temple, and she to her own house. 'I shall drive out in the park at five as usual,' she said as she left him. I heard no more. They drove away in different directions, and I went off to make my own arrangements."

"Which are?"

"Some cold beef and a glass of beer," he answered, ringing the bell. "I have been too busy to think of food, and I am likely to be busier still this evening. By the way, Doctor, I shall want your co-operation."

"I shall be delighted."

"You don't mind breaking the law?"

"Not in the least."

"Nor running a chance of arrest?"

"Not in a good cause."

"Oh, the cause is excellent!"

"Then I am your man."

"I was sure that I might rely on you."

"But what is it you wish?"

"When Mrs. Turner has brought in the tray I will make it clear to you. Now," he said as he turned hungrily on the simple fare that our landlady had provided, "I must discuss it while I eat, for I have not much time. It is nearly five now. In two hours we must be on the scene of action. Miss Irene, or Madame, rather, returns from her drive at seven. We must be at Briony Lodge to meet her."

"And what then?"

"You must leave that to me. I have already arranged what is to occur. There is only one point on which I must insist. You must not interfere, come what may. You understand?"

"I am to be neutral?"

"To do nothing whatever. There will probably be some small unpleasantness. Do not join in it. It will end in my being conveyed into the house. Four or five minutes afterwards the sitting-room window will open. You are to station yourself close to that open window."

"Yes."

"You are to watch me, for I will be visible to you."

"Yes."

"And when I raise my hand—so—you will throw into the room what I give you to throw, and will, at the same time, raise the cry of fire. You quite follow me?"

"Entirely."

"It is nothing very formidable," he said, taking a long cig-ar-shaped roll from his pocket. "It is an ordinary plumber's smoke-rocket, fitted with a cap at either end to make it self-lighting. Your task is confined to that. When you raise your cry of fire, it will be taken up by quite a number of people. You may then walk to the end of the street, and I will rejoin you in ten minutes. I hope that I have made myself clear?"

"I am to remain neutral, to get near the window, to watch you, and at the signal to throw in this object, then to raise the cry of fire, and to wait you at the corner of the street."

"Precisely."

"Then you may entirely rely on me."

"That is excellent. I think, perhaps, it is almost time that I prepare for the new role I have to play."

He disappeared into his bedroom and returned in a few minutes in the character of an amiable and simple-minded Nonconformist clergyman. His broad black hat, his baggy trousers, his white tie, his sympathetic smile, and general look of peering and benevolent curiosity were such as Mr. John Hare alone could have equalled. It was not merely that Holmes changed his costume. His expression, his manner, his very soul seemed to vary with every fresh part that he assumed. The stage lost a fine actor, even as science lost an acute reasoner, when he became a specialist in crime.

It was a quarter past six when we left Baker Street, and it still wanted ten minutes to the hour when we found our-selves in Serpentine Avenue. It was already dusk, and the lamps were just being lighted as we paced up and down in front of Briony Lodge, waiting for the coming of its occupant. The house was just such as I had pictured it from Sherlock Holmes' succinct description, but the locality appeared to be less private than I expected. On the contrary, for a small street in a quiet neighbourhood, it was remarkably animated. There was a group of shabbily dressed men smoking and laughing in a corner, a scissors-grinder with his wheel, two guardsmen who were flirting with a nurse-girl, and several well-dressed young men who were lounging up and down with cigars in their mouths.

"You see," remarked Holmes, as we paced to and fro in front of the house, "this marriage rather simplifies matters. The photograph becomes a double-edged weapon now. The chances are that she would be as averse to its being seen by Mr. Godfrey Norton, as our client is to its coming to the eyes of his princess. Now the question is—Where are we to find the photograph?"

"Where, indeed?"

"It is most unlikely that she carries it about with her. It is cabinet size. Too large for easy concealment about a woman's dress. She knows that the King is capable of having her waylaid and searched. Two attempts of the sort have already been made. We may take it, then, that she does not carry it about with her."

"Where, then?"

"Her banker or her lawyer. There is that double possibility. But I am inclined to think neither. Women are naturally secretive, and they like to do their own secreting. Why should she hand it over to anyone else? She could trust her own guardianship, but she could not tell what indirect or political influence might be brought to bear upon a business man. Besides, remember that she had resolved to use it within a few days. It must be where she can lay her hands upon it. It must be in her own house."

"But it has twice been burgled."

"Pshaw! They did not know how to look."

"But how will you look?"

"I will not look."

"What then?"

"I will get her to show me."

"But she will refuse."

"She will not be able to. But I hear the rumble of wheels. It is her carriage. Now carry out my orders to the letter."

As he spoke the gleam of the side-lights of a carriage came round the curve of the avenue. It was a smart little landau which rattled up to the door of Briony Lodge. As it pulled up, one of the loafing men at the corner dashed forward to open the door in the hope of earning a copper, but was elbowed away by another loafer, who had rushed up with the same intention. A fierce quarrel broke out, which was increased by the two guardsmen, who took sides with one of the loungers, and by the scissors-grinder, who was equally hot upon the other side. A blow was struck, and in an instant the lady, who had stepped from her carriage, was the centre of a little knot of flushed and struggling men, who struck savagely at each other with their fists and sticks. Holmes dashed into the crowd to protect the lady; but just as he reached her he gave a cry and dropped to the ground, with the blood running freely down his face. At his fall the guardsmen took to their heels in one direction and the loungers in the other, while a number of better-dressed people, who had watched the scuffle without taking part in it, crowded in to help the lady and to attend to the injured man. Irene Adler, as I will still call her, had hurried up the steps; but she stood at the top with her superb figure outlined against the lights of the hall, looking back into the street.

"Is the poor gentleman much hurt?" she asked.

"He is dead," cried several voices.

"No, no, there's life in him!" shouted another. "But he'll be gone before you can get him to hospital."

"He's a brave fellow," said a woman. "They would have had the lady's purse and watch if it hadn't been for him. They were a gang, and a rough one, too. Ah, he's breathing now."

"He can't lie in the street. May we bring him in, marm?"

"Surely. Bring him into the sitting-room. There is a comfortable sofa. This way, please!"

Slowly and solemnly he was borne into Briony Lodge and laid out in the principal room, while I still observed the proceedings from my post by the window. The lamps had been lit, but the blinds had not been drawn, so that I could see Holmes as he lay upon the couch. I do not know whether he was seized with compunction at that moment for the part he was playing, but I know that I never felt more heartily ashamed of myself in my life than when I saw the beautiful creature against whom I was conspiring, or the grace and kindliness with which she waited upon the injured man. And yet it would be the blackest treachery to Holmes to draw back now from the part which he had intrusted to me. I hardened my heart, and took the smoke-rocket from under my ulster. After all, I thought, we are not injuring her. We are but preventing her from injuring another.

Holmes had sat up upon the couch, and I saw him motion like a man who is in need of air. A maid rushed across and threw open the window. At the same instant I saw him raise his hand and at the signal I tossed my rocket into the room with a cry of "Fire!" The word was no sooner out of my mouth than the whole crowd of spectators, well dressed and ill—gentlemen, ostlers, and servant-maids—joined in a general shriek of "Fire!" Thick clouds of smoke curled through the room and out at the open window. I caught a glimpse of rushing figures, and a moment later the voice of Holmes from within assuring them that it was a false alarm. Slipping through the shouting crowd I made my way to the corner of the street, and in ten minutes was rejoiced to find my friend's arm in mine, and to get away from the scene of uproar. He walked swiftly and in silence for some few minutes until we had turned down one of the quiet streets which lead towards the Edgeware Road.

"You did it very nicely, Doctor," he remarked. "Nothing could have been better. It is all right."

"You have the photograph?"

"I know where it is."

"And how did you find out?"

"She showed me, as I told you she would."

"I am still in the dark."

"I do not wish to make a mystery," said he, laughing. "The matter was perfectly simple. You, of course, saw that every-one in the street was an accomplice. They were all engaged for the evening."

"I guessed as much."

"Then, when the row broke out, I had a little moist red paint in the palm of my hand. I rushed forward, fell down, clapped my hand to my face, and became a piteous spectacle. It is an old trick."

"That also I could fathom."

"Then they carried me in. She was bound to have me in. What else could she do? And into her sitting-room, which was the very room which I suspected. It lay between that and her bedroom, and I was determined to see which. They laid me on a couch, I motioned for air, they were compelled to open the window, and you had your chance."

"How did that help you?"

"It was all-important. When a woman thinks that her house is on fire, her instinct is at once to rush to the thing which she values most. It is a perfectly overpowering impulse, and I have more than once taken advantage of it. In the case of the Darlington substitution scandal it was of use to me, and also in the Arnsworth Castle business. A married woman grabs at her baby; an unmarried one reaches for her jewel-box. Now it was clear to me that our lady of to-day had nothing in the house more precious to her than what we are in quest of. She would rush to secure it. The alarm of fire was admirably done. The smoke and shouting were enough to shake nerves of steel. She responded beautifully. The photograph is in a recess behind a sliding panel just above the right bell-pull. She was there in an instant, and I caught a glimpse of it as she half-drew it out. When I cried out that it was a false alarm, she replaced it, glanced at the rocket, rushed from the room, and I have not seen her since. I rose, and, making my excuses, escaped from the house. I hesitated whether to attempt to secure the photograph at once; but the coachman had come in, and as he was watching me narrowly it seemed safer to wait. A little over-precipitance may ruin all."

"And now?" I asked.

"Our quest is practically finished. I shall call with the King to-morrow, and with you, if you care to come with us. We will be shown into the sitting-room to wait for the lady, but it is probable that when she comes she may find neither us nor the photograph. It might be a satisfaction to his Majesty to regain it with his own hands."

"And when will you call?"

"At eight in the morning. She will not be up, so that we shall have a clear field. Besides, we must be prompt, for this marriage may mean a complete change in her life and habits. I must wire to the King without delay."

We had reached Baker Street and had stopped at the door. He was searching his pockets for the key when someone passing said:

"Good-night, Mister Sherlock Holmes."

There were several people on the pavement at the time, but the greeting appeared to come from a slim youth in an ulster who had hurried by.

"I've heard that voice before," said Holmes, staring down the dimly lit street. "Now, I wonder who the deuce that could have been."

III

I slept at Baker Street that night, and we were engaged upon our toast and coffee in the morning when the King of Bohemia rushed into the room.

"You have really got it!" he cried, grasping Sherlock Holmes by either shoulder and looking eagerly into his face.

"Not yet."

"But you have hopes?"

"I have hopes."

"Then, come. I am all impatience to be gone."

"We must have a cab."

"No, my brougham is waiting."

"Then that will simplify matters." We descended and started off once more for Briony Lodge.

"Irene Adler is married," remarked Holmes.

"Married! When?"

"Yesterday."

"But to whom?"

"To an English lawyer named Norton."

"But she could not love him."

"I am in hopes that she does."

"And why in hopes?"

"Because it would spare your Majesty all fear of future annoyance. If the lady loves her husband, she does not love your Majesty. If she does not love your Majesty, there is no reason why she should interfere with your Majesty's plan."

"It is true. And yet—Well! I wish she had been of my own station! What a queen she would have made!" He relapsed into a moody silence, which was not broken until we drew up in Serpentine Avenue.

The door of Briony Lodge was open, and an elderly woman stood upon the steps. She watched us with a sardonic eye as we stepped from the brougham.

"Mr. Sherlock Holmes, I believe?" said she.

"I am Mr. Holmes," answered my companion, looking at her with a questioning and rather startled gaze.

"Indeed! My mistress told me that you were likely to call. She left this morning with her husband by the 5.15 train from Charing Cross for the Continent."

"What!" Sherlock Holmes staggered back, white with chagrin and surprise. "Do you mean that she has left England?"

"Never to return."

"And the papers?" asked the King hoarsely. "All is lost."

"We shall see." He pushed past the servant and rushed into the drawing-room, followed by the King and myself.

The furniture was scattered about in every direction, with dismantled shelves and open drawers, as if the lady had hurriedly ransacked them before her flight. Holmes rushed at the bell-pull, tore back a small sliding shutter, and, plunging in his hand, pulled out a photograph and a letter. The photograph was of Irene Adler herself in evening dress, the letter was superscribed to 'Sherlock Holmes, Esq. To be left till called for.' My friend tore it open and we all three read it together.

It was dated at midnight of the preceding night and ran in this way:

"My dear Mr. Sherlock Holmes:

"You really did it very well. You took me in completely. Until after the alarm of fire, I had not a suspicion. But then, when I found how I had betrayed myself, I began to think. I had been warned against you months ago. I had been told that if the King employed an agent it would certainly be you. And your address had been given me. Yet, with all this, you made me reveal what you wanted to know. Even after I became suspicious, I found it hard to think evil of such a dear, kind old clergyman. But, you know, I have been trained as an actress myself. Male costume is nothing new to me. I often take advantage of the freedom which it gives. I sent John, the coachman, to watch you, ran upstairs, got into my walking-clothes, as I call them, and came down just as you departed.

"Well, I followed you to your door, and so made sure that I was really an object of interest to the celebrated Mr. Sherlock Holmes. Then I, rather imprudently, wished you good-night, and started for the Temple to see my husband.

"We both thought the best resource was flight, when pursued by so formidable an antagonist; so you will find the nest empty when you call to-morrow. As to the photograph, your client may rest in peace. I love and am loved by a better man than he. The King may do what he will without hindrance from one whom he has cruelly wronged. I keep it only to safeguard myself, and to preserve a weapon which will always secure me from any steps which he might take in the future. I leave a photograph which he might care to possess; and I remain, dear Mr. Sherlock Holmes,

Very truly yours,

Irene Norton, née Adler."

"What a woman—oh, what a woman!" cried the King of Bohemia, when we had all three read this epistle. "Did I not tell you how quick and resolute she was? Would she not have made an admirable queen? Is it not a pity that she was not on my level?"

"From what I have seen of the lady she seems indeed to be on a very different level to your Majesty," said Holmes coldly. "I am sorry that I have not been able to bring your Majesty's business to a more successful conclusion."

"On the contrary, my dear sir," cried the King; "nothing could be more successful. I know that her word is inviolate. The photograph is now as safe as if it were in the fire."

"I am glad to hear your Majesty say so."

"I am immensely indebted to you. Pray tell me in what way I can reward you. This ring—" He slipped an emerald snake ring from his finger and held it out upon the palm of his hand.

"Your Majesty has something which I should value even more highly," said Holmes.

"You have but to name it."

"This photograph!"

The King stared at him in amazement.

"Irene's photograph!" he cried. "Certainly, if you wish it."

"I thank your Majesty. Then there is no more to be done in the matter. I have the honour to wish you a very good-morning." He bowed, and, turning away without observing the hand which the King had stretched out to him, he set off in my company for his chambers.

And that was how a great scandal threatened to affect the kingdom of Bohemia, and how the best plans of Mr. Sherlock Holmes were beaten by a woman's wit. He used to make merry over the cleverness of women, but I have not heard him do it of late. And when he speaks of Irene Adler, or when he refers to her photograph, it is always under the honourable title of *the woman.*

PART III

Horror & the Supernatural

EDGAR ALLAN POE

Edgar Allan Poe (1809–1849) was an American poet, critic, and pioneer of the macabre whose tales forged the modern short story. Orphaned young and raised by a foster family that never formally adopted him, he briefly attended the University of Virginia before gambling debts drove him to enlist in the army under an alias. Discharged, he turned to writing full-time amid poverty and loss. His beloved wife, Virginia, died of tuberculosis in 1847, echoing the consumptive heroines in his work. Poe invented the detective genre with his character C. Auguste Dupin in *The Murders in the Rue Morgue* (1841), delved into psychological terror, and crafted Gothic masterpieces laced with rhythm and dread. He died mysteriously in Baltimore at forty, found delirious in borrowed clothes; theories range from alcohol to rabies, but his raven-shadowed legacy endures.

THE BLACK CAT

EDGAR ALLAN POE

First published in *The Saturday Evening Post*, 1843.

For the most wild, yet most homely narrative which I am about to pen, I neither expect nor solicit belief. Mad indeed would I be to expect it, in a case where my very senses reject their own evidence. Yet, mad am I not—and very surely do I not dream. But to-morrow I die, and to-day I would unburthen my soul. My immediate purpose is to place before the world, plainly, succinctly, and without comment, a series of mere household events. In their consequences, these events have terrified—have tortured—have destroyed me. Yet I will not attempt to expound them. To me, they have presented little but horror—to many they will seem less terrible than *barroques*. Hereafter, perhaps, some intellect may be found which will reduce my phantasm to the common-place—some intellect more calm, more logical, and far less excitable than my own, which will perceive, in the circumstances I detail with awe, nothing more than an ordinary succession of very natural causes and effects.

From my infancy I was noted for the docility and humanity of my disposition. My tenderness of heart was even so conspicuous as to make me the jest of my companions. I was especially fond of animals, and was indulged by my parents with a great variety of pets. With these I spent most of my time, and never was so happy as when feeding and caressing them. This peculiarity of character grew with my growth, and in my manhood, I derived from it one of my principal sources of pleasure. To those who have cherished an affection for a faithful and sagacious dog, I need hardly be at the trouble of explaining the nature or the intensity of the gratification thus derivable. There is something in the unselfish and self-sacrificing love of a brute, which goes directly to the heart of him who has had frequent occasion to test the paltry friendship and gossamer fidelity of mere *Man*.

I married early, and was happy to find in my wife a disposition not uncongenial with my own. Observing my partiality for domestic pets, she lost no opportunity of procuring those of the most agreeable kind. We had birds, goldfish, a fine dog, rabbits, a small monkey, and *a cat*.

This latter was a remarkably large and beautiful animal, entirely black, and sagacious to an astonishing degree. In speaking of his intelligence, my wife, who at heart was not a little tinctured with superstition, made frequent allusion to the ancient popular notion, which regarded all black cats as witches in disguise. Not that she was ever *serious* upon this point—and I mention the matter at all for no better reason than that it happens, just now, to be remembered.

Pluto—this was the cat's name—was my favorite pet and playmate. I alone fed him, and he attended me wherever I went about the house. It was even with difficulty that I could prevent him from following me through the streets.

Our friendship lasted, in this manner, for several years, during which my general temperament and character—through the instrumentality of the Fiend Intemperance—had (I blush to confess it) experienced a radical alteration for the worse. I grew, day by day, more moody, more irritable, more regardless of the feelings of others. I suffered myself to use intemperate language to my wife. At length, I even offered her personal violence. My pets, of course, were made to feel the change in my disposition. I not only neglected, but ill-used them. For Pluto, however, I still retained sufficient regard to restrain me from maltreating him, as I made no scruple of maltreating the rabbits, the monkey, or even the dog, when by accident, or through affection, they came in my way. But my disease grew upon me—for what disease is like Alcohol!—and at length even Pluto, who was now becoming old, and consequently somewhat peevish—even Pluto began to experience the effects of my ill temper.

One night, returning home, much intoxicated, from one of my haunts about town, I fancied that the cat avoided my presence. I seized him; when, in his fright at my violence, he inflicted a slight wound upon my hand with his teeth. The fury of a demon instantly possessed me. I knew myself no longer. My original soul seemed, at once, to take its flight from my body and a more than fiendish malevolence, gin-nurtured, thrilled every fibre of my frame. I took from my waistcoat pocket a penknife, opened it, grasped the poor beast by the throat, and deliberately cut one of its eyes from the socket! I blush, I burn, I shudder, while I pen the damnable atrocity.

When reason returned with the morning—when I had slept off the fumes of the night's debauch—I experienced a sentiment half of horror, half of remorse, for the crime of which I had been guilty; but it was, at best, a feeble and equivocal feeling, and the soul remained untouched. I again plunged into excess, and soon drowned in wine all memory of the deed.

In the meantime the cat slowly recovered. The socket of the lost eye presented, it is true, a frightful appearance, but he no longer appeared to suffer any pain. He went about the house as usual, but, as might be expected, fled in extreme terror at my approach. I had so much of my old heart left, as to be at first grieved by this evident dislike on the part of a creature which had once so loved me. But this feeling soon gave place to irritation. And then came, as if to my final and irrevocable overthrow, the spirit of PERVERSENESS. Of this spirit philosophy takes no account. Yet I am not more sure that my soul lives, than I am that perverseness is one of the primitive impulses of the human heart—one of the indivisible primary faculties, or sentiments, which give di-rection to the character of Man. Who has not, a hundred times, found himself committing a vile or a silly action, for no other reason than because he knows he should not? Have we not a perpetual inclination, in the teeth of our best judgment, to violate that which is *Law*, merely because we understand it to be such? This spirit of perverseness, I say, came to my final overthrow. It was this unfathomable longing of the soul *to vex itself*—to offer violence to its own nature—to do wrong for the wrong's sake only—that urged me to continue and finally to consummate the injury I had inflicted upon the unoffending brute. One morning, in cool blood, I slipped a noose about its neck and hung it to the limb of a tree;—hung it with the tears streaming from my eyes, and with the bitterest remorse at my heart;—hung it *because* I knew that it had loved me, and *because* I felt it had given me no reason of offence;—hung it *because* I knew that in so doing I was committing a sin—a deadly sin that would so jeopardize my immortal soul as to place it—if such a thing wore possible—even beyond the reach of the infinite mercy of the Most Merciful and Most Terrible God.

On the night of the day on which this cruel deed was done, I was aroused from sleep by the cry of fire. The curtains of my bed were in flames. The whole house was blazing. It was with great difficulty that my wife, a servant, and myself, made our escape from the conflagration. The destruction was complete. My entire worldly wealth was swallowed up, and I resigned myself thenceforward to despair.

I am above the weakness of seeking to establish a sequence of cause and effect, between the disaster and the atrocity. But I am detailing a chain of facts—and wish not to leave even a possible link imperfect. On the day succeeding the fire, I visited the ruins. The walls, with one exception, had fallen in. This exception was found in a compartment wall, not very thick, which stood about the middle of the house, and against which had rested the head of my bed. The plastering had here, in great measure, resisted the action of the fire—a fact which I attributed to its having been recently spread. About this wall a dense crowd were collected, and many persons seemed to be examining a particular portion of it with very minute and eager attention. The words "strange!" "singular!" and other similar expressions, excited my curiosity. I approached and saw, as if graven in *bas relief* upon the white surface, the figure of a gigantic *cat*. The impression was given with an accuracy truly marvellous. There was a rope about the animal's neck.

When I first beheld this apparition—for I could scarcely regard it as less—my wonder and my terror were extreme. But at length reflection came to my aid. The cat, I remembered, had been hung in a garden adjacent to the house. Upon the alarm of fire, this garden had been immediately filled by the crowd—by some one of whom the animal must have been cut from the tree and thrown, through an open window, into my chamber. This had probably been done with the view of arousing me from sleep. The falling of other walls had compressed the victim of my cruelty into the substance of the freshly-spread plaster; the lime of which, with the flames, and the *ammonia* from the carcass, had then accomplished the portraiture as I saw it.

Although I thus readily accounted to my reason, if not altogether to my conscience, for the startling fact just detailed, it did not the less fail to make a deep impression upon my fancy. For months I could not rid myself of the phantasm of the cat; and, during this period, there came back into my spirit a half-sentiment that seemed, but was not, remorse. I went so far as to regret the loss of the animal, and to look about me, among the vile haunts which I now habitually frequented, for another pet of the same species, and of somewhat similar appearance, with which to supply its place.

One night as I sat, half stupefied, in a den of more than infamy, my attention was suddenly drawn to some black object, reposing upon the head of one of the immense hogsheads of gin, or of rum, which constituted the chief furniture of the apartment. I had been looking steadily at the top of this hogshead for some minutes, and what now caused me surprise was the fact that I had not sooner perceived the object thereupon. I approached it, and touched it with my hand. It was a black cat—a very large one—fully as large as Pluto, and closely resembling him in every respect but one. Pluto had not a white hair upon any portion of his body; but this cat had a large, although indefinite splotch of white, covering nearly the whole region of the breast. Upon my touching him, he immediately arose, purred loudly, rubbed against my hand, and appeared delighted with my notice. This, then, was the very creature of which I was in search. I at once offered to purchase it of the landlord; but this person made no claim to it—knew nothing of it—had never seen it before.

I continued my caresses, and, when I prepared to go home, the animal evinced a disposition to accompany me. I permitted it to do so; occasionally stooping and patting it as I proceeded. When it reached the house it domesticated itself at once, and became immediately a great favorite with my wife.

For my own part, I soon found a dislike to it arising within me. This was just the reverse of what I had anticipated; but—I know not how or why it was—its evident fondness for myself rather disgusted and annoyed. By slow degrees, these feelings of disgust and annoyance rose into the bitterness of hatred. I avoided the creature; a certain sense of shame, and the remembrance of my former deed of cruelty, preventing me from physically abusing it. I did not, for some weeks, strike, or otherwise violently ill use it; but gradually—very gradually—I came to look upon it with unutterable loathing, and to flee silently from its odious presence, as from the breath of a pestilence.

What added, no doubt, to my hatred of the beast, was the discovery, on the morning after I brought it home, that, like Pluto, it also had been deprived of one of its eyes. This circumstance, however, only endeared it to my wife, who, as I have already said, possessed, in a high degree, that humanity of feeling which had once been my distinguishing trait, and the source of many of my simplest and purest pleasures.

With my aversion to this cat, however, its partiality for myself seemed to increase. It followed my footsteps with a pertinacity which it would be difficult to make the reader comprehend. Whenever I sat, it would crouch beneath my chair, or spring upon my knees, covering me with its loathsome caresses. If I arose to walk it would get between my feet and thus nearly throw me down, or, fastening its long and sharp claws in my dress, clamber, in this manner, to my breast. At such times, although I longed to destroy it with a blow, I was yet withheld from so doing, partly by a memory of my former crime, but chiefly—let me confess it at once—by absolute dread of the beast.

This dread was not exactly a dread of physical evil—and yet I should be at a loss how otherwise to define it. I am almost ashamed to own—yes, even in this felon's cell, I am almost ashamed to own—that the terror and horror with which the animal inspired me, had been heightened by one of the merest chimaeras it would be possible to conceive. My wife had called my attention, more than once, to the character of the mark of white hair, of which I have spoken, and which constituted the sole visible difference between the strange beast and the one I had destroyed. The reader will remember that this mark, although large, had been originally very indefinite; but, by slow degrees—degrees nearly imperceptible, and which for a long time my reason struggled to reject as fanciful—it had, at length, assumed a rigorous distinctness of outline. It was now the representation of an object that I shudder to name—and for this, above all, I loathed, and dreaded, and would have rid myself of the monster *had I dared*—it was now, I say, the image of a hideous—of a ghastly thing—of the GALLOWS!—oh, mournful and terrible engine of Horror and of Crime—of Agony and of Death!

And now was I indeed wretched beyond the wretchedness of mere Humanity. And *a brute beast* —whose fellow I had contemptuously destroyed—*a brute beast* to work out for *me*—for me a man, fashioned in the image of the High God—so much of insufferable woe! Alas! neither by day nor by night knew I the blessing of rest any more! During the former the creature left me no moment alone, and in the latter I started hourly from dreams of unutterable fear to find the hot breath of *the thing* upon my face, and its vast weight—an incarnate nightmare that I had no power to shake off—incumbent eternally upon my *heart*!

Beneath the pressure of torments such as these, the feeble remnant of the good within me succumbed. Evil thoughts became my sole intimates—the darkest and most evil of thoughts. The moodiness of my usual temper increased to hatred of all things and of all mankind; while, from the sudden, frequent, and ungovernable outbursts of a fury to which I now blindly abandoned myself, my uncomplaining wife, alas, was the most usual and the most patient of sufferers.

One day she accompanied me, upon some household errand, into the cellar of the old building which our poverty compelled us to inhabit. The cat followed me down the steep stairs, and, nearly throwing me headlong, exasperated me to madness. Uplifting an axe, and forgetting, in my wrath, the childish dread which had hitherto stayed my hand, I aimed a blow at the animal which, of course, would have proved instantly fatal had it descended as I wished. But this blow was arrested by the hand of my wife. Goaded, by the interference, into a rage more than demoniacal, I withdrew my arm from her grasp and buried the axe in her brain. She fell dead upon the spot, without a groan.

This hideous murder accomplished, I set myself forthwith, and with entire deliberation, to the task of concealing the body. I knew that I could not remove it from the house, either by day or by night, without the risk of being observed by the neighbors. Many projects entered my mind. At one period I thought of cutting the corpse into minute fragments, and destroying them by fire. At another, I resolved to dig a grave for it in the floor of the cellar. Again, I deliberated about casting it in the well in the yard—about packing it in a box, as if merchandise, with the usual arrangements, and so getting a porter to take it from the house. Finally I hit upon what I considered a far better expedient than either of these. I determined to wall it up in the cellar—as the monks of the middle ages are recorded to have walled up their victims.

For a purpose such as this the cellar was well adapted. Its walls were loosely constructed, and had lately been plastered throughout with a rough plaster, which the dampness of the atmosphere had prevented from hardening. Moreover, in one of the walls was a projection, caused by a false chimney, or fireplace, that had been filled up, and made to resemble the red of the cellar. I made no doubt that I could readily displace the bricks at this point, insert the corpse, and wall the whole up as before, so that no eye could detect any thing suspicious. And in this calculation I was not deceived. By means of a crow-bar I easily dislodged the bricks, and, having carefully deposited the body against the inner wall, I propped it in that position, while, with little trouble, I re-laid the whole structure as it originally stood. Having procured mortar, sand, and hair, with every possible precaution, I prepared a plaster which could not be distinguished from the old, and with this I very carefully went over the new brickwork. When I had finished, I felt satisfied that all was right. The wall did not present the slightest appearance of having been disturbed. The rubbish on the floor was picked up with the minutest care. I looked around triumphantly, and said to myself: "Here at least, then, my labor has not been in vain."

My next step was to look for the beast which had been the cause of so much wretchedness; for I had, at length, firmly resolved to put it to death. Had I been able to meet with it, at the moment, there could have been no doubt of its fate; but it appeared that the crafty animal had been alarmed at the violence of my previous anger, and forebore to present itself in my present mood. It is impossible to describe, or to imagine, the deep, the blissful sense of relief which the absence of the detested creature occasioned in my bosom. It did not make its appearance during the night; and thus for one night at least, since its introduction into the house, I soundly and tranquilly slept; aye, slept even with the burden of murder upon my soul!

The second and the third day passed, and still my tormentor came not. Once again I breathed as a freeman. The monster, in terror, had fled the premises forever! I should behold it no more! My happiness was supreme! The guilt of my dark deed disturbed me but little. Some few inquiries had been made, but these had been readily answered. Even a search had been instituted—but of course nothing was to be discovered. I looked upon my future felicity as secured.

Upon the fourth day of the assassination, a party of the police came, very unexpectedly, into the house, and proceeded again to make rigorous investigation of the premises. Secure, however, in the inscrutability of my place of concealment, I felt no embarrassment whatever. The officers bade me accompany them in their search. They left no nook or corner unexplored. At length, for the third or fourth time, they descended into the cellar. I quivered not in a muscle. My heart beat calmly as that of one who slumbers in innocence. I walked the cellar from end to end. I folded my arms upon my bosom, and roamed easily to and fro. The police were thoroughly satisfied and prepared to depart. The glee at my heart was too strong to be restrained. I burned to say if but one word, by way of triumph, and to render doubly sure their assurance of my guiltlessness.

"Gentlemen," I said at last, as the party ascended the steps, "I delight to have allayed your suspicions. I wish you all health, and a little more courtesy. By the bye, gentlemen, this—this is a very well-constructed house." (In the rabid desire to say something easily, I scarcely knew what I uttered at all.)—"I may say an *excellently* well-constructed house. These walls—are you going, gentlemen?—these walls are solidly put together;" and here, through the mere phrenzy of bravado, I rapped heavily, with a cane which I held in my hand, upon that very portion of the brick-work behind which stood the corpse of the wife of my bosom.

But may God shield and deliver me from the fangs of the Arch-Fiend! No sooner had the reverberation of my blows sunk into silence, than I was answered by a voice from within the tomb!—by a cry, at first muffled and broken, like the sobbing of a child, and then quickly swelling into one long, loud, and continuous scream, utterly anomalous and inhuman—a howl—a wailing shriek, half of horror and half of triumph, such as might have arisen only out of hell, conjointly from the throats of the damned in their agony and of the demons that exult in the damnation.

Of my own thoughts it is folly to speak. Swooning, I staggered to the opposite wall. For one instant the party upon the stairs remained motionless, through extremity of terror and of awe. In the next, a dozen stout arms were toiling at the wall. It fell bodily. The corpse, already greatly decayed and clotted with gore, stood erect before the eyes of the spectators. Upon its head, with red extended mouth and solitary eye of fire, sat the hideous beast whose craft had seduced me into murder, and whose informing voice had consigned me to the hangman. I had walled the monster up within the tomb!

WILKIE COLLINS

Wilkie Collins (1824–1889) was a master storyteller whose intricately plotted tales of deception and dread helped invent the modern mystery. A protégé and collaborator of Charles Dickens, he trained as a lawyer before abandoning the bar for fiction, contributing serialised tales to Dickens's magazines. Collins championed social reform in his work, exposing injustices such as marital inequality and opium addiction, drawing partly on his own laudanum use. His novels *The Woman in White* and *The Moonstone* shaped both Gothic horror and detective fiction, earning him the title "grandfather of the English detective novel." He wrote of secrets behind polite society, the kind that make even a gentleman's nightcap feel dangerous.

A TERRIBLY STRANGE BED

WILKIE COLLINS

First published in *Household Words*, 1852.

Shortly after my education at college was finished, I happened to be staying at Paris with an English friend. We were both young men then, and lived, I am afraid, rather a wild life, in the delightful city of our sojourn. One night we were idling about the neighbourhood of the Palais Royal, doubtful to what amusement we should next betake ourselves. My friend proposed a visit to Frascati's; but his suggestion was not to my taste. I knew Frascati's, as the French saying is, by heart; had lost and won plenty of five-franc pieces there, merely for amusement's sake, until it was amusement no longer, and was thoroughly tired, in fact, of all the ghastly respectabilities of such a social anomaly as a respectable gambling-house.

'For Heaven's sake,' said I to my friend, 'let us go somewhere where we can see a little genuine, blackguard, poverty-stricken gaming, with no false gingerbread glitter thrown over it all. Let us get away from fashionable Frascati's, to a house where they don't mind letting in a man with a ragged coat, or a man with no coat, ragged or otherwise.'

'Very well,' said my friend, 'we needn't go out of the Palais Royal to find the sort of company you want. Here's the place just before us—as blackguard a place, by all report, as you could possibly wish to see.'

In another minute we arrived at the door, and entered the house, the back of which you have drawn in your sketch.

When we got upstairs, and had left our hats and sticks with the doorkeeper, we were admitted into the chief gambling-room. We did not find many people assembled there. But, few as the men were who looked up at us on our entrance, they were all types—lamentably true types—of their respective classes.

We had come to see blackguards; but these men were something worse. There is a comic side, more or less appreciable, in all blackguardism—here there was nothing but tragedy—mute, weird tragedy. The quiet in the room was horrible. The thin, haggard, long-haired young man, whose sunken eyes fiercely watched the turning up of the cards, never spoke; the flabby, fat-faced, pimply player, who pricked his piece of pasteboard perseveringly, to register how often black won, and how often red—never spoke; the dirty, wrinkled old man, with the vulture eyes and the darned great-coat, who had lost his last sou, and still looked on desperately, after he could play no longer—never spoke. Even the voice of the croupier sounded as if it were strangely dulled and thickened in the atmosphere of the room. I had entered the place to laugh, but the spectacle before me was something to weep over. I soon found it necessary to take refuge in excitement from the depression of spirits which was fast stealing on me. Unfortunately I sought the nearest excitement, by going to the table and beginning to play. Still more unfortunately, as the event will show, I won—won prodigiously; won incredibly; won at such a rate that the regular players at the table crowded round me, and, staring at my stakes with hungry, superstitious eyes, whispered to one another that the English stranger was going to break the bank.

The game was *Rouge et Noir*. I had played at it in every city in Europe, without, however, the care or the wish to study the Theory of Chances—that philosopher's stone of all gamblers! And a gambler, in the strict sense of the word, I had never been. I was heart-whole from the corroding passion for play. My gaming was a mere idle amusement. I never resorted to it by necessity, because I never knew what it was to want money. I never practised it so incessantly as to lose more than I could afford, or to gain more than I could coolly pocket without being thrown off my balance by my good luck. In short, I had hitherto frequented gambling-tables—just as I frequented ball-rooms and opera-houses—because they amused me, and because I had nothing better to do with my leisure hours.

But on this occasion it was very different—now, for the first time in my life, I felt what the passion for play really was. My success first bewildered, and then, in the most literal meaning of the word, intoxicated me. Incredible as it may appear, it is nevertheless true that I only lost when I attempted to estimate chances, and played according to previous calculation. If I left everything to luck, and staked without any care or consideration, I was sure to win—to win in the face of every recognised probability in favour of the bank. At first some of the men present ventured their money safely enough on my colour; but I speedily increased my stakes to sums which they dared not risk. One after another they left off playing, and breathlessly looked on at my game.

Still, time after time, I staked higher and higher, and still won. The excitement in the room rose to fever pitch. The silence was interrupted by a deep-muttered chorus of oaths and exclamations in different languages, every time the gold was shovelled across to my side of the table—even the imperturbable croupier dashed his rake on the floor in a fury of astonishment at my success. But one man present preserved his self-possession, and that man was my friend. He came to my side, and, whispering in English, begged me to leave the place, satisfied with what I had already gained. I must do him the justice to say that he repeated his warnings and entreaties several times, and only left me and went away after I had rejected his advice (I was, to all intents and purposes, gambling drunk) in terms which rendered it impossible for him to address me again that night.

Shortly after he had gone, a hoarse voice behind me cried: 'Permit me, my dear sir—permit me to restore to their proper place two napoleons which you have dropped. Wonderful luck, sir! I pledge you my word of honour, as an old soldier, in the course of my long experience in this sort of thing, I never saw such luck as yours—never! Go on, sir—sacré mille bombes! Go on boldly, and break the bank!'

I turned round and saw, nodding and smiling at me with inveterate civility, a tall man, dressed in a frogged and braided surtout.

If I had been in my senses, I should have considered him, personally, as being rather a suspicious specimen of an old soldier. He had goggling, bloodshot eyes, mangy moustaches, and a broken nose. His voice betrayed a barrack-room intonation of the worst order, and he had the dirtiest pair of hands I ever saw—even in France. These little personal peculiarities exercised, however, no repelling influence on me. In the mad excitement, the reckless triumph of that moment, I was ready to fraternise with anybody who encouraged me in my game. I accepted the old soldier's offered pinch of snuff, clapped him on the back, and swore he was the honestest fellow in the world—the most glorious relic of the Grand Army that I had ever met with.

'Go on!' cried my military friend, snapping his fingers in ecstasy. 'Go on, and win! Break the bank—mille tonnerres! my gallant English comrade, break the bank!'

And I did go on—went on at such a rate that, in another quarter of an hour, the croupier called out, 'Gentlemen, the bank has discontinued for to-night.' All the notes, and all the gold in that bank, now lay in a heap under my hands; the whole floating capital of the gambling-house was waiting to pour into my pockets!

'Tie up the money in your pocket-handkerchief, my worthy sir,' said the old soldier, as I wildly plunged my hands into my heap of gold. 'Tie it up, as we used to tie up a bit of dinner in the Grand Army; your winnings are too heavy for any breeches-pockets that ever were sewed. There! that's it—shovel them in, notes and all! Crédié! what luck! Stop! another napoleon on the floor! Ah! sacré petit polisson de Napoléon! have I found thee at last? Now then, sir—two tight double knots each way, with your honourable permission, and the money's safe. Feel it! feel it, fortunate sir! Hard and round as a cannon-ball—ah, bah! if they had only fired such cannon-balls at us at Austerlitz—nom d'une pipe! if they only had! And now, as an ancient grenadier, as an ex-brave of the French army, what remains for me to do? I ask what? Simply this: to entreat my valued English friend to drink a bottle of champagne with me, and toast the goddess Fortune in foaming goblets before we part!'

Excellent ex-brave! Convivial ancient grenadier! Champagne by all means! An English cheer for an old soldier! Hurrah! hurrah! Another English cheer for the goddess Fortune! Hurrah! hurrah! hurrah!

'Bravo! the Englishman; the amiable, gracious Englishman, in whose veins circulates the vivacious blood of France! Another glass? Ah, bah!—the bottle is empty! Never mind! *Vive le vin!* I, the old soldier, order another bottle, and half a pound of bonbons with it!'

'No, no, ex-brave; never—ancient grenadier! Your bottle last time; my bottle this. Behold it! Toast away! The French Army! the great Napoleon! the present company! the croupier! the honest croupier's wife and daughters—if he has any! the ladies generally! everybody in the world!'

By the time the second bottle of champagne was emptied, I felt as if I had been drinking liquid fire—my brain seemed all aflame. No excess in wine had ever had this effect on me before in my life. Was it the result of a stimulant acting upon my system when I was in a highly excited state? Was my stomach in a particularly disordered condition? Or was the champagne amazingly strong?

'Ex-brave of the French Army!' cried I, in a mad state of exhilaration, 'I am on fire! How are you? You have set me on fire! Do you hear, my hero of Austerlitz? Let us have a third bottle of champagne to put the flame out!'

The old soldier wagged his head, rolled his goggle-eyes until I expected to see them slip out of their sockets, placed his dirty forefinger by the side of his broken nose, solemnly ejaculated 'Coffee!' and immediately ran off into an inner room.

The word pronounced by the eccentric veteran seemed to have a magical effect on the rest of the company present. With one accord they all rose to depart. Probably they had expected to profit by my intoxication; but, finding that my new friend was benevolently bent on preventing me from getting dead drunk, they had now abandoned all hope of thriving pleasantly on my winnings. Whatever their motive might be, at any rate they went away in a body.

When the old soldier returned and sat down again opposite to me at the table, we had the room to ourselves. I could see the croupier, in a sort of vestibule which opened out of it, eating his supper in solitude. The silence was now deeper than ever.

A sudden change, too, had come over the ex-brave. He assumed a portentously solemn look; and when he spoke to me again, his speech was ornamented by no oaths, enforced by no finger-snapping, enlivened by no apostrophes or ex-clamations.

'Listen, my dear sir,' said he, in mysteriously confidential tones, 'listen to an old soldier's advice. I have been to the mistress of the house (a very charming woman, with a genius for cookery!) to impress on her the necessity of making us some particularly strong and good coffee. You must drink this coffee in order to get rid of your little amiable exaltation of spirits before you think of going home—you must, my good and gracious friend! With all that money to take home to-night, it is a sacred duty to yourself to have your wits about you. You are known to be a winner to an enormous extent by several gentlemen present to-night, who, in a certain point of view, are very worthy and excellent fellows; but they are mortal men, my dear sir, and they have their amiable weaknesses. Need I say more? Ah, no, no! you understand me! Now, this is what you must do—send for a cabriolet when you feel quite well again—draw up all the windows when you get into it—and tell the driver to take you home only through the large and well-lighted thoroughfares. Do this; and you and your money will be safe. Do this; and to-morrow you will thank an old soldier for giving you a word of honest advice.'

Just as the ex-brave ended his oration in very lachrymose tones, the coffee came in, ready poured out in two cups. My attentive friend handed me one of the cups with a bow. I was parched with thirst, and drank it off at a draught. Almost instantly afterwards I was seized with a fit of giddiness, and felt more completely intoxicated than ever. The room whirled round and round furiously; the old soldier seemed to be regularly bobbing up and down before me like the piston of a steam-engine. I was half-deafened by a violent singing in my ears; a feeling of utter bewilderment, helplessness, idiocy, overcame me. I rose from my chair, holding on by the table to keep my balance, and stammered out that I felt dreadfully unwell—so unwell that I did not know how I was to get home.

'My dear friend,' answered the old soldier—and even his voice seemed to be bobbing up and down as he spoke—'my dear friend, it would be madness to go home in your state; you would be sure to lose your money; you might be robbed and murdered with the greatest ease. I am going to sleep here; do you sleep here too—they make up capital beds in this house—take one; sleep off the effects of the wine, and go home safely with your winnings to-morrow—to-morrow, in broad daylight.'

I had but two ideas left: one, that I must never let go hold of my handkerchief full of money; the other, that I must lie down somewhere immediately, and fall off into a comfortable sleep. So I agreed to the proposal about the bed, and took the offered arm of the old soldier, carrying my money with my disengaged hand. Preceded by the croupier, we passed along some passages and up a flight of stairs into the bedroom which I was to occupy. The ex-brave shook me warmly by the hand, proposed that we should breakfast together, and then, followed by the croupier, left me for the night.

I ran to the wash-hand stand; drank some of the water in my jug; poured the rest out, and plunged my face into it; then sat down in a chair and tried to compose myself. I soon felt better. The change for my lungs from the fetid atmosphere of the gambling-room to the cool air of the apartment I now occupied, the almost equally refreshing change for my eyes from the glaring gaslights of the salon to the dim, quiet flicker of one bedroom-candle, aided wonderfully the restorative effects of cold water. The giddiness left me, and I began to feel a little like a reasonable being again.

My first thought was of the risk of sleeping all night in a gambling-house; my second, of the still greater risk of trying to get out after the house was closed, and of going home alone at night through the streets of Paris with a large sum of money about me. I had slept in worse places than this on my travels; so I determined to lock, bolt, and barricade my door, and take my chance till the next morning.

Accordingly I secured myself against all intrusion; looked under the bed, and into the cupboard; tried the fastening of the window; and then, satisfied that I had taken every proper precaution, pulled off my upper clothing, put my light—which was a dim one—on the hearth among a feathery litter of wood-ashes, and got into bed, with the handkerchief full of money under my pillow.

I soon felt not only that I could not go to sleep, but that I could not even close my eyes. I was wide awake, and in a high fever. Every nerve in my body trembled—every one of my senses seemed to be preternaturally sharpened. I tossed and rolled, and tried every kind of position, and perseveringly sought out the cold corners of the bed, and all to no purpose. Now I thrust my arms over the clothes; now I poked them under the clothes; now I violently shot my legs straight out down to the bottom of the bed; now I convulsively coiled them up as near my chin as they would go; now I shook out my crumpled pillow, changed it to the cool side, patted it flat, and lay down quietly on my back; now I fiercely doubled it in two, set it up on end, thrust it against the board of the bed, and tried a sitting posture. Every effort was in vain; I groaned with vexation as I felt that I was in for a sleepless night.

What could I do? I had no book to read. And yet, unless I found out some method of diverting my mind, I felt certain that I was in the condition to imagine all sorts of horrors—to rack my brain with forebodings of every possible and im- possible danger—in short, to pass the night in suffering all conceivable varieties of nervous terror.

I raised myself on my elbow and looked about the room—which was brightened by a lovely moonlight pour- ing straight through the window—to see if it contained any pictures or ornaments that I could at all clearly distinguish. While my eyes wandered from wall to wall, a remembrance of Le Maistre's delightful little book, *Voyage autour de ma Chambre*, occurred to me. I resolved to imitate the French author, and find occupation and amusement enough to relieve the tedium of my wakefulness, by making a mental inventory of every article of furniture I could see, and by following up to their sources the multitude of associations which even a chair, a table, or a wash-hand stand may be made to call forth.

In the nervous unsettled state of my mind at that moment, I found it much easier to make my inventory than to make my reflections, and thereupon soon gave up all hope of thinking in Le Maistre's fanciful track—or, indeed, of thinking at all. I looked about the room at the different articles of furniture, and did nothing more.

There was, first, the bed I was lying in—a four-post bed, of all things in the world to meet with in Paris—yes, a thorough clumsy British four-poster, with the regular top lined with chintz—the regular fringed valance all round—the regular stifling, unwholesome curtains, which I remembered having mechanically drawn back against the posts without particularly noticing the bed when I first got into the room. Then there was the marble-topped wash-hand stand, from which the water I had spilt, in my hurry to pour it out, was still dripping, slowly and more slowly, on to the brick floor. Then two small chairs, with my coat, waistcoat, and trousers flung on them. Then a large elbow-chair covered with dirty white dimity, with my cravat and shirt collar thrown over the back. Then a chest of drawers with two of the brass handles off, and a tawdry, broken china inkstand placed on it by way of ornament for the top. Then the dressing-table, adorned by a very small looking-glass and a very large pincushion. Then the window—an unusually large window. Then a dark old picture, which the feeble candle dimly showed me. It was a picture of a fellow in a high Spanish hat, crowned with a plume of towering feathers—a swarthy, sinister ruffian, looking upward, shading his eyes with his hand, and looking intently upward—it might be at some tall gallows at which he was going to be hanged. At any rate, he had the appearance of thoroughly deserving it.

This picture put a kind of constraint upon me to look upward too—at the top of the bed. It was a gloomy and not an interesting object, and I looked back at the picture. I counted the feathers in the man's hat—they stood out in relief—three white, two green. I observed the crown of his hat, which was of conical shape, according to the fashion supposed to have been favoured by Guido Fawkes. I wondered what he was looking up at. It couldn't be at the stars; such a desperado was neither astrologer nor astronomer. It must be at the high gallows, and he was going to be hanged presently. Would the executioner come into possession of his conical-crowned hat and plume of feathers? I counted the feathers again—three white, two green.

While I still lingered over this very improving and intellectual employment, my thoughts insensibly began to wander. The moonlight shining into the room reminded me of a certain moonlight night in England—the night after a picnic party in a Welsh valley. Every incident of the drive homeward, through lovely scenery which the moonlight made lovelier than ever, came back to my remembrance, though I had never given the picnic a thought for years; though, if I had tried to recollect it, I could certainly have recalled little or nothing of that scene long past. Of all the wonderful faculties that help to tell us we are immortal, which speaks the sublime truth more eloquently than memory?

Here was I, in a strange house of the most suspicious character, in a situation of uncertainty, and even of peril, which might seem to make the cool exercise of my recollection almost out of the question; nevertheless, remembering, quite involuntarily, places, people, conversations, minute circumstances of every kind, which I had thought forgotten for ever; which I could not possibly have recalled at will, even under the most favourable auspices. And what cause had produced in a moment the whole of this strange, complicated, mysterious effect? Nothing but some rays of moonlight shining in at my bedroom window.

I was still thinking of the picnic—of our merriment on the drive home—of the sentimental young lady who would quote *Childe Harold* because it was moonlight. I was absorbed by these past scenes and past amusements, when, in an instant, the thread on which my memories hung snapped asunder; my attention immediately came back to present things more vividly than ever, and I found myself, I neither knew why nor wherefore, looking hard at the picture again.

Looking for what?

Good God! the man had pulled his hat down on his brows! No! the hat itself was gone! Where was the conical crown? Where the feathers—three white, two green? Not there! In place of the hat and feathers, what dusky object was it that now hid his forehead, his eyes, his shading hand?

Was the bed moving?

I turned on my back and looked up. Was I mad? drunk? dreaming? giddy again? or was the top of the bed really moving down—sinking slowly, regularly, silently, horribly, right down throughout the whole of its length and breadth—right down upon me, as I lay underneath?

My blood seemed to stand still. A deadly paralysing coldness stole all over me as I turned my head round on the pillow and determined to test whether the bed-top was really moving or not, by keeping my eye on the man in the picture.

The next look in that direction was enough. The dull, black, frowzy outline of the valance above me was within an inch of being parallel with his waist. I still looked breathlessly. And steadily and slowly—very slowly—I saw the figure, and the line of frame below the figure, vanish, as the valance moved down before it.

I am, constitutionally, anything but timid. I have been on more than one occasion in peril of my life, and have not lost my self-possession for an instant; but when the conviction first settled on my mind that the bed-top was really moving—was steadily and continuously sinking down upon me—I looked up, shuddering, helpless, panic-stricken, beneath the hideous machinery for murder which was advancing closer and closer to suffocate me where I lay.

I looked up, motionless, speechless, breathless. The candle, fully spent, went out; but the moonlight still brightened the room. Down and down, without pausing and without sounding, came the bed-top, and still my panic-terror seemed to bind me faster and faster to the mattress on which I lay—down and down it sank, till the dusty odour from the lining of the canopy came stealing into my nostrils.

At that final moment the instinct of self-preservation star-tled me out of my trance, and I moved at last. There was just room for me to roll myself sidewise off the bed. As I dropped noiselessly to the floor, the edge of the murderous canopy touched me on the shoulder.

Without stopping to draw my breath, without wiping the cold sweat from my face, I rose instantly on my knees to watch the bed-top. I was literally spellbound by it. If I had heard footsteps behind me, I could not have turned round; if a means of escape had been miraculously provided for me, I could not have moved to take advantage of it. The whole life in me was, at that moment, concentrated in my eyes.

It descended—the whole canopy, with the fringe round it, came down—down—close down; so close that there was not room now to squeeze my finger between the bed-top and the bed. I felt at the sides, and discovered that what had appeared to me from beneath to be the ordinary light canopy of a four-post bed was in reality a thick, broad mattress, the substance of which was concealed by the valance and its fringe. I looked up and saw the four posts rising hideously bare. In the middle of the bed-top was a huge wooden screw that had evidently worked it down through a hole in the ceiling, just as ordinary presses are worked down on the substance selected for compression.

The frightful apparatus moved without making the faintest noise. There had been no creaking as it came down; there was now not the faintest sound from the room above. Amid a dead and awful silence I beheld before me—in the nine-teenth century, and in the civilised capital of France—such a machine for secret murder by suffocation as might have existed in the worst days of the Inquisition, in the lonely inns among the Harz Mountains, in the mysterious tribunals of Westphalia! Still, as I looked on it, I could not move, I could hardly breathe, but I began to recover the power of thinking, and in a moment I discovered the murderous conspiracy framed against me in all its horror.

My cup of coffee had been drugged, and drugged too strongly. I had been saved from being smothered by having taken an overdose of some narcotic. How I had chafed and fretted at the fever fit which had preserved my life by keeping me awake! How recklessly I had confided myself to the two wretches who had led me into this room, determined, for the sake of my winnings, to kill me in my sleep by the surest and most horrible contrivance for secretly accomplishing my destruction! How many men, winners like me, had slept, as I had proposed to sleep, in that bed, and had never been seen or heard of more! I shuddered at the bare idea of it.

But, ere long, all thought was again suspended by the sight of the murderous canopy moving once more. After it had remained on the bed—as nearly as I could guess—about ten minutes, it began to move up again. The villains who worked it from above evidently believed that their purpose was now accomplished. Slowly and silently, as it had descended, that horrible bed-top rose towards its former place. When it reached the upper extremities of the four posts, it reached the ceiling too. Neither hole nor screw could be seen; the bed became in appearance an ordinary bed again—the canopy an ordinary canopy—even to the most suspicious eyes.

Now, for the first time, I was able to move—to rise from my knees—to dress myself in my upper clothing—and to consider how I should escape. If I betrayed by the smallest noise that the attempt to suffocate me had failed, I was certain to be murdered. Had I made any noise already? I listened intently, looking towards the door.

No! no footsteps in the passage outside—no sound of a tread, light or heavy, in the room above—absolute silence everywhere. Besides locking and bolting my door, I had moved an old wooden chest against it, which I had found under the bed. To remove this chest (my blood ran cold as I thought of what its contents might be!) without making some disturbance was impossible; and, moreover, to think of escaping through the house, now barred up for the night, was sheer insanity. Only one chance was left me—the window. I stole to it on tiptoe.

My bedroom was on the first floor, above an entresol, and looked into a back street. I raised my hand to open the window, knowing that on that action hung, by the merest hair's breadth, my chance of safety. They keep vigilant watch in a house of murder. If any part of the frame cracked, if the hinge creaked, I was a lost man! It must have occupied me at least five minutes, reckoning by time—five hours, reckoning by suspense—to open that window. I succeeded in doing it silently—in doing it with all the dexterity of a house-breaker—and then looked down into the street. To leap the distance beneath me would be almost certain destruction.

Next I looked round at the sides of the house. Down the left side ran a thick water-pipe—it passed close by the outer edge of the window. The moment I saw the pipe I knew I was saved. My breath came and went freely for the first time since I had seen the canopy of the bed moving down upon me!

To some men the means of escape which I had discovered might have seemed difficult and dangerous enough—to me the prospect of slipping down the pipe into the street did not suggest even a thought of peril. I had always been accustomed, by the practice of gymnastics, to keep up my school-boy powers as a daring and expert climber, and knew that my head, hands, and feet would serve me faithfully in any hazards of ascent or descent. I had already got one leg over the window-sill when I remembered the handkerchief filled with money under my pillow. I could well have afforded to leave it behind me, but I was revengefully determined that the miscreants of the gambling-house should miss their plunder as well as their victim. So I went back to the bed and tied the heavy handkerchief at my back by my cravat.

Just as I had made it tight and fixed it in a comfortable place, I thought I heard a sound of breathing outside the door. The chill feeling of horror ran through me again as I listened. No! dead silence still in the passage—I had only heard the night air blowing softly into the room. The next moment I was on the window-sill—and the next I had a firm grip on the water-pipe with my hands and knees.

I slid down into the street easily and quietly, as I thought I should, and immediately set off at the top of my speed to a branch *Préfecture* of Police, which I knew was situated in the immediate neighbourhood.

A *sous-préfet*, and several picked men among his subordinates, happened to be up, maturing, I believe, some scheme for discovering the perpetrator of a mysterious murder which all Paris was talking of just then. When I began my story, in a breathless hurry and in very bad French, I could see that the *sous-préfet* suspected me of being a drunken Englishman who had robbed somebody; but he soon altered his opinion as I went on, and before I had anything like concluded, he shoved all the papers before him into a drawer, put on his hat, supplied me with another (for I was bareheaded), ordered a file of soldiers, desired his expert followers to get ready all sorts of tools for breaking open doors and ripping up brick flooring, and took my arm, in the most friendly and familiar manner possible, to lead me with him out of the house.

I will venture to say that when the *sous-préfet* was a little boy, and was taken for the first time to the play, he was not half as much pleased as he was now at the job in prospect for him at the gambling-house!

Away we went through the streets, the *sous-préfet* cross-examining and congratulating me in the same breath as we marched at the head of our formidable *posse comitatus*. Sentinels were placed at the back and front of the house the moment we got to it; a tremendous battery of knocks was directed against the door; a light appeared at a window; I was told to conceal myself behind the police—then came more knocks and a cry of 'Open in the name of the law!'

At that terrible summons bolts and locks gave way before an invisible hand, and the moment after the *sous-préfet* was in the passage, confronting a waiter half-dressed and ghastly pale. This was the short dialogue which immediately took place:

'We want to see the Englishman who is sleeping in this house.'

'He went away hours ago.'

'He did no such thing. His friend went away; he remained. Show us to his bedroom!'

'I swear to you, Monsieur le *Sous-préfet*, he is not here! he—'

'I swear to you, Monsieur le *Garçon*, he is. He slept here—he didn't find your bed comfortable—he came to us to complain of it—here he is among my men—and here am I ready to look for a flea or two in his bedstead. Renaudin!' (calling to one of the subordinates, and pointing to the waiter) 'Collar that man and tie his hands behind him. Now then, gentlemen, let us walk upstairs!'

Every man and woman in the house was secured—the 'old soldier' the first. Then I identified the bed in which I had slept, and then we went into the room above.

No object that was at all extraordinary appeared in any part of it. The *sous-préfet* looked round the place, commanded everybody to be silent, stamped twice on the floor, called for a candle, looked attentively at the spot he had stamped on, and ordered the flooring there to be carefully taken up. This was done in no time. Lights were produced, and we saw a deep raftered cavity between the floor of this room and the ceiling of the room beneath. Through this cavity there ran perpendicularly a sort of case of iron thickly greased; and inside the case appeared the screw, which communicated with the bed-top below.

Extra lengths of screw, freshly oiled; levers covered with felt; all the complete upper works of a heavy press—constructed with infernal ingenuity so as to join the fixtures below, and, when taken to pieces again, to go into the smallest possible compass—were next discovered and pulled out on the floor. After some little difficulty the *sous-préfet* succeeded in putting the machinery together, and, leaving his men to work it, descended with me to the bedroom. The smothering canopy was then lowered, but not so noiselessly as I had seen it lowered. When I mentioned this to the *sous-préfet*, his answer, simple as it was, had a terrible significance.

'My men,' said he, 'are working down the bed-top for the first time—the men whose money you won were in better practice.'

We left the house in the sole possession of two police agents—every one of the inmates being removed to prison on the spot. The *sous-préfet*, after taking down my *procès-verbal* in his office, returned with me to my hotel to get my passport.

'Do you think,' I asked, as I gave it to him, 'that any men have really been smothered in that bed, as they tried to smother me?'

'I have seen dozens of drowned men laid out at the Morgue,' answered the *sous-préfet*, 'in whose pocket-books were found letters stating that they had committed suicide in the Seine because they had lost everything at the gaming table. Do I know how many of those men entered the same gambling-house that you entered? Won as you won? Took that bed as you took it? Slept in it? Were smothered in it? And were privately thrown into the river, with a letter of explanation written by the murderers and placed in their pocket-books? No man can say how many or how few have suffered the fate from which you have escaped. The people of the gambling-house kept their bedstead machinery a secret from us—even from the police! The dead kept the rest of the secret for them. Good-night, or rather good-morning, Monsieur Faulkner! Be at my office again at nine o'clock—in the meantime, *au revoir!*'

The rest of my story is soon told. I was examined and re-examined; the gambling-house was strictly searched all through from top to bottom; the prisoners were separately interrogated; and two of the less guilty among them made a confession. I discovered that the old soldier was the master of the gambling-house—justice discovered that he had been drummed out of the army as a vagabond years ago; that he had been guilty of all sorts of villainies since; that he was in possession of stolen property, which the owners identified; and that he, the croupier, another accomplice, and the woman who had made my cup of coffee, were all in the secret of the bedstead.

There appeared some reason to doubt whether the inferior persons attached to the house knew anything of the suffocating machinery; and they received the benefit of that doubt, by being treated simply as thieves and vagabonds. As for the old soldier and his two head myrmidons, they went to the galleys; the woman who had drugged my coffee was imprisoned for I forget how many years; the regular attendants at the gambling-house were considered "suspicious" and placed under surveillance; and I became, for one whole week (which is a long time) the head "lion" in Parisian society.

My adventure was dramatised by three illustrious play-makers, but never saw theatrical daylight; for the censorship forbade the introduction on the stage of a correct copy of the gambling-house bedstead.

One good result was produced by my adventure, which any censorship must have approved: it cured me of ever again trying *Rouge et Noir* as an amusement. The sight of a green cloth, with packs of cards and heaps of money on it, will henceforth be for ever associated in my mind with the sight of a bed canopy descending to suffocate me in the silence and darkness of the night.

ROBERT LOUIS STEVENSON

Robert Louis Stevenson (1850–1894) was a Scottish novelist, poet, and essayist whose imagination spanned both high-seas adventure and the dark recesses of the mind. Frail in health from childhood, he traveled widely through Europe and the Pacific in search of kinder climates, transforming his travels into enduring stories. A trained lawyer who chose the pen over the bar, he found global fame with *Treasure Island* (1883), inspired by a map he sketched for his stepson on a rainy holiday. *The Strange Case of Dr. Jekyll and Mr. Hyde* (1886) broke new ground, blending Gothic terror with sharp psychological insight. He finally settled in Samoa, where locals knew him as *Tusitala* ("Teller of Tales"). He died suddenly at forty-four. His work continues to inspire modern swashbucklers and psychological thrillers.

THE BODY-SNATCHER

ROBERT LOUIS STEVENSON

First published in *The Pall Mall Gazette*, 1884.

Every night in the year, four of us sat in the small parlour of the George at Debenham—the undertaker, and the landlord, and Fettes, and myself. Sometimes there would be more; but blow high, blow low, come rain or snow or frost, we four would be each planted in his own particular arm-chair. Fettes was an old drunken Scotchman, a man of education obviously, and a man of some property, since he lived in idleness. He had come to Debenham years ago, while still young, and by a mere continuance of living had grown to be an adopted townsman. His blue camlet cloak was a local antiquity, like the church-spire. His place in the parlour at the George, his absence from church, his old, crapulous, disreputable vices, were all things of course in Debenham. He had some vague Radical opinions and some fleeting infidelities, which he would now and again set forth and emphasise with tottering slaps upon the table. He drank rum—five glasses regularly every evening; and for the greater portion of his nightly visit to the George sat, with his glass in his right hand, in a state of melancholy alcoholic saturation.

We called him the Doctor, for he was supposed to have some special knowledge of medicine, and had been known, upon a pinch, to set a fracture or reduce a dislocation; but beyond these slight particulars, we had no knowledge of his character and antecedents.

One dark winter night—it had struck nine some time before the landlord joined us—there was a sick man in the George, a great neighbouring proprietor suddenly struck down with apoplexy on his way to Parliament; and the great man's still greater London doctor had been telegraphed to his bedside. It was the first time that such a thing had happened in Debenham, for the railway was but newly open, and we were all proportionately moved by the occurrence.

'He's come,' said the landlord, after he had filled and lighted his pipe.

'He?' said I. 'Who?—not the doctor?'

'Himself,' replied our host.

'What is his name?'

'Doctor Macfarlane,' said the landlord.

Fettes was far through his third tumbler, stupidly fuddled, now nodding over, now staring mazily around him; but at the last word he seemed to awaken, and repeated the name 'Macfarlane' twice, quietly enough the first time, but with sudden emotion at the second.

'Yes,' said the landlord, 'that's his name, Doctor Wolfe Macfarlane.'

Fettes became instantly sober; his eyes awoke, his voice became clear, loud, and steady, his language forcible and earnest. We were all startled by the transformation, as if a man had risen from the dead.

'I beg your pardon,' he said, 'I am afraid I have not been paying much attention to your talk. Who is this Wolfe Macfarlane?' And then, when he had heard the landlord out, 'It cannot be, it cannot be,' he added; 'and yet I would like well to see him face to face.'

'Do you know him, Doctor?' asked the undertaker, with a gasp.

'God forbid!' was the reply. 'And yet the name is a strange one; it were too much to fancy two. Tell me, landlord, is he old?'

'Well,' said the host, 'he's not a young man, to be sure, and his hair is white; but he looks younger than you.'

'He is older, though; years older. But,' with a slap upon the table, 'it's the rum you see in my face—rum and sin. This man, perhaps, may have an easy conscience and a good digestion. Conscience! Hear me speak. You would think I was some good, old, decent Christian, would you not? But no, not I; I never canted. Voltaire might have canted if he'd stood in my shoes; but the brains'—with a rattling fillip on his bald head—'the brains were clear and active, and I saw and made no deductions.'

'If you know this doctor,' I ventured to remark, after a somewhat awful pause, 'I should gather that you do not share the landlord's good opinion.'

Fettes paid no regard to me.

'Yes,' he said, with sudden decision, 'I must see him face to face.'

There was another pause, and then a door was closed rather sharply on the first floor, and a step was heard upon the stair.

'That's the doctor,' cried the landlord. 'Look sharp, and you can catch him.'

It was but two steps from the small parlour to the door of the old George Inn; the wide oak staircase landed almost in the street; there was room for a Turkey rug and nothing more between the threshold and the last round of the descent; but this little space was every evening brilliantly lit up, not only by the light upon the stair and the great signal-lamp below the sign, but by the warm radiance of the bar-room window. The George thus brightly advertised itself to passers-by in the cold street. Fettes walked steadily to the spot, and we, who were hanging behind, beheld the two men meet, as one of them had phrased it, face to face. Dr. Macfarlane was alert and vigorous. His white hair set off his pale and placid, although energetic, countenance. He was richly dressed in the finest of broadcloth and the whitest of linen, with a great gold watch-chain, and studs and spectacles of the same precious material. He wore a broad-folded tie, white and speckled with lilac, and he carried on his arm a comfortable driving-coat of fur. There was no doubt but he became his years, breathing, as he did, of wealth and consideration; and it was a surprising contrast to see our parlour sot—bald, dirty, pimpled, and robed in his old camlet cloak—confront him at the bottom of the stairs.

'Macfarlane!' he said somewhat loudly, more like a herald than a friend.

The great doctor pulled up short on the fourth step, as though the familiarity of the address surprised and some-what shocked his dignity.

'Toddy Macfarlane!' repeated Fettes.

The London man almost staggered. He stared for the swiftest of seconds at the man before him, glanced behind him with a sort of scare, and then in a startled whisper, 'Fettes!' he said, 'You!'

'Ay,' said the other, 'me! Did you think I was dead too? We are not so easy shut of our acquaintance.'

'Hush, hush!' exclaimed the doctor. 'Hush, hush! this meeting is so unexpected—I can see you are unmanned. I hardly knew you, I confess, at first; but I am overjoyed—overjoyed to have this opportunity. For the present it must be how-d'ye-do and good-bye in one, for my fly is waiting, and I must not fail the train; but you shall—let me see—yes—you shall give me your address, and you can count on early news of me. We must do something for you, Fettes. I fear you are out at elbows; but we must see to that for auld lang syne, as once we sang at suppers.'

'Money!' cried Fettes; 'money from you! The money that I had from you is lying where I cast it in the rain.'

Dr. Macfarlane had talked himself into some measure of superiority and confidence, but the uncommon energy of this refusal cast him back into his first confusion.

A horrible, ugly look came and went across his almost venerable countenance. 'My dear fellow,' he said, 'be it as you please; my last thought is to offend you. I would intrude on none. I will leave you my address, however—'

'I do not wish it—I do not wish to know the roof that shelters you,' interrupted the other. 'I heard your name; I feared it might be you; I wished to know if, after all, there were a God; I know now that there is none. Begone!'

He still stood in the middle of the rug, between the stair and doorway; and the great London physician, in order to escape, would be forced to step to one side. It was plain that he hesitated before the thought of this humiliation. White as he was, there was a dangerous glitter in his spectacles; but while he still paused uncertain, he became aware that the driver of his fly was peering in from the street at this unusual scene and caught a glimpse at the same time of our little body from the parlour, huddled by the corner of the bar. The presence of so many witnesses decided him at once to flee. He crouched together, brushing on the wainscot, and made a dart like a serpent, striking for the door. But his tribulation was not yet entirely at an end, for even as he was passing Fettes clutched him by the arm and these words came in a whisper, and yet painfully distinct, 'Have you seen it again?'

The great rich London doctor cried out aloud with a sharp, throttling cry; he dashed his questioner across the open space, and, with his hands over his head, fled out of the door like a detected thief. Before it had occurred to one of us to make a movement the fly was already rattling toward the station. The scene was over like a dream, but the dream had left proofs and traces of its passage. Next day the servant found the fine gold spectacles broken on the threshold, and that very night we were all standing breathless by the bar-room window, and Fettes at our side, sober, pale, and resolute in look.

'God protect us, Mr. Fettes!' said the landlord, coming first into possession of his customary senses. 'What in the universe is all this? These are strange things you have been saying.'

Fettes turned toward us; he looked us each in succession in the face. 'See if you can hold your tongues,' said he. 'That man Macfarlane is not safe to cross; those that have done so already have repented it too late.'

And then, without so much as finishing his third glass, far less waiting for the other two, he bade us good-bye and went forth, under the lamp of the hotel, into the black night.

We three turned to our places in the parlour, with the big red fire and four clear candles; and as we recapitulated what had passed, the first chill of our surprise soon changed into a glow of curiosity. We sat late; it was the latest session I have known in the old George. Each man, before we parted, had his theory that he was bound to prove; and none of us had any nearer business in this world than to track out the past of our condemned companion, and surprise the secret that he shared with the great London doctor. It is no great boast, but I believe I was a better hand at worming out a story than either of my fellows at the George; and perhaps there is now no other man alive who could narrate to you the following foul and unnatural events.

In his young days Fettes studied medicine in the schools of Edinburgh. He had talent of a kind, the talent that picks up swiftly what it hears and readily retails it for its own. He worked little at home; but he was civil, attentive, and intelligent in the presence of his masters. They soon picked him out as a lad who listened closely and remembered well; nay, strange as it seemed to me when I first heard it, he was in those days well favoured, and pleased by his exterior. There was, at that period, a certain extramural teacher of anatomy, whom I shall here designate by the letter K. His name was subsequently too well known. The man who bore it skulked through the streets of Edinburgh in disguise, while the mob that applauded at the execution of Burke called loudly for the blood of his employer. But Mr. K— was then at the top of his vogue; he enjoyed a popularity due partly to his own talent and address, partly to the incapacity of his rival, the university professor. The students, at least, swore by his name, and Fettes believed himself, and was believed by others, to have laid the foundations of success when he had acquired the favour of this meteorically famous man. Mr. K— was a *bon vivant* as well as an accomplished teacher; he liked a sly illusion no less than a careful preparation. In both capacities Fettes enjoyed and deserved his notice, and by the second year of his attendance he held the half-regular position of second demonstrator or sub-assistant in his class.

In this capacity the charge of the theatre and lecture-room devolved in particular upon his shoulders. He had to answer for the cleanliness of the premises and the conduct of the other students, and it was a part of his duty to supply, receive, and divide the various subjects. It was with a view to this last—at that time very delicate—affair that he was lodged by Mr. K— in the same wynd, and at last in the same building, with the dissecting-rooms. Here, after a night of turbulent pleasures, his hand still tottering, his sight still misty and confused, he would be called out of bed in the black hours before the winter dawn by the unclean and desperate interlopers who supplied the table. He would open the door to these men, since infamous throughout the land. He would help them with their tragic burden, pay them their sordid price, and remain alone, when they were gone, with the unfriendly relics of humanity. From such a scene he would return to snatch another hour or two of slumber, to repair the abuses of the night, and refresh himself for the labours of the day.

Few lads could have been more insensible to the impressions of a life thus passed among the ensigns of mortality. His mind was closed against all general considerations. He was incapable of interest in the fate and fortunes of another, the slave of his own desires and low ambitions. Cold, light, and selfish in the last resort, he had that modicum of prudence, miscalled morality, which keeps a man from inconvenient drunkenness or punishable theft. He coveted, besides, a measure of consideration from his masters and his fellow-pupils, and he had no desire to fail conspicuously in the external parts of life. Thus he made it his pleasure to gain some distinction in his studies, and day after day rendered unimpeachable eye-service to his employer, Mr. K—. For his day of work he indemnified himself by nights of roaring, blackguardly enjoyment; and when that balance had been struck, the organ that he called his conscience declared itself content.

The supply of subjects was a continual trouble to him as well as to his master. In that large and busy class, the raw material of the anatomists kept perpetually running out; and the business thus rendered necessary was not only unpleasant in itself, but threatened dangerous consequences to all who were concerned. It was the policy of Mr. K— to ask no questions in his dealings with the trade. 'They bring the body, and we pay the price,' he used to say, dwelling on the alliteration—'*quid pro quo*.' And, again, and somewhat profanely, 'Ask no questions,' he would tell his assistants, 'for conscience' sake.' There was no understanding that the subjects were provided by the crime of murder. Had that idea been broached to him in words, he would have recoiled in horror; but the lightness of his speech upon so grave a matter was, in itself, an offence against good manners, and a temptation to the men with whom he dealt. Fettes, for instance, had often remarked to himself upon the singular freshness of the bodies. He had been struck again and again by the hang-dog, abominable looks of the ruffians who came to him before the dawn; and putting things together clearly in his private thoughts, he perhaps attributed a meaning too immoral and too categorical to the unguarded counsels of his master. He understood his duty, in short, to have three branches: to take what was brought, to pay the price, and to avert the eye from any evidence of crime.

One November morning this policy of silence was put sharply to the test. He had been awake all night with a racking toothache—pacing his room like a caged beast or throwing himself in fury on his bed—and had fallen at last into that profound, uneasy slumber that so often follows on a night of pain, when he was awakened by the third or fourth angry repetition of the concerted signal. There was a thin, bright moonshine; it was bitter cold, windy, and frosty; the town had not yet awakened, but an indefinable stir already preluded the noise and business of the day. The ghouls had come later than usual, and they seemed more than usually eager to be gone. Fettes, sick with sleep, lighted them upstairs. He heard their grumbling Irish voices through a dream; and as they stripped the sack from their sad merchandise he leaned dozing, with his shoulder propped against the wall; he had to shake himself to find the men their money. As he did so his eyes lighted on the dead face. He started; he took two steps nearer, with the candle raised.

'God Almighty!' he cried. 'That is Jane Galbraith!'

The men answered nothing, but they shuffled nearer the door.

'I know her, I tell you,' he continued. 'She was alive and hearty yesterday. It's impossible she can be dead; it's impossible you should have got this body fairly.'

'Sure, sir, you're mistaken entirely,' said one of the men.

But the other looked Fettes darkly in the eyes, and demanded the money on the spot.

It was impossible to misconceive the threat or to exaggerate the danger. The lad's heart failed him. He stammered some excuses, counted out the sum, and saw his hateful visitors depart. No sooner were they gone than he hastened to confirm his doubts. By a dozen unquestionable marks he identified the girl he had jested with the day before. He saw, with horror, marks upon her body that might well betoken violence. A panic seized him, and he took refuge in his room. There he reflected at length over the discovery that he had made; considered soberly the bearing of Mr. K—'s instructions and the danger to himself of interference in so serious a business, and at last, in sore perplexity, determined to wait for the advice of his immediate superior, the class assistant.

This was a young doctor, Wolfe Macfarlane, a high favourite among all the reckless students, clever, dissipated, and unscrupulous to the last degree. He had travelled and studied abroad. His manners were agreeable and a little forward. He was an authority on the stage, skilful on the ice or the links with skate or golf-club; he dressed with nice audacity, and, to put the finishing touch upon his glory, he kept a gig and a strong trotting-horse. With Fettes he was on terms of intimacy; indeed, their relative positions called for some community of life; and when subjects were scarce the pair would drive far into the country in Macfarlane's gig, visit and desecrate some lonely graveyard, and return before dawn with their booty to the door of the dissecting-room.

On that particular morning Macfarlane arrived somewhat earlier than his wont. Fettes heard him, and met him on the stairs, told him his story, and showed him the cause of his alarm. Macfarlane examined the marks on her body.

'Yes,' he said with a nod, 'it looks fishy.'

'Well, what should I do?' asked Fettes.

'Do?' repeated the other. 'Do you want to do anything? Least said soonest mended, I should say.'

'Some one else might recognise her,' objected Fettes. 'She was as well known as the Castle Rock.'

'We'll hope not,' said Macfarlane, 'and if anybody does—well, you didn't, don't you see, and there's an end. The fact is, this has been going on too long. Stir up the mud, and you'll get K— into the most unholy trouble; you'll be in a shocking box yourself. So will I, if you come to that. I should like to know how any one of us would look, or what the devil we should have to say for ourselves, in any Christian witness-box. For me, you know there's one thing certain—that, practically speaking, all our subjects have been murdered.'

'Macfarlane!' cried Fettes.

'Come now!' sneered the other. 'As if you hadn't suspected it yourself!'

'Suspecting is one thing—'

'And proof another. Yes, I know; and I'm as sorry as you are this should have come here,' tapping the body with his cane. 'The next best thing for me is not to recognise it; and,' he added coolly, 'I don't. You may, if you please. I don't dictate, but I think a man of the world would do as I do; and I may add, I fancy that is what K— would look for at our hands. The question is, Why did he choose us two for his assistants? And I answer, because he didn't want old wives.'

This was the tone of all others to affect the mind of a lad like Fettes. He agreed to imitate Macfarlane. The body of the unfortunate girl was duly dissected, and no one remarked or appeared to recognise her.

One afternoon, when his day's work was over, Fettes dropped into a popular tavern and found Macfarlane sitting with a stranger. This was a small man, very pale and dark, with coal-black eyes. The cut of his features gave a promise of intellect and refinement which was but feebly realised in his manners, for he proved, upon a nearer acquaintance, coarse, vulgar, and stupid. He exercised, however, a very remarkable control over Macfarlane; issued orders like the Great Bashaw; became inflamed at the least discussion or delay, and commented rudely on the servility with which he was obeyed. This most offensive person took a fancy to Fettes on the spot, plied him with drinks, and honoured him with unusual confidences on his past career. If a tenth part of what he confessed were true, he was a very loathsome rogue; and the lad's vanity was tickled by the attention of so experienced a man.

'I'm a pretty bad fellow myself,' the stranger remarked, 'but Macfarlane is the boy—Toddy Macfarlane I call him. Toddy, order your friend another glass.' Or it might be, 'Toddy, you jump up and shut the door.' 'Toddy hates me,' he said again. 'Oh yes, Toddy, you do!'

'Don't you call me that confounded name,' growled Macfarlane.

'Hear him! Did you ever see the lads play knife? He would like to do that all over my body,' remarked the stranger.

'We medicals have a better way than that,' said Fettes. 'When we dislike a dead friend of ours, we dissect him.'

Macfarlane looked up sharply, as though this jest were scarcely to his mind.

The afternoon passed. Gray, for that was the stranger's name, invited Fettes to join them at dinner, ordered a feast so sumptuous that the tavern was thrown into commotion, and when all was done commanded Macfarlane to settle the bill. It was late before they separated; the man Gray was incapably drunk. Macfarlane, sobered by his fury, chewed the cud of the money he had been forced to squander and the slights he had been obliged to swallow. Fettes, with various liquors singing in his head, returned home with devious footsteps and a mind entirely in abeyance. Next day Macfarlane was absent from the class, and Fettes smiled to himself as he imagined him still squiring the intolerable Gray from tavern to tavern. As soon as the hour of liberty had struck he posted from place to place in quest of his last night's companions. He could find them, however, nowhere; so returned early to his rooms, went early to bed, and slept the sleep of the just.

At four in the morning he was awakened by the well-known signal. Descending to the door, he was filled with astonishment to find Macfarlane with his gig, and in the gig one of those long and ghastly packages with which he was so well acquainted.

'What?' he cried. 'Have you been out alone? How did you manage?'

But Macfarlane silenced him roughly, bidding him turn to business. When they had got the body upstairs and laid it on the table, Macfarlane made at first as if he were going away. Then he paused and seemed to hesitate; and then, 'You had better look at the face,' said he, in tones of some constraint. 'You had better,' he repeated, as Fettes only stared at him in wonder.

'But where, and how, and when did you come by it?' cried the other.

'Look at the face,' was the only answer.

Fettes was staggered; strange doubts assailed him. He looked from the young doctor to the body, and then back again. At last, with a start, he did as he was bidden. He had almost expected the sight that met his eyes, and yet the shock was cruel. To see, fixed in the rigidity of death and naked on that coarse layer of sackcloth, the man whom he had left well clad and full of meat and sin upon the threshold of a tavern, awoke, even in the thoughtless Fettes, some of the terrors of the conscience. It was a *cras tibi* which re-echoed in his soul, that two whom he had known should have come to lie upon these icy tables. Yet these were only secondary thoughts. His first concern regarded Wolfe. Unprepared for a challenge so momentous, he knew not how to look his comrade in the face. He durst not meet his eye, and he had neither words nor voice at his command.

It was Macfarlane himself who made the first advance. He came up quietly behind and laid his hand gently but firmly on the other's shoulder.

'Richardson,' said he, 'may have the head.'

Now Richardson was a student who had long been anxious for that portion of the human subject to dissect. There was no answer, and the murderer resumed: 'Talking of business, you must pay me; your accounts, you see, must tally.'

Fettes found a voice, the ghost of his own: 'Pay you!' he cried. 'Pay you for that?'

'Why, yes, of course you must. By all means and on every possible account, you must,' returned the other. 'I dare not give it for nothing, you dare not take it for nothing; it would compromise us both. This is another case like Jane Galbraith's. The more things are wrong the more we must act as if all were right. Where does old K— keep his money?'

'There,' answered Fettes hoarsely, pointing to a cupboard in the corner.

'Give me the key, then,' said the other, calmly, holding out his hand.

There was an instant's hesitation, and the die was cast. Macfarlane could not suppress a nervous twitch, the infinitesimal mark of an immense relief, as he felt the key between his fingers. He opened the cupboard, brought out pen and ink and a paper-book that stood in one compartment, and separated from the funds in a drawer a sum suitable to the occasion.

'Now, look here,' he said, 'there is the payment made—first proof of your good faith: first step to your security. You have now to clinch it by a second. Enter the payment in your book, and then you for your part may defy the devil.'

The next few seconds were for Fettes an agony of thought; but in balancing his terrors it was the most immediate that triumphed. Any future difficulty seemed almost welcome if he could avoid a present quarrel with Macfarlane. He set down the candle which he had been carrying all this time, and with a steady hand entered the date, the nature, and the amount of the transaction.

'And now,' said Macfarlane, 'it's only fair that you should pocket the lucre. I've had my share already. By the bye, when a man of the world falls into a bit of luck, has a few shillings extra in his pocket—I'm ashamed to speak of it, but there's a rule of conduct in the case. No treating, no purchase of expensive class-books, no squaring of old debts; borrow, don't lend.'

'Macfarlane,' began Fettes, still somewhat hoarsely, 'I have put my neck in a halter to oblige you.'

'To oblige me?' cried Wolfe. 'Oh, come! You did, as near as I can see the matter, what you downright had to do in self-defence. Suppose I got into trouble, where would you be? This second little matter flows clearly from the first. Mr. Gray is the continuation of Miss Galbraith. You can't begin and then stop. If you begin, you must keep on beginning; that's the truth. No rest for the wicked.'

A horrible sense of blackness and the treachery of fate seized hold upon the soul of the unhappy student.

'My God!' he cried, 'but what have I done? and when did I begin? To be made a class assistant—in the name of reason, where's the harm in that? Service wanted the position; Service might have got it. Would *he* have been where I am now?'

'My dear fellow,' said Macfarlane, 'what a boy you are! What harm *has* come to you? What harm *can* come to you if you hold your tongue? Why, man, do you know what this life is? There are two squads of us—the lions and the lambs. If you're a lamb, you'll come to lie upon these tables like Gray or Jane Galbraith; if you're a lion, you'll live and drive a horse like me, like K—, like all the world with any wit or courage.

You're staggered at the first. But look at K—! My dear fellow, you're clever, you have pluck. I like you, and K— likes you. You were born to lead the hunt; and I tell you, on my honour and my experience of life, three days from now you'll laugh at all these scarecrows like a High School boy at a farce.'

And with that Macfarlane took his departure and drove off up the wynd in his gig to get under cover before daylight. Fettes was thus left alone with his regrets. He saw the miserable peril in which he stood involved. He saw, with inexpressible dismay, that there was no limit to his weakness, and that, from concession to concession, he had fallen from the arbiter of Macfarlane's destiny to his paid and helpless accomplice. He would have given the world to have been a little braver at the time, but it did not occur to him that he might still be brave. The secret of Jane Galbraith and the cursed entry in the day-book closed his mouth.

Hours passed; the class began to arrive; the members of the unhappy Gray were dealt out to one and to another, and received without remark. Richardson was made happy with the head; and before the hour of freedom rang Fettes trembled with exultation to perceive how far they had already gone toward safety.

For two days he continued to watch, with increasing joy, the dreadful process of disguise.

On the third day Macfarlane made his appearance. He had been ill, he said; but he made up for lost time by the energy with which he directed the students. To Richardson in particular he extended the most valuable assistance and advice, and that student, encouraged by the praise of the demonstrator, burned high with ambitious hopes, and saw the medal already in his grasp.

Before the week was out Macfarlane's prophecy had been fulfilled. Fettes had outlived his terrors and had forgotten his baseness. He began to plume himself upon his courage, and had so arranged the story in his mind that he could look back on these events with an unhealthy pride. Of his accomplice he saw but little. They met, of course, in the business of the class; they received their orders together from Mr. K—. At times they had a word or two in private, and Macfarlane was from first to last particularly kind and jovial. But it was plain that he avoided any reference to their common secret; and even when Fettes whispered to him that he had cast in his lot with the lions and foresworn the lambs, he only signed to him smilingly to hold his peace.

At length an occasion arose which threw the pair once more into a closer union. Mr. K— was again short of subjects; pupils were eager, and it was a part of this teacher's pretensions to be always well supplied. At the same time there came the news of a burial in the rustic graveyard of Glencorse. Time has little changed the place in question. It stood then, as now, upon a cross road, out of call of human habitations, and buried fathom deep in the foliage of six cedar trees. The cries of the sheep upon the neighbouring hills, the streamlets upon either hand, one loudly singing among pebbles, the other dripping furtively from pond to pond, the stir of the wind in mountainous old flowering chestnuts, and once in seven days the voice of the bell and the old tunes of the precentor, were the only sounds that disturbed the silence around the rural church. The Resurrection Man—to use a byname of the period—was not to be deterred by any of the sanctities of customary piety. It was part of his trade to despise and desecrate the scrolls and trumpets of old tombs, the paths worn by the feet of worshippers and mourners, and the offerings and the inscriptions of bereaved affection. To rustic neighbourhoods, where love is more than commonly tenacious, and where some bonds of blood or fellowship unite the entire society of a parish, the body-snatcher, far from being repelled by natural respect, was attracted by the ease and safety of the task. To bodies that had been laid in earth, in joyful expectation of a far different awakening, there came that hasty, lamp-lit, terror-haunted resurrection of the spade and mattock. The coffin was forced, the cerements torn, and the melancholy relics, clad in sackcloth, after being rattled for hours on moonless byways, were at length exposed to uttermost indignities before a class of gaping boys.

Somewhat as two vultures may swoop upon a dying lamb, Fettes and Macfarlane were to be let loose upon a grave in that green and quiet resting-place. The wife of a farmer, a woman who had lived for sixty years, and been known for nothing but good butter and a godly conversation, was to be rooted from her grave at midnight and carried, dead and naked, to that far-away city that she had always honoured with her Sunday's best; the place beside her family was to be empty till the crack of doom; her innocent and almost venerable members to be exposed to that last curiosity of the anatomist.

Late one afternoon the pair set forth, well wrapped in cloaks and furnished with a formidable bottle. It rained without remission—a cold, dense, lashing rain. Now and again there blew a puff of wind, but these sheets of falling water kept it down. Bottle and all, it was a sad and silent drive as far as Penicuik, where they were to spend the evening. They stopped once, to hide their implements in a thick bush not far from the churchyard, and once again at the Fisher's Tryst, to have a toast before the kitchen fire and vary their nips of whisky with a glass of ale. When they reached their journey's end the gig was housed, the horse was fed and comforted, and the two young doctors in a private room sat down to the best dinner and the best wine the house afforded. The lights, the fire, the beating rain upon the window, the cold, incongruous work that lay before them, added zest to their enjoyment of the meal. With every glass their cordiality increased. Soon Macfarlane handed a little pile of gold to his companion.

'A compliment,' he said. 'Between friends these little d–d accommodations ought to fly like pipe-lights.'

Fettes pocketed the money, and applauded the sentiment to the echo. 'You are a philosopher,' he cried. 'I was an ass till I knew you. You and K— between you, by the Lord Harry! but you'll make a man of me.'

'Of course we shall,' applauded Macfarlane. 'A man? I tell you, it required a man to back me up the other morning. There are some big, brawling, forty-year-old cowards who would have turned sick at the look of the d–d thing; but not you—you kept your head. I watched you.'

'Well, and why not?' Fettes thus vaunted himself. 'It was no affair of mine. There was nothing to gain on the one side but disturbance, and on the other I could count on your gratitude, don't you see?' And he slapped his pocket till the gold pieces rang.

Macfarlane somehow felt a certain touch of alarm at these unpleasant words. He may have regretted that he had taught his young companion so successfully, but he had no time to interfere, for the other noisily continued in this boastful strain:—

'The great thing is not to be afraid. Now, between you and me, I don't want to hang—that's practical; but for all cant, Macfarlane, I was born with a contempt. Hell, God, Devil, right, wrong, sin, crime, and all the old gallery of curiosities—they may frighten boys, but men of the world, like you and me, despise them. Here's to the memory of Gray!'

It was by this time growing somewhat late. The gig, according to order, was brought round to the door with both lamps brightly shining, and the young men had to pay their bill and take the road. They announced that they were bound for Peebles, and drove in that direction till they were clear of the last houses of the town; then, extinguishing the lamps, returned upon their course, and followed a by-road toward Glencorse. There was no sound but that of their own passage, and the incessant, strident pouring of the rain. It was pitch dark; here and there a white gate or a white stone in the wall guided them for a short space across the night; but for the most part it was at a foot pace, and almost groping, that they picked their way through that resonant blackness to their solemn and isolated destination. In the sunken woods that traverse the neighbourhood of the burying-ground the last glimmer failed them, and it became necessary to kindle a match and re-illumine one of the lanterns of the gig. Thus, under the dripping trees, and environed by huge and moving shadows, they reached the scene of their unhallowed labours.

They were both experienced in such affairs, and powerful with the spade; and they had scarce been twenty minutes at their task before they were rewarded by a dull rattle on the coffin lid. At the same moment Macfarlane, having hurt his hand upon a stone, flung it carelessly above his head. The grave, in which they now stood almost to the shoulders, was close to the edge of the plateau of the graveyard; and the gig lamp had been propped, the better to illuminate their labours, against a tree, and on the immediate verge of the steep bank descending to the stream. Chance had taken a sure aim with the stone. Then came a clang of broken glass; night fell upon them; sounds alternately dull and ringing announced the bounding of the lantern down the bank, and its occasional collision with the trees. A stone or two, which it had dislodged in its descent, rattled behind it into the profundities of the glen; and then silence, like night, resumed its sway; and they might bend their hearing to its utmost pitch, but naught was to be heard except the rain, now marching to the wind, now steadily falling over miles of open country.

They were so nearly at an end of their abhorred task that they judged it wisest to complete it in the dark. The coffin was exhumed and broken open; the body inserted in the dripping sack and carried between them to the gig; one mounted to keep it in its place, and the other, taking the horse by the mouth, groped along by wall and bush until they reached the wider road by the Fisher's Tryst. Here was a faint, diffused radiancy, which they hailed like daylight; by that they pushed the horse to a good pace and began to rattle along merrily in the direction of the town.

They had both been wetted to the skin during their operations, and now, as the gig jumped among the deep ruts, the thing that stood propped between them fell now upon one and now upon the other. At every repetition of the horrid contact each instinctively repelled it with the greater haste; and the process, natural although it was, began to tell upon the nerves of the companions. Macfarlane made some ill-favoured jest about the farmer's wife, but it came hollowly from his lips, and was allowed to drop in silence. Still their unnatural burden bumped from side to side; and now the head would be laid, as if in confidence, upon their shoulders, and now the drenching sack-cloth would flap icily about their faces. A creeping chill began to possess the soul of Fettes. He peered at the bundle, and it seemed somehow larger than at first. All over the country-side, and from every degree of distance, the farm dogs accompanied their passage with tragic ululations; and it grew and grew upon his mind that some unnatural miracle had been accomplished, that some nameless change had befallen the dead body, and that it was in fear of their unholy burden that the dogs were howling.

'For God's sake,' said he, making a great effort to arrive at speech, 'for God's sake, let's have a light!'

Seemingly Macfarlane was affected in the same direction; for, though he made no reply, he stopped the horse, passed the reins to his companion, got down, and proceeded to kindle the remaining lamp. They had by that time got no farther than the cross-road down to Auchenclinny. The rain still poured as though the deluge were returning, and it was no easy matter to make a light in such a world of wet and darkness. When at last the flickering blue flame had been transferred to the wick and began to expand and clarify, and shed a wide circle of misty brightness round the gig, it be-came possible for the two young men to see each other and the thing they had along with them. The rain had moulded the rough sacking to the outlines of the body underneath;

the head was distinct from the trunk, the shoulders plainly modelled; something at once spectral and human riveted their eyes upon the ghastly comrade of their drive.

For some time Macfarlane stood motionless, holding up the lamp. A nameless dread was swathed, like a wet sheet, about the body, and tightened the white skin upon the face of Fettes; a fear that was meaningless, a horror of what could not be, kept mounting to his brain. Another beat of the watch, and he had spoken. But his comrade forestalled him.

'That is not a woman,' said Macfarlane, in a hushed voice.

'It was a woman when we put her in,' whispered Fettes.

'Hold that lamp,' said the other. 'I must see her face.'

And as Fettes took the lamp his companion untied the fastenings of the sack and drew down the cover from the head. The light fell very clear upon the dark, well-moulded features and smooth-shaven cheeks of a too familiar countenance, often beheld in dreams of both of these young men. A wild yell rang up into the night; each leaped from his own side into the roadway: the lamp fell, broke, and was extinguished; and the horse, terrified by this unusual commotion, bounded and went off toward Edinburgh at a gallop, bearing along with it, sole occupant of the gig, the body of the dead and long-dissected Gray.

F. Marion Crawford (1854–1909)

F. Marion Crawford (1854–1909) was an American novelist and scholar best remembered for his elegantly crafted tales of the uncanny. Born in Italy to an artistic New England family, he studied Sanskrit and literature at Harvard and in Rome before turning to fiction. His works often merged cosmopolitan sophistication with shrewd psychological insight, exploring the thin border between the rational and the supernatural. Crawford wrote more than forty novels and numerous ghost stories marked by restraint and atmosphere rather than gore. His most celebrated tale, *The Upper Berth*, transforms a shipboard mystery into one of the most chilling hauntings in English fiction, praised by M. R. James and H. P. Lovecraft alike for its masterful tension and realism.

THE UPPER BERTH

F. Marion Crawford

First published in *The Broken Shaft: Tales in Mid-Ocean*, 1886.

I

Somebody asked for the cigars. We had talked long, and the conversation was beginning to languish; the tobacco smoke had got into the heavy curtains, the wine had got into those brains which were liable to become heavy, and it was already perfectly evident that, unless somebody did something to rouse our oppressed spirits, the meeting would soon come to its natural conclusion, and we, the guests, would speedily go home to bed—and most certainly to sleep.

No one had said anything very remarkable; it may be that no one had anything very remarkable to say. Jones had given us every particular of his last hunting adventure in Yorkshire. Mr Tompkins, of Boston, had explained at elaborate length those working principles by the due and careful maintenance of which the Atchison, Topeka, and Santa Fé Railroad not only extended its territory, increased its departmental influence, and transported live stock without starving them to death before the day of actual delivery, but also had for years succeeded in deceiving those passengers who bought its tickets into the fallacious belief that the corporation aforesaid was really able to transport human life without destroying it.

Signor Tombola had endeavoured to persuade us, by arguments which we took no trouble to oppose, that the unity of his country in no way resembled the average modern torpedo—carefully planned, constructed with all the skill of the greatest European arsenals, but, when constructed, destined to be directed by feeble hands into a region where it must undoubtedly explode, unseen, unfeared, and unheard, into the illimitable wastes of political chaos.

It is unnecessary to go into further details. The conversation had assumed proportions which would have bored Prometheus on his rock, driven Tantalus to distraction, and impelled Ixion to seek relaxation in the simple but instructive dialogues of Herr Ollendorff, rather than submit to the greater evil of listening to our talk. We had sat at table for hours; we were bored, we were tired, and nobody showed signs of moving.

Somebody called for cigars. We all instinctively looked towards the speaker. Brisbane was a man of five-and-thirty years of age, and remarkable for those gifts which chiefly attract the attention of men. He was a strong man. The external proportions of his figure presented nothing extraordinary to the common eye, though his size was above the average. He was a little over six feet in height and moderately broad in the shoulder; he did not appear to be stout, but, on the other hand, he was certainly not thin. His small head was supported by a strong and sinewy neck; his broad muscular hands appeared to possess a peculiar skill in breaking walnuts without the assistance of the ordinary cracker, and, seeing him in profile, one could not help remarking the extraordinary breadth of his sleeves and the unusual thickness of his chest. He was one of those men who are commonly spoken of among men as *deceptive*—that is to say, that though he looked exceedingly strong, he was in reality very much stronger than he looked.

Of his features I need say little. His head is small, his hair is thin, his eyes are blue, his nose is large, he has a small moustache, and a square jaw. Everybody knows Brisbane, and when he asked for a cigar everybody looked at him.

"It is a very singular thing," said Brisbane.

Everybody stopped talking. Brisbane's voice was not loud, but possessed a peculiar quality of penetrating general conversation, and cutting it like a knife. Everybody listened. Brisbane, perceiving that he had attracted their general attention, lit his cigar with great equanimity.

"It is very singular," he continued, "that thing about ghosts. People are always asking whether anybody has seen a ghost. I have."

"Bosh! What, you? You don't mean to say so, Brisbane? Well, for a man of his intelligence!"

A chorus of exclamations greeted Brisbane's remarkable statement. Everybody called for cigars, and Stubbs the butler suddenly appeared from the depths of nowhere with a fresh bottle of dry champagne. The situation was saved; Brisbane was going to tell a story.

"I am an old sailor," said Brisbane, "and as I have to cross the Atlantic pretty often, I have my favourites. Most men have their favourites. I have seen a man wait in a Broadway bar for three-quarters of an hour for a particular car which he liked. I believe the bar-keeper made at least one-third of his living by that man's preference. I have a habit of waiting for certain ships when I am obliged to cross that duck-pond. It may be a prejudice, but I was never cheated out of a good passage but once in my life. I remember it very well; it was a warm morning in June, and the Custom House officials, who were hanging about waiting for a steamer already on her way up from the Quarantine, presented a peculiarly hazy and thoughtful appearance."

"One hundred and five, lower berth," said I, in the business-like tone peculiar to men who think no more of crossing the Atlantic than taking a whisky cocktail at downtown Delmonico's."

The steward took my portmanteau, great coat, and rug. I shall never forget the expression of his face. Not that he turned pale. It is maintained by the most eminent divines that even miracles cannot change the course of nature. I have no hesitation in saying that he did not turn pale; but, from his expression, I judged that he was either about to shed tears, to sneeze, or to drop my portmanteau. As the latter contained two bottles of particularly fine old sherry presented to me for my voyage by my old friend Snigginson van Pickyns, I felt extremely nervous. But the steward did none of these things.

"Well, I'm d——d!" said he in a low voice, and led the way.

I supposed my Hermes, as he led me to the lower regions, had had a little grog, but I said nothing, and followed him. One hundred and five was on the port side, well aft. There was nothing remarkable about the state-room. The lower berth, like most of those upon the *Kamtschatka*, was double. There was plenty of room; there was the usual washing apparatus, calculated to convey an idea of luxury to the mind of a North-American Indian; there were the usual inefficient racks of brown wood, in which it is more easy to hang a large-sized umbrella than the common tooth-brush of commerce. Upon the uninviting mattresses were carefully folded together those blankets which a great modern humorist has aptly compared to cold buckwheat cakes. The question of towels was left entirely to the imagination. The glass decanters were filled with a transparent liquid faintly tinged with brown, but from which an odor less faint, but not more pleasing, ascended to the nostrils, like a far-off sea-sick reminiscence of oily machinery. Sad-coloured curtains half-closed the upper berth. The hazy June daylight shed a faint illumination upon the desolate little scene. Ugh! how I hate that state-room!

The steward deposited my traps and looked at me, as though he wanted to get away—probably in search of more passengers and more fees. It is always a good plan to start in favour with those functionaries, and I accordingly gave him certain coins there and then.

"I'll try and make yer comfortable all I can," he remarked, as he put the coins in his pocket. Nevertheless, there was a doubtful intonation in his voice which surprised me. Possibly his scale of fees had gone up, and he was not satisfied; but on the whole I was inclined to think that, as he himself would have expressed it, he was "the better for a glass." I was wrong, however, and did the man injustice.

II

Nothing especially worthy of mention occurred during that day. We left the pier punctually, and it was very pleasant to be fairly under way, for the weather was warm and sultry, and the motion of the steamer produced a refreshing breeze. Everybody knows what the first day at sea is like. People pace the decks and stare at each other, and occasionally meet acquaintances whom they did not know to be on board. There is the usual uncertainty as to whether the food will be good, bad, or indifferent, until the first two meals have put the matter beyond a doubt; there is the usual uncertainty about the weather, until the ship is fairly off Fire Island.

The tables are crowded at first, and then suddenly thinned. Pale-faced people spring from their seats and precipitate themselves towards the door, and each old sailor breathes more freely as his sea-sick neighbour rushes from his side, leaving him plenty of elbow-room and an unlimited command over the mustard.

One passage across the Atlantic is very much like another, and we who cross very often do not make the voyage for the sake of novelty. Whales and icebergs are indeed always objects of interest; but, after all, one whale is very much like another whale, and one rarely sees an iceberg at close quarters. To the majority of us the most delightful moment of the day on board an ocean steamer is when we have taken our last turn on deck, have smoked our last cigar, and, having succeeded in tiring ourselves, feel at liberty to turn in with a clear conscience.

On that first night of the voyage I felt particularly lazy, and went to bed in One Hundred and Five rather earlier than I usually do. As I turned in, I was amazed to see that I was to have a companion. A portmanteau, very like my own, lay in the opposite corner, and in the upper berth had been deposited a neatly folded rug with a stick and umbrella. I had hoped to be alone, and I was disappointed; but I wondered who my room-mate was to be, and I determined to have a look at him.

Before I had been long in bed he entered. He was, as far as I could see, a very tall man, very thin, very pale, with sandy hair and whiskers and colourless grey eyes. He had about him, I thought, an air of rather dubious fashion—the sort of man you might see in Wall Street, without being able precisely to say what he was doing there; the sort of man who frequents the Café Anglais, who always seems to be alone and who drinks champagne; you might meet him on a race-course, but he would never appear to be doing anything there either. A little over-dressed—a little odd. There are three or four of his kind on every ocean steamer.

I made up my mind that I did not care to make his acquaintance, and I went to sleep saying to myself that I would study his habits in order to avoid him. If he rose early, I would rise late; if he went to bed late, I would go to bed early. I did not care to know him. If you once know people of that kind, they are always turning up. Poor fellow! I need not have taken the trouble to come to so many decisions about him, for I never saw him again after that first night in One Hundred and Five.

I was sleeping soundly when I was suddenly waked by a loud noise. To judge from the sound, my room-mate must have sprung with a single leap from the upper berth to the floor. I heard him fumbling with the latch and bolt of the door, which opened almost immediately, and then I heard his footsteps as he ran at full speed down the passage, leaving the door open behind him. The ship was rolling a little, and I expected to hear him stumble or fall, but he ran as though he were running for his life.

The door swung on its hinges with the motion of the vessel, and the sound annoyed me. I got up and shut it, and groped my way back to my berth in the darkness. I went to sleep again; but I have no idea how long I slept.

When I awoke it was still quite dark, but I felt a disagreeable sensation of cold, and it seemed to me that the air was damp. You know the peculiar smell of a cabin which has been wet with sea-water. I covered myself up as well as I could and dozed off again, framing complaints to be made the next day, and selecting the most powerful epithets in the language. I could hear my room-mate turn over in the upper berth. He had probably returned while I was asleep. Once I thought I heard him groan, and I argued that he was sea-sick. That is particularly unpleasant when one is below. Nevertheless, I dozed off and slept till early daylight.

The ship was rolling heavily, much more than on the previous evening, and the grey light which came in through the porthole changed in tint with every movement according as the angle of the vessel's side turned the glass sea-wards or sky-wards. It was very cold—unaccountably so for the month of June. I turned my head and looked at the porthole, and saw, to my surprise, that it was wide open and hooked back. I believe I swore audibly. Then I got up and shut it. As I turned back I glanced at the upper berth. The curtains were drawn close together; my companion had probably felt cold as well as I.

It struck me that I had slept enough. The state-room was uncomfortable, though, strange to say, I could not smell the dampness which had annoyed me in the night. My room-mate was still asleep—an excellent opportunity for avoiding him—so I dressed at once and went on deck. The day was warm and cloudy, with an oily smell on the water. It was seven o'clock as I came out—much later than I had imagined.

I came across the doctor, who was taking his first sniff of the morning air. He was a young man from the west of Ireland—a tremendous fellow, with black hair and blue eyes, already inclined to be stout; he had a happy-go-lucky, healthy look about him which was rather attractive.

"Fine morning," I remarked, by way of introduction.

"Well," said he, eyeing me with an air of ready interest, "it's a fine morning and it's not a fine morning. I don't think it's much of a morning."

"Well, no—it is not so very fine," said I.

"It's just what I call *fuggly* weather," replied the doctor.

"It was very cold last night, I thought," I remarked. "However, when I looked about, I found that the porthole was wide open. I had not noticed it when I went to bed. And the state-room was damp, too."

"Damp!" said he. "Whereabouts are you?"

"One Hundred and Five——"

To my surprise the doctor started visibly, and stared at me.

"What is the matter?" I asked.

"Oh—nothing," he answered; "only everybody has complained of that state-room for the last three trips."

"I shall complain too," I said. "It has certainly not been properly aired. It is a shame!"

"I don't believe it can be helped," answered the doctor. "I believe there is something—well, it is not my business to frighten passengers."

"You need not be afraid of frightening me," I replied. "I can stand any amount of damp. If I should get a bad cold I will come to you."

I offered the doctor a cigar, which he took and examined very critically.

"It is not so much the damp," he remarked. "However, I dare say you will get on very well. Have you a room-mate?"

"Yes; a deuce of a fellow, who bolts out in the middle of the night and leaves the door open."

Again the doctor glanced curiously at me. Then he lit the cigar and looked grave.

"Did he come back?" he asked presently.

"Yes. I was asleep, but I waked up and heard him moving. Then I felt cold and went to sleep again. This morning I found the porthole open."

"Look here," said the doctor, quietly, "I don't care much for this ship. I don't care a rap for her reputation. I tell you what I will do. I have a good-sized place up here. I will share it with you, though I don't know you from Adam."

I was very much surprised at the proposition. I could not imagine why he should take such a sudden interest in my welfare. However, his manner as he spoke of the ship was peculiar.

"You are very good, doctor," I said. "But really, I believe even now the cabin could be aired, or cleaned out, or something. Why do you not care for the ship?"

"We are not superstitious in our profession, sir," replied the doctor. "But the sea makes people so. I don't want to prejudice you, and I don't want to frighten you, but if you will take my advice you will move in here. I would as soon see you overboard," he added, "as know that you or any other man was to sleep in One Hundred and Five."

"Good gracious! Why?" I asked.

"Just because on the last three trips the people who have slept there actually have gone overboard," he answered gravely.

The intelligence was startling and exceedingly unpleasant, I confess.

We played whist in the evening, and I went to bed late. I will confess now that I felt a disagreeable sensation when I entered my state-room. I could not help thinking of the tall man I had seen on the previous night, who was now dead, drowned, tossing about in the long swell two or three hundred miles astern. His face rose very distinctly before me as I undressed, and I even went so far as to draw back the curtains of the upper berth, as though to persuade myself that he was actually gone. I also bolted the door of the state-room.

Suddenly I became aware that the porthole was open and fastened back. This was more than I could stand. I hastily threw on my dressing-gown and went in search of Robert, the steward of my passage. I was very angry, I remember, and when I found him I dragged him roughly to the door of One Hundred and Five, and pushed him towards the open porthole.

"What the deuce do you mean, you scoundrel, by leaving that port open every night? Don't you know it is against the regulations? Don't you know that if the ship heeled and the water began to come in, ten men could not shut it? I will report you to the captain, you blackguard, for endangering the ship!"

The man trembled and turned pale, and then began to shut the round glass plate with the heavy brass fittings.

"Why don't you answer me?" I said, roughly.

"If you please, sir," faltered Robert, "there's nobody on board as can keep this 'ere port shut at night. You can try it yourself, sir. I ain't a-going to stop hany longer on board o' this vessel, sir; I ain't, indeed. But if I was you, sir, I'd just clear out and go and sleep with the surgeon, or something, I would. Look 'ere, sir, is that fastened what you may call securely, or not, sir? Try it, sir—see if it will move a hinch."

I tried the port, and found it perfectly tight.

"Well, sir," continued Robert, triumphantly, "I wager my reputation as a A1 steward, that in 'arf an hour it will be open again—fastened back, too, sir, that's the horful thing—fastened back!"

I examined the great screw and the looped nut that ran on it.

"If I find it open in the night, Robert, I will give you a sovereign. It is not possible. You may go."

"Soverin' did you say, sir? Very good, sir. Thank ye, sir. Good night, sir. Pleasant reepose, sir, and all manner of hinchantin' dreams, sir."

Robert scuttled away, delighted at being released. Of course I thought he was trying to account for his negligence by a silly story, intended to frighten me, and I disbelieved him. The consequence was that he got his sovereign, and I spent a very peculiarly unpleasant night.

I went to bed, and five minutes after I had rolled myself up in my blankets the inexorable Robert extinguished the light that burned steadily behind the ground-glass pane near the door. I lay quite still in the dark, trying to go to sleep, but I soon found that impossible. It had been some satisfaction to be angry with the steward, and the diversion had banished that unpleasant sensation I had at first experienced when

I thought of the drowned man who had been my chum; but I was no longer sleepy, and I lay awake for some time, occasionally glancing at the porthole, which I could just see from where I lay, and which, in the darkness, looked like a faintly luminous soup-plate suspended in blackness.

I believe I must have lain there for an hour, and, as I remember, I was just dozing into sleep when I was roused by a draught of cold air and by distinctly feeling the spray of the sea blown upon my face. I started to my feet, and, not having allowed in the dark for the motion of the ship, I was instantly thrown violently across the state-room upon the couch which was placed beneath the porthole. I recovered myself immediately, however, and climbed upon my knees. The porthole was again wide open and fastened back!

Now these things are facts. I was wide awake when I got up, and I should certainly have been waked by the fall had I still been dozing. Moreover, I bruised my elbows and knees badly, and the bruises were there on the following morning to testify to the fact, if I myself had doubted it. The porthole was wide open and fastened back—a thing so unaccountable that I remember very well feeling astonishment rather than fear when I discovered it.

I at once closed the plate again and screwed down the loop nut with all my strength. It was very dark in the state-room. I reflected that the port had certainly been opened within an hour after Robert had first shut it in my presence, and I determined to watch it and see whether it would open again. Those brass fittings are very heavy and by no means easy to move; I could not believe that the clump had been turned by the shaking of the screw.

I stood peering out through the thick glass at the alternate white and grey streaks of the sea that foamed beneath the ship's side. I must have remained there a quarter of an hour. Suddenly, as I stood, I distinctly heard something moving behind me in one of the berths, and a moment afterwards, just as I turned instinctively to look—though I could, of course, see nothing in the darkness—I heard a very faint groan.

I sprang across the state-room and tore the curtains of the upper berth aside, thrusting in my hands to discover if there were any one there. There *was* some one.

I remember that the sensation as I put my hands forward was as though I were plunging them into the air of a damp cellar, and from behind the curtain came a gust of wind that smelled horribly of stagnant sea-water. I laid hold of something that had the shape of a man's arm, but was smooth, and wet, and icy cold. But suddenly, as I pulled, the creature sprang violently forward against me—a clammy, oozy mass, as it seemed to me, heavy and wet, yet endowed with a sort of supernatural strength.

I reeled across the state-room, and in an instant the door opened and the thing rushed out. I had not had time to be frightened, and quickly recovering myself, I sprang through the door and gave chase at the top of my speed, but I was too late. Ten yards before me I could see—I am sure I saw it—a dark shadow moving in the dimly lighted passage, quickly as the shadow of a fast horse thrown before a dog-cart by the lamp on a dark night. But in a moment it had disappeared, and I found myself holding on to the polished rail that ran along the bulkhead where the passage turned towards the companion. My hair stood on end, and the cold perspiration rolled down my face.

Still I doubted my senses, and pulled myself together. It was absurd, I thought. The Welsh rare-bit I had eaten had disagreed with me; I had been in a nightmare. I made my way back to my state-room, and entered it with an effort. The whole place smelled of stagnant sea-water, as it had when I had waked on the previous evening. It required my utmost strength to go in and grope among my things for a box of wax-lights.

As I lighted a railway reading-lantern which I always carry in case I want to read after the lamps are out, I perceived that the porthole was again open, and a sort of creeping horror began to take possession of me which I never felt before, nor wish to feel again. But I got a light and proceeded to examine the upper berth, expecting to find it drenched with sea-water.

But I was disappointed. The bed had been slept in, and the smell of the sea was strong; but the bedding was as dry as a bone. I fancied that Robert had not had the courage to make the bed after the accident of the previous night—it had all been a hideous dream. I drew the curtains back as far as I could and examined the place very carefully. It was perfectly dry. But the porthole was open again.

With a sort of dull bewilderment of horror, I closed it and screwed it down, and, thrusting my heavy stick through the brass loop, wrenched it with all my might till the thick metal began to bend under the pressure. Then I hooked my reading-lantern into the red velvet at the head of the couch and sat down to recover my senses if I could. I sat there all night, unable to think of rest—hardly able to think at all. But the porthole remained closed, and I did not believe it would now open again without the application of a considerable force.

III

The morning dawned at last, and I dressed myself slowly, thinking over all that had happened in the night. It was a beautiful day, and I went on deck, glad to get out in the early, pure sunshine and to smell the breeze from the blue water, so different from the noisome, stagnant odour from my state-room. Instinctively I turned aft, towards the surgeon's cabin. There he stood, with a pipe in his mouth, taking his morning airing precisely as on the preceding day.

"Good-morning," said he, quietly, but looking at me with evident curiosity.

"Doctor, you were quite right," said I. "There is something wrong about that place."

"I thought you would change your mind," he answered, rather triumphantly. "You have had a bad night, eh? Shall I make you a pick-me-up? I have a capital recipe."

"No, thanks," I cried. "But I would like to tell you what happened."

I then tried to explain as clearly as possible precisely what had occurred, not omitting to state that I had been scared as I had never been scared in my whole life before. I dwelt particularly on the phenomenon of the porthole, which was a fact to which I could testify, even if the rest had been an illusion.

"You seem to think I am likely to doubt the story," said the doctor, smiling at the detailed account of the state of the porthole. "I do not doubt it in the least. I renew my invitation to you. Bring your traps here, and take half my cabin."

"Come and take half of mine for one night," I said. "Help me to get at the bottom of this thing."

"You will get to the bottom of something else if you try," answered the doctor.

"What?" I asked.

"The bottom of the sea. I am going to leave the ship. It is not canny."

"Then you will not help me to find out——"

"Not I," said the doctor, quickly. "It is my business to keep my wits about me—not to go fiddling about with ghosts and things."

"Do you really believe it is a ghost?" I inquired, rather contemptuously.

But as I spoke I remembered very well the horrible sensation of the supernatural which had got possession of me during the night.

"Have you any reasonable explanation of these things to offer?" he asked. "No; you have not. Well, you say you will find an explanation. I say that you won't, sir, simply because there is not any."

"But, my dear sir," I retorted, "do you, a man of science, mean to tell me that such things cannot be explained?"

"I do," he answered stoutly. "And, if they could, I would not be concerned in the explanation."

The captain was one of those splendidly tough and cheerful specimens of seafaring humanity whose combined courage, hardihood, and calmness in difficulty lead them naturally into high positions of trust. He was not the man to be led away by an idle tale, and the mere fact that he was willing to join me in the investigation was proof that he thought there was something seriously wrong which could not be accounted for on ordinary theories, nor laughed down as a common superstition. To some extent, too, his reputation was at stake, as well as the reputation of the ship. It is no light thing to lose passengers overboard, and he knew it.

About ten o'clock that evening, as I was smoking a last cigar, he came up to me and drew me aside from the beat of the other passengers who were patrolling the deck in the warm darkness.

"This is a serious matter, Mr Brisbane," he said. "We must make up our minds either way—to be disappointed or to have a pretty rough time of it. You see, I cannot afford to laugh at the affair, and I will ask you to sign your name to a statement of whatever occurs. If nothing happens to-night we will try it again to-morrow and next day. Are you ready?"

So we went below and entered the state-room. As we went in I could see Robert the steward, who stood a little further down the passage, watching us with his usual grin, as though certain that something dreadful was about to happen. The captain closed the door behind us and bolted it.

"Supposing we put your portmanteau before the door," he suggested. "One of us can sit on it. Nothing can get out then. Is the port screwed down?"

I found it as I had left it in the morning. Indeed, without using a lever, as I had done, no one could have opened it. I drew back the curtains of the upper berth so that I could see well into it. By the captain's advice I lighted my reading-lantern and placed it so that it shone upon the white sheets above. He insisted upon sitting on the portmanteau, declaring that he wished to be able to swear that he had sat before the door.

Then he requested me to search the state-room thoroughly—an operation very soon accomplished, as it consisted merely in looking beneath the lower berth and under the couch below the porthole. The spaces were quite empty.

"It is impossible for any human being to get in," I said, "or for any human being to open the port."

"Very good," said the captain, calmly. "If we see anything now, it must be either imagination or something supernatural."

I sat down on the edge of the lower berth.

"The first time it happened," said the captain, crossing his legs and leaning back against the door, "was in March. The passenger who slept here, in the upper berth, turned out to have been a lunatic—at all events, he was known to have been a little touched, and he had taken his passage without the knowledge of his friends. He rushed out in the middle of the night and threw himself overboard, before the officer who had the watch could stop him. We stopped and lowered a boat; it was a quiet night, just before that heavy weather came on; but we could not find him. Of course his suicide was afterwards accounted for on the ground of his insanity."

"I suppose that often happens?" I remarked, rather absently.

"Not often—no," said the captain; "never before in my experience, though I have heard of it happening on board other ships. Well, as I was saying, that occurred in March. On the very next trip—what are you looking at?" he asked, stopping suddenly in his narration.

I believe I gave no answer. My eyes were riveted upon the porthole. It seemed to me that the brass loop-nut was beginning to turn very slowly upon the screw—so slowly, however, that I was not sure it moved at all. I watched it intently, fixing its position in my mind and trying to ascertain whether it changed. Seeing where I was looking, the captain looked too.

"It moves!" he exclaimed, in a tone of conviction. "No, it does not," he added, after a minute.

"If it were the jarring of the screw," said I, "it would have opened during the day; but I found it this evening jammed tight as I left it this morning."

I rose and tried the nut. It was certainly loosened, for by an effort I could move it with my hands.

"The queer thing," said the captain, "is that the second man who was lost is supposed to have got through that very port. We had a terrible time over it. It was in the middle of the night, and the weather was very heavy; there was an alarm that one of the ports was open and the sea running in. I came below and found everything flooded, the water pouring in every time she rolled, and the whole port swinging from the top bolts—not the porthole in the middle. Well, we managed to shut it, but the water did some damage. Ever since that the place smells of sea-water from time to time. We supposed the passenger had thrown himself out, though the Lord only knows how he did it. The steward kept telling me that he could not keep anything shut here. Upon my word—I can smell it now, cannot you?"

"Yes—distinctly," I said, and I shuddered as that same odour of stagnant sea-water grew stronger in the cabin. "Now, to smell like this, the place must be damp," I continued, "and yet when I examined it with the carpenter this morning every-thing was perfectly dry. It is most extraordinary—hallo!"

My reading-lantern, which had been placed in the upper berth, was suddenly extinguished. There was still a good deal of light from the pane of ground glass near the door, behind which loomed the regulation lamp. The ship rolled heavily, and the curtain of the upper berth swung far out into the state-room and back again. I rose quickly from my seat on the edge of the bed, and the captain at the same moment started to his feet with a loud cry of surprise. I had turned with the intention of taking down the lantern to examine it, when I heard his exclamation, and immediately afterwards his call for help.

I sprang towards him. He was wrestling with all his might with the brass loop of the port. It seemed to turn against his hands in spite of all his efforts. I caught up my cane—a heavy oak stick I always used to carry—and thrust it through the ring and bore on it with all my strength. But the strong wood snapped suddenly, and I fell upon the couch. When I rose again the port was wide open, and the captain was standing with his back against the door, pale to the lips.

"There is something in that berth!" he cried, in a strange voice, his eyes almost starting from his head. "Hold the door, while I look—it shall not escape us, whatever it is!"

But instead of taking his place, I sprang upon the lower bed and seized something which lay in the upper berth.

It was something ghostly—horrible beyond words—and it moved in my grip. It was like the body of a man long drowned, and yet it moved, and had the strength of ten men living; but I gripped it with all my might—the slippery, oozy, horrible thing. The dead white eyes seemed to stare at me out of the dusk; the putrid odour of rank sea-water was about it, and its shiny hair hung in foul wet curls over its dead face. I wrestled with the dead thing; it thrust itself upon me and forced me back and nearly broke my arms; it wound its corpse's arms about my neck—the living death—and overpowered me, so that I, at last, cried aloud and fell, and left my hold.

As I fell, the thing sprang across me, and seemed to throw itself upon the captain. When I last saw him on his feet his face was white and his lips set. It seemed to me that he struck a violent blow at the dead being, and then he, too, fell forward upon his face, with an inarticulate cry of horror.

The thing paused an instant, seeming to hover over his prostrate body, and I could have screamed again for very fright, but I had no voice left. The thing vanished suddenly, and it seemed to my disturbed senses that it made its exit through the open port, though how that was possible, considering the smallness of the aperture, is more than any one can tell.

I lay a long time upon the floor, and the captain lay beside me. At last I partially recovered my senses and moved, and I instantly knew that my arm was broken—the small bone of the left forearm near the wrist. I got upon my feet somehow, and with my remaining hand I tried to raise the captain. He groaned and moved, and at last came to himself. He was not hurt, but he seemed badly stunned.

"Well, do you want to hear any more? There is nothing more. That is the end of my story."

IV

The carpenter carried out his scheme of running half a dozen four-inch screws through the door of One Hundred and Five; and if ever you take a passage in the *Kamtschatka,* you may ask for a berth in that state-room. You will be told that it is engaged—yes, it is engaged by that dead thing.

I finished the trip in the surgeon's cabin. He doctored my broken arm, and advised me not to "fiddle about with ghosts and things" any more. The captain was very silent, and never sailed again in that ship, though it is still running. And I will not sail in her either. It was a very disagreeable experience, and I was very badly frightened, which is a thing I do not like.

That is all. That is how I saw a ghost—if it was a ghost. It was dead, anyhow.

GABRIEL-ERNEST

SAKI

First published in *The Westminster Gazette*, 1909.

"There is a wild beast in your woods," said the artist Cunningham, as he was being driven to the station. It was the only remark he had made during the drive, but as Van Cheele had talked incessantly his companion's silence had not been noticeable.

"A stray fox or two and some resident weasels. Nothing more formidable," said Van Cheele.

The artist said nothing.

"What did you mean about a wild beast?" said Van Cheele later, when they were on the platform.

"Nothing. My imagination. Here is the train," said Cunningham.

That afternoon Van Cheele went for one of his frequent rambles through his woodland property. He had a stuffed bittern in his study, and knew the names of quite a number of wild flowers, so his aunt had possibly some justification in describing him as a great naturalist. At any rate, he was a great walker. It was his custom to take mental notes of

everything he saw during his walks, not so much for the purpose of assisting contemporary science as to provide topics
for conversation afterwards. When the bluebells began to
show themselves in flower he made a point of informing
every one of the fact; the season of the year might have
warned his hearers of the likelihood of such an occurrence,
but at least they felt that he was being absolutely frank with
them.

What Van Cheele saw on this particular afternoon was,
however, something far removed from his ordinary range of
experience. On a shelf of smooth stone overhanging a deep
pool in the hollow of an oak coppice a boy of about sixteen lay
asprawl, drying his wet brown limbs luxuriously in the sun.
His wet hair, parted by a recent dive, lay close to his head,
and his light-brown eyes, so light that there was an almost
tigerish gleam in them, were turned towards Van Cheele with
a certain lazy watchfulness. It was an unexpected apparition, and Van Cheele found himself engaged in the novel
process of thinking before he spoke. Where on earth could
this wild-looking boy hail from? The miller's wife had lost a
child some two months ago, supposed to have been swept
away by the mill-race, but that had been a mere baby, not a
half-grown lad.

"What are you doing there?" he demanded.

"Obviously, sunning myself," replied the boy.

"Where do you live?"

"Here, in these woods."

"You can't live in the woods," said Van Cheele.

"They are very nice woods," said the boy, with a touch of
patronage in his voice.

"But where do you sleep at night?"

"I don't sleep at night; that's my busiest time."

Van Cheele began to have an irritated feeling that he was grappling with a problem that was eluding him.

"What do you feed on?" he asked.

"Flesh," said the boy, and he pronounced the word with slow relish, as though he were tasting it.

"Flesh! What Flesh?"

"Since it interests you, rabbits, wild-fowl, hares, poultry, lambs in their season, children when I can get any; they're usually too well locked in at night, when I do most of my hunting. It's quite two months since I tasted child-flesh."

Ignoring the chaffing nature of the last remark Van Cheele tried to draw the boy on the subject of possible poaching operations.

"You're talking rather through your hat when you speak of feeding on hares." (Considering the nature of the boy's toilet the simile was hardly an apt one.) "Our hillside hares aren't easily caught."

"At night I hunt on four feet," was the somewhat cryptic response.

"I suppose you mean that you hunt with a dog?" hazarded Van Cheele.

The boy rolled slowly over on to his back, and laughed a weird low laugh, that was pleasantly like a chuckle and disagreeably like a snarl.

"I don't fancy any dog would be very anxious for my company, especially at night."

Van Cheele began to feel that there was something positively uncanny about the strange-eyed, strange-tongued youngster.

"I can't have you staying in these woods," he declared authoritatively.

"I fancy you'd rather have me here than in your house," said the boy.

The prospect of this wild, nude animal in Van Cheele's primly ordered house was certainly an alarming one.

"If you don't go. I shall have to make you," said Van Cheele.

The boy turned like a flash, plunged into the pool, and in a moment had flung his wet and glistening body half-way up the bank where Van Cheele was standing. In an otter the movement would not have been remarkable; in a boy Van Cheele found it sufficiently startling. His foot slipped as he made an involuntarily backward movement, and he found himself almost prostrate on the slippery weed-grown bank, with those tigerish yellow eyes not very far from his own. Almost instinctively he half raised his hand to his throat. They boy laughed again, a laugh in which the snarl had nearly driven out the chuckle, and then, with another of his astonishing lightning movements, plunged out of view into a yielding tangle of weed and fern.

"What an extraordinary wild animal!" said Van Cheele as he picked himself up. And then he recalled Cunningham's remark "There is a wild beast in your woods."

Walking slowly homeward, Van Cheele began to turn over in his mind various local occurrences which might be traceable to the existence of this astonishing young savage.

Something had been thinning the game in the woods lately, poultry had been missing from the farms, hares were growing unaccountably scarcer, and complaints had reached him of lambs being carried off bodily from the hills. Was it possible that this wild boy was really hunting the countryside in company with some clever poacher dogs? He had spoken of hunting "four-footed" by night, but then, again, he had hinted strangely at no dog caring to come near him, "especially at night." It was certainly puzzling. And then, as Van Cheele ran his mind over the various depredations that had been committed during the last month or two, he came suddenly to a dead stop, alike in his walk and his speculations. The child missing from the mill two months ago—the accepted theory was that it had tumbled into the mill-race and been swept away; but the mother had always declared she had heard a shriek on the hill side of the house, in the opposite direction from the water. It was unthinkable, of course, but he wished that the boy had not made that uncanny remark about child-flesh eaten two months ago. Such dreadful things should not be said even in fun.

Van Cheele, contrary to his usual wont, did not feel disposed to be communicative about his discovery in the wood. His position as a parish councillor and justice of the peace seemed somehow compromised by the fact that he was harbouring a personality of such doubtful repute on his property; there was even a possibility that a heavy bill of damages for raided lambs and poultry might be laid at his door. At dinner that night he was quite unusually silent.

"Where's your voice gone to?" said his aunt. "One would think you had seen a wolf."

Van Cheele, who was not familiar with the old saying, thought the remark rather foolish; if he *had* seen a wolf on his property his tongue would have been extraordinarily busy with the subject.

At breakfast next morning Van Cheele was conscious that his feeling of uneasiness regarding yesterday's episode had not wholly disappeared, and he resolved to go by train to the neighbouring cathedral town, hunt up Cunningham, and learn from him what he had really seen that had prompted the remark about a wild beast in the woods. With this resolution taken, his usual cheerfulness partially returned, and he hummed a bright little melody as he sauntered to the morning-room for his customary cigarette. As he entered the room the melody made way abruptly for a pious invocation. Gracefully asprawl on the ottoman, in an attitude of almost exaggerated repose, was the boy of the woods. He was drier than when Van Cheele had last seen him, but no other alteration was noticeable in his toilet.

"How dare you come here?" asked Van Cheele furiously.

"You told me I was not to stay in the woods," said the boy calmly.

"But not to come here. Supposing my aunt should see you!"

And with a view to minimising that catastrophe, Van Cheele hastily obscured as much of his unwelcome guest as possible under the folds of a *Morning Post*. At that moment his aunt entered the room.

"This is a poor boy who has lost his way—and lost his memory. He doesn't know who he is or where he comes from," explained Van Cheele desperately, glancing apprehensively at the waif's face to see whether he was going to add inconvenient candour to his other savage propensities.

Miss Van Cheele was enormously interested.

"Perhaps his underlinen is marked," she suggested.

"He seems to have lost most of that, too," said Van Cheele, making frantic little grabs at the *Morning Post* to keep it in its place.

A naked homeless child appealed to Miss Van Cheele as warmly as a stray kitten or derelict puppy would have done.

"We must do all we can for him," she decided, and in a very short time a messenger, dispatched to the rectory, where a page-boy was kept, had returned with a suit of pantry clothes, and the necessary accessories of shirt, shoes, collar, etc. Clothed, clean, and groomed, the boy lost none of his uncanniness in Van Cheele's eyes, but his aunt found him sweet.

"We must call him something till we know who he really is," she said. "Gabriel-Ernest, I think; those are nice suitable names."

Van Cheele agreed, but he privately doubted whether they were being grafted on to a nice suitable child. His misgivings were not diminished by the fact that his staid and elderly spaniel had bolted out of the house at the first incoming of the boy, and now obstinately remained shivering and yapping at the farther end of the orchard, while the canary, usually as vocally industrious as Van Cheele himself, had put itself on an allowance of frightened cheeps. More than ever he was resolved to consult Cunningham without loss of time.

As he drove off to the station his aunt was arranging that Gabriel-Ernest should help her to entertain the infant members of her Sunday-school class at tea that afternoon.

Cunningham was not at first disposed to be communicative.

"My mother died of some brain trouble," he explained, "so you will understand why I am averse to dwelling on anything of an impossibly fantastic nature that I may see or think that I have seen."

"But what *did* you see?" persisted Van Cheele.

"What I thought I saw was something so extraordinary that no really sane man could dignify it with the credit of having actually happened. I was standing, the last evening I was with you, half-hidden in the hedge-growth by the orchard gate, watching the dying glow of the sunset. Suddenly I became aware of a naked boy, a bather from some neighbouring pool, I took him to be, who was standing out on the bare hillside also watching the sunset. His pose was so suggestive of some wild faun of Pagan myth that I instantly wanted to engage him as a model, and in another moment I think I should have hailed him. But just then the sun dipped out of view, and all the orange and pink slid out of the landscape, leaving it cold and grey. And at the same moment an astounding thing happened—the boy vanished too!"

"What! vanished away into nothing?" asked Van Cheele excitedly.

"No; that is the dreadful part of it," answered the artist; "on the open hillside where the boy had been standing a second ago, stood a large wolf, blackish in colour, with gleaming fangs and cruel, yellow eyes. You may think—"

But Van Cheele did not stop for anything as futile as thought. Already he was tearing at top speed towards the station. He dismissed the idea of a telegram. "Gabriel-Ernest is a werewolf" was a hopelessly inadequate effort at conveying the situation, and his aunt would think it was a code message to which he had omitted to give her the key. His one hope was that he might reach home before sundown. The cab which he chartered at the other end of the railway journey bore him with what seemed exasperating slowness along the country roads, which were pink and mauve with the flush of the sinking sun. His aunt was putting away some unfinished jams and cake when he arrived.

"Where is Gabriel-Ernest?" he almost screamed.

"He is taking the little Toop child home," said his aunt. "It was getting so late, I thought it wasn't safe to let it go back alone. What a lovely sunset, isn't it?"

But Van Cheele, although not oblivious of the glow in the western sky, did not stay to discuss its beauties. At a speed for which he was scarcely geared he raced along the narrow lane that led to the home of the Toops. On one side ran the swift current of the mill-stream, on the other rose the stretch of bare hillside. A dwindling rim of red sun showed still on the skyline, and the next turning must bring him in view of the ill-assorted

couple he was pursuing. Then the colour went suddenly out of things, and a grey light settled itself with a quick shiver over the landscape. Van Cheele heard a shrill wail of fear, and stopped running.

Nothing was ever seen again of the Toop child or Gabriel-Ernest, but the latter's discarded garments were found lying in the road so it was assumed that the child had fallen into the water, and that the boy had stripped and jumped in, in a vain endeavour to save it. Van Cheele and some workmen who were near by at the time testified to having heard a child scream loudly just near the spot where the clothes were found. Mrs. Toop, who had eleven other children, was decently resigned to her bereavement, but Miss Van Cheele sincerely mourned her lost foundling. It was on her initiative that a memorial brass was put up in the parish church to "Gabriel-Ernest, an unknown boy, who bravely sacrificed his life for another."

Van Cheele gave way to his aunt in most things, but he flatly refused to subscribe to the Gabriel-Ernest memorial.

PART IV

Romance & Redemption

MARK TWAIN

Mark Twain (1835–1910) was the pen name of Samuel Langhorne Clemens, an American author, humorist, satirist, and moral observer whose wit and storytelling reshaped American literature. Born in Missouri along the Mississippi River, he apprenticed as a printer and piloted steamboats, adopting "Mark Twain" from the river call for safe depth, before the Civil War steered him toward journalism, lecturing, and far-flung travels from Hawaii to the Mediterranean. His breakthrough novels *The Adventures of Tom Sawyer* (1876) and *Adventures of Huckleberry Finn* (1884), hailed by Hemingway as the wellspring of modern American literature, captured a nation's raw voice, blending boyish mischief with sharp social critique. Twain battled debt with tireless lecture tours, synchronized his birth and death to the passage of Halley's Comet, and left behind a legacy quoted in classrooms and courtrooms alike. His irreverent spark still ignites films, stages, and bestselling editions around the world.

THE £1,000,000 BANK-NOTE

MARK TWAIN

First published in *The Century Magazine*, 1893.

When I was twenty-seven years old, I was a mining-broker's clerk in San Francisco, and an expert in all the details of stock traffic. I was alone in the world, and had nothing to depend upon but my wits and a clean reputation; but these were setting my feet in the road to eventual fortune, and I was content with the prospect.

My time was my own after the afternoon board, Saturdays, and I was accustomed to put it in on a little sail-boat on the bay. One day I ventured too far, and was carried out to sea. Just at nightfall, when hope was about gone, I was picked up by a small brig which was bound for London. It was a long and stormy voyage, and they made me work my passage without pay, as a common sailor. When I stepped ashore in London my clothes were ragged and shabby, and I had only a dollar in my pocket. This money fed and sheltered me twenty-four hours. During the next twenty-four I went without food and shelter.

About ten o'clock on the following morning, seedy and hungry, I was dragging myself along Portland Place, when a child that was passing, towed by a nursemaid, tossed a luscious big pear—minus one bite—into the gutter. I stopped, of course, and fastened my desiring eye on that muddy treasure. My mouth watered for it, my stomach craved it, my whole being begged for it. But every time I made a move to get it some passing eye detected my purpose, and of course I straightened up, then, and looked indifferent, and pretended that I hadn't been thinking about the pear at all. This same thing kept happening and happening, and I couldn't get the pear. I was just getting desperate enough to brave all the shame, and to seize it, when a window behind me was raised, and a gentleman spoke out of it, saying:

'Step in here, please.'

I was admitted by a gorgeous flunkey, and shown into a sumptuous room where a couple of elderly gentlemen were sitting. They sent away the servant, and made me sit down. They had just finished their breakfast, and the sight of the remains of it almost overpowered me. I could hardly keep my wits together in the presence of that food, but as I was not asked to sample it, I had to bear my trouble as best I could.

Now, something had been happening there a little before, which I did not know anything about until a good many days afterwards, but I will tell you about it now. Those two old brothers had been having a pretty hot argument a couple of days before, and had ended by agreeing to decide it by a bet, which is the English way of settling everything.

You will remember that the Bank of England once issued two notes of a million pounds each, to be used for a special purpose connected with some public transaction with a foreign country. For some reason or other only one of these had been used and cancelled; the other still lay in the vaults of the Bank. Well, the brothers, chatting along, happened to get to wondering what might be the fate of a perfectly honest and intelligent stranger who should be turned adrift in London without a friend, and with no money but that million-pound bank-note, and no way to account for his being in possession of it. Brother A said he would starve to death; Brother B said he wouldn't. Brother A said he couldn't offer it at a bank or anywhere else, because he would be arrested on the spot. So they went on disputing till Brother B said he would bet twenty thousand pounds that the man would live thirty days, any way, on that million, and keep out of jail, too. Brother A took him up. Brother B went down to the Bank and bought that note. Just like an Englishman, you see; pluck to the backbone. Then he dictated a letter, which one of his clerks wrote out in a beautiful round hand, and then the two brothers sat at the window a whole day watching for the right man to give it to.

They saw many honest faces go by that were not intelligent enough; many that were intelligent but not honest enough; many that were both, but the possessors were not poor enough, or, if poor enough, were not strangers. There was always a defect, until I came along; but they agreed that I filled the bill all around; so they elected me unanimously, and there I was, now, waiting to know why I was called in. They began to ask me questions about myself, and pretty soon they had my story. Finally they told me I would answer their purpose. I said I was sincerely glad, and asked what it was. Then one of them handed me an envelope, and said I would find the explanation inside. I was going to open it, but he said no; take it to my lodgings, and look it over carefully, and not be hasty or rash. I was puzzled, and wanted to discuss the matter a little further, but they didn't; so I took my leave, feeling hurt and insulted to be made the butt of what was apparently some kind of a practical joke, and yet obliged to put up with it, not being in circumstances to resent affronts from rich and strong folk.

I would have picked up the pear, now, and eaten it before all the world, but it was gone; so I had lost that by this unlucky business, and the thought of it did not soften my feeling towards those men. As soon as I was out of sight of that house I opened my envelope, and saw that it contained money! My opinion of those people changed, I can tell you! I lost not a moment, but shoved note and money into my vest-pocket, and broke for the nearest cheap eating-house. Well, how I did eat! When at last I couldn't hold any more, I took out my money and unfolded it, took one glimpse and nearly fainted. Five millions of dollars! Why, it made my head swim.

I must have sat there stunned and blinking at the note as much as a minute before I came rightly to myself again. The first thing I noticed, then, was the landlord. His eye was on the note, and he was petrified. He was worshipping, with all his body and soul, but he looked as if he couldn't stir hand or foot. I took my cue in a moment, and did the only rational thing there was to do. I reached the note towards him, and said carelessly:

'Give me the change, please.'

Then he was restored to his normal condition, and made a thousand apologies for not being able to break the bill, and I couldn't get him to touch it. He wanted to look at it, and keep on looking at it; he couldn't seem to get enough of it to quench the thirst of his eye, but he shrank from touching it as if it had been something too sacred for poor common clay to handle. I said:

'I am sorry if it is an inconvenience, but I must insist. Please change it; I haven't anything else.'

But he said that wasn't any matter; he was quite willing to let the trifle stand over till another time. I said I might not be in his neighbourhood again for a good while; but he said it was of no consequence, he could wait, and, moreover, I could have anything I wanted, any time I chose, and let the account run as long as I pleased. He said he hoped he wasn't afraid to trust as rich a gentleman as I was, merely because I was of a merry disposition, and chose to play larks on the public in the matter of dress. By this time another customer was entering, and the landlord hinted to me to put the monster out of sight; then he bowed me all the way to the door, and I started straight for that house and those brothers, to correct the mistake which had been made before the police should hunt me up, and help me do it. I was pretty nervous, in fact pretty badly frightened, though, of course, I was no way in fault; but I knew men well enough to know that when they find they've given a tramp a million-pound bill when they thought it was a one-pounder, they are in a frantic rage against him instead of quarrelling with their own near-sightedness, as they ought. As I approached the house my excitement began to abate, for all was quiet there, which made me feel pretty sure the blunder was not discovered yet. I rang. The same servant appeared. I asked for those gentlemen.

'They are gone.' This in the lofty, cold way of that fellow's tribe.

'Gone? Gone where?'

'On a journey.'

'But whereabouts?'

'To the Continent, I think.'

'The Continent?'

'Yes, sir.'

'Which way—by what route?'

'I can't say, sir.'

'When will they be back?'

'In a month, they said.'

'A month! Oh, this is awful! Give me some sort of idea of how to get a word to them. It's of the last importance.'

'I can't, indeed. I've no idea where they've gone, sir.'

'Then I must see some member of the family.'

'Family's away too; been abroad months—in Egypt and India, I think.'

'Man, there's been an immense mistake made. They'll be back before night. Will you tell them I've been here, and that I will keep coming till it's all made right, and they needn't be afraid?'

'I'll tell them, if they come back, but I am not expecting them. They said you would be here in an hour to make inquiries, but I must tell you it's all right, they'll be here on time and expect you.'

So I had to give it up and go away. What a riddle it all was! I was like to lose my mind. They would be here 'on time.' What could that mean? Oh, the letter would explain, maybe. I had forgotten the letter; I got it out and read it. This is what it said:

'You are an intelligent and honest man, as one may see by your face. We conceive you to be poor and a stranger. Enclosed you will find a sum of money. It is lent to you for thirty days, without interest. Report at this house at the end of that time. I have a bet on you. If I win it you shall have any situation that is in my gift—any, that is, that you shall be able to prove yourself familiar with and competent to fill.'

No signature, no address, no date.

Well, here was a coil to be in! You are posted on what had preceded all this, but I was not. It was just a deep, dark puzzle to me. I hadn't the least idea what the game was, nor whether harm was meant me or a kindness. I went into a park, and sat down to try to think it out, and to consider what I had best do.

At the end of an hour, my reasonings had crystallised into this verdict.

Maybe those men mean me well, maybe they mean me ill; no way to decide that—let it go. They've got a game, or a scheme, or an experiment of some kind on hand; no way to determine what it is—let it go. There's a bet on me; no way to find out what it is—let it go. That disposes of the indeterminable quantities; the remainder of the matter is tangible, solid, and may be classed and labelled with certainty. If I ask the Bank of England to place this bill to the credit of the man it belongs to, they'll do it, for they know him, although I don't; but they will ask me how I came in possession of it, and if I tell the truth, they'll put me in the asylum, naturally, and a lie will land me in jail. The same result would follow if I tried to bank the bill anywhere or to borrow money on it. I have got to carry this immense burden around until those men come back, whether I want to or not. It is useless to me, as useless as a handful of ashes, and yet I must take care of it, and watch over it, while I beg my living. I couldn't give it away, if I should try, for neither honest citizen nor highwayman would accept it or meddle with it for anything. Those brothers are safe. Even if I lose their bill, or burn it, they are still safe, because they can stop payment, and the Bank will make them whole; but meantime, I've got to do a month's suffering without wages or profit—unless I help win that bet, whatever it may be, and get that situation that I am promised. I should like to get that; men of their sort have situations in their gift that are worth having.

I got to thinking a good deal about that situation. My hopes began to rise high. Without doubt the salary would be large. It would begin in a month; after that I should be all right. Pretty soon I was feeling first-rate. By this time I was tramping the streets again. The sight of a tailor-shop gave me a sharp longing to shed my rags, and to clothe myself decently once more. Could I afford it? No; I had nothing in the world but a million pounds. So I forced myself to go on by. But soon I was drifting back again. The temptation persecuted me cruelly. I must have passed that shop back and forth six times during that manful struggle. At last I gave in; I had to. I asked if they had a misfit suit that had been thrown on their hands. The fellow I spoke to nodded his head towards another fellow, and gave me no answer. I went to the indicated fellow, and he indicated another fellow with his head, and no words. I went to him, and he said:

"Tend to you presently."

I waited till he was done with what he was at, then he took me into a back room, and overhauled a pile of rejected suits, and selected the rattiest one for me. I put it on. It didn't fit, and wasn't in any way attractive, but it was new, and I was anxious to have it; so I didn't find any fault, but said with some diffidence:

'It would be an accommodation to me if you could wait some days for the money. I haven't any small change about me.'

The fellow worked up a most sarcastic expression of countenance, and said:

'Oh, you haven't? Well, of course, I didn't expect it. I'd only expect gentlemen like you to carry large change.'

I was nettled, and said:

'My friend, you shouldn't judge a stranger always by the clothes he wears. I am quite able to pay for this suit; I simply didn't wish to put you to the trouble of changing a large note.'

He modified his style a little at that, and said, though still with something of an air:

'I didn't mean any particular harm, but as long as rebukes are going, I might say it wasn't quite your affair to jump to the conclusion that we couldn't change any note that you might happen to be carrying around. On the contrary, we can.'

I handed the note to him, and said:

'Oh, very well; I apologise.'

He received it with a smile, one of those large smiles which goes all around over, and has folds in it, and wrinkles, and spirals, and looks like the place where you have thrown a brick in a pond; and then in the act of his taking a glimpse of the bill this smile froze solid, and turned yellow, and looked like those wavy, wormy spreads of lava which you find hardened on little levels on the side of Vesuvius. I never before saw a smile caught like that, and perpetuated. The man stood there holding the bill, and looking like that, and the proprietor hustled up to see what was the matter, and said briskly:

'Well, what's up? what's the trouble? what's wanting?'

I said, 'There isn't any trouble. I'm waiting for my change.'

'Come, come; get him his change, Tod; get him his change.'

Tod retorted: 'Get him his change! It's easy to say, sir; but look at the bill yourself.'

The proprietor took a look, gave a low, eloquent whistle, then made a dive for the pile of rejected clothing, and began to snatch it this way and that, talking all the time excitedly, and as if to himself:

'Sell an eccentric millionaire such an unspeakable suit as that! Tod's a fool—a born fool. Always doing something like this. Drives every millionaire away from this place, because he can't tell a millionaire from a tramp, and never could. Ah, here's the thing I'm after. Please get those things off, sir, and throw them in the fire. Do me the favour to put on this shirt and this suit; it's just the thing, the very thing—plain, rich, modest, and just ducally nobby; made to order for a foreign prince—you may know him, sir, his Serene Highness the Hospodar of Halifax; had to leave it with us and take a mourning-suit because his mother was going to die—which she didn't. But that's all right; we can't always have things the way we—that is, the way they—there! trousers all right, they fit you to a charm, sir; now the waistcoat: aha, right again! now the coat—lord! look at that, now! Perfect, the whole thing! I never saw such a triumph in all my experience.'

I expressed my satisfaction.

'Quite right, sir, quite right; it'll do for a makeshift, I'm bound to say. But wait till you see what we'll get up for you on your own measure. Come, Tod, book and pen; get at it. Length of leg, 32'—and so on. Before I could get in a word he had measured me, and was giving orders for dress-suits, morning suits, shirts, and all sorts of things. When I got a chance I said:

'But, my dear sir, I can't give these orders, unless you can wait indefinitely, or change the bill.'

'Indefinitely! It's a weak word, sir, a weak word. Eternally—that's the word, sir. Tod, rush these things through, and send them to the gentleman's address without any waste of time. Let the minor customers wait. Set down the gentleman's address and——'

'I'm changing my quarters. I will drop in and leave the new address.'

'Quite right, sir, quite right. One moment—let me show you out, sir. There—good day, sir, good day.'

Well, don't you see what was bound to happen? I drifted naturally into buying whatever I wanted, and asking for change. Within a week I was sumptuously equipped with all needful comforts and luxuries, and was housed in an expensive private hotel in Hanover Square. I took my dinners there, but for breakfast I stuck by Harris's humble feeding-house, where I had got my first meal on my million-pound bill. I was the making of Harris. The fact had gone all abroad that the foreign crank who carried million-pound bills in his vest-pocket was the patron saint of the place. That was enough. From being a poor, struggling, little hand-to-mouth enterprise, it had become celebrated, and overcrowded with customers. Harris was so grateful that he forced loans upon me, and would not be denied; and so, pauper as I was, I had money to spend, and was living like the rich and the great. I judged that there was going to be a crash by and by, but I was in, now, and must swim across or drown. You see there was just that element of impending disaster to give a serious side, a sober side, yes, a tragic side, to a state of things which would otherwise have been purely ridiculous. In the night, in the dark, the tragedy part was always to the front, and always warning, always threatening; and so I moaned and tossed, and sleep was hard to find. But in the cheerful daylight the tragedy element faded out and disappeared, and I walked on air, and was happy to giddiness, to intoxication, you may say.

And it was natural; for I had become one of the notorieties of the metropolis of the world, and it turned my head, not just a little, but a good deal. You could not take up a newspaper, English, Scotch, or Irish, without finding in it one or more references to the 'vest-pocket million-pounder' and his latest doings and sayings. At first, in these mentions, I was at the bottom of the personal gossip column; next, I was listed above the knights, next above the baronets, next above the barons, and so on, and so on, climbing steadily, as my notoriety augmented, until I reached the highest altitude possible, and there I remained, taking precedence of all dukes not royal, and of all ecclesiastics except the Primate of all England. But, mind, this was not fame; as yet I had achieved only notoriety. Then came the climaxing stroke—the accolade, so to speak—which in a single instance transmuted the perishable dross of notoriety into the enduring gold of fame: 'Punch' caricatured me! Yes, I was a made man, now: my place was established. I might be joked about still, but reverently, not hilariously, not rudely; I could be smiled at, but not laughed at. The time for that had gone by. 'Punch' pictured me all a-flutter with rags, dickering with a beefeater for the Tower of London. Well, you can imagine how it was with a young fellow who had never been taken notice of before, and now all of a sudden couldn't say a thing that wasn't taken up and repeated everywhere; couldn't stir abroad without constantly overhearing the remark flying from lip to lip, 'There he goes; that's him!' couldn't take his breakfast without a crowd to look on; couldn't appear in an opera-box without concentrating there the fire of a thousand lorgnettes. Why, I just swam in glory all day long—that is the amount of it.

You know, I even kept my old suit of rags, and every now and then appeared in them, so as to have the old pleasure of buying trifles, and being insulted, and then shooting the scoffer dead with the million-pound bill. But I couldn't keep that up. The illustrated papers made the outfit so familiar that when I went out in it I was at once recognised and followed by a crowd, and if I attempted a purchase the man would offer me his whole shop on credit before I could pull my note on him.

About the tenth day of my fame I went to fulfil my duty to my flag by paying my respects to the American minister. He received me with the enthusiasm proper in my case, upbraided me for being so tardy in my duty, and said that there was only one way to get his forgiveness, and that was to take the seat at his dinner-party that night made vacant by the illness of one of his guests. I said I would, and we got to talking. It turned out that he and my father had been schoolmates in boyhood, Yale students together later, and always warm friends up to my father's death. So then he required me to put in at his house all the odd time I might have to spare, and I was very willing, of course.

In fact I was more than willing; I was glad. When the crash should come, he might somehow be able to save me from total destruction; I didn't know how, but he might think of a way, maybe. I couldn't venture to unbosom myself to him at this late date, a thing which I would have been quick to do in the beginning of this awful career of mine in London. No, I couldn't venture it now; I was in too deep; that is, too deep for me to be risking revelations to so new a friend, though not clear beyond my depth, as I looked at it. Because, you see, with all my borrowing, I was carefully keeping within my means—I mean within my salary. Of course I couldn't know what my salary was going to be, but I had a good enough basis for an estimate in the fact that, if I won the bet, I was to have choice of any situation in that rich old gentleman's gift provided I was competent—and I should certainly prove competent; I hadn't any doubt about that. And as to the bet, I wasn't worrying about that; I had always been lucky. Now, my estimate of the salary was six hundred to a thousand a year; say, six hundred for the first year, and so on up year by year, till I struck the upper figure by proved merit. At present I was only in debt for my first year's salary. Everybody had been trying to lend me money, but I had fought off the most of them on one pretext or another; so this indebtedness represented only £300 borrowed money, the other £300 represented my keep and my purchases. I believed my second year's salary would carry me through the rest of the month if I went on being cautious and economical, and I intended to look sharply out for that. My month ended, my employer back from his journey, I should be all right once more, for I should at once divide the two years' salary among my creditors by assignment, and get right down to my work.

It was a lovely dinner party of fourteen. The Duke and Duchess of Shoreditch, and their daughter the Lady Anne-Grace-Eleanor-Ce-leste-and-so-forth-and-so-forth-de-Bohun, the Earl and Countess of Newgate, Viscount Cheapside, Lord and Lady Blatherskite, some untitled people of both sexes, the minister and his wife and daughter, and his daughter's visiting friend, an English girl of twenty-two, named Portia Langham, whom I fell in love with in two minutes, and she with me—I could see it without glasses. There was still another guest, an American—but I am a little ahead of my story. While the people were still in the drawing-room, whetting up for dinner, and coldly inspecting the late comers, the servant announced:

'Mr. Lloyd Hastings.'

The moment the usual civilities were over, Hastings caught sight of me, and came straight with cordially outstretched hand; then stopped short when about to shake, and said with an embarrassed look:

'I beg your pardon, sir, I thought I knew you.'

'Why, you do know me, old fellow.'

'No! Are you the—the——?'

'Vest-pocket monster? I am, indeed. Don't be afraid to call me by my nickname; I'm used to it.'

'Well, well, well, this is a surprise. Once or twice I've seen your own name coupled with the nickname, but it never occurred to me that you could be the Henry Adams referred to. Why, it isn't six months since you were clerking away for Blake Hopkins in Frisco on a salary, and sitting up nights on an extra allowance, helping me arrange and verify the Gould and Curry Extension papers and statistics. The idea of your being in London, and a vast millionaire, and a colossal celebrity! Why, it's the Arabian Nights come again. Man, I can't take it in at all; can't realise it; give me time to settle the whirl in my head.'

'The fact is, Lloyd, you are no worse off than I am. I can't realise it myself.'

'Dear me, it is stunning, now, isn't it? Why, it's just three months to-day since we went to the Miners' restaurant——'

'No; the What Cheer.'

'Right, it was the What Cheer; went there at two in the morning, and had a chop and coffee after a hard six hours' grind over those Extension papers, and I tried to persuade you to come to London with me, and offered to get leave of absence for you and pay all your expenses, and give you something over if I succeeded in making the sale; and you would not listen to me, said I wouldn't succeed, and you couldn't afford to lose the run of business and be no end of time getting the hang of things again when you got back home. And yet here you are. How odd it all is! How did you happen to come, and whatever did give you this incredible start?'

'Oh, just an accident. It's a long story—a romance, a body may say. I'll tell you all about it, but not now.'

'When?'

'The end of this month.'

'That's more than a fortnight yet. It's too much of a strain on a person's curiosity. Make it a week.'

'I can't. You'll know why, by and by. But how's the trade getting along?'

His cheerfulness vanished like a breath, and he said with a sigh:

'You were a true prophet, Hal, a true prophet. I wish I hadn't come. I don't want to talk about it.'

'But you must. You must come and stop with me to-night, when we leave here, and tell me all about it.'

'Oh, may I? Are you in earnest?' and the water showed in his eyes.

'Yes; I want to hear the whole story, every word.'

'I'm so grateful! Just to find a human interest once more, in some voice and in some eye, in me and affairs of mine, after what I've been through here—lord! I could go down on my knees for it!'

He gripped my hand hard, and braced up, and was all right and lively after that for the dinner—which didn't come off. No; the usual thing happened, the thing that is always happening under that vicious and aggravating English system—the matter of precedence couldn't be settled, and so there was no dinner. Englishmen always eat dinner before they go out to dinner, because they know the risks they are running; but nobody ever warns the stranger, and so he walks placidly into the trap. Of course nobody was hurt this time, because we had all been to dinner, none of us being novices except Hastings, and he having been informed by the minister at the time that he invited him that in deference to the English custom he had not provided any dinner. Everybody took a lady and processioned down to the dining-room, because it is usual to go through the motions; but there the dispute began. The Duke of Shoreditch wanted to take precedence, and sit at the head of the table, holding that he outranked a minister who represented merely a nation and not a monarch; but I stood for my rights, and refused to yield. In the gossip column I ranked all dukes not royal, and said so, and claimed precedence of this one. It couldn't be settled, of course, struggle as we might and did, he finally (and injudiciously) trying to play birth and antiquity, and I 'seeing' his Conqueror and 'raising' him with Adam, whose direct posterity I was, as shown by my name, while he was of a collateral branch, as shown by his, and by his recent Norman origin; so we all processioned back to the drawing-room again and had a perpendicular lunch—plate of sardines and a strawberry, and you group yourself and stand up and eat it. Here the religion of precedence is not so strenuous; the two persons of highest rank chuck up a shilling, the one that wins has first go at his strawberry, and the loser gets the shilling. The next two chuck up, then the next two, and so on. After refreshment, tables were brought, and we all played cribbage, sixpence a game. The English never play any game for amusement. If they can't make something or lose something—they don't care which—they won't play.

We had a lovely time; certainly two of us had, Miss Langham and I. I was so bewitched with her that I couldn't count my hands if they went above a double sequence; and when I struck home I never discovered it, and started up the outside row again, and would have lost the game every time, only the girl did the same, she being in just my condition, you see; and consequently neither of us ever got out, or cared to wonder why we didn't; we only just knew we were happy, and didn't wish to know anything else, and didn't want to be interrupted. And I told her—I did indeed—told her I loved her; and she—well, she blushed till her hair turned red, but she liked it; she said she did. Oh, there was never such an evening! Every time I pegged I put on a postscript; every time she pegged she acknowledged receipt of it, counting the hands the same. Why, I couldn't even say, 'Two for his heels,' without adding, 'My, how sweet you do look!' And she would say, 'Fifteen two, fifteen four, fifteen six, and a pair are eight, and eight are sixteen—do you think so?' peeping out aslant from under her lashes, you know, so sweet and cunning. Oh, it was just too-too!

Well, I was perfectly honest and square with her; told her I hadn't a cent in the world but just the million-pound note she'd heard so much talk about, and it didn't belong to me; and that started her curiosity, and then I talked low, and told her the whole history right from the start, and it nearly killed her, laughing. What in the nation she could find to laugh about, I couldn't see, but there it was; every half minute some new detail would fetch her, and I would have to stop as much as a minute and a half to give her a chance to settle down again. Why, she laughed herself lame, she did indeed; I never saw anything like it. I mean I never saw a painful story—a story of a person's troubles and worries and fears—produce just that kind of effect before. So I loved her all the more, seeing she could be so cheerful when there wasn't anything to be cheerful about; for I might soon need that kind of wife, you know, the way things looked. Of course I told her we should have to wait a couple of years, till I could catch up on my salary; but she didn't mind that, only she hoped I would be as careful as possible in the matter of expenses, and not let them run the least risk of trenching on our third year's pay. Then she began to get a little worried, and wondered if we were making any mistake, and starting the salary on a higher figure for the first year than I would get. This was good sense, and it made me feel a little less confident than I had been feeling before; but it gave me a good business idea, and I brought it frankly out.

'Portia, dear, would you mind going with me that day, when I confront those old gentlemen?'

She shrank a little, but said:

'N-o; if my being with you would help hearten you. But—would it be quite proper, do you think?'

'No, I don't know that it would; in fact, I'm afraid it wouldn't; but, you see, there's so much dependent upon it that——'

'Then I'll go anyway, proper or improper,' she said, with a beautiful and generous enthusiasm. 'Oh, I shall be so happy to think I'm helping.'

'Helping, dear? Why, you'll be doing it all. You're so beautiful, and so lovely, and so winning, that with you there I can pile our salary up till I break those good old fellows, and they'll never have the heart to struggle.'

Sho! you should have seen the rich blood mount, and her happy eyes shine!

'You wicked flatterer! There isn't a word of truth in what you say, but still I'll go with you. Maybe it will teach you not to expect other people to look with your eyes.'

Were my doubts dissipated? Was my confidence restored? You may judge by this fact: privately I raised my salary to twelve hundred the first year on the spot. But I didn't tell her; I saved it for a surprise.

All the way home I was in the clouds, Hastings talking, I not hearing a word. When he and I entered my parlour he brought me to myself with his fervent appreciations of my manifold comforts and luxuries.

'Let me just stand here a little and look my fill! Dear me, it's a palace; it's just a palace! And in it everything a body could desire, including cozy coal fire and supper standing ready. Henry, it doesn't merely make me realise how rich you are; it makes me realise to the bone, to the marrow, how poor I am—how poor I am—and how miserable, how defeated, routed, annihilated!'

Plague take it! this language gave me the cold shudders. It scared me broad awake, and made me comprehend that I was standing on a half-inch crust, with a crater underneath. I didn't know I had been dreaming—that is, I hadn't been allowing myself to know it for a while back; but now—oh, dear! Deep in debt, not a cent in the world, a lovely girl's happiness or woe in my hands, and nothing in front of me but a salary which might never—oh, would never—materialise! Oh, oh, oh, I am ruined past hope; nothing can save me!

'Henry, the mere unconsidered drippings of your daily income would——'

'Oh, my daily income! Here, down with this hot Scotch, and cheer up your soul. Here's with you! Or, no—you're hungry; sit down and——'

'Not a bite for me; I'm past it. I can't eat, these days; but I'll drink with you till I drop. Come!'

'Barrel for barrel, I'm with you! Ready! Here we go! Now, then, Lloyd, unreel your story while I brew.'

'Unreel it? What, again?'

'Again? What do you mean by that?'

'Why, I mean do you want to hear it over again?'

'Do I want to hear it over again? This is a puzzler. Wait; don't take any more of that liquid. You don't need it.'

'Look here, Henry, you alarm me. Didn't I tell you the whole story on the way here?'

'You?'

'Yes, I.'

'I'll be hanged if I heard a word of it.'

'Henry, this is a serious thing. It troubles me. What did you take up yonder at the minister's?'

Then it all flashed on me, and I owned up, like a man.

'I took the dearest girl in this world—prisoner!'

So then he came with a rush, and we shook, and shook, and shook till our hands ached; and he didn't blame me for not having heard a word of a story which had lasted while we walked three miles. He just sat down then, like the patient, good fellow he was, and told it all over again. Synopsised, it amounted to this: He had come to England with what he thought was a grand opportunity; he had an 'option' to sell the Gould and Curry Extension for the 'locators' of it, and keep all he could get over a million dollars. He had worked hard, had pulled every wire he knew of, had left no honest expedient untried, had spent nearly all the money he had in the world, had not been able to get a solitary capitalist to listen to him, and his option would run out at the end of the month. In a word, he was ruined. Then he jumped up and cried out:

'Henry, you can save me! You can save me, and you're the only man in the universe that can. Will you do it? Won't you do it?'

'Tell me how. Speak out, my boy.'

'Give me a million and my passage home for my 'option'! Don't, don't refuse!'

I was in a kind of agony. I was right on the point of coming out with the words, 'Lloyd, I'm a pauper myself—absolutely penniless, and in debt!' But a white-hot idea came flaming through my head, and I gripped my jaws together, and calmed myself down till I was as cold as a capitalist. Then I said, in a commercial and self-possessed way:

'I will save you, Lloyd——'

'Then I'm already saved! God be merciful to you for ever! If ever I——'

'Let me finish, Lloyd. I will save you, but not in that way; for that would not be fair to you, after your hard work, and the risks you've run. I don't need to buy mines; I can keep my capital moving, in a commercial centre like London, without that; it's what I'm at, all the time; but here is what I'll do. I know all about that mine, of course; I know its immense value, and can swear to it if anybody wishes it. You shall sell out inside of the fortnight for three millions cash, using my name freely, and we'll divide, share and share alike.'

Do you know, he would have danced the furniture to kindling-wood, in his insane joy, and broken everything on the place, if I hadn't tripped him up and tied him.

Then he lay there, perfectly happy, saying:

'I may use your name! Your name—think of it! Man, they'll flock in droves, these rich Londoners; they'll fight for that stock! I'm a made man, I'm a made man for ever, and I'll never forget you as long as I live!'

In less than twenty-four hours London was abuzz! I hadn't anything to do, day after day, but sit at home, and say to all comers:

'Yes; I told him to refer to me. I know the man and I know the mine. His character is above reproach, and the mine is worth far more than he asks for it.'

Meantime I spent all my evenings at the minister's with Portia. I didn't say a word to her about the mine; I saved it for a surprise. We talked salary; never anything but salary and love; sometimes love, sometimes salary, sometimes love and salary together. And my! the interest the minister's wife and daughter took in our little affair, and the endless ingenuities they invented to save us from interruption, and to keep the minister in the dark and unsuspicious—well, it was just lovely of them!

When the month was up, at last, I had a million dollars to my credit in the London and County Bank, and Hastings was fixed in the same way. Dressed at my level best, I drove by the house in Portland Place, judged by the look of things that my birds were home again, went on towards the minister's and got my precious, and we started back, talking salary with all our might. She was so excited and anxious that it made her just intolerably beautiful. I said:

'Dearie, the way you're looking it's a crime to strike for a salary a single penny under three thousand a year.'

'Henry, Henry, you'll ruin us!'

'Don't you be afraid. Just keep up those looks, and trust to me. It'll all come out right.'

So, as it turned out, I had to keep bolstering up her courage all the way. She kept pleading with me, and saying:

'Oh, please remember that if we ask for too much we may get no salary at all; and then what will become of us, with no way in the world to earn our living?'

We were ushered in by that same servant, and there they were, the two old gentlemen. Of course they were surprised to see that wonderful creature with me, but I said:

'It's all right, gentlemen; she is my future stay and help-mate.'

And I introduced them to her, and called them by name. It didn't surprise them; they knew I would know enough to consult the directory. They seated us, and were very polite to me, and very solicitous to relieve her from embarrassment, and put her as much at her ease as they could. Then I said:

'Gentlemen, I am ready to report.'

'We are glad to hear it,' said my man, 'for now we can decide the bet which my brother Abel and I made. If you have won for me, you shall have any situation in my gift. Have you the million-pound note?'

'Here it is, sir,' and I handed it to him.

'I've won!' he shouted, and slapped Abel on the back. 'Now what do you say, brother?'

'I say he did survive, and I've lost twenty thousand pounds. I never would have believed it.'

'I've a further report to make,' I said, 'and a pretty long one. I want you to let me come soon, and detail my whole month's history; and I promise you it's worth hearing. Meantime, take a look at that.'

'What, man! Certificate of deposit for £200,000? Is it yours?'

'Mine! I earned it by thirty days' judicious use of that little loan you let me have. And the only use I made of it was to buy trifles and offer the bill in change.'

'Come, this is astonishing! It's incredible, man!'

'Never mind, I'll prove it. Don't take my word unsupported.'

But now Portia's turn was come to be surprised. Her eyes were spread wide, and she said:

'Henry, is that really your money? Have you been fibbing to me?'

'I have indeed, dearie. But you'll forgive me, I know.'

She put up an arch pout, and said:

'Don't you be so sure. You are a naughty thing to deceive me so!'

'Oh, you'll get over it, sweetheart, you'll get over it; it was only fun, you know. Come, let's be going.'

'But wait, wait! The situation, you know. I want to give you the situation,' said my man.

'Well,' I said, 'I'm just as grateful as I can be, but really I don't want one.'

'But you can have the very choicest one in my gift.'

'Thanks again, with all my heart; but I don't even want that one.'

'Henry, I'm ashamed of you. You don't half thank the good gentleman. May I do it for you?'

'Indeed you shall, dear, if you can improve it. Let us see you try.'

She walked to my man, got up in his lap, put her arm round his neck, and kissed him right on the mouth. Then the two old gentlemen shouted with laughter, but I was dumfounded, just petrified, as you may say. Portia said:

'Papa, he has said you haven't a situation in your gift that he'd take; and I feel just as hurt as——'

'My darling! is that your papa?'

'Yes; he's my step-papa, and the dearest one that ever was. You understand now, don't you, why I was able to laugh when you told me at the minister's, not knowing my relationships, what trouble and worry papa's and Uncle Abel's scheme was giving you?'

Of course I spoke right up, now, without any fooling, and went straight to the point.

'Oh, my dearest dear sir, I want to take back what I said. You have got a situation open that I want.'

'Name it.'

'Son-in-law.'

'Well, well, well! But you know, if you haven't ever served in that capacity, you of course can't furnish recommendations of a sort to satisfy the conditions of the contract, and so——'

'Try me—oh, do, I beg of you! Only just try me thirty or forty years, and if——'

'Oh, well, all right; it's but a little thing to ask. Take her along.'

Happy, we too? There are not words enough in the unabridged to describe it. And when London got the whole history, a day or two later, of my month's adventures with that bank-note, and how they ended, did London talk, and have a good time? Yes.

My Portia's papa took that friendly and hospitable bill back to the Bank of England and cashed it; then the Bank cancelled it and made him a present of it, and he gave it to us at our wedding, and it has always hung in its frame in the sacredest place in our home, ever since. For it gave me my Portia. But for it I could not have remained in London, would not have appeared at the minister's, never should have met her. And so I always say, 'Yes, it's a million-pounder, as you see; but it never made but one purchase in its life, and then got the article for only about a tenth part of its value.'

THE LAST LEAF

O. HENRY

First published in *The New York World*, 1905.

In a little district west of Washington Square the streets have run crazy and broken themselves into small strips called "places." These "places" make strange angles and curves. One Street crosses itself a time or two. An artist once discovered a valuable possibility in this street. Suppose a collector with a bill for paints, paper and canvas should, in traversing this route, suddenly meet himself coming back, without a cent having been paid on account!

So, to quaint old Greenwich Village the art people soon came prowling, hunting for north windows and eighteenth-century gables and Dutch attics and low rents. Then they imported some pewter mugs and a chafing dish or two from Sixth Avenue, and became a "colony."

At the top of a squatty, three-story brick Sue and Johnsy had their studio. "Johnsy" was familiar for Joanna. One was from Maine; the other from California. They had met at the table d'hôte of an Eighth Street "Delmonico's," and found their tastes in art, chicory salad and bishop sleeves so congenial that the joint studio resulted.

That was in May. In November a cold, unseen stranger, whom the doctors called Pneumonia, stalked about the colony, touching one here and there with his icy fingers. Over on the east side this ravager strode boldly, smiting his victims by scores, but his feet trod slowly through the maze of the narrow and moss-grown "places."

Mr. Pneumonia was not what you would call a chivalric old gentleman. A mite of a little woman with blood thinned by California zephyrs was hardly fair game for the red-fisted, short-breathed old duffer. But Johnsy he smote; and she lay, scarcely moving, on her painted iron bedstead, looking through the small Dutch window-panes at the blank side of the next brick house.

One morning the busy doctor invited Sue into the hallway with a shaggy, grey eyebrow.

"She has one chance in - let us say, ten," he said, as he shook down the mercury in his clinical thermometer. " And that chance is for her to want to live. This way people have of lining-up on the side of the undertaker makes the entire pharmacopoeia look silly. Your little lady has made up her mind that she's not going to get well. Has she anything on her mind?"

"She - she wanted to paint the Bay of Naples some day." said Sue.

"Paint? - bosh! Has she anything on her mind worth think-ing twice - a man for instance?"

"A man?" said Sue, with a jew's-harp twang in her voice. "Is a man worth - but, no, doctor; there is nothing of the kind."

"Well, it is the weakness, then," said the doctor. "I will do all that science, so far as it may filter through my efforts, can accomplish. But whenever my patient begins to count the carriages in her funeral procession I subtract 50 per cent from the curative power of medicines. If you will get her to ask one question about the new winter styles in cloak sleeves I will promise you a one-in-five chance for her, instead of one in ten."

After the doctor had gone Sue went into the workroom and cried a Japanese napkin to a pulp. Then she swaggered into Johnsy's room with her drawing board, whistling ragtime.

Johnsy lay, scarcely making a ripple under the bedclothes, with her face toward the window. Sue stopped whistling, thinking she was asleep.

She arranged her board and began a pen-and-ink drawing to illustrate a magazine story. Young artists must pave their way to Art by drawing pictures for magazine stories that young authors write to pave their way to Literature.

As Sue was sketching a pair of elegant horseshow riding trousers and a monocle of the figure of the hero, an Idaho cowboy, she heard a low sound, several times repeated. She went quickly to the bedside.

Johnsy's eyes were open wide. She was looking out the window and counting - counting backward.

"Twelve," she said, and little later "eleven"; and then "ten," and "nine"; and then "eight" and "seven", almost together.

Sue look solicitously out of the window. What was there to count? There was only a bare, dreary yard to be seen, and the blank side of the brick house twenty feet away. An old, old ivy vine, gnarled and decayed at the roots, climbed half way up the brick wall. The cold breath of autumn had stricken its leaves from the vine until its skeleton branches clung, almost bare, to the crumbling bricks.

"What is it, dear?" asked Sue.

"Six," said Johnsy, in almost a whisper. "They're falling faster now. Three days ago there were almost a hundred. It made my head ache to count them. But now it's easy. There goes another one. There are only five left now."

"Five what, dear? Tell your Sudie."

"Leaves. On the ivy vine. When the last one falls I must go, too. I've known that for three days. Didn't the doctor tell you?"

"Oh, I never heard of such nonsense," complained Sue, with magnificent scorn. "What have old ivy leaves to do with your getting well? And you used to love that vine so, you naughty girl. Don't be a goosey. Why, the doctor told me this morning that your chances for getting well real soon were - let's see exactly what he said - he said the chances were ten to one! Why, that's almost as good a chance as we have in New York when we ride on the street cars or walk past a new building. Try to take some broth now, and let Sudie go back to her drawing, so she can sell the editor man with it, and buy port wine for her sick child, and pork chops for her greedy self."

"You needn't get any more wine," said Johnsy, keeping her eyes fixed out the window. "There goes another. No, I don't want any broth. That leaves just four. I want to see the last one fall before it gets dark. Then I'll go, too."

"Johnsy, dear," said Sue, bending over her, "will you promise me to keep your eyes closed, and not look out the window until I am done working? I must hand those drawings in by to-morrow. I need the light, or I would draw the shade down."

"Couldn't you draw in the other room?" asked Johnsy, coldly.

"I'd rather be here by you," said Sue. "Beside, I don't want you to keep looking at those silly ivy leaves."

"Tell me as soon as you have finished," said Johnsy, closing her eyes, and lying white and still as fallen statue, "because I want to see the last one fall. I'm tired of waiting. I'm tired of thinking. I want to turn loose my hold on everything, and go sailing down, down, just like one of those poor, tired leaves."

"Try to sleep," said Sue. "I must call Behrman up to be my model for the old hermit miner. I'll not be gone a minute. Don't try to move 'til I come back."

Old Behrman was a painter who lived on the ground floor beneath them. He was past sixty and had a Michael Angelo's Moses beard curling down from the head of a satyr along with the body of an imp. Behrman was a failure in art. Forty years he had wielded the brush without getting near enough to touch the hem of his Mistress's robe. He had been always about to paint a masterpiece, but had never yet begun it. For several years he had painted nothing except now and then a daub in the line of commerce or advertising. He earned a little by serving as a model to those young artists in the colony who could not pay the price of a professional. He drank gin to excess, and still talked of his coming masterpiece. For the rest he was a fierce little old man, who scoffed terribly at softness in any one, and who regarded himself as especial mastiff-in-waiting to protect the two young artists in the studio above.

Sue found Behrman smelling strongly of juniper berries in his dimly lighted den below. In one corner was a blank canvas on an easel that had been waiting there for twenty-five years to receive the first line of the masterpiece. She told him of Johnsy's fancy, and how she feared she would, indeed, light and fragile as a leaf herself, float away, when her slight hold upon the world grew weaker.

Old Behrman, with his red eyes plainly streaming, shouted his contempt and derision for such idiotic imaginings.

"Vass!" he cried. "Is dere people in de world mit der foolishness to die because leafs dey drop off from a confounded vine? I haf not heard of such a thing. No, I will not pose as a model for your fool hermit-dunderhead. Vy do you allow dot silly pusiness to come in der brain of her? Ach, dot poor leetle Miss Yohnsy."

"She is very ill and weak," said Sue, "and the fever has left her mind morbid and full of strange fancies. Very well, Mr. Behrman, if you do not care to pose for me, you needn't. But I think you are a horrid old - old flibbertigibbet."

"You are just like a woman!" yelled Behrman. "Who said I will not pose? Go on. I come mit you. For half an hour I haf peen trying to say dot I am ready to pose. Gott! dis is not any blace in which one so goot as Miss Yohnsy shall lie sick. Some day I vill baint a masterpiece, and ve shall all go away. Gott! yes."

Johnsy was sleeping when they went upstairs. Sue pulled the shade down to the window-sill, and motioned Behrman into the other room. In there they peered out the window fearfully at the ivy vine. Then they looked at each other for a moment without speaking. A persistent, cold rain was falling, mingled with snow. Behrman, in his old blue shirt, took his seat as the hermit miner on an upturned kettle for a rock.

When Sue awoke from an hour's sleep the next morning she found Johnsy with dull, wide-open eyes staring at the drawn green shade.

"Pull it up; I want to see," she ordered, in a whisper.

Wearily Sue obeyed.

But, lo! after the beating rain and fierce gusts of wind that had endured through the livelong night, there yet stood out against the brick wall one ivy leaf. It was the last one on the vine. Still dark green near its stem, with its serrated edges tinted with the yellow of dissolution and decay, it hung bravely from the branch some twenty feet above the ground.

"It is the last one," said Johnsy. "I thought it would surely fall during the night. I heard the wind. It will fall to-day, and I shall die at the same time."

"Dear, dear!" said Sue, leaning her worn face down to the pillow, "think of me, if you won't think of yourself. What would I do?"

But Johnsy did not answer. The lonesomest thing in all the world is a soul when it is making ready to go on its mysterious, far journey. The fancy seemed to possess her more strongly as one by one the ties that bound her to friendship and to earth were loosed.

The day wore away, and even through the twilight they could see the lone ivy leaf clinging to its stem against the wall. And then, with the coming of the night the north wind was again loosed, while the rain still beat against the windows and pattered down from the low Dutch eaves.

When it was light enough Johnsy, the merciless, commanded that the shade be raised.

The ivy leaf was still there.

Johnsy lay for a long time looking at it. And then she called to Sue, who was stirring her chicken broth over the gas stove.

"I've been a bad girl, Sudie," said Johnsy. "Something has made that last leaf stay there to show me how wicked I was. It is a sin to want to die. You may bring a me a little broth now, and some milk with a little port in it, and - no; bring me a hand-mirror first, and then pack some pillows about me, and I will sit up and watch you cook."

An hour later she said:

"Sudie, some day I hope to paint the Bay of Naples."

The doctor came in the afternoon, and Sue had an excuse to go into the hallway as he left.

"Even chances," said the doctor, taking Sue's thin, shaking hand in his. "With good nursing you'll win." And now I must see another case I have downstairs. Behrman, his name is - some kind of an artist, I believe. Pneumonia, too. He is an old, weak man, and the attack is acute. There is no hope for him; but he goes to the hospital to-day to be made more comfortable."

The next day the doctor said to Sue: "She's out of danger. You won. Nutrition and care now - that's all."

And that afternoon Sue came to the bed where Johnsy lay, contentedly knitting a very blue and very useless woollen shoulder scarf, and put one arm around her, pillows and all.

"I have something to tell you, white mouse," she said. "Mr. Behrman died of pneumonia to-day in the hospital. He was ill only two days. The janitor found him the morning of the first day in his room downstairs helpless with pain. His shoes and clothing were wet through and icy cold. They couldn't imagine where he had been on such a dreadful night. And then they found a lantern, still lighted, and a ladder that had been dragged from its place, and some scattered brushes, and a palette with green and yellow colours mixed on it, and - look out the window, dear, at the last ivy leaf on the wall. Didn't you wonder why it never fluttered or moved when the wind blew? Ah, darling, it's Behrman's masterpiece - he painted it there the night that the last leaf fell."

F. Scott Fitzgerald

F. Scott Fitzgerald (1896–1940) was an American novelist and short-story writer whose lyrical prose and romantic sensibility defined the Jazz Age. Born in St. Paul, Minnesota, he attended Princeton before joining the U.S. Army during World War I. Fearing he might die in battle, he wrote feverishly, producing the early draft of what would later become his first novel, *This Side of Paradise*. The awareness of his own mortality would echo throughout his work, infusing it with a sense of urgency, beauty, and loss. Fitzgerald found instant fame after the war, and his later masterpiece *The Great Gatsby* (1925) secured his place among America's finest stylists. His writing shimmers with longing, music, and the ache of lost youth. Fitzgerald's own battles with alcohol and financial ruin shadowed his later years, yet his evocation of fleeting beauty and lost illusions endures in bestselling editions and silver-screen revivals worldwide.*The Offshore Pirate* (1920) is an early romantic adventure where charm, rebellion, and desire collide beneath the bright sun of new beginnings.

THE OFFSHORE PIRATE

F. SCOTT FITZGERALD

First published in *The Saturday Evening Post*, 1920.

I

This unlikely story begins on a sea that was a blue dream, as colorful as blue-silk stockings, and beneath a sky as blue as the irises of children's eyes. From the western half of the sky the sun was shying little golden disks at the sea—if you gazed intently enough you could see them skip from wave tip to wave tip until they joined a broad collar of golden coin that was collecting half a mile out and would eventually be a dazzling sunset. About half-way between the Florida shore and the golden collar a white steam-yacht, very young and graceful, was riding at anchor and under a blue-and-white awning aft a yellow-haired girl reclined in a wicker settee reading The Revolt of the Angels, by Anatole France.

She was about nineteen, slender and supple, with a spoiled alluring mouth and quick gray eyes full of a radiant curiosity. Her feet, stockingless, and adorned rather than clad in blue-satin slippers which swung nonchalantly from her toes, were perched on the arm of a settee adjoining the one she occupied. And as she read she intermittently regaled herself by a faint application to her tongue of a half-lemon that she held in her hand. The other half, sucked dry, lay on the deck at her feet and rocked very gently to and fro at the almost imperceptible motion of the tide.

The second half-lemon was well-nigh pulpless and the golden collar had grown astonishing in width, when suddenly the drowsy silence which enveloped the yacht was broken by the sound of heavy footsteps and an elderly man topped with orderly gray hair and clad in a white-flannel suit appeared at the head of the companionway. There he paused for a moment until his eyes became accustomed to the sun, and then seeing the girl under the awning he uttered a long even grunt of disapproval.

If he had intended thereby to obtain a rise of any sort he was doomed to disappointment. The girl calmly turned over two pages, turned back one, raised the lemon mechanically to tasting distance, and then very faintly but quite unmistakably yawned.

"Ardita!" said the gray-haired man sternly.

Ardita uttered a small sound indicating nothing.

"Ardita!" he repeated. "Ardita!"

Ardita raised the lemon languidly, allowing three words to slip out before it reached her tongue.

"Oh, shut up."

"Ardita!"

"What?"

"Will you listen to me—or will I have to get a servant to hold you while I talk to you?"

The lemon descended very slowly and scornfully.

"Put it in writing."

"Will you have the decency to close that abominable book and discard that damn lemon for two minutes?"

"Oh, can't you lemme alone for a second?"

"Ardita, I have just received a telephone message from the shore—"

"Telephone?" She showed for the first time a faint interest.

"Yes, it was—"

"Do you mean to say," she interrupted wonderingly, "'at they let you run a wire out here?"

"Yes, and just now—"

"Won't other boats bump into it?"

"No. It's run along the bottom. Five min—"

"Well, I'll be darned! Gosh! Science is golden or something—isn't it?"

"Will you let me say what I started to?"

"Shoot!"

"Well it seems—well, I am up here—" He paused and swallowed several times distractedly. "Oh, yes. Young woman, Colonel Moreland has called up again to ask me to be sure to bring you in to dinner. His son Toby has come all the way from New York to meet you and he's invited several other young people. For the last time, will you—"

"No," said Ardita shortly, "I won't. I came along on this darn cruise with the one idea of going to Palm Beach, and you knew it, and I absolutely refuse to meet any darn old colonel or any darn young Toby or any darn old young people or to set foot in any other darn old town in this crazy state. So you either take me to Palm Beach or else shut up and go away."

"Very well. This is the last straw. In your infatuation for this man.—a man who is notorious for his excesses—a man your father would not have allowed to so much as mention your name—you have rejected the demi-monde rather than the circles in which you have presumably grown up. From now on—"

"I know," interrupted Ardita ironically, "from now on you go your way and I go mine. I've heard that story before. You know I'd like nothing better."

"From now on," he announced grandiloquently, "you are no niece of mine. I—"

"O-o-o-oh!" The cry was wrung from Ardita with the agony of a lost soul. "Will you stop boring me! Will you go 'way! Will you jump overboard and drown! Do you want me to throw this book at you!"

"If you dare do any—"

Smack! The Revolt of the Angels sailed through the air, missed its target by the length of a short nose, and bumped cheerfully down the companionway.

The gray-haired man made an instinctive step backward and then two cautious steps forward. Ardita jumped to her five feet four and stared at him defiantly, her gray eyes blazing.

"Keep off!"

"How dare you!" he cried.

"Because I darn please!"

"You've grown unbearable! Your disposition—"

"You've made me that way! No child ever has a bad disposition unless it's her fancy's fault! Whatever I am, you did it."

Muttering something under his breath her uncle turned and, walking forward called in a loud voice for the launch. Then he returned to the awning, where Ardita had again seated herself and resumed her attention to the lemon.

"I am going ashore," he said slowly. "I will be out again at nine o'clock to-night. When I return we start back to New York, wither I shall turn you over to your aunt for the rest of your natural, or rather unnatural, life." He paused and looked at her, and then all at once something in the utter childness of her beauty seemed to puncture his anger like an inflated tire, and render him helpless, uncertain, utterly fatuous.

"Ardita," he said not unkindly, "I'm no fool. I've been round. I know men. And, child, confirmed libertines don't reform until they're tired—and then they're not themselves—they're husks of themselves." He looked at her as if expecting agreement, but receiving no sight or sound of it he continued. "Perhaps the man loves you—that's possible. He's loved many women and he'll love many more. Less than a month ago, one month, Ardita, he was involved in a notorious affair with that red-haired woman, Mimi Merril; promised to give her the diamond bracelet that the Czar of Russia gave his mother. You know—you read the papers."

"Thrilling scandals by an anxious uncle," yawned Ardita. "Have it filmed. Wicked clubman making eyes at virtuous flapper. Virtuous flapper conclusively vamped by his lurid past. Plans to meet him at Palm Beach. Foiled by anxious uncle."

"Will you tell me why the devil you want to marry him?"

"I'm sure I couldn't say," said Ardita shortly. "Maybe because he's the only man I know, good or bad, who has an imagination and the courage of his convictions. Maybe it's to get away from the young fools that spend their vacuous hours pursuing me around the country. But as for the famous Russian bracelet, you can set your mind at rest on that score.

He's going to give it to me at Palm Beach—if you'll show a little intelligence."

"How about the—red-haired woman?"

"He hasn't seen her for six months," she said angrily. "Don't you suppose I have enough pride to see to that? Don't you know by this time that I can do any darn thing with any darn man I want to?"

She put her chin in the air like the statue of France Aroused, and then spoiled the pose somewhat by raising the lemon for action.

"Is it the Russian bracelet that fascinates you?"

"No, I'm merely trying to give you the sort of argument that would appeal to your intelligence. And I wish you'd go 'way," she said, her temper rising again. "You know I never change my mind. You've been boring me for three days until I'm about to go crazy. I won't go ashore! Won't! Do you hear? Won't!"

"Very well," he said, "and you won't go to Palm Beach either. Of all the selfish, spoiled, uncontrolled disagreeable, impossible girl I have—"

Splush! The half-lemon caught him in the neck. Simultaneously came a hail from over the side.

"The launch is ready, Mr. Farnam."

Too full of words and rage to speak, Mr. Farnam cast one utterly condemning glance at his niece and, turning, ran swiftly down the ladder.

II

Five o'clock robed down from the sun and plumped soundlessly into the sea. The golden collar widened into a glittering island; and a faint breeze that had been playing with the edges of the awning and swaying one of the dangling blue slippers became suddenly freighted with song. It was a chorus of men in close harmony and in perfect rhythm to an accompanying sound of oars dealing the blue writers. Ardita lifted her head and listened.

"Carrots and Peas,
Beans on their knees,
Pigs in the seas,
Lucky fellows!
Blow us a breeze,
Blow us a breeze,
Blow us a breeze,
With your bellows."

Ardita's brow wrinkled in astonishment. Sitting very still she listened eagerly as the chorus took up a second verse.

"Onions and beans,
Marshalls and Deans,
Goldbergs and Greens
And Costellos.
Blow us a breeze,
Blow us a breeze,
Blow us a breeze,
With your bellows."

With an exclamation she tossed her book to the desk, where it sprawled at a straddle, and hurried to the rail. Fifty feet away a large rowboat was approaching containing seven men, six of them rowing and one standing up in the stern keeping time to their song with an orchestra leader's baton.

"Oysters and Rocks,
Sawdust and socks,

Who could make clocks
Out of cellos?—"

The leader's eyes suddenly rested on Ardita, who was leaning over the rail spellbound with curiosity. He made a quick
movement with his baton and the singing instantly ceased.
She saw that he was the only white man in the boat—the six
rowers were negroes.

"Narcissus ahoy!" he called politely.

"What's the idea of all the discord?" demanded Ardita
cheerfully. "Is this the varsity crew from the county nut
farm?"

By this time the boat was scraping the side of the yacht and
a great bulking negro in the bow turned round and grasped
the ladder. Thereupon the leader left his position in the stern
and before Ardita had realized his intention he ran up the
ladder and stood breathless before her on the deck.

"The women and children will be spared!" he said briskly.
"All crying babies will be immediately drowned and all males
put in double irons!" Digging her hands excitedly down into
the pockets of her dress Ardita stared at him, speechless with
astonishment. He was a young man with a scornful mouth
and the bright blue eyes of a healthy baby set in a dark
sensitive face. His hair was pitch black, damp and curly—the
hair of a Grecian statue gone brunette. He was trimly built,
trimly dressed, and graceful as an agile quarter-back.

"Well, I'll be a son of a gun!" she said dazedly.

They eyed each other coolly.

"Do you surrender the ship?"

"Is this an outburst of wit?" demanded Ardita. "Are you an
idiot—or just being initiated to some fraternity?"

"I asked you if you surrendered the ship."

"I thought the country was dry," said Ardita disdainfully. "Have you been drinking finger-nail enamel? You better get off this yacht!"

"What?" the young man's voice expressed incredulity.

"Get off the yacht! You heard me!"

He looked at her for a moment as if considering what she had said.

"No," said his scornful mouth slowly; "No, I won't get off the yacht. You can get off if you wish."

Going to the rail be gave a curt command and immediately the crew of the rowboat scrambled up the ladder and ranged themselves in line before him, a coal-black and burly darky at one end and a miniature mulatto of four feet nine at to other. They seemed to be uniformly dressed in some sort of blue costume ornamented with dust, mud, and tatters; over the shoulder of each was slung a small, heavy-looking white sack, and under their arms they carried large black cases apparently containing musical instruments.

"'Ten-*shun*!" commanded the young man, snapping his own heels together crisply. "Right *driss*! Front! Step out here, Babe!"

The smallest Negro took a quick step forward and saluted.

"Take command, go down below, catch the crew and tie 'em up—all except the engineer. Bring him up to me. Oh, and pile those bags by the rail there."

"Yas-suh!"

Babe saluted again and wheeling about motioned for the five others to gather about him. Then after a short whispered consultation they all filed noiselessly down the companion-way.

"Now," said the young man cheerfully to Ardita, who had witnessed this last scene in withering silence, "if you will swear on your honor as a flapper—which probably isn't worth much—that you'll keep that spoiled little mouth of yours tight shut for forty-eight hours, you can row yourself ashore in our rowboat."

"Otherwise what?"

"Otherwise you're going to sea in a ship."

With a little sigh as for a crisis well passed, the young man sank into the settee Ardita had lately vacated and stretched his arms lazily. The corners of his mouth relaxed appreciatively as he looked round at the rich striped awning, the polished brass, and the luxurious fittings of the deck. His eye felt on the book, and then on the exhausted lemon.

"Hm," he said, "Stonewall Jackson claimed that lemon-juice cleared his head. Your head feel pretty clear?"

Ardita disdained to answer.

"Because inside of five minutes you'll have to make a clear decision whether it's go or stay."

He picked up the book and opened it curiously.

"The Revolt of the Angels. Sounds pretty good. French, eh?" He stared at her with new interest "You French?"

"No."

"What's your name?"

"Farnam."

"Farnam what?"

"Ardita Farnam."

"Well Ardita, no use standing up there and chewing out the insides of your mouth. You ought to break those nervous habits while you're young. Come over here and sit down."

Ardita took a carved jade case from her pocket, extracted a cigarette and lit it with a conscious coolness, though she knew her hand was trembling a little; then she crossed over with her supple, swinging walk, and sitting down in the other settee blew a mouthful of smoke at the awning.

"You can't get me off this yacht," she raid steadily; "and you haven't got very much sense if you think you'll get far with it. My uncle'll have wirelesses zigzagging all over this ocean by half past six."

"Hm."

She looked quickly at his face, caught anxiety stamped there plainly in the faintest depression of the mouth's corners.

"It's all the same to me," she said, shrugging her shoulders. "'Tisn't my yacht. I don't mind going for a coupla hours' cruise. I'll even lend you that book so you'll have something to read on the revenue boat that takes you up to Sing-Sing."

He laughed scornfully.

"If that's advice you needn't bother. This is part of a plan arranged before I ever knew this yacht existed. If it hadn't been this one it'd have been the next one we passed anchored along the coast."

"Who are you?" demanded Ardita suddenly. "And what are you?"

"You've decided not to go ashore?"

"I never even faintly considered it."

"We're generally known," he said "all seven of us, as Curtis Carlyle and his Six Black Buddies late of the Winter Garden and the Midnight Frolic."

"You're singers?"

"We were until to-day. At present, due to those white bags you see there we're fugitives from justice and if the reward offered for our capture hasn't by this time reached twenty thousand dollars I miss my guess."

"What's in the bags?" asked Ardita curiously.

"Well," he said "for the present we'll call it—mud—Florida mud."

III

Within ten minutes after Curtis Carlyle's interview with a very frightened engineer the yacht Narcissus was under way, steaming south through a balmy tropical twilight. The little mulatto, Babe, who seems to have Carlyle's implicit confidence, took full command of the situation. Mr. Farnam's valet and the chef, the only members of the crew on board except the engineer, having shown fight, were now reconsidering, strapped securely to their bunks below. Trombone Mose, the biggest negro, was set busy with a can of paint obliterating the name Narcissus from the bow, and substituting the name Hula Hula, and the others congregated aft and became intently involved in a game of craps.

Having given order for a meal to be prepared and served on deck at seven-thirty, Carlyle rejoined Ardita, and, sinking back into his settee, half closed his eyes and fell into a state of profound abstraction.

Ardita scrutinized him carefully—and classed him immediately as a romantic figure. He gave the effect of towering self-confidence erected on a slight foundation—just under the surface of each of his decisions she discerned a hesitancy that was in decided contrast to the arrogant curl of his lips.

"He's not like me," she thought "There's a difference some-where." Being a supreme egotist Ardita frequently thought about herself; never having had her egotism disputed she did it entirely naturally and with no detraction from her unquestioned charm. Though she was nineteen she gave the effect of a high-spirited precocious child, and in the present glow of her youth and beauty all the men and women she had known were but driftwood on the ripples of her temperament. She had met other egotists—in fact she found that selfish people bored her rather less than unselfish peo-ple—but as yet there had not been one she had not eventually defeated and brought to her feet.

But though she recognized an egotist in the settee, she felt none of that usual shutting of doors in her mind which meant clearing ship for action; on the contrary her instinct told her that this man was somehow completely pregnable and quite defenseless. When Ardita defied convention—and of late it had been her chief amusement—it was from an intense desire to be herself, and she felt that this man, on the contrary, was preoccupied with his own defiance.

She was much more interested in him than she was in her own situation, which affected her as the prospect of a matineé might affect a ten-year-old child. She had implicit confidence in her ability to take care of herself under any and all circumstances.

The night deepened. A pale new moon smiled misty-eyed upon the sea, and as the shore faded dimly out and dark clouds were blown like leaves along the far horizon a great haze of moonshine suddenly bathed the yacht and spread an avenue of glittering mail in her swift path. From time to time there was the bright flare of a match as one of them lighted a cigarette, but except for the low under-tone of the throbbing engines and the even wash of the waves about the stern the yacht was quiet as a dream boat star-bound through the heavens. Round them bowed the smell of the night sea, bringing with it an infinite languor.

Carlyle broke the silence at last.

"Lucky girl," he sighed "I've always wanted to be rich—and buy all this beauty."

Ardita yawned.

"I'd rather be you," she said frankly.

"You would—for about a day. But you do seem to possess a lot of nerve for a flapper."

"I wish you wouldn't call me that."

"Beg your pardon."

"As to nerve," she continued slowly, "it's my one redeeming feature. I'm not afraid of anything in heaven or earth."

"Hm, I am."

"To be afraid," said Ardita, "a person has either to be very great and strong—or else a coward. I'm neither." She paused for a moment, and eagerness crept into her tone. "But I want to talk about you. What on earth have you done—and how did you do it?"

"Why?" he demanded cynically. "Going to write a movie, about me?"

"Go on," she urged. "Lie to me by the moonlight. Do a fabulous story."

A negro appeared, switched on a string of small lights under the awning, and began setting the wicker table for supper. And while they ate cold sliced chicken, salad, arti-chokes and strawberry jam from the plentiful larder below, Carlyle began to talk, hesitatingly at first, but eagerly as he saw she was interested. Ardita scarcely touched her food as she watched his dark young face—handsome, ironic faintly ineffectual.

He began life as a poor kid in a Tennessee town, he said, so poor that his people were the only white family in their street. He never remembered any white children—but there were inevitably a dozen pickaninnies streaming in his trail, passionate admirers whom he kept in tow by the vividness of his imagination and the amount of trouble he was always getting them in and out of. And it seemed that this association diverted a rather unusual musical gift into a strange channel.

There had been a colored woman named Belle Pope Calhoun who played the piano at parties given for white children—nice white children that would have passed Curtis Carlyle with a sniff. But the ragged little "poh white" used to sit beside her piano by the hour and try to get in an alto with one of those kazoos that boys hum through. Before he was thirteen he was picking up a living teasing ragtime out of a battered violin in little cafés round Nashville. Eight years later the ragtime craze hit the country, and he took six darkies on the Orpheum circuit. Five of them were boys he had grown up with; the other was the little mulatto, Babe Divine, who was a wharf nigger round New York, and long before that a plantation hand in Bermuda, until he stuck an eight-inch stiletto in his master's back. Almost before Carlyle realized his good fortune he was on Broadway, with offers of engagements on all sides, and more money than he had ever dreamed of.

It was about then that a change began in his whole attitude, a rather curious, embittering change. It was when he realized that he was spending the golden years of his life gibbering round a stage with a lot of black men. His act was good of its kind—three trombones, three saxophones, and Carlyle's flute—and it was his own peculiar sense of rhythm that made all the difference; but he began to grow strangely sensitive about it, began to hate the thought of appearing, dreaded it from day to day.

They were making money—each contract he signed called for more—but when he went to managers and told them that he wanted to separate from his sextet and go on as a regular pianist, they laughed at him and told him he was crazy—it would be an artistic suicide. He used to laugh afterward at the phrase "artistic suicide." They all used it.

Half a dozen times they played at private dances at three thousand dollars a night, and it seemed as if these crystallized all his distaste for his mode of livelihood. They took place in clubs and houses that he couldn't have gone into in the daytime. After all, he was merely playing to rôle of the eternal monkey, a sort of sublimated chorus man. He was sick of the very smell of the theatre, of powder and rouge and the chatter of the greenroom, and the patronizing approval of the boxes. He couldn't put his heart into it any more. The idea of a slow approach to the luxury of leisure drove him wild. He was, of course, progressing toward it, but, like a child, eating his ice-cream so slowly that he couldn't taste it at all.

He wanted to have a lot of money and time and opportunity to read and play, and the sort of men and women round him that he could never have—the kind who, if they thought of him at all, would have considered him rather contemptible; in short he wanted all those things which he was beginning to lump under the general head of aristocracy, an aristocracy which it seemed almost any money could buy except money made as he was making it. He was twenty-five then, without family or education or any promise that he would succeed in a business career. He began speculating wildly, and within three weeks he had lost every cent he had saved.

Then the war came. He went to Plattsburg, and even there his profession followed him. A brigadier-general called him up to headquarters and told him he could serve his country better as a band leader—so he spent the war entertaining celebrities behind the line with a headquarters band. It was not so bad—except that when the infantry came limping back from the trenches he wanted to be one of them. The sweat and mud they wore seemed only one of those ineffable symbols of aristocracy that were forever eluding him.

"It was the private dances that did it. After I came back from the war the old routine started. We had an offer from a syndicate of Florida hotels. It was only a question of time then."

He broke off and Ardita looked at him expectantly, but he shook his head.

"No," he said, "I'm going to tell you about it. I'm enjoying it too much, and I'm afraid I'd lose a little of that enjoyment if I shared it with anyone else. I want to hang on to those few breathless, heroic moments when I stood out before them all and let them know I was more than a damn bobbing, squawking clown."

From up forward came suddenly the low sound of singing. The negroes had gathered together on the deck and their voices rose together in a haunting melody that soared in poignant harmonics toward the moon. And Ardita listens in enchantment.

"Oh down—
oh down,
Mammy wanna take me down milky way,
Oh down,
oh down,
Pappy say to-morra-a-a-ah
But mammy say to-day,
Yes—mammy say to-day!"

Carlyle sighed and was silent for a moment looking up at the gathered host of stars blinking like arc-lights in the warm sky. The negroes' song had died away to a plaintive humming and it seemed as if minute by minute the brightness and the great silence were increasing until he could almost hear the midnight toilet of the mermaids as they combed their silver dripping curls under the moon and gossiped to each other of the fine wrecks they lived on the green opalescent avenues below.

"You see," said Carlyle softly, "this is the beauty I want. Beauty has got to be astonishing, astounding—it's got to burst in on you like a dream, like the exquisite eyes of a girl."

He turned to her, but she was silent.

"You see, don't you, Anita—I mean, Ardita?"

Again she made no answer. She had been sound asleep for some time.

IV

In the dense sun-flooded noon of next day a spot in the sea before them resolved casually into a green-and-gray islet, apparently composed of a great granite cliff at its northern end which slanted south through a mile of vivid coppice and grass to a sandy beach melting lazily into the surf. When Ardita, reading in her favorite seat, came to the last page of The Revolt of the Angels, and slamming the book shut looked up and saw it, she gave a little cry of delight, and called to Carlyle, who was standing moodily by the rail.

"Is this it? Is this where you're going?"

Carlyle shrugged his shoulders carelessly.

"You've got me." He raised his voice and called up to the acting skipper: "Oh, Babe, is this your island?"

The mulatto's miniature head appeared from round the corner of the deck-house.

"Yas-suh! This yeah's it."

Carlyle joined Ardita.

"Looks sort of sporting, doesn't it?"

"Yes," she agreed; "but it doesn't look big enough to be much of a hiding-place."

"You still putting your faith in those wirelesses your uncle was going to have zigzagging round?"

"No," said Ardita frankly. "I'm all for you. I'd really like to see you make a get-away."

He laughed.

"You're our Lady Luck. Guess we'll have to keep you with us as a mascot—for the present anyway."

"You couldn't very well ask me to swim back," she said coolly. "If you do I'm going to start writing dime novels founded on that interminable history of your life you gave me last night."

He flushed and stiffened slightly.

"I'm very sorry I bored you."

"Oh, you didn't—until just at the end with some story about how furious you were because you couldn't dance with the ladies you played music for."

He rose angrily.

"You have got a darn mean little tongue."

"Excuse me," she said melting into laughter, "but I'm not used to having men regale me with the story of their life ambitions—especially if they've lived such deathly platonic lives."

"Why? What do men usually regale you with?"

"Oh, they talk about me," she yawned. "They tell me I'm the spirit of youth and beauty."

"What do you tell them?"

"Oh, I agree quietly."

"Does every man you meet tell you he loves you?"

Ardita nodded.

"Why shouldn't he? All life is just a progression toward, and then a recession from, one phrase—'I love you.'"

Carlyle laughed and sat down.

"That's very true. That's—that's not bad. Did you make that up?"

"Yes—or rather I found it out. It doesn't mean anything especially. It's just clever."

"It's the sort of remark," he said gravely, "that's typical of your class."

"Oh," she interrupted impatiently, "don't start that lecture on aristocracy again! I distrust people who can be intense at this hour in the morning. It's a mild form of insanity—a sort of breakfast-food jag. Morning's the time to sleep, swim, and be careless."

Ten minutes later they had swung round in a wide circle as if to approach the island from the north.

"There's a trick somewhere," commented Ardita thoughtfully. "He can't mean just to anchor up against this cliff."

They were heading straight in now toward the solid rock, which must have been well over a hundred feet tall, and not until they were within fifty yards of it did Ardita see their objective. Then she clapped her hands in delight. There was a break in the cliff entirely hidden by a curious overlapping of rock, and through this break the yacht entered and very slowly traversed a narrow channel of crystal-clear water between high gray walls. Then they were riding at anchor in a miniature world of green and gold, a gilded bay smooth as glass and set round with tiny palms, the whole resembling the mirror lakes and twig trees that children set up in sand piles.

"Not so darned bad!" cried Carlyle excitedly.

"I guess that little coon knows his way round this corner of the Atlantic."

His exuberance was contagious, and Ardita became quite jubilant.

"It's an absolutely sure-fire hiding-place!"

"Lordy, yes! It's the sort of island you read about."

The rowboat was lowered into the golden lake and they pulled to shore.

"Come on," said Carlyle as they landed in the slushy sand, "we'll go exploring."

The fringe of palms was in turn ringed in by a round mile of flat, sandy country. They followed it south and brushing through a farther rim of tropical vegetation came out on a pearl-gray virgin beach where Ardita kicked of her brown golf shoes—she seemed to have permanently abandoned stockings—and went wading. Then they sauntered back to the yacht, where the indefatigable Babe had luncheon ready for them. He had posted a lookout on the high cliff to the north to watch the sea on both sides, though he doubted if the entrance to the cliff was generally known—he had never even seen a map on which the island was marked.

"What's its name," asked Ardita—"the island, I mean?"

"No name 'tall," chuckled Babe. "Reckin she jus' island, 'at's all."

In the late afternoon they sat with their backs against great boulders on the highest part of the cliff and Carlyle sketched for her his vague plans. He was sure they were hot after him by this time. The total proceeds of the coup he had pulled off and concerning which he still refused to enlighten her, he estimated as just under a million dollars. He counted on lying up here several weeks and then setting off southward, keeping well outside the usual channels of travel rounding the Horn and heading for Callao, in Peru. The details of coaling and provisioning he was leaving entirely to Babe who, it seemed, had sailed these seas in every capacity from cabin-boy aboard a coffee trader to virtual first mate on a Brazilian pirate craft, whose skipper had long since been hung.

"If he'd been white he'd have been king of South America long ago," said Carlyle emphatically. "When it comes to intelligence he makes Booker T. Washington look like a moron. He's got the guile of every race and nationality whose blood is in his veins, and that's half a dozen or I'm a liar. He worships me because I'm the only man in the world who can play better ragtime than he can. We used to sit together on the wharfs down on the New York water-front, he with a bassoon and me with an oboe, and we'd blend minor keys in African harmonics a thousand years old until the rats would crawl up the posts and sit round groaning and squeaking like dogs will in front of a phonograph."

Ardita roared.

"How you can tell 'em!"

Carlyle grinned.

"I swear that's the gos—"

"What you going to do when you get to Callao?" she interrupted.

"Take ship for India. I want to be a rajah. I mean it. My idea is to go up into Afghanistan somewhere, buy up a palace and a reputation, and then after about five years appear in England with a foreign accent and a mysterious past. But India first. Do you know, they say that all the gold in the world drifts very gradually back to India. Something fascinating about that to me. And I want leisure to read—an immense amount."

"How about after that?"

"Then," he answered defiantly, "comes aristocracy. Laugh if you want to—but at least you'll have to admit that I know what I want—which I imagine is more than you do."

"On the contrary," contradicted Ardita, reaching in her pocket for her cigarette case, "when I met you I was in the midst of a great uproar of all my friends and relatives because I did know what I wanted."

"What was it?"

"A man."

He started.

"You mean you were engaged?"

"After a fashion. If you hadn't come aboard I had every intention of slipping ashore yesterday evening—how long ago it seems—and meeting him in Palm Beach. He's waiting there for me with a bracelet that once belonged to Catherine of Russia. Now don't mutter anything about aristocracy," she put in quickly. "I liked him simply because he had had an imagination and the utter courage of his convictions."

"But your family disapproved, eh?"

"What there is of it—only a silly uncle and a sillier aunt. It seems he got into some scandal with a red-haired woman name Mimi something—it was frightfully exaggerated, he said, and men don't lie to me—and anyway I didn't care what he'd done; it was the future that counted. And I'd see to that. When a man's in love with me he doesn't care for other amusements. I told him to drop her like a hot cake, and he did."

"I feel rather jealous," said Carlyle, frowning—and then he laughed. "I guess I'll just keep you along with us until we get to Callao. Then I'll lend you enough money to get back to the States. By that time you'll have had a chance to think that gentleman over a little more."

"Don't talk to me like that!" fired up Ardita. "I won't tolerate the parental attitude from anybody! Do you understand me?" He chuckled and then stopped, rather abashed, as her cold anger seemed to fold him about and chill him.

"I'm sorry," he offered uncertainly.

"Oh, don't apologize! I can't stand men who say 'I'm sorry' in that manly, reserved tone. Just shut up!"

A pause ensued, a pause which Carlyle found rather awkward, but which Ardita seemed not to notice at all as she sat contentedly enjoying her cigarette and gazing out at the shining sea. After a minute she crawled out on the rock and lay with her face over the edge looking down. Carlyle, watching her, reflected how it seemed impossible for her to assume an ungraceful attitude.

"Oh, look," she cried. "There's a lot of sort of ledges down there. Wide ones of all different heights."

"We'll go swimming to-night!" she said excitedly. "By moonlight."

"Wouldn't you rather go in at the beach on the other end?"

"Not a chance. I like to dive. You can use my uncle's bathing suit, only it'll fit you like a gunny sack, because he's a very flabby man. I've got a one-piece that's shocked the natives all along the Atlantic coast from Biddeford Pool to St. Augustine."

"I suppose you're a shark."

"Yes, I'm pretty good. And I look cute too. A sculptor up at Rye last summer told me my calves are worth five hundred dollars."

There didn't seem to be any answer to this, so Carlyle was silent, permitting himself only a discreet interior smile.

V

When the night crept down in shadowy blue and silver they threaded the shimmering channel in the rowboat and, tying it to a jutting rock, began climbing the cliff together. The first shelf was ten feet up, wide, and furnishing a natural diving platform. There they sat down in the bright moonlight and watched the faint incessant surge of the waters almost stilled now as the tide set seaward.

"Are you happy?" he asked suddenly.

She nodded.

"Always happy near the sea. You know," she went on, "I've been thinking all day that you and I are somewhat alike. We're both rebels—only for different reasons. Two years ago, when I was just eighteen and you were—"

"Twenty-five."

"—well, we were both conventional successes. I was an utterly devastating débutante and you were a prosperous musician just commissioned in the army—"

"Gentleman by act of Congress," he put in ironically.

"Well, at any rate, we both fitted. If our corners were not rubbed off they were at least pulled in. But deep in us both was something that made us require more for happiness. I didn't know what I wanted. I went from man to man, restless, impatient, month by month getting less acquiescent and more dissatisfied. I used to sit sometimes chewing at the insides of my mouth and thinking I was going crazy—I had a frightful sense of transiency. I wanted things now—now—now! Here I was—beautiful—I am, aren't I?"

"Yes," agreed Carlyle tentatively.

Ardita rose suddenly.

"Wait a second. I want to try this delightful-looking sea."

She walked to the end of the ledge and shot out over the sea, doubling up in mid-air and then straightening out and entering to water straight as a blade in a perfect jack-knife dive.

In a minute her voice floated up to him.

"You see, I used to read all day and most of the night. I began to resent society—"

"Come on up here," he interrupted. "What on earth are you doing?"

"Just floating round on my back. I'll be up in a minute. Let me tell you. The only thing I enjoyed was shocking people; wearing something quite impossible and quite charming to a fancy-dress party, going round with the fastest men in New York, and getting into some of the most hellish scrapes imaginable."

The sounds of splashing mingled with her words, and then he heard her hurried breathing as she began climbing up side to the ledge.

"Go on in!" she called

Obediently he rose and dived. When he emerged, dripping, and made the climb he found that she was no longer on the ledge, but after a second frightened he heard her light laughter from another shelf ten feet up. There he joined her and they both sat quietly for a moment, their arms clasped round their knees, panting a little from the climb.

"The family were wild," she said suddenly. "They tried to marry me off. And then when I'd begun to feel that after all life was scarcely worth living I found something"—her eyes went skyward exultantly—"I found something!"

Carlyle waited and her words came with a rush.

"Courage—just that; courage as a rule of life, and something to cling to always. I began to build up this enormous faith in myself. I began to see that in all my idols in the past some manifestation of courage had unconsciously been the thing that attracted me. I began separating courage from the other things of life. All sorts of courage—the beaten, bloody prize-fighter coming up for more—I used to make men take me to prize-fights; the déclassé woman sailing through a nest of cats and looking at them as if they were mud under her feet; the liking what you like always; the utter disregard for other people's opinions—just to live as I liked always and to die in my own way— Did you bring up the cigarettes?"

He handed one over and held a match for her gently.

"Still," Ardita continued, "the men kept gathering—old men and young men, my mental and physical inferiors, most of them, but all intensely desiring to have me—to own this rather magnificent proud tradition I'd built up round me. Do you see?"

"Sort of. You never were beaten and you never apologized."

"Never!"

She sprang to the edge, poised for a moment like a crucified figure against the sky; then describing a dark parabola plunked without a slash between two silver ripples twenty feet below.

Her voice floated up to him again.

"And courage to me meant ploughing through that dull gray mist that comes down on life—not only overriding people and circumstances but overriding the bleakness of living. A sort of insistence on the value of life and the worth of transient things."

She was climbing up now, and at her last words her head, with the damp yellow hair slicked symmetrically back appeared on his level.

"All very well," objected Carlyle. "You can call it courage, but your courage is really built, after all, on a pride of birth. You were bred to that defiant attitude. On my gray days even courage is one of the things that's gray and lifeless."

She was sitting near the edge, hugging her knees and gazing abstractedly at the white moon; he was farther back, crammed like a grotesque god into a niche in the rock.

"I don't want to sound like Pollyanna," she began, "but you haven't grasped me yet. My courage is faith—faith in the eternal resilience of me—that joy'll come back, and hope and spontaneity. And I feel that till it does I've got to keep my lips shut and my chin high, and my eyes wide—not necessarily any silly smiling. Oh, I've been through hell without a whine quite often—and the female hell is deadlier than the male."

"But supposing," suggested Carlyle, "that before joy and hope and all that came back the curtain was drawn on you for good?"

Ardita rose, and going to the wall climbed with some difficulty to the next ledge, another ten or fifteen feet above.

"Why," she called back "then I'd have won!"

He edged out till he could see her.

"Better not dive from there! You'll break your back," he said quickly.

She laughed.

"Not I!"

Slowly she spread her arms and stood there swan-like, radiating a pride in her young perfection that lit a warm glow in Carlyle's heart.

"We're going through the black air with our arms wide and our feet straight out behind like a dolphin's tail, and we're going to think we'll never hit the silver down there till suddenly it'll be all warm round us and full of little kissing, caressing waves."

Then she was in the air, and Carlyle involuntarily held his breath. He had not realized that the dive was nearly forty feet. It seemed an eternity before he heard the swift compact sound as she reached the sea.

And it was with his glad sigh of relief when her light watery laughter curled up the side of the cliff and into his anxious ears that he knew he loved her.

VI

Time, having no axe to grind, showered down upon them three days of afternoons. When the sun cleared the port-hole of Ardita's cabin an hour after dawn she rose cheerily, donned her bathing-suit, and went up on deck. The negroes would leave their work when they saw her, and crowd, chuckling and chattering, to the rail as she floated, an agile minnow, on and under the surface of the clear water. Again in the cool of the afternoon she would swim—and loll and smoke with Carlyle upon the cliff; or else they would lie on their sides in the sands of the southern beach, talking little, but watching the day fade colorfully and tragically into the infinite langour of a tropical evening.

And with the long, sunny hours Ardita's idea of the episode as incidental, madcap, a sprig of romance in a desert of reality, gradually left her. She dreaded the time when he would strike off southward; she dreaded all the eventualities that presented themselves to her; thoughts were suddenly troublesome and decisions odious. Had prayers found place in the pagan rituals of her soul she would have asked of life only to be unmolested for a while, lazily acquiescent to the ready, naïf flow of Carlyle's ideas, his vivid boyish imagination, and the vein of monomania that seemed to run crosswise through his temperament and colored his every action.

But this is not a story of two on an island, nor concerned primarily with love bred of isolation. It is merely the presentation of two personalities, and its idyllic setting among the palms of the Gulf Stream is quite incidental. Most of us are content to exist and breed and fight for the right to do both, and the dominant idea, the foredoomed attest to control one's destiny, is reserved for the fortunate or unfortunate few. To me the interesting thing about Ardita is the courage that will tarnish with her beauty and youth.

"Take me with you," she said late one night as they sat lazily in the grass under the shadowy spreading palms. The negroes had brought ashore their musical instruments, and the sound of weird ragtime was drifting softly over on the warm breath of the night. "I'd love to reappear in ten years, as a fabulously wealthy high-caste Indian lady," she continued.

Carlyle looked at her quickly.

"You can, you know."

She laughed.

"Is it a proposal of marriage? Extra! Ardita Farnam becomes pirate's bride. Society girl kidnapped by ragtime bank robber."

"It wasn't a bank."

"What was it? Why won't you tell me?"

"I don't want to break down your illusions."

"My dear man, I have no illusions about you."

"I mean your illusions about yourself."

She looked up in surprise.

"About myself! What on earth have I got to do with whatever stray felonies you've committed?"

"That remains to be seen."

She reached over and patted his hand.

"Dear Mr. Curtis Carlyle," she said softly, "are you in love with me?"

"As if it mattered."

"But it does—because I think I'm in love with you."

He looked at her ironically.

"Thus swelling your January total to half a dozen," he suggested. "Suppose I call your bluff and ask you to come to India with me?"

"Shall I?"

He shrugged his shoulders.

"We can get married in Callao."

"What sort of life can you offer me? I don't mean that unkindly, but seriously; what would become of me if the people who want that twenty-thousand-dollar reward ever catch up with you?"

"I thought you weren't afraid."

"I never am—but I won't throw my life away just to show one man I'm not."

"I wish you'd been poor. Just a little poor girl dreaming over a fence in a warm cow country."

"Wouldn't it have been nice?"

"I'd have enjoyed astonishing you—watching your eyes open on things. If you only wanted things! Don't you see?"

"I know—like girls who stare into the windows of jewelry-stores."

"Yes—and want the big oblong watch that's platinum and has diamonds all round the edge. Only you'd decide it was too expensive and choose one of white gold for a hundred dollar. Then I'd say: 'Expensive? I should say not!' And we'd go into the store and pretty soon the platinum one would be gleaming on your wrist."

"That sounds so nice and vulgar—and fun, doesn't it?" murmured Ardita.

"Doesn't it? Can't you see us travelling round and spending money right and left, and being worshipped by bell-boys and waiters? Oh, blessed are the simple rich for they inherit the earth!"

"I honestly wish we were that way."

"I love you, Ardita," he said gently.

Her face lost its childish look for moment and became oddly grave.

"I love to be with you," she said, "more than with any man I've ever met. And I like your looks and your dark old hair, and the way you go over the side of the rail when we come ashore. In fact, Curtis Carlyle, I like all the things you do when you're perfectly natural. I think you've got nerve and you know how I feel about that. Sometimes when you're around I've been tempted to kiss you suddenly and tell you that you were just an idealistic boy with a lot of caste nonsense in his head. Perhaps if I were just a little bit older and a little more bored I'd go with you. As it is, I think I'll go back and marry—that other man."

Over across the silver lake the figures of the negroes writhed and squirmed in the moonlight like acrobats who, having been too long inactive, must go through their tacks from sheer surplus energy. In single file they marched, weaving in concentric circles, now with their heads thrown back, now bent over their instruments like piping fauns. And from trombone and saxophone ceaselessly whined a blended melody, sometimes riotous and jubilant, sometimes haunting and plaintive as a death-dance from the Congo's heart.

"Let's dance," cried Ardita. "I can't sit still with that perfect jazz going on."

Taking her hand he led her out into a broad stretch of hard sandy soil that the moon flooded with great splendor. They floated out like drifting moths under the rich hazy light, and as the fantastic symphony wept and exulted and wavered and despaired Ardita's last sense of reality dropped away, and she abandoned her imagination to the dreamy summer scents of tropical flowers and the infinite starry spaces overhead, feeling that if she opened her eyes it would be to find herself dancing with a ghost in a land created by her own fancy.

"This is what I should call an exclusive private dance," he whispered.

"I feel quite mad—but delightfully mad!"

"We're enchanted. The shades of unnumbered generations of cannibals are watching us from high up on the side of the cliff there."

"And I'll bet the cannibal women are saying that we dance too close, and that it was immodest of me to come without my nose-ring."

They both laughed softly—and then their laughter died as over across the lake they heard the trombones stop in the middle of a bar, and the saxophones give a startled moan and fade out.

"What's the matter?" called Carlyle.

After a moment's silence they made out the dark figure of a man rounding the silver lake at a run. As he came closer they saw it was Babe in a state of unusual excitement. He drew up before them and gasped out his news in a breath.

"Ship stan'in' off sho' 'bout half a mile suh. Mose, he uz on watch, he say look's if she's done ancho'd."

"A ship—what kind of a ship?" demanded Carlyle anxiously.

Dismay was in his voice, and Ardita's heart gave a sudden wrench as she saw his whole face suddenly droop.

"He say he don't know, suh."

"Are they landing a boat?"

"No, suh."

"We'll go up," said Carlyle.

They ascended the hill in silence, Ardita's hand still resting in Carlyle's as it had when they finished dancing. She felt it clinch nervously from time to time as though he were unaware of the contact, but though he hurt her she made no attempt to remove it. It seemed an hour's climb before they reached the top and crept cautiously across the silhouetted plateau to the edge of the cliff. After one short look Carlyle involuntarily gave a little cry. It was a revenue boat with six-inch guns mounted fore and aft.

"They know!" he said with a short intake of breath. "They know! They picked up the trail somewhere."

"Are you sure they know about the channel? They may be only standing by to take a look at the island in the morning. From where they are they couldn't see the opening in the cliff."

"They could with field-glasses," he said hopelessly. He looked at his wrist-watch. "It's nearly two now. They won't do anything until dawn, that's certain. Of course there's always the faint possibility that they're waiting for some other ship to join; or for a coaler."

"I suppose we may as well stay right here."

The hour passed and they lay there side by side, very silently, their chins in their hands like dreaming children. In back of them squatted the negroes, patient, resigned, acquiescent, announcing now and then with sonorous snores that not even the presence of danger could subdue their unconquerable African craving for sleep.

Just before five o'clock Babe approached Carlyle. There were half a dozen rifles aboard the Narcissus he said. Had it been decided to offer no resistance?

A pretty good fight might be made, he thought, if they worked out some plan.

Carlyle laughed and shook his head.

"That isn't a Spic army out there, Babe. That's a revenue boat. It'd be like a bow and arrow trying to fight a machine-gun. If you want to bury those bags somewhere and take a chance on recovering them later, go on and do it. But it won't work—they'd dig this island over from one end to the other. It's a lost battle all round, Babe."

Babe inclined his head silently and turned away, and Carlyle's voice was husky as he turned to Ardita.

"There's the best friend I ever had. He'd die for me, and be proud to, if I'd let him."

"You've given up?"

"I've no choice. Of course there's always one way out—the sure way—but that can wait. I wouldn't miss my trial for anything—it'll be an interesting experiment in notoriety. 'Miss Farnam testifies that the pirate's attitude to her was at all times that of a gentleman.'"

"Don't!" she said. "I'm awfully sorry."

When the color faded from the sky and lustreless blue changed to leaden gray a commotion was visible on the ship's deck, and they made out a group of officers clad in white duck, gathered near the rail. They had field-glasses in their hands and were attentively examining the islet.

"It's all up," said Carlyle grimly.

"Damn," whispered Ardita. She felt tears gathering in her eyes "We'll go back to the yacht," he said. "I prefer that to being hunted out up here like a 'possum."

Leaving the plateau they descended the hill, and reaching the lake were rowed out to the yacht by the silent negroes. Then, pale and weary, they sank into the settees and waited.

Half an hour later in the dim gray light the nose of the revenue boat appeared in the channel and stopped, evidently fearing that the bay might be too shallow. From the peaceful look of the yacht, the man and the girl in the settees, and the negroes lounging curiously against the rail, they evidently judged that there would be no resistance, for two boats were lowered casually over the side, one containing an officer and six bluejackets, and the other, four rowers and in the stern two gray-haired men in yachting flannels. Ardita and Carlyle stood up, and half unconsciously started toward each other.

Then he paused and putting his hand suddenly into his pocket he pulled out a round, glittering object and held it out to her.

"What is it?" she asked wonderingly.

"I'm not positive, but I think from the Russian inscription inside that it's your promised bracelet."

"Where—where on earth—"

"It came out of one of those bags. You see, Curtis Carlyle and his Six Black Buddies, in the middle of their performance in the tea-room of the hotel at Palm Beach, suddenly changed their instruments for automatics and held up the crowd. I took this bracelet from a pretty, overrouged woman with red hair."

Ardita frowned and then smiled.

"So that's what you did! You *have* got nerve!"

He bowed.

"A well-known bourgeois quality," he said.

And then dawn slanted dynamically across the deck and flung the shadows reeling into gray corners. The dew rose and turned to golden mist, thin as a dream, enveloping them until they seemed gossamer relics of the late night, infinitely transient and already fading. For a moment sea and sky were breathless, and dawn held a pink hand over the young mouth of life—then from out in the lake came the complaint of a rowboat and the swish of oars.

Suddenly against the golden furnace low in the east their two graceful figures melted into one, and he was kissing her spoiled young mouth.

"It's a sort of glory," he murmured after a second.

She smiled up at him.

"Happy, are you?"

Her sigh was a benediction—an ecstatic surety that she was youth and beauty now as much as she would ever know. For another instant life was radiant and time a phantom and their strength eternal—then there was a bumping, scraping sound as the rowboat scraped alongside.

Up the ladder scrambled the two gray-haired men, the officer and two of the sailors with their hands on their revolvers. Mr. Farnam folded his arms and stood looking at his niece.

"So," he said nodding his head slowly.

With a sigh her arms unwound from Carlyle's neck, and her eyes, transfigured and far away, fell upon the boarding party. Her uncle saw her upper lip slowly swell into that arrogant pout he knew so well.

"So," he repeated savagely. "So this is your idea of—of romance. A runaway affair, with a high-seas pirate."

Ardita glanced at him carelessly.

"What an old fool you are!" she said quietly.

"Is that the best you can say for yourself?"

"No," she said as if considering. "No, there's something else. There's that well-known phrase with which I have ended most of our conversations for the past few years—'Shut up!'"

And with that she turned, included the two old men, the officer, and the two sailors in a curt glance of contempt, and walked proudly down the companionway.

But had she waited an instant longer she would have heard a sound from her uncle quite unfamiliar in most of their interviews. He gave vent to a whole-hearted amused chuckle, in which the second old man joined.

The latter turned briskly to Carlyle, who had been regarding this scene with an air of cryptic amusement.

"Well Toby," he said genially, "you incurable, hare-brained romantic chaser of rainbows, did you find that she was the person you wanted?"

Carlyle smiled confidently.

"Why—naturally," he said "I've been perfectly sure ever since I first heard tell of her wild career. That'd why I had Babe send up the rocket last night."

"I'm glad you did," said Colonel Moreland gravely. "We've been keeping pretty close to you in case you should have trouble with those six strange niggers. And we hoped we'd find you two in some such compromising position," he sighed. "Well, set a crank to catch a crank!"

"Your father and I sat up all night hoping for the best—or perhaps it's the worst. Lord knows you're welcome to her, my boy. She's run me crazy. Did you give her the Russian bracelet my detective got from that Mimi woman?"

Carlyle nodded.

"Sh!" he said. "She's coming on deck."

Ardita appeared at the head of the companionway and gave a quick involuntary glance at Carlyle's wrists. A puzzled look passed across her face. Back aft the negroes had begun to sing, and the cool lake, fresh with dawn, echoed serenely to their low voices.

"Ardita," said Carlyle unsteadily.

She swayed a step toward him.

"Ardita," he repeated breathlessly, "I've got to tell you the—the truth. It was all a plant, Ardita. My name isn't Carlyle. It's Moreland, Toby Moreland. The story was invented, Ardita, invented out of thin Florida air."

She stared at him, bewildered, amazement, disbelief, and anger flowing in quick waves across her face. The three men held their breaths. Moreland, Senior, took a step toward her; Mr. Farnam's mouth dropped a little open as he waited, panic-stricken, for the expected crash.

But it did not come. Ardita's face became suddenly radiant, and with a little laugh she went swiftly to young Moreland and looked up at him without a trace of wrath in her gray eyes.

"Will you swear," she said quietly "That it was entirely a product of your own brain?"

"I swear," said young Moreland eagerly.

She drew his head down and kissed him gently.

"What an imagination!" she said softly and almost enviously. "I want you to lie to me just as sweetly as you know how for the rest of my life."

The negroes' voices floated drowsily back, mingled in an air that she had heard them singing before.

"Time is a thief;
Gladness and grief
Cling to the leaf
As it yellows—"

"What was in the bags?" she asked softly.

"Florida mud," he answered. "That was one of the two true things I told you."

"Perhaps I can guess the other one," she said; and reaching up on her tiptoes she kissed him softly in the illustration.

ACKNOWLEDGEMENTS

There are many people who contributed to the creation of this collection. First and foremost, I'd like to thank my wife, Jaqueline, and our two children, Caio and Bianca, whose love, patience, and sharp instincts as my first readers make everything I write possible.

In my journey as a writer and publisher, I've been fortunate to receive generous guidance and input from family and friends, especially Nick Macpherson, Penny Macpherson, Greg Nicholas, Alana McGuire, Richard Amey, Dejvi and Corinne Malesic, Michael Altieri, and Luana and Andrew Jones.

I'm also deeply grateful for the professional support and encouragement from David Morrell, Robert Dugoni, and David Caesar.

I want to thank the independent booksellers and librarians whose support has been incredible, especially Sasha Cattapan, Maria Neumann, and Jennifer Dwyer.

Finally, I'd like to thank you, dear reader, for joining me on this journey through some of the world's finest short stories. If you enjoyed the collection, I'd be grateful if you left a short review or shared it with another story lover.

About the Editor

Jonathan Macpherson is the author of the crime fiction novels *Brazen Violations*, *Prior Violations*, and *Outback Creed*. He also writes children's fiction under the name J. Macpherson, and is the author of the *Rotto!* series, about a quick witted-quokka.

For more information, visit jonathanmacpherson.com. For his children's books, visit jfmbooks.com.